The
Silver Swimmers

By

Jenny Thomas

ISBN: 978-1-9999435-0-9

I owe a huge debt of gratitude to my friend, Judith Mcgirr, who designed the cover. Thank you Judy!

Published by
Calon Publishing

This is Jenny's second novel. The first was 'Over Streams and Squirrel Woods,' written under the pseudonym Alys Williams and from which the descriptions of dementia behavior, which she had observed in her mother, have been taken and repeated here.

'The centre of me is always and eternally a terrible pain – a curious wild pain – a searching for something transfigured and infinite.'
Bertrand Russell Oct 23rd 1916

'All my past life is mine no more;
The flying hours are gone;
Like transitory dreams given o'er
Whose images are kept in store
By memory alone.'
John Wilmot, Earl of Rochester. 'Love and Life, A Song.

List of main Characters – in order of appearance

Laura 64
5ft 10ins. Slim. Shoulder length, dark hair. Retired from being Head of Humanities in an FE college. Daughter: Daisy twenty-six, who is model like with auburn hair and freckles like her father. She has four-year-old twins Lily and Ruby. Dan moved in when she was thirteen.

Dan 62
6ft 2ins. Skinny with clothes hanger shoulders. Thick, dark, curly hair with silver strands. Just retired from being an analyst in a city bank. Learning to paint. Parents are ninety-two and ninety-six.

Marie 61
5ft 5ins. Thick, dark, wavy hair. Ethnic style sense. A medical doctor. Worked for Medicin sans Frontieres. She and Arun, a Burmese doctor set up a hospice in Mandalay. He had a fatal heart attack. She returned to her flat in London.

Beth 62
5ft 1ins. Overweight. Thin, brown hair, streaked with grey. Wears baggy, loose clothes. A Housewife. Three children: Hugh thirty-two, an accountant living with Lucy. Harriet twenty-seven doing VSO. Jake twenty-three, living at home.

Annie 66
5ft 4ins. Bleached, short blonde hair. A cookery writer and TV presenter. Former county tennis player and Laura's partner.

Martin 67, 5ft 8ins. slim, pale, receding hairline. A harbour design engineer and DIY expert. He and Annie have a son, Ben, in Chicago.

Helen 62

5ft. 5ins. Shoulder length, thick, wavy, red/greying hair, freckled skin. Deep, husky voice. Educational psychologist working in local schools.

James 65

5ft 9ins. An overweight, balding lawyer married to Beth. Retires during the year of this story. Mother Sybil.

Phillip 62

5ft 9ins. Shoulder length curly dark hair with silver streaks, which he wears in a ponytail. Flexible, sinewy, neat body. A Psychotherapist.

Terry 66

5ft 6ins. Brown, greying frizzy hair with highlights, a little overweight. Retiring from an educational charity 'Cultural Access'. Breast cancer five years ago. Married to Leonard, a retired architect. fifteen years older. Son, David.

Lynne 68

5ft 7ins. Thick, curly, greying hair, heavy boned. A physiotherapist, who works from home. Shared a flat with Laura and Jo. Mother Betty, eighty-eight lives with her.

Jo 64

5ft 9ins. Shoulder length, naturally fair hair, voluptuous. Ex-husband, Ed, Daughter, Jessica. She met Laura at University.

Frances 58

5ft. 4ins. Thin, short mousey greying hair, Delicate, small, face and big shoulders. Made redundant from her law firm.

Chapter 1. September

'Hither each man's pleasure draws him, young and old alike...here the limbs of the weary are refreshed with gentle swimming.'
Millerd's Map of Bristol. (1673)

L aura stirred in her sleep, as Daniel woke suddenly with a fizzing, vibrating, brightly coloured scene in his head. This was it *exactly*. It needed to be sketched now before it vanished.

The house was dark and silent. He had no idea of the time. Sliding soundlessly out of bed, so as not to disturb Laura, he felt for his sweater and shorts on the chair and shivering in the chill, crept towards the door, his vision already fading like a dream.

A creak on the stairs woke her. "Dan?" A creak again and a gangly shadow appeared at the bedroom door. She felt a stab of love.

"Have you had an idea?"

"Mmm." The silver streaks in his thick, curly hair glinted in the light from the landing, such a gentle, familiar face. "Go back to sleep." More creaks, a door being quietly opened, the sound of the alarm code being punched in, she turned over and snuggled down.

Three hours later

"A cup of tea?" Laura asked of the frozen statue standing in front of a canvas in his loft studio. "Mmm, thanks," soft brown eyes clouded, far away, she may as well have been the cat, if they'd had one.

Out of the door, it was a chill, misty morning. The smell of damp autumn leaves was fresh, sharp, expectant. She ducked underneath some spider's threads sparkling in a sudden ray of pale sunlight and carried on down her path and left up the road. Past the large red brick semi-detached houses spreading like rampant ivy over what were once rivers, woods and farmland. The Victorian and Edwardian middle classes had built them with large rooms, front and back gardens and decorative detail. Some were now divided up into small flats and bedsits like numbers 42 to 46. Unknown people came and went

1

behind their undrawn heavy curtains or grubby nets, their wheelie bins in disordered display around their cars. Numbers 50 to 62 were neglected and overgrown, drifts of leaves under trees, the pavement strewn with crab apples and smashed pears. From then on there were gardens where effort and thought combined to give passers-by much pleasure.

Marie was kneeling by a flowerbed, a bucket of weeds at her side, her dark curls pulled back by plaited coloured thread. She stood up, brushing leaves from her jeggings and embroidered fitted jacket, an ethnic style icon with dark olive skin and a dazzling smile. Laura immediately felt ordinary in the jeans and fleece, which had become her uniform since she had retired, and curled into herself a little. She carried her height without conviction, always having been taller than her girl friends.

"The last of the lavender," Marie said, holding out a tiny aromatic hand-stitched bag. "It needed a haircut," she added.

Laura's eyes were drawn to the deeply etched groove between Marie's nose and mouth, which had appeared with her smile. Her lovely face was wrinkle free, just this one dark aperture, perhaps a secret way into her mysterious, elusive psyche. If only, she thought and smiled back. "Thanks, you're the ultimate giver."

They hugged and crossed the road, clicked open the gate of 67 and pressed the doorbell. There was a muffled shout, then, "I'm ready, just looking for my thingies," from the other side of the door. The two early risers grinned knowingly at one another. There was a minute of complete silence then the sound of scuffling and at last the door opened. Beth was pulling on her rather battered brown jacket over her red corduroy flares and grey polo neck, checking in her swimming bag and pockets for her locker pound, hanging her keys around her neck and they were off to Annie's.

The bedroom curtains were closed and a gentle push of the doorbell brought Martin to the door. "She had a bad night. She's gone back to bed," he said apologetically, and "Have a good swim," to their retreating backs.

"Can't remember the last time she came," muttered Beth.

"Mmm it's been weeks. Think she's lost interest," Laura agreed.

2

"She doesn't sleep very well. She's on Twitter, Facebook and eBay, doing crosswords or writing her column half the night."

It was Friday, Helen's late start day. She was waiting at the end of the road, her shoulder length, thick, greying hair tucked under one of the woolly hats she had knitted, in a similar pink to her cardigan coat.

They set off briskly on their twenty minute walk to the Leisure Centre, not as usual discussing the films, plays or exhibitions they had seen, because Beth was telling them a long involved story about George and Peggy, whom they had never met or indeed heard of before.

The water sparkled in the sunlight through the glass roof, as blue as the sky and the bushes of lavender on the raised bed outside. Laura swum up and down in the medium lane, preoccupied with Marie's age-denoting groove. Her routine was to swim for around twenty-five minutes, alternating strokes between crawl, back crawl and breast stroke. Marie did relaxed, graceful crawl for ten minutes, then elegant backstroke for five and some water exercises. Helen crawled in the fast lane and Beth usually breast stroked slowly, but strenuously in the unlaned area, around the gaggle of Asian women standing in the water, talking, their long hair trailing wet and mermaid like.

When I worked, Laura thought, I was too busy to think about getting older. She smiled to herself thinking about a young woman who had come up to her in the gym the previous week, to tell her how great she looked.

Then, when she had thanked her, she had said: "Yes, great for you age." Very deflating. Some younger swimmers with clear, flawless faces passed, breast stroking in the other direction in the fast lane. Young people have a softness, a fluidity, they glow, she thought. Perhaps our youthful radiance is our real persona, our soul?

There's something so fixed and set about the appearance of us older people. Apart from all the lines, furrows and sagging, crepey flesh, we become solidified… as if our radiance has been drawn inside leaving only the occasional gleam or glow. She remembered the look of puzzlement and distaste on teenage Daisy's face when she caught her Grandmother giggling girlishly as she shared a joke with an old

3

boyfriend. Daisy had looked perplexed as if she had seen a mirage, as the impression of youth left with her smile.

"How many more?" called Marie, treading water in the next lane. "Beth's had enough."

They swam back down the pool, waved to Helen, climbed out and joined Beth in the shower. "I've got someone coming to look at the boiler at 9.30," she said apologetically. Neither friend bothered to say, "Why doesn't James deal with it, now he's semi-retired?"

They knew that Beth was in charge of the house, the garden, the children, now grown up, the pets, which had come and gone and they had even seen her cleaning the car and taking it for a service. James had married to have someone to organise his life while he became entirely absorbed in his legal cases. "Nothing gets done unless I do it. The children wouldn't have got to school on time, have done their homework, have had hobbies and friends…nothing would get mended, the house cleaned," she often said.

"Doesn't he do man jobs, like digging the garden or bleeding the radiators?" Laura had asked.

"James?" Beth had looked exasperated. "He'll lay the table, serve drinks to friends and help in the garden sometimes. He will do little things if I ask him, but I sound like my mother or a primary school teacher if I complain that he should notice what needs doing without me telling him. We took roles when we got married and they've never changed. It's easier to get on with it myself. I married him knowing that he didn't want me to work, but somehow I've never managed to get on top of things like those 'yummy mummies' in exercise gear I see walking their children to school and then popping off to the gym."

She waved the feeble hair dryer over her grey streaked, nameless colour hair while the other three collected up their clothes and put on their shoes.

Beth arrived back just in time to see the boiler man drive up. The part he had brought was fitted quickly and he was gone. Taking her swimming things upstairs, she picked up last night's camomile tea mugs from the bedside tables, looked out at the garden and sighed. The hedges and grass needed cutting and she must get trays of

4

dianthus and pansies to cheer up the autumn beds. There had always been too much to do. She heard the shower going off and sighed again. Why couldn't James help more now that he was only going in to the office twice a week? Though it could be worse. He could be like Phillip, touching up any woman who would let him. To be fair, James had been a faithful husband. She looked down at the mess of journals and newspapers on his side of the bed and shuffled them into a pile. There was the sound of the bathroom door and James appeared, a short sighted pink faced mole with a towel wrapped under his large white stomach.

"Have you seen my glasses?" he asked. She picked them up from the floor, but then smiling placed them on his bedside table and moving towards him, wrapped her arms around his warm softness. He enveloped her, his towel dropping to the floor and surprisingly that old tingling sensation shot through her as she touched the still damp hair in his groin and they edged carefully towards the bed.

Helen reached home to see Phillip standing on their doorstep just about to lock the door. "CCQI policy meeting?" she asked. He nodded. They gave one another a peck on the cheek and she let herself in to have some herb tea and toast and look at a case file, before she drove to Hazelmere, one of the junior schools for which she was the educational psychologist.

Marie opened her front door and picked up her post. Her heart did a cartwheel as she saw an envelope from Medecins Sans Frontieres. No, it wouldn't be a posting, they would have rung or emailed. It must be the newsletter. Would she go to the Scientific Day conference this year? Let's see who the speakers are…Itching to rip it open, she delayed the pleasure by determinedly walking forward into the kitchen and putting on the kettle, Sadi mewing after her.

Five minutes later and she was carrying her coffee, warmed flat bread and goat cheese into her conservatory. Putting them down on a small inlaid table, she opened one of the arched windows, so that a little breeze fluttered the beautiful scarves over the lampshades and embroidered shawls covering the rattan chairs. Settling amongst a pile of kilims and pillows on the tiled floor, she carefully undid the seal and slid out the contents, looking across at a framed photograph on the table. "I'll just do one more stint with MSF, Arun shall I? Not the Middle East again though. Africa?"

"You're late Mummy. I wanted to get to college early," Daisy said accusingly as Laura arrived back home. "Lily and Ruby are watching C Beebies. They can have fruit and porridge now, but then nothing else before lunch."

"Am I fetching them from school and putting them to bed?" Laura asked, anticipating the reply.

"I'm meeting Ames after college. She's got a temp job near Oxford Street."

A quick peck and Daisy was gone. The girls had heard her come in.

"Nana, we're hungry," Ruby wrapped herself around her grandmother.

"Hello Nana, can we have a cake?" called Lily from the armchair.

"How about a little bowl of porridge and blueberries?"

"Not soft ones," said fussy Lily.

"Yes, yes, Nana, and honey please." Ruby followed Laura into the kitchen.

She looked out of the window to see Daniel taking down the runner bean sticks and dying foliage.

"Nana, Nana, let me see." Ruby was jumping up and down, wanting to be lifted.

"Dan," she shouted, "Dan!"

He was too far away to hear, so opening the back door, the three year old pushed her feet into her wellingtons and ran to 'help' him.

After lunch, Dan returned from taking the girls to their afternoon school session to find a sad-faced Laura standing at the sink washing up. He wound his arms around her waist.

"How is the great novel going?" he asked teasingly.

"I must speak to her. This can't go on indefinitely. I haven't worked for more than forty years to take on another almost full time job, when I thought that for the first time in my life there was going to be time for me." She picked up the towel and twisted round to face him. "Don't you need a nap? You must have got up before five?"

"If you have one with me?" His brown eyes twinkled.

Her tension eased. He really was still very handsome, his greying curly hair falling around his delicate features. He had never fitted in to the tough city environment, but found niches where his reliability and hard work obtained respect. He had always been offered long contracts. And now at last he could concentrate on painting, well when their time was not sucked up by the children, much as they loved them.

He buried his face in her hair and nuzzled her ear. She felt her pent up resentment melt away, and hand in hand they went upstairs.

Terry had been to the opticians to pick up her new glasses. She wore them home on the bus, staring eagerly around with her newly brilliant eye-sight. Calling in at number 25, she asked Laura to join the U3A art class with her.

"Oh, no thanks, I'm just not interested in drawing or painting. I'm useless at it." Laura was absorbed in cooking a meal for the twins. She made her friend some tea, cut her a piece of apple cake, then went back to stirring a cheese sauce. Terry sat at the farmhouse table near the window and found herself marvelling at the petals on the peony picture on her mug of tea and the dust on an orchid leaf on the windowsill, exclaiming at the detail revealed to her.

Laura looked up from the saucepan. "You had glasses before. Surely these aren't making that much difference?"

"I hadn't realised how poor my eyesight had become. That's working with computers for you."

Laura pushed the saucepan off the heat and came and sat down, to prepare runner beans. Terry hoped that Laura was not seeing her as clearly as she could now see her. "I haven't been able to see detail for a while. I feel naked now and knowing that everyone could see me this clearly is unnerving!. Can I ask you something?"

"You have my almost undivided attention till Dan and the girls get back."

"Well, you know that I've been part time, winding down and breaking in my replacement. Do you, you know…do you ever fancy anyone else?"

Laura looked at her closely. Terry was attractive, quite tall and voluptuous though a little overweight. She had had highlights in her greying hair and the frizz had been tamed to gentle curls. There was a glow about her.

"Well, I'm not a good one to ask. I seem to have lost my sex drive, but when I get the urge I still fancy Dan more than anyone I've come across. Come on tell me, who's this person?"

"He's called Tony. He was CEO of a Hedge Fund and when he retired thought he'd work part time for a charity. Perhaps I'm imagining it, but I get quite horny when he looks at me. I haven't had sex for years, we stopped when Leonard was in his sixties and anyway it wasn't that great for me. He never really seemed to notice. I know I should be grateful that he loves me so much, but any attraction and excitement have long gone. I hate myself, but Tony makes me feel like I remember feeling when I was young…"

Laura poured her another cup of tea. "More cake?"

Terry looked longingly at the apple sponge, "It's delicious, but I need to get rid of some of this." She squeezed a roll of flesh around her middle.

Laura thought about Leonard, a tall, almost bald eighty year old, with prodigious energy for doing jobs around the house and very leftie views. A rather stiff inflexible loner, with few friends outside his wife and son. She got up to put the beans on to cook and drain the spinach pasta. "You're giving me goose pimples. What are you going to do? You're retiring before you want to because Leonard wants you to spend more time with him. You can't have an affair once you've left because you'd never be able to go off on your own without huge lies. If you're going to do it, you'd better get on with it."

Terry smiled. "Perhaps I'm being ridiculous and fantasising, but I can't think about anything else and I don't know what to do about it. This may be my last chance for having a sexual relationship. It's all down hill from here."

The front door opened and two noisy children came down the

hall with Dan. "Nana, Nana, look what we did today."

"Sorry, Terry, we'll have to talk about this another time. Didn't you say you were going to start swimming with us?"

"Yes, I'm rubbish at it, but I should start some sort of exercise regime."

Chapter 2. October. The nameless existential Dread

'Season of mists and mellow fruitfulness'
John Keats 'To Autumn.' (1795 – 1821).

Laura had had a bad night. This wasn't how she had envisaged her retirement. Who am I now? Nana? Mainly Nana. What if I never, ever, write that novel? All those years of teaching with no time to write more than articles. But I love them so much...

She dragged herself out of bed at 7.30, dressed and went downstairs to see Dan making himself tea.

"I'm off to the pool now. You're making the porridge today, don't forget."

He sighed. "Yes, I'm sure Daisy will remind me."

Out of the door, the pearl grey sky threatened rain. It felt cold and damp. The trees were yellowing fast and red and gold leaves drifted down. The forecast was showers. Should they drive? But no, the sun came out palely as she arrived at Marie and Beth's end of the street.

"Let's risk it," Marie said. "They're often wrong."

The pool was busy. The water churning with flailing bodies and in the large non-laned area, was a group of older Asian men, either standing in the middle, chatting, or swimming slowly across the width. No chance of doing lengths of back crawl there. She joined a procession in the medium lane, Beth went into the slow and Marie the fast.

By the time they came out, the sun was skimming along the edge of an angry black sky.

"It looks as if it's going to pour," said Marie. "Time for head down striding."

"So, have you given up swimming?" Laura had called in on her way home from the pool. Annie was in her raffishly short, white dressing gown and they were drinking green tea at the kitchen table.

"You know what I'm like. I get bored with things and I wasn't losing weight."

Laura did indeed know that Annie quickly lost interest in non-competitive activities. Writing articles, making TV series, radio talks and playing county and club tennis gave her the variety and challenge she craved, but swimming up and down had soon paled.

"You said how much better you felt, fitter and more flexible."

"I'm not going any more, the changing rooms are disgusting, the chlorine ruins my hair, I've picked up verrucas and you've had ringworm twice. *And* you've had conjunctivitis loads of times and gone deaf."

"Yes, but with those ear plugs the hospital made for me and goggles, I may be in my own world, but I don't get problems any more. It really lifts my mood. You say you're a bit depressed, come and try the cure!"

"It messes up my hair. I'd have to go on days when I'm going to have it done."

Laura looked across at Annie's dyed blonde, smooth helmet. "I can see your grey roots."

"Well I'm going later, after the belly dancing class and I've got a winter league match tonight. It would have been too much for one day, and I'm not sleeping. I wrote my Daily News column in the middle of the night last night and did the Times crossword." Her sand-blasted eyes registered her sleep deprivation. She rubbed them and blinked, but they stayed dry and stinging. "Anyway, I preferred it when there was just you and me. Beth bangs on too much. I'm not interested in her beige life, her trivial domestic smuggery, her girl powerlessness!"

That's a bit harsh, Laura thought. The main topic of our conversation so far is how difficult it is to fit in your hair appointment.

"Do you want some toast?"

"Are you having any?"

"No. I'm dieting again. I always seem to put on weight when it gets cold. Why don't you come and try the class?" She wondered if she would carry on with it. Everyone but Annie had seemed to be able to go into a trance, circling, whirling and wriggling around the hall with their eyes closed.

"How was it for you?" the overweight instructor had asked at the end. "Do you feel mischievous, open, younger?"

Perhaps she had better give it one more go. She had had to pay for the term.

"No thanks on both counts, I'd better get back, Dan will have made porridge. It's not fair to leave him with the children for too long. Anyway, I'm sure I'd be hopeless at belly dancing"

"Daisy's stuck the journalism course then?" Annie's cold blue eyes narrowed. "I don't think these courses help you get a job in the industry. Is she applying for anything?"

"I don't think so, not at the moment."

"She wasn't interested in that consumer research job at the BBC I told her about. I hope she knows what she's doing."

Laura looked out at the lovely garden. Martin was up a ladder, pruning the climbing rose. It was true, Annie had found Daisy quite a few openings, free-lancing in the industry for so many years, meant she could call in favours.

"Shall we have a game one evening? If we start at six we should get a court."

Laura nodded. "Perhaps next Thursday?"

"So you can't play any evening before that?" Annie asked in the impatient, sharp tone she used when displeased. Laura felt as if she were being pierced by icy needles. "You're busy every single night?"

"Well, I'll see you at choir, but there's a lecture at Somerset House, baby sitting and book group this week..." Laura said feebly.

Sitting by the table, his long body folded into the chair next to Lily, Dan was swooping a spoon about her face, exhorting her to open her mouth so the baby bunny could go into her home. Lily made a huge, wide mouth, but bit the spoon as it arrived, so porridge dribbled down her chin. She giggled.

Ruby was sitting on the floor playing with the farm and train set. "Look Nana," she shouted, jumping up and pointing at her empty plate on the table. "I eated it all up!"

Laura pulled her still damp, shoulder length dark hair back into a scrunchy, and smiled at her, thinking about when the twins and Daisy had moved in and the tsunami of cases, plastic bags and toys which had swept into the formerly orderly kitchen. She wiped Ruby's mouth and hands with a wet flannel, remembering what Daisy had said yesterday.

"You're always hoovering, tidying, cleaning, fussing, mess isn't important! Why don't you have a cleaning lady? Because you're a megalomaniac that's why. You have to control everything."

"I don't think by cleaning I'm in control," Laura had said mildly.

"Ha, if I was to move anything by a couple of inches in this house, you'd notice. We live here by your rules. You make all the decisions, from what we eat, when to change sheets to what plants and décor we have. I've got a room, but you disapprove of how I live in it. You're a control freak!"

"Why are you attacking me?"

"Oh, I'm just in a bad mood," Daisy had said and walked out into the garden. But actually it was because she envied her mother's energy and enthusiasm for life and how she had coped as a single parent, working full time, yet making her own bread and cakes and nourishing dishes from cheap ingredients. She grew vegetables and flowers, had dinner parties, played sport, *and* kept the house clean! Until she had come back home, Daisy had lived in a small flat, and after Femi had left, she had found it difficult to manage even with a cleaner.

Four more weeks and then retirement, Terry thought. How am I going to live this last part of my life? She strode along the street with strides as long as her straight skirt allowed. She felt good. Slowing down to look at her reflection in the shop windows, she thought that she looked younger than her age, though not slim. No, not slim, but this morning she had picked out a black t-shirt with little cap sleeves, black trousers and a purple jacket and her mirror had told her that with new caramel highlights in her mass of curls, she looked stylish and striking.

Through Green Park, people rushing past, heading for buses

or tubes, others on bikes, runners, mothers dragging reluctant children. Out onto Piccadilly and down White Horse Street to the wine bar. She had promised Leonard that she would not be home later than 7.30. That gives me an hour and a half, she thought.

Opening the door, she saw Bella immediately. Her oldest friend, her friend from schooldays. They met whenever Bella came up to London. Within minutes she had turned the conversation around to telling her about Tony.

"I've been working just mornings for five weeks, breaking in this guy who's taking over from me. He's sixty, wife died, children grown up and wanted a little job. He's rather attractive."

Bella looked at her closely. "You fancy him?"

"He looks at me as if we share a secret and is a bit flirty and suggestive at times. I can feel my heart racing, my body flooding with excitement, well, desire I guess," she blushed. "Then a week last Monday we went to a conference in the Ramsden hotel near Euston. We made polite conversation over lunch then we were going down in the lift together and I was tired, so I closed my eyes. The lift stopped and I opened them and he was staring at me. It made me feel really shaky I'm sure I saw naked desire there. Then the lift doors opened and I went right and he went left down the Euston Rd. I feel so awkward and yes, churned up having to work so closely with him. When we touch accidentally, I can see it's like an electric shock for him too."

"Interesting. Do you still love Leonard?"

"I don't know any more. We seem to be like brother and sister. No sex for donkey's years. There's no joy, no fun. Of course after forty-five years I can't imagine life without him, but is this enough? He's never wanted friends, just David and me. He doesn't have a social life except through me."

Bella looked irritated. "He's always provided for you, given you a lovely home, but you're going to be like Rapunzel. You deserve a better retirement than being suffocated by an old man. Come on holiday with me for a start. Derek would rather go to a golf resort with his cronies!"

"Leonard would never understand. He'd be mortified if I said I

14

wanted a holiday without him!"

"So your life has to be unhappy to make him happy. Why don't you put your foot down, threaten to leave him?"

"I couldn't…could I?"

"I haven't a clue. Work out where you could live and how much money you'd have to live on."

"I haven't been on my own since I was in college."

"Well check out this Tony guy. See if he's free and up for a relationship."

"Bella you're such a bad girl, you shouldn't encourage me."

"Remember life's never perfect. Everyone's going to have their pluses and minuses. You have to decide on balance what is most important for you. Maybe this Tony will give you everything, passion, stimulation, companionship. Perhaps he's the man for you. You'll never know till you try him out."

Terry barely noticed her homeward journey. Her head was whirling. I can't ask Tony straight out if he wants a relationship, she thought. He's never going to show interest while I'm living with Leonard. If I was single? Wouldn't it be better than living the rest of my life wondering if I had spent most of it with the wrong person? She was at her front door and suddenly her legs were weak and she did not know where she was. She hung onto the doorknob, then just as quickly she was Ok and able to open the door. "What was that?" she wondered, a stroke? Am I that stressed? "Hello, Leonard," she called. The wall clock was ticking and the tiffany lamp on the hall table was colouring the framed photograph of David and Leonard with beautiful patterns. It had been taken last Christmas, their faces repeated the same handsome features, only one grey and lined, the skin puffy a bit like a mushroom, the other like he used to look.

She filled the kettle through the spout, spraying water everywhere as she gazed out of the window at Tosca, next doors cat, tensing to spring at something in the hellebores. Leonard leapt up to mop it away.

"Thanks, can't do anything right today."

"Sit down, you've gone so pale."

15

Terry subsided onto a chair and put her head in her hands. How was she going to tell Leonard, her husband for three quarters of her life, that she was considering leaving him? Leaving their comfortable, predictable existence.

"What's wrong?" Leonard put his arm around her shoulders.

"I don't know… nothing…just a bit tired." Her head was ringing with: I can't do it. I can't!

Later, Terry stuck her fork into her last mouthful of salad, trout and Dauphinoise potatoes. She was trying to explain to Leonard why it had been difficult to teach Tony everything in a short time. Even after she officially left in December, she would probably have to pop in to the office occasionally for the handover to work successfully. Leonard was not really listening. He was sitting looking out of the window at the rain, sipping his sparkling water. He was irritatingly rather deaf and refused to wear a hearing aid, so often floated off into his private world.

He sat back, belching quietly. Sometimes she had the feeling that they had stopped communicating years earlier and perhaps he realised this too, as half way through sentences, he often stopped, stuck on a multiple memory track. Every subject seemed like a re-tread. She put down her fork and shifted her position on her chair, but he was scraping his knife around and round his plate to catch every last morsel. This action had always infuriated David. "Stop it, Dad, it's disgusting!" he would say.

Laura struggled down the road towards Beth's and Helen's houses. The bossy wind was bullying the trees, leaves flew wildly and swirled beneath her feet. In Beths' hall bare branches clicked against the window like skeletons fingers.

She was rubbing her left shoulder. "It's been stiff and painful for a couple of days, perhaps I shouldn't swim. It might make it worse. Is this what being old and decrepit is going to be like?"

"Well, you're ready to go now. When we come back, why don't we make an appointment for you to see Lynne? She's such an experienced physio. Let her tell you if you should lay off swimming."

The pool was crowded again and by the time that they returned there was almost a gale with black clouds above. The twigs and branches on the pavements were portents of another winter.

Two afternoons later they were walking to Lynne's practice. She worked from home. It was a perfect day, sunny, warm and cloudless, the trees red and gold, leaves thick underfoot

"Didn't you share a flat with Lynne when you started teaching?" asked Beth.

"Yes, when we were in our twenties, with another friend, Jo, who's just moved into Clarendon Road. Her mother Betty lives here now, she wasn't managing at home and Lynne says she's getting quite frail and forgetful."

They turned the corner and walked up a tree-lined street of well maintained Edwardian houses. "Has she lived here long?"

"Twenty years or so. She bought it with Ken, but he died after a few years." She pushed open the gate and rung the bell. A tall, well-built woman in loose trousers and a tunic top, with thick, salt and pepper hair and a rather sad face opened the oak and lead-paned door. Laura and Lynne hugged and then Beth was ushered into the treatment room.

"Mum's around somewhere. She's looking forward to seeing you," said Lynne before turning her full attention on Beth.

"Hello Betty." Laura kissed her soft, powdery face. They sat on the bench under the climbing rose, still flowering in the weak October sun.

"No luck again," Betty said, taking a crumpled lottery ticket out of her pocket, seemingly perplexed and astonished that she had failed to predict the six numbers. "There's a good show on in the West End, 'Martha' or 'Matilda.' Shall we go?"

"You're still going to West End matinees are you? I'm afraid the afternoons are difficult for me, except for today, Fridays. I have to take the twins to school and very often pick them up after. Can we walk around the garden? I'd love to have a closer look." Betty shuffled her bottom to the edge of the seat and, putting her hands on an arm, gradually eased herself upright. Reaching for her stick, she shuffled slowly down the path. The front of her skirt was grubby from kneeling. It was longer at the front and her cardigan hung very short at the back because of her forward stoop. Her grey hair was cut in a bob like most older women. She looks like an old long legged bird, like Lynne and I will look in twenty years, Laura thought.

"See the back of that bed? I can't get at it. It's choked with ivy and ground elder." Betty looked up with desolation at Laura. "My balance, my walking's not what it was. My feet, my hands, my brain don't seem to belong to me anymore. And you know how I loved to read, but I just can't concentrate to even finish a page now. Who was it who said: 'Getting old doesn't suit sissies'?"

"Wasn't it someone like Bette Davis? Jo's the one for remembering quotes."

Betty smiled. Her faded hazel eyes were red rimmed. "Oh yes, she was always quoting someone, was it, was it..."

"Oscar Wilde," said Laura. "She started a PhD in something to do with him."

After half an hour, Lynne called them in and Betty pottered off to help get the tea. This seemed to take all her energy as she nodded off a few minutes after sitting down, her cat Sophie on her lap.

"She's not the person she was," said Laura.

Lynne nodded. "She's stiff, shaky, sees things on top of one another and hallucinates. Her boyfriend did so much for her that her problems were disguised. I didn't realise she couldn't use her cooker any more or knit, or even put on the TV. When he died I arranged carers to come morning and evening to help her wash and dress and booked a cleaner. The local authority fixed up meals on wheels, fitted grab rails, raised her chair and toilet seat and put in a door lock intercom. But she still wasn't really coping on her own. Now she's even weaker and if I let her out she'll disappear for the whole of the day, slowly wandering the West End till late at night. She's eighty-eight and going off her head."

"Poor, poor Betty, no more a maths czar and wonderful, complicated knitwear designer," murmured Laura.

Lynne was cutting large slices of carrot cake for them.

"A tiny piece for me, please Lynne. I'm always hoping to get thinner," Beth said quickly.

"You'll regret it. She's a brilliant cake-maker," said Laura. "Do you know Jo has moved into a flat in Clarendon Road?"

Lynne passed her a slab of cake. "Oh, you said she was looking round here. Watch out North London men…"

"What about you? You can go on double dates."

"Me? Can't be bothered any more with jumping through all the hoops, playing all the games and trying to pass all the tests in a new relationship. I've given up on men, especially the married ones who grope you in the kitchen when you're trying to be helpful and do their washing up. They get angry when you tell them to piss off and anyway their wives think I was leading them on. I'm overweight, overburdened with Mum and over men," she said feelingly.

Sex is over rated anyway, she thought. All those meaningless couplings. A scene from a party on the deck of a yacht in Greece flashed into her head. He had seemed nice and wasn't unattractive. Sex followed on his grubby bed in an airless messy cabin. There was all the interminable thrusting and I was soaked in his sweat. It was obvious that it was as important and enjoyable to him as a visit to a gym. Was sex ever worth the effort!

They talked about Jo and how hard she was taking her divorce. "She seems to be drinking rather a lot," Laura observed.

Lynne looked irritated. "I think people who are rich stop their emotional development. They've got money, so people suck up to them and they think they can do what they want. She needs a bit of hardship, a dose of realism, she's become a spoilt madam suffering from glistening self love!"

"I think she knows that money and spending it don't make you happy," Laura said in Jo's defence.

"Hallelulia, and she's what, sixty-four? Beautiful people have an unearned pass to life's top table. Her philosophy of life has become sex, designer clothes and her terrifying steel capped toothpicks, Manolos or whatever they're called. Is there anything about her that's real? She's breathtakingly self-absorbed, a gyrating piece of billtong. And if she's still having 'treatments' she must look as if she's been pickaxed from a glacier." There was a horrified pause in the conversation. Laura remembered too late that Lynne had always been hard on Jo. Beth's eyes were unfocused and Laura could see that she was planning dinner or similar, she hated unpleasantness.

Lynne continued as if she had not assassinated her friend's character. "I'd like to cut down on patients and I'll have to if Mum gets much worse, but I've still got some mortgage to pay. I hate myself for getting so annoyed at her 'otherness'. Where has my charming, friendly, clever mother gone? She can't learn how to open the front door or put on the television and 'I don't mind, you choose,' she says whenever I ask her anything. She's become so tentative and eager to please, so accepting and dependent, she's suffocating me. I can't let her go out on her own, because she might not find her way back. If I take her out, she gets swollen feet and she's not really enjoying it, she's got this blank, trance like expression. I'm getting house bound and panicky about my life being so restricted, doing so little. I hate myself when I speak in a harsh tone and am impatient with her. I don't want to be this person. I imagined myself behaving with understanding and tenderness, not continual anger." She ran her fingers through her thick hair so it stood up and framed her face.

"She's actually rather attractive if she didn't look so fierce and tired," Beth thought.

On their way home Beth asked, "Don't you dread the time when you're forced to become a burden on other people?"

"God, yes," Laura said feelingly. "Lynne hasn't got a partner to share supporting her Mum and Betty must feel so lonely, helpless and scared of what's in front of her."

"Do you think that being snapped at is making her lose confidence?"

"Could be. Lynne's a lovely, kind hearted girl, but she can be forthright and impatient, so yes, it could be making her worse."

"My Mum got a little, no, very selfish, unreasonable, demanding and bad tempered, Betty is so sweet. Lynne's lucky," said Beth.

"Yes but you never had to actually live with her."

"No, true. Has Lynne got children?"

"No, and she's an only child."

20

"Look, there's Jo, coming out of Sainsbury's. Jo!" Laura shouted, but she had shot round the corner.

"Oh, so that's who you and Lynne were talking about," said Beth. "Did you know her before you flat shared?"

"Yes, we were at Bristol together, on the same English course, then MA's. Jo did hers on Oscar Wilde. She should have done a PhD. She's a very clever girl, and all light and dazzle and a huge appetite for life. Men can't resist her blonde rippling hair, huge boobs and lovely smile. She married Ed, and had Jessica. That's a quick synopsis."

"When did they move here?"

"Not Ed. He caught her in their bed with some Italian guy and it wasn't the first time. She's so highly sexed, she can't help herself…always needed sex and always taken too many risks. He's divorcing her."

"Were they the friends with an estate in Sussex, where you used to go for weekends?"

"Yes, well done. Hollybridge Manor. Lovely house, very grand. Heavy, carved front door, high ceilings with wonderful mouldings, beautiful fire-grates with real fires, oak floors with oriental rugs, a minstrels gallery. Ed had a barn converted into a spa with a pool, a Jacuzzi, sauna and a masseur coming in when they had weekend parties. There were flat screen TVs in every room, a chef and housekeeper. We never really fitted in. We didn't want to ride or shoot and no-one else wanted to walk."

"What a life she must have had!"

"She's not in a good state. She really did love Ed."

"What about the daughter, where's she?"

"Jess is working in New York. I think she's back this week for her graduation. I'm hoping she can get Jo to pull herself together. She's not taking much notice of me."

"She's younger than Daisy then?"

"No, she did modelling for a few years. She's a stunning looking girl, but she got fed up with the life and decided to go to University." They talked about their daughters, Daisy and Harriet.

Sleeping alone had proved to be difficult for Jo. She kept

waking at dawn with the birdsong and then tossing through the endless hours till it was time to get up. Get up? What was she getting up for? Sometimes she would listen to the World Service, or read, but mostly she was too tired, depressed and hung over so lay listening to the siren call of the blackbirds and the pigeon's mocking coo, thinking how much she missed Ed. She would have flashbacks to their best moments, but mostly to scenes from their increasingly strained relationship. She remembered every detail of their last evening. They ate Oakham chicken, rosemary potatoes and fruit salad and drunk the 'Gascogne' white wine – the £10 'dine for 2' offer, which she had hastily bought in M&S, on the way home. In silence, as they had done for some time. He was exhausted and preoccupied with work matters, while she was relaxed and replete from an afternoon shopping and a quick visit to Antons' city flat. Why did I invite him the next day? Ed often came back early on Fridays. It was a death wish. I had it coming though, she thought. She lay there squirming in pain at the memory, as she had done so many times since. Opening her eyes, she felt the bashing of a hundred tiny hammers against her skull. Recently, only red wine seemed to dull this, the smouldering tension in her stomach, and the agonising pain in her head. Taking a deep breath, she rolled over and sat up carefully, wondering how her insides would cope. She immediately felt her stomach heave. Edging her legs out of bed, her head spinning with every tiny movement, she almost crawled to the bathroom and threw up in the toilet, then slid down and passed out on the cold tiles.

She must have managed to get back to bed, because next morning she woke with a massive headache, and no idea of the time or day. All she could think of was having a drink and all the bottles on the floor were empty. She could smell herself, stale sweat, alcohol and sick? When did she last change her clothes? Staggering out of her bedroom, she was heading down the corridor towards the kitchen, when she heard the key in the lock.

"Up are you?" Jess shut the door behind her. "You stink mother. I can smell you from here. Go and have a shower. It's clean in there now. I cleared up your puke which was all over the floor."

Jo's head felt so light that it could float away. She leaned sideways against the cool wall.

"I'm going to catch the train. You are obviously not in a fit state to come."

Oh God, it's her graduation ceremony today. "Let me just get dressed."

"You're absolutely not coming. You stink of alcohol, you can hardly stand up and you've got big black bags under your eyes and filthy hair. I'm not taking you anywhere. I'd be ashamed."

Hot tears sprang into Jo's eyes and erupted like burning lava down her face.

"Oh cry, why don't you. Feel sorry for yourself again and have another drink, because that's all you can do lately!"

"Don't be so cruel. I'm really sorry."

"I wanted to be proud of you today. I thought you'd be proud of me, getting a first! Fiona could have come, but it's too late to ask Dad to bring her now. You disgust me mother. I've had it feeling sorry for you. Dad did the right thing leaving you." She stormed past Jo and into her bedroom, emerging again with her case. "I'm going to catch my train now and if there isn't a total turn round when I get back, I'm out of here for good!"

The door slammed. Jo staggered around the boxes of empty bottles, the exercise bike and the crates of shoes, books and other things in the hall that she still had not unpacked, to the mirror and looked at herself. Her much envied naturally fair shoulder length hair was in greasy rats' tails. Her skin was grey and dead looking. She widened her grey eyes trying to pull up the puffiness beneath them. I'm sixty-four, on my own and a grunting, wrecked slob. Am I trying to kill myself? Is this who I really am? Into the lounge and there were more boxes, dirty dishes, empty bottles. No wonder Jess was disgusted, coming back to this. She gazed around. It's not a bad flat. I didn't even unpack or try to make a home. She stared mournfully through the window at the dead looking box topiary and flowering bushes in their pewter pots. What were they called? 'Cloud pruned' or something. That's £250 wasted. I need to get a gardener for the patio and a cleaner. Her beautiful 'Smallbone' and 'Poggenpohl' kitchen had hardly been used. She opened the fridge and a rotting, sour smell floated out. Shutting it hurriedly, she looked in the bread bin, a whole, mouldering loaf. I've finally become the hedonistic slut that propriety and staff stopped me being for the last twenty-five years. She picked up a wine bottle, a mouthful left. Determinedly she put it down and switched the kettle on.

I've been drowning in self-pity. Laura's the only friend who ever bothers to contact me. She made herself a black coffee and sat at the expensive polished white table that could expand to seat twelve. I've got to be a better mother, a good friend, support Jess more. Drink doesn't change anything and I've got the rest of my life to live. I've got two days to get myself together for when she gets back and I must.

Keeping Jess's disgusted face and her words in her head to drive her on, she had a shower, made a mountain of dirty clothes, towels and sheets ready to wash, rang a cleaning agency, Alcoholics Anonymous and Laura. "Can you show me how to use the washing machine?" was her first question when Laura and Dan knocked at the door.

Frances lay on her back in bed, staring at the darkness. Combing methodically through her memory to replay scenes from her working life, relishing every detail as a reminder of what she had been. She knew that she should not be doing it, she should be planning her future, yet her job had been everything to her and it kept seeping back into her thoughts. Why me? What can I do with my life now?

She was the daughter of a Vicar, brought up in the Manse. Her father had taught her that she should pray for patience, kindness and gratitude, but her heart was broken. She could no longer pray; her life was over. All she could think was: "Dear God, why have you been so cruel to me. I loved my job and thought that I had respect from my colleagues…"

Most Sundays and today at five am when the tubes started, still grey with sleep, she had gone back to stare up at the blank faced, glassy building, where she had spent most of her life working. It was unbelievable that she would never walk in there again. Her glass walled office had felt like home. There were blinds if one needed privacy with a client and she could turn on white noise to prevent being overheard outside the room. Her stomach lurched and the indignity of not being able to go in and sit at her desk, turned her into ice. She knew all the sandwich bars, bought ready suppers, could get anything she wanted in this so familiar territory. I even liked working late, she thought. I'd swivel my chair so I could see the darkening streets with bright lights coming on in every office block.

If you love your job, believe in it, sacrificed for it, it would dominate your life and it did mine, I can't deny it. But that's it, the horizon in my life is a ceiling and I'm there. I'm not going to be a Chief Executive, or even a senior partner. I'm a childless, unemployed singleton. She paced around the square, watching her office window from every angle. The rain had cleared and the early morning sun aflamed the block a dazzling gold. She suddenly felt ashamed. What if one of my colleagues came in early and saw me hanging around like a ghost? She hurried down a side street onto the embankment, leaned on the wall and stared into the black water through the faint low mist still clinging on.

She was still standing motionless, dreaming as the arriving crowds of workers brushed past her. A bus was approaching, going to 'Worlds End.' Should I finish it all? Big Ben chimed in the distance. Was that seven? Better get away from here. Cold and stiff she retreated to the tube and home.

Later, she went to a lunchtime concert at St Martin-in-the-Fields. An old lady sat next to her, tapping her arthritic fingers on her score and smiling with delight. What makes her so happy? Couples were all around them, holding hands, leaning towards one another.

Everyone thinks that I love single life, that I've have no desires, that I'm too old and set in my ways and I'm not interested in men. Could I be? I know I'm not attractive, I'm ordinary, a medium sort of person. Medium height, medium weight, medium colour hair….

Chapter 3. October. Meals with Friends

'The leaves are falling, falling from trees
in dying gardens far above us; as if their slow
free-fall was the sky declining.'
Robin Robertson. 'Fall' (1955 -)

Laura hurried up the street towards the tube station. The sun shone through the delicate branches of the autumnal plane trees. Everything was so beautiful that she felt almost drunk. It was Friday, her free day.

"Where are you off to then?" Daniel had asked.

"That photography exhibition Annie wants to see."

Daniel was incredulous. "But you don't like photography!"

"I expect I'll get something from it and Annie is so keen."

"I don't understand why she can snap her fingers and you are there for her."

"I'm worried that she's not very happy at the moment. We can have a talk at the same time."

Later:

"Why can't you change your mind and play in matches with me? We were invincible for twenty odd years," Annie asked. They were sitting, drinking tea and sharing a dark chocolate tartlet, in the National Portrait Gallery café.

It was true, they had been a good team. Laura had had a long reach, killer serve and demon volley, whereas Annie could ground stroke all day and dashed about the court, retrieving everything. She had made the openings for Laura to put away.

"You know why. My reactions and movement have gone downhill. You're amazing that you still feel so competitive."

"It's part of who I am, isn't it? It's coming up to fifty years of playing county if you count the juniors and the vets. You eat the rest. I just wanted a taste, you know I only have to look at cake to..." she puffed out her cheeks.

"Well, I'm happy not playing competitively now. I'd prefer to have single knocks for exercise. I don't want to depress myself playing doubles. You've always needed to feel frantically busy, packing your day with activity, diving at life, with your projects, deadlines, appointments, classes, matches. It's as if you're scared to have a moment to be relaxed and philosophical."

Annie gave Laura a cold stare.

"I've got to keep on top of things. I'm not going to start going backwards!"

"Life's like tennis, you're not going to win every time. You're going to have to accept, we're getting older. It was incredibly painful for me to walk away from my department. I'd built it from almost nothing, but I've never gone back, don't want to know how it is now. I'm trying to reset my sights on something completely different. Perhaps you need to be planning what you're going to do when you retire?"

Annie's shoulders slumped a little. "Mmm, perhaps you're right. I've been thinking a lot of how tired of everything I am. I've been working for over forty years in a dog eat dog competitive world, having to keep coming up with new stuff to keep ahead, brought up Ben, played club and county tennis matches and yes, thrown myself at life, but I'm starting to feel old, clapped out. I read other food journalists' entries on Facebook, can I keep being out there in front? It's getting harder and harder. I'm desperate for the stillness and warmth of my bed, but I haven't been sleeping through the night since I don't know when. I'm up, writing my column, doing crosswords, so I'm irritable and have toddler tantrums if I get behind a slow driver or am not served instantly in a shop. And what's happened to my concentration? Even selling things on ebay I keep forgetting my password and have to make up another and a user name and code name and by the time I've decided when the bidding can start from and for how long, I've spent half a day on it and had no takers!"

"Can't you try and calm down, Annie, prioritise, organise, relax a bit. Nobody's keeping score, just you."

Laura was doing housework. If only the words would flow out lyrically, meaningfully. She had had some deeply satisfying times as a teacher, not better than having Daisy or meeting Dan of course, but writing would give worth and meaning to her retirement, this dream she has of creating a novel.

Her obedient duster flew over the mantelpiece and small tables, lifting any dust and rubbing out little finger-marks as she thought about the choices people make after retirement. Some people think living in London is dirty, noisy and expensive, uncontrollably chaotic, with frustrating deficiencies and they retire to the country. I would miss all those things that fire up my imagination: people watching, imagining the ghosts of all the past eras, those meadows, streams and farms, buried beneath the concrete and under that, the remains of Roman life as much as twenty feet below! This city's so stimulating and exciting. The posh bits, the parks, the gouged scars of criss crossing railway lines, derelict buildings, mansion blocks, the smell, the pollution of too many humans and their detritus. She ran the duster along the top of the kitchen door, ugh, filthy, too much dust and dirt, but I never want to leave its endless options and possibilities...

She heard the phone and her heart sank. Three pm and she had barely started writing. It would be Daisy asking her to pick up the children, though Thursdays and Fridays are not her days to fetch or feed. "Hello Mum, I don't think I can get back in time, can you pop over to the school?"

Recently she had made up reasons not to, been evasive. She had better go this time. "Yes."

"Perhaps you could give them supper and a bath. I'll be back by six."

"Yes, Ok, bye." She put the phone back, hoping that she had not been too short with Daisy, but no writing again today...Not that she *has* to write, it's just a hobby after all, but it is what she has always wanted to do. Looking at the clock, she realised with annoyance that there wasn't time to buy more food. They would not like fresh tuna and sprouting seed salad. She would have to make something up.

Ruby saw her opening the gate to the school playground and ran towards her, round face and soft brown eyes like a little dusky cherub.

Laura swept her into her arms and they rubbed noses, giggling because Ruby's was runny. Lily had seen her, but was busy playing aeroplanes, whizzing round and round, making sure she was out of reach. "Nana, Nana," Ruby sang, "isn't Lily naughty?"

Laura was thinking of her own childhood, where she had run free in the country, damming streams, climbing trees, racing through the bracken. Children in London played in manicured gardens where they were only allowed in certain places. They were unaware of real nature, of the fact that without huge effort their surroundings would be back to waist high thistles, ragwort and nettles, rampant bindweed and traveller's joy.

She loved them intensely and had been unprepared for the powerful feelings of pure love welling inside her. She had read somewhere that life with children was life in colour, while without them it was black and white.

After a long bath, answering twenty-five hundred questions about why some toys sank and where birds slept, the water was almost cold before they could be persuaded to get out. She read them 'The Inside Duck', in bed. Their lips moved as they remembered the familiar lines.

"Hi Lynne, how are you? What was that shouting when you picked up the phone?"

"Sorry Laurs, but Mum just dropped a bottle of milk on the floor."

"Shall I ring back later?"

No, I've mopped up most of it. I'm having fun with all manner of captivating activities, hoovering, bloody dusting, making a casserole while considering my responses to well crafted discourses from my mother, but I can have a quick chat."

"Now, now," said Laura. "Betty was telling me last week how powerful and strong you were and how you've smacked her when she did stupid things, as if that were to be admired! I was quite shocked. I know I don't have to live with her, but you said yourself you felt upset when you lost your temper."

"I know, I know, but she's getting worse. She's been diagnosed with Dementia with Lewy bodies. We can't even go out now because she leaves damp patches if she sits down. She's getting frustrated and angry at being in so much and when I've got patients I'm wondering what she's doing all the time. I made a biological decision not to have kids, all those nappies and toddler sick, but it's like having one now! Someone, somewhere is living the life I should have had. I had so many dreams and instead I'm a pensioner living with my demented mother!"

"I was going to ask you if you two wanted to come for supper on Thursday? We could talk about it, while Dan shows Betty his paintings or something?"

Lynne had a quick shower. It was almost time to get Betty up. She rubbed herself dry and reached for the body lotion, her brain busy with questions of money and debt and if she would ever have sex again. The lotion was smooth and cool as she rubbed it gently into her skin. It was getting drier, more wrinkled, the last vestiges of youth, withering away. "Bye, bye thickening ankles and receding gums stage, hello thin, greying hair and loose hanging flesh phase." The mirror was thankfully too steamed up to see her reflection. She reached for her M&S capacious underwear. "I really should buy something a bit sexier." Putting her towel on the heated rail, she went down stairs to make tea for Betty. The clock in the hall was ticking, the sun was shining in through the stained glass above the door, onto the vase of golden chrysanthemums. Life was not that bad and at least she did not have to cook supper tonight.

They had eaten the parmagiano and then the salmon, watercress sauce, beetroot mash and a mix of green vegetables and were pausing before the lemon pudding. Betty had been playing with her food and endlessly wiping a trickle of saliva from the corner of her mouth. Then she had gone into a deep sleep, her head back and her mouth open. "Mum, mum, wake up, eat your nice supper." Lynne had tried to wake her, but she had gone into a quieter, distant place and could not hear.

"She seems to be retreating inside herself with less and less interest in anything. She's frailer, more tired, can't remember new information and sleeps most of the day. Her life is dwindling away," Lynne said sadly

"What are you going to do? You can't manage your patients and Betty," Dan asked.

"That's true. Her memory is terrible, it's a tangled mess. She's got perfect recall of her childhood and school friends, poems she learnt then, but of the here and now, she remembers nothing. My world has shrunk, like hers, her friends have faded away and so have some of mine. Perhaps because I'm tired of them giving me advice. Has she tried sudoku, or crossword puzzles, or counting backwards in seven's? they say. 'Use it or lose it.' I'm getting really sarky, why do they think a few minutes in a mind gym is going to make a difference? She had the most creative, agile mind of anyone I've known, and it's not because she didn't use it, the opposite in fact.

I'm going to have to put her in a nursing home that's just round the corner from me. Then I can go and see her every day and not worry about what she's doing all the time."

Laura didn't know what to say. Betty was a highly intelligent, proud woman, who had always said: "Don't put me in a Home. Shoot me first!"

Pale sun shining, frost on the grass and squirrels busily collecting for whatever was ahead. The trees had shed most of their brown and gold leaves and a biting wind, was whipping them into eddies. There was a squawking overhead and Helen looked up to see six tropical green parakeets darting between the trees. "They used to be confined to the Barnes/Twickenham area. They're taking over London."

"Terry says she might come with us next week," said Laura.

"Oh good, but thought she hated swimming?"

"Yeh, but she says she needs to have some exercise and she's only part time now. I keep telling her she's supposed to do thirty minutes of exercise five times a week…to be fit and healthy, and she's intrigued by all the interesting women we chat to in the changing room"

"I saw Leonard the other day He doesn't look over eighty does he?"

"Absolutely not. Great hair, hardly white and so thick. Not sure he's a bundle of fun though, he doesn't seem to like going out much. Except to play golf, but only with Terry . Come on, let's cross."

"Hasn't he been retired for years?"

"Maybe twenty-five? More perhaps. He's always got DIY projects on the go, their house is immaculate, very modern. You should see their kitchen! It's all glass, black metal and stainless steel, polished concrete floor, minimalist, efficient. And, he's a non-smoking, teetotal, non-meat eater, so Terry really loves a drink and meat when she's out."

"Poor Terry. Wasn't he an engineer?"

"Yes, in Kuala Lumpur, they often talk in Malay, they were there for so long. She's really loved her job running that educational charity, after all those years of not being particularly challenged. I don't think she should be retiring, just because he wants her to be around more. Oh, damn, there's a queue and we're late."

Rain was splashing from the broken gutter onto the pot of pansies, scattering the soil and making a pool. I should move the pot, Terry thought, then absentmindedly wandered away to get the lunch. It was so cold. They had agreed not to put on the heating until six pm every day. She was going to miss the warmth of her office at work. There was the sound of a key in the lock.

"Did you get soaked?"

"Not too bad." He put down the shopping.

"I was sopping when I got back. The soup's hot."

"I'll just put these away."

He unpacked his rucksack and took off his wet boots and anorak. He was wearing an ancient cardigan and baggy walking trousers. Why can't he ever look smart? She thought, ladling out the soup and cutting bread. They moved around one another companionably as only two people with no sexual interest in one another can do.

"I'll replace that gutter tomorrow if this rain stops," he said.

That evening, table laid, the food ready, heating on, they sat sipping drinks with Laura and Dan. Terry seemed a bit switched off. She was polite and hospitable, but definitely as if part of her were somewhere else. Laura's heart had sunk when they had arrived. She could smell fish. It sunk even further when Terry carried four trout triumphantly out of the kitchen, complete with their heads and tails. Leonard dexterously filleted them and looked across at Terry a few times, but she was oblivious. "Terry," he barked and pointed to the mess on the serving plate. She shook her head as if to clear it and jumped up saying "I'll get a bowl for the skeletons."

Laura ate her salad, but was not doing well with her fish. Every mouthful of flesh seemed infested with bones. She was desperate to spit it all out and had to think hard about other things, not to retch. Leonard was espousing his rigid left wing views to a laid back, politely attentive Daniel. "Paying for privileged access shouldn't be allowed, not private health care or education or even 'speedy boarding'. They mean that the wealthy and rest of us live increasingly separate lives and shared citizenship is eroded."

She and Terry had been discussing tomato blight.

"Hasn't that always been the case?" Daniel asked mildly.

But Leonard had started on his other pet hate, paying tips and bonuses. "Financial incentives destroy good and selfless behaviour."

Laura's plate resembled a war zone. She had tried to squash the fish together, so it appeared that she had eaten most of it. Something's up with Terry, she thought as she caught her smiling to herself. She's miles away, where? With that guy at work?

Phillip went to professional meetings on Thursdays and Helen had invited Beth and Laura for supper. Helen and Beth had met almost thirty years ago when they had both moved to the estate but once Beth started child rearing and meeting other mothers at the school gates, Helen had dropped out of her world and mind, to re-enter it recently. No-one liked to ask why she and Phillip had never had children.

"Wine, fruit juice or Badoit?" Helen asked when they arrived.

"Tap water is fine," said Beth.

"It's full of hormones and human and animal waste."

"Ok, Badoit then. I try not to drink wine except with food."

"Red for me," added Laura. "Thanks. How's your shoulder, Beth?"

"The exercises seem to have done the trick, thank you. I'm coming swimming tomorrow."

Helen knew that neither of her friends approved of her smoking. "So sorry," she murmured. Her hand with three large jade rings hovered over a delicately carved musical cigarette box. "Do you mind if I just have two or three drags? Work is quite stressful at the moment, Yvonne has retired and Chioma's on maternity leave." They shook their heads and she reached for an elegant lighter set in rosewood.

"Little conscience gifts?" thought Beth, then felt guilty. The room was full of presents from Phillip's visits to conferences all over the world, but it did not seem cluttered, such was its cosy, pretty, style. Pink lampshades and lacy chair backs, embroidered cushions and pink and white rugs on the oak floor. Helen was wearing quite a low cut dress revealing freckled skin and an ample bosom. The photographs on the piano were of a slim, lithe Helen. She must have had her pick, with her looks: brown eyes, thick, glossy auburn hair and husky, sexy voice, Beth concluded. "Are you sure you want to go part time? Don't you wish you'd gone for the principal psychologist job?"

They were sitting at the laid table, after carrying the food in from the kitchen.

Helen took a spoonful of minted little potatoes. "I just felt too old, to be managing the budget cuts, attending more meetings, organising the EP team, dealing with difficult parents and head teachers...the rest of the department are in their twenties or early thirties. But now Marta has taken over, I feel that we've tried the all the initiatives she's suggesting, said all the same things and made all the same mistakes before. *And* because of cuts, no one has replaced a colleague on maternity leave or one who has left, so I've had to take on extra schools. I've had enough. I want to go part time, be less involved." She passed around the dish of broccoli florets and broad beans and popped back into her tasteful shrine of lime washed oak cupboards, aga cooker, eau de nil walls and subtle lighting, for a refill.

34

Re-emerging, she handed Laura the filled dish. "I've been working ever since we moved into this house. I could spend more time here and do some travelling if I could cut my hours down."

"You'd be cutting your pension down too, wouldn't you? Isn't it based on your final salary?"

"Not if I take it next spring, when I'm sixty five, then top it up with some part time and have less paperwork. I know we could manage if I retired, but I need to work a little for me." Tears were pricking her eyes. "I want to enjoy my life and do things, see things, before I get too old and my health starts disintegrating. Before Mum went into the home she wasn't coping, her house was a mess and needed repairs and her lovely garden was a jungle. She was too weak to do more than sit in the same clothes she went to bed in. It took ten minutes for her to come to the door and then another ten to open the six locks. That state can't be a million years away for me."

Laura sipped the velvety, fruity wine appreciatively. "Yes, it's so hard. We all want our lives to go on forever and hang on to what we know, then it all gets too much. Should we be down sizing now, or joining 'Exit'?" She took some more lamb and the talk moved to the closure of the News of the World and the integrity of journalists.

"What do you think is necessary for a happy retirement, Laura? You always seem happy?" Helen asked over the pudding.

"A positive attitude and good health. Having ambitions and interests, yes, and different ones from your partner. The worst thing is probably to think it's a time for doing nothing and relaxing. You see people slowing down too much, feeling useless and losing their energy and self pride." She grinned and lifted her glass. "It's such a special age. Retirement is the age of opportunity when you can hopefully achieve whatever you have been dreaming about."

"So, when you're part time…" Beth helped herself to another spoonful of rhubarb fool as she brought the conversation back to Helen. "You'll be able to go to exhibitions and concerts and join the choir. Laura says you don't have to be able to sing."

"Or the book group. You have to be able to read," smiled Laura. "We don't want flakey people not having time to read the monthly choices."

35

"I may try both," said Helen, getting up to clear away the dishes.

She wondered later what she was really going to do. She had said what she thought they wanted to hear, but did she really want to work part time, join a choir and book club and get used to her empty bed? What *was* she going to do about Phillip? Her scream echoed around the house. "Could I chuck him out, can I manage my life, my finances, without him?"

Marie had spent the morning gardening, accompanied by squeals and shouts from next door's children, playing badminton. It was a mild, pleasant day and she had cut the grass for the last time before the spring, raked up the leaves and piled them on top of the summer's prunings in the wild area behind the fruit trees at the end of the garden. Ready to light a bonfire at dusk.

She felt unsettled, she had completed the MSF CRN forms, been in to see the HR department and said not Burma again, and hopefully not to a war zone. She still had nightmares of the emergency hospital tents, the stench of suffering, of human meat in her nose, lights swinging on wires in the operating theatre, sucking power from the ambulances, the sounds of screaming, suffering, having to cut chop, and stitch…all those cut off limbs. She had had an acceptance email, but no posting had yet been offered. Her initial euphoria was dimming and she wondered if she was too old, if she should put that life out of her mind…there was plenty of locum tenens GP work…

The book she had been scribbling in was leather bound, its blank pages were smooth, soft and inviting for writing. She pushed it away. Her sad thoughts were now in the book, instead of in her head. Opposite was Arun's favourite chair. Sometimes she could swear that he was sitting there, reading. "Don't feed the pain with these hallucinations," she told herself. "Life can be good again, just different."

The towering waves of black grief, which had stormed above her head had crashed down when she had got back to London. She had thought she would die too, but no, here she was, living, sort of anyway, with her tender, beautiful memories.

She looked at her watch. I'd better have a shower and get

dressed. What shall I wear? Fran's friends are well heeled, sophisticated, I'd better not look too ethnic. It's ridiculous at my age to be apprehensive about a lunch party and worry about wearing the right thing. I'll make some notes on that interesting article about the economy, some of them are bound to be bankers. I suppose I'm lucky. Older single women don't often get invited out, there aren't many tame older single men to balance the table plan.

Having chosen a black shift dress with a heavily embroidered little jacket, she took the tube to Islington. Out of the station and down the traffic choked main road she walked, past endless shops with bowls of rotting fruit and veg on stands taking up half the pavement. Turning the corner, it was so quiet.

In David and Fran's street blank-faced houses, either dripped with wisteria or had bay trees in pots behind their wrought iron railings. Looming beyond them were council high rises. A cruising car with throbbing music was coming nearer and nearer. She felt a chest-bursting explosion as it swept past. Then the road was hers again.

She remembered their beautiful stained glass door, here it was, and rung the bell.

David opened the door, embraced her and took the bouquet of hydrangeas, "How kind, lovely to see you," and she was inside on the polished parquet floor, being kissed by Fran and ushered through the french doors into their small, elegant formal garden. "It's not too cold at the moment, but we'll go in for lunch. Will, this is Marie, can you give her a glass of champagne please."

Marie took the glass from a plumpish, nice looking man, probably in his fifties, wearing expensive looking chinos, polo shirt and blazer. She had learnt to live compassionately and harmoniously with Arun and given up intoxicating substances. She hadn't changed her ideas or beliefs, but hey, she needed something to help her get through this. Two other couples were chatting in a group. One she had definitely met before, Tricia...Tessa and Bob? What on earth are their names? Weren't they boring and self-opinionated? Stop it Marie. It's a lovely day, the garden looks beautiful, birds are singing in the trees, it can't be all bad.

"You remember Brian and Tess?" said Fran, propelling them

37

towards her. Within minutes she had found that they had just returned from Sri Lanka and Brian proceeded to list place names, dates and a day-by-day account of their holiday. Tess, impatient at not getting the opportunity to tell her side of their adventure, side-lined Will. There was no escape for either of them.

In an effort to get away from his next subjects of 'Mad Men', 'The Wire', and their clips on 'YouTube' and his apparent unconcern that she had no interest in them, she sidled sideways, but, as if to the manor born, without seeming to pause for breath Brian and Tess swopped victims. Marie listened patiently to Tess's account of her superb time management and organisation with five children. She oozed smug domestic imperialism, secure in the knowledge that no woman's life was better or more fascinating than her own. They're a conceited, charmless, self-indulgent couple, she thought, feeling spiteful and mean.

For lunch, Marie was seated between Brian and the other man, a lawyer called Nigel. The conversation ebbed and flowed around her. She turned her bright, interested face towards Nigel, wondering how much longer she could pretend to be fascinated by his monologue. By the time that they had finished the main course, Brian and Nigel were competing for the floor, sometimes across her, she wondered if they would notice if she sunk under the table.

To her surprise, Will offered her a lift home and she found herself agreeing to a walk the next day.

Laura, in an effort to get Jo out of her flat, asked her for supper when Dan was playing squash. She poured glasses of Shiraz and put a tuna salad down between them. "This is like old times at university, except that the wine and food are rather better. How are you feeling now?" she asked, pulling a chair up to the table.

Jo took a long swig from her glass. "I'm just a bit lost. I keep dreaming that I've jumped from a Hollybridge window thinking I could fly, and I soar briefly then hurtle to the ground, which wakes me up, terrified and shaking. I'm drinking too much and live on takeaways. I'm not being freaky Laurs, but I'm hyper-aware of our mortality…we're getting to the end!" She made a comic-sad face.

"Don't be so dramatic. You've got years of fun ahead of you. Stop feeling sorry for yourself. Everyone gets depressed some times. You're a privileged, clever, attractive girl with your health and enough money to live comfortably."

"Yeh, you're right, I'm pathetic. It's just that it feels like only yesterday that I was sexually attractive to men and life was sheer fun…Ok, I'm not in elasticated stockings and getting meals on wheels yet…but if I stop plucking the hairs out of my chin, I'll have a luxurious beard and my joints are stiff and creaky in the morning…My body is racing ahead of me. I'm not ready to be old."

Laura nodded, "Well, I can't move in tennis like I could, my reactions are slow, slow, god I see the ball late, and I need my glasses for choir." She looked at her friend, at her eyes like stirred mud, full lips, her stupendous exposed breasts like huge suet puddings. She had always worn low cut tops, her olive skin was so unusual for a blonde. "Well you're looking pretty young to me, how do you do it?"

"Alcohol, Botox, a little surgical help and good genes." She leaned over and refilled her glass again. "What was that maxim? 'You can't turn back the clock, but you can wind it up again?' I've always taken it for granted that I could attract men, but perhaps those days are gone? Why does it take a man to validate me to make me want to keep in shape…to enjoy life, anyway?"

"Do more things. I keep asking you to come swimming."

"Mmm, could do." An answer, which sucked the air out of Laura's suggestion. Jo knew she would not be up in time, she could not shake her depression with her reduced life. She had tried to persuade herself that 18a Cranford Road was a sweet little flat, but in reality all the fireplaces and Edwardian features had been ripped out and the lounge, patio and her bedroom faced cold north. With the money I spent on surgery I could have bought a nice house, she thought.

"It's all your fault, Mother." Jess would say if she complained.

This realisation made her pain even worse. She had been too cocky, too sure of Ed's love. It had made her behave too outrageously. Her grief at her behaviour was sometimes overwhelming. She would lie in bed, groaning like an injured animal.

And the thought of him now playing happy families with Fiona, that wig on a stick posh girl and her two daughters...

"Ed seemed to have set himself up quickly."

Laura must have been reading her thoughts. She topped up her glass. "You don't know how badly I treated him. He must have been thinking for a long time about leaving me. I never cooked anything, just warmed up those convenience meals. I drunk too much and flirted with everyone."

Laura grimaced. "You've always been hit on though."

"I asked for it." A vision of his eyes that day he told her he was leaving was in her head. They had a poisonous hatred. All civility and love had gone and she could see there was no going back. "I think we should make a go of it until Jess finishes University, it's not fair on her," she had said.

"How thoughtful," he had replied. "You should have thought about that before. She's not stupid, you've never bothered to hide your appalling behaviour."

A vision of Jess aged sixteen catching her on the couch with Sebastien flashed into her head. "You're sick, why don't you act your age? You're nearly a pensioner, it's gross! The general idea is that when you get married, you're faithful, you settle down with your partner, my father, not shop around for sex thrills! You're disgusting."

She shook her head to drive the memory away. "I do love you Laurs. You're my only friend, you're part of the fabric of my life."

"What happened to all those weekend friends?"

"No-one so much as rung me after we started divorce proceedings." She picked up the salad bowl and emptied the remainder onto her plate. Then looked up, "Oh, I'm so sorry Laurs, how rude of me." She offered her plate to her friend.

Laura smiled. "No honestly, go ahead, there's still tons of rocket in the garden. I get a sick of eating it and it won't last through a frost."

There was a silence as if their conversation had hit a speed bump. They looked around the kitchen with hazy smiles, both searching their brains for safer topics.

Chapter 4. November. Sour thoughts

'We know not what sores may be running into the waters while we are bathing and what sort of matter we may thus imbibe!'
Tobias Smollett
'The Expedition of Humphry Clinker.' (1721-1771).

Laura was in her bedroom, hastily pulling on her bathing costume. The heating had only just come on. A chilly drizzle was spattering the windowpanes, spreading its fine gauze, making the sodden garden blurred and mysterious. The phone rang. Who is ducking out now, Laura wondered, or offering to drive rather than walk?

Five minutes later and she was driving herself. None of her friends were coming, none of her usual acquaintances were in the changing room or pool and the lane for medium speed swimmers had eight people slowly following one another round and round. Laura got into the big unlaned area, where the non-swimmers and exercisers clung to the edges, stood chatting or made short excursions, their sausage floats tucked under their arms. She started to plough up and down next to the fast lane, where no-one else had ventured, feeling sour and a bit depressed. Why am I swimming on Monday anyway? There are far more contaminants in the water after the weekend. She was speculating about the amount of particles of faeces, urine, dead skin cells and hair and was half way down the pool when a little woman got in and determinedly breast stroked towards her. Laura kept going; surely she had seen that she was already swimming down against the rope lane divider and would move over; there was room for them not to collide. But then, she never gave way. She had infuriated most of Laura's friends by swimming at them. Three quarters of the way down the pool Laura stopped and stood up in the water. "I'll move shall I?" she asked sarcastically to the face in front of her. The woman ignored her and made no attempt to make a detour. What is her problem? Laura fumed as she got out of the way. She had a choice, go and swim somewhere else, or get out. She did the latter, wondering if she would be banned if she had slapped her.

Annie was up before dawn sitting at the kitchen table with a cup of hot water, studying the kitchen. Two companies had sent designers who had measured and plotted the arrangement of the units and sent suggestions and quotes. Their prices were much of a muchness. She had to decide between walnut, oak or maple and silver, white or cream appliances.

She wrestled with the decision for an hour or so, then shut the file to be reviewed later and got on with an article for the Daily News. Looking out of her bedroom window after her morning shower, she saw Laura's car going past towards home, waited five minutes then gave her a ring. "Are you coming to Bicester village on Friday, Laura? I got a Jonathan Saunders dress half price last time."

"Mmm, not keen. I went a year or so ago and there were only tiny or very big sizes, which is what you'd expect really."

Martin waved from the door. "Hang on a minute, Laurs. Where are you going, Martin?"

"I'm just going round to Ray's to help him sort out the plumbing for his walk-in shower room. I'll be back at tea time."

"You're a fool, Martin. He's taking advantage of you. Tell him to get a plumber."

He hunched forward miserably, his thin frame folding into itself as if she were administering a blow. "I've said I'd help and he's lonely since Alice left him." He ran his fingers through his thin, grey, carefully combed hair. He always seemed to have a nervous urgency, be moving, changing his weight distribution, checking his watch or adjusting his glasses. If Annie allowed herself to think about these irritating habits, they drove her mad. She waved him away and carried on her conversation with Laura. "He's impossible, *I* want a new walk-in. He's built that workbench in the shed with racks and racks of shelving to store his tools, varnishes, glues, paints, brushes, plugs, you name it. They're all neatly stacked. Why's he wasting time doing someone else's jobs?"

"Give him a break, Annie. He pampers to most of your whims. You're a lucky girl!"

They finished their conversation and Laura put down the phone thinking about Martin's attributes of gentleness, modesty and kindness which Annie seemed to interpret as naivety, inadequacy and weakness. She constantly did what no human being should ever do to another, destroyed his dignity and self-belief.

Later, as Laura dusted, mopped and vacuumed the lounge she was still thinking about Annie's dominant, short fuse character. At school she had been Head Girl and played in all the teams. She liked to be in charge, she liked to win. They had met in their early twenties, playing county matches against one another and then teamed up when they found themselves at the same London club.

Martin was gentle and mild mannered. Laura wondered if he had lacked the edge required in his working environment. Four years ago, it had been suggested to him that he took early retirement, while still being available, if needed, in his specialist area, harbour design. Other more aggressively self-promoting engineers had taken over his field in recent years.

They had been married for nearly forty years and he called himself 'Annie's devoted swain.' Her response was to give him a daily bashing, belittling everything he said, putting him down and ripping out his soul to wave it like a flag. It's tragic, Laura thought.

Then again, no one knows the whole story. Perhaps Martin doesn't mind being subjugated. Surely though, what matters even more than love is respect. Caring how the other one feels, wanting to know what they think and finding it interesting and important. Contempt is a killer. She finished her vacuuming and wound the flex onto the Dyson to carry it upstairs to clean the bedrooms, before she went to fetch the twins.

She had bumped into Martin in Sainsbury's yesterday. He was always quiet, but he had seemed distracted and reserved and there was something else she could not quite put her finger on, something different about him. He seemed to have taken to starting a conversation then withdrawing into himself, hunching forward miserably silent. His balding head, his wrinkly forgettable face and slight stature ensured that he was not someone you would notice, though if anyone did they would see his soft brown eyes and his sweet smile. He could be talked about as 'poor old' and be treated with indifference, but his appearance was deceiving. He was like water that trickled through your hands, but wears away rocks, sweet and seemingly easy to handle, but enduring and probably stubborn to have stayed with Annie so long. And he was the perfect husband. Solicitous, supportive, practical, calm and hard working. Their house and garden were immaculate. He constantly worked on improvement projects; a northwest facing beautiful conservatory, ensuite bathrooms for every bedroom and a Bang and Olufsen system relaying music to almost every room in the house.

She wondered if he was depressed at no longer working at the job he loved or was it Annie's constant bullying, or his son's 'coming out'? Were any of those phantoms flickering at the back of his brain?

They chitchatted about the weather, then Laura asked, "Are you Ok Martin? Is anything wrong?"

"No, no, I'm fine. It's just…just Annie's a bit hyper at the moment."

"Martin, you know I love Annie, but don't let her get away with bullying you. She's a full on compulsive controller. Don't kow tow to her. She gets over it if you say no to her sometimes."

"Yes…she wasn't always like this, you know. I don't think she can help herself. She gets so worked up," he said weakly, obviously feeling guilty at talking about her, even to one of her best friends. "I'd better go. Bye Laura."

Dan was on his way to the tube. It was early evening, but already windows no longer slept, but were bright with light. He was thinking how much nicer life had been before Daisy had moved back in, he had found the change very unsettling. Daisy and the children had gone from being occasional visitors during the last four years, to being omnipresent. In the three months now since he had retired, the house had become noisy and felt smaller. Even his airy, light attic studio, his retreat, wasn't sacrosanct, or the cellar where he did odd jobs. Laura would often need him for something or one of the twins would be shuffling down the steep stairs on their bottoms: "Dan, Dan, I help you. Let me see?"

Daisy was slowly coming up the road towards him, carrying her usual skinny latte, and wearing only a sloppy sweater, black tights and a pair of spike-trim ankle boots. She looked like a model with her coltish legs and bee-stung lips. Laura must have looked similar. "Your mother is waiting to go out to choir," he said hopefully. She raised her eyebrows and sailed on.

Laura enjoyed choir. She had an average voice, but singing gave her an endorphin rush, it uplifted her and banished tiredness and any feelings of depression. She stood with the sopranos because they invariably sang the tune. The bases were note bashing. They looked like a group of old bears growling at the moon. Around her she could hear the squeaky, high pitched chit-chat of her fellow sopranos. Mathew gave them a warning look and then they were concentrating totally on enunciating at speed through 'Carol of the Bells'.

The next evening, Laura had put the twins to bed and was sitting in the conservatory finishing off their supper of macaroni cheese, french beans and roasted vegetables, her insoluble situation going round and round in her head. She sipped a glass of Merlot, gazed out at the darkening garden and agonised about being unable to communicate with Daisy. Other mothers and daughters seemed to be always on the phone to one another or going out on shopping trips, but Daisy had been self-contained and shut off ever since Daniel had moved in. She's a lovely, friendly, clever and articulate girl and kind and thoughtful to her friends. Why can't we be close and loving like we used to be? I can't say anything right to her. When I told her how rebellious and wanting to hurt Mum I'd been when I was young, she was so sarcastic and deriding. "Oh, is this the 'it's a phase, you'll grow out of it' theory?' 'Cos if it is, forget it, you might have, but I'm different."

That awful time she lied to me about applying for University…

"Why didn't you send off your application Daisy?"

"I don't want any more fucking education. I'm not going to University and that's that."

"Then what are you going to do?"

"That's my decision."

"But Daisy, you're so clever and you'll have such fun!"

"I'm going to write a novel."

"You could always take that up later in life, get a career first?"

"I am no longer a child, Mother." Her tone had been intended to freeze. "You obviously don't understand how I want to live my life, so I am not discussing it."

"There's no money in writing. Earning a living and being able to support yourself should be your first priority. There's plenty of time in later life for writing, you'll have more to write about."

"You don't get it, how awful you are," Daisy had shouted. "Daniel says you bang on until you get your way."

"No I don't," I had replied, but I had had a suspicion that it was true; he could sometimes be very perceptive.

Daisy had scraped her spoon around the yoghourt pot. "You're impossible, Mother, exasperating. Not everyone wants to be a workhorse. I don't have your stamina and drive. I want to do it my way, back off."

Her voice had been harsh, so Laura had braced herself. "Can we discuss it later when I come home from work."

"That would be pointless. Anyway I'm out tonight. Just give up, Mum, you're not going to win this one." She had got up, tossed the pot into the washing up bowl for Dan to wash and recycle and stomped up to her bedroom.

Have I been wrong, trying to guide her? Too prescriptive? I wish someone had tried to help me when I was her age...

Why did I keep believing that everything would turn out for the best? Ok, she did go to University in the end. But was I blind and self-deceiving letting Dan into our home? I kept hoping that her pain would go away, but it never did. So now she's getting her own back. I remember over-hearing her saying to Jess how home had become an alien place. 'They'd both be at work and the house would be quiet when I surfaced, but it wasn't my haven any more, a cuckoo was in my nest. I'd go down the stairs, knowing every creak, every mark on the paintwork, every stain on the carpet, my home had been my refuge, but it had been invaded.' She'd said.

What should I have done?

The forecast gale arrived in the night. Laura thrashed around, sleeping fitfully until her alarm went off. Fumbling for the clock, she groaned, feeling battered and headachey. It was dark and she could hear sheets of rain against the window. Pulling the duvet over her head, she tried to relax, but after a few minutes the phone rang. It was Beth.

"It's nearly stopped, it's clearing up, you are coming, aren't you?"

Ten minutes later and Beth, Helen, and Laura were picking their way through pavements littered with twigs, broken branches, rubbish and upturned wheely bins. The trees were still being terrorized and the pale sun came and went between black clouds.

Laura bent down and caught a couple of plastic water bottles, careering along in front of them. "Damn plastic bottles! What pisses me off are all those people who walk around clutching them and swigging water every so often, to 'hydrate'! Water's free from the tap. They're just slaves to marketing. Then they throw them in the bin, so they can travel half way round the world to be burnt or something in China. Grr." This was one of Laura's hobby horses.

"That reminds me, I had a little note from Harriet yesterday," Beth said.

"How is Rwanda?" asked Helen.

"She's back in three weeks, but she's enjoyed teaching. I'm hoping she'll be a bit more laid back about life now."

"Do you think she'll want to teach?"

"Not sure. She's pretty keen on saving the planet. Shopping with her is exhausting. She examines every item and works out the variety with the least food miles!"

"Very laudable, but…" said Laura.

"Well I do try and buy local, go to Farmers Markets even though it's expensive and anyway the heating and lighting used to ripen the tomatoes in this country probably produce more carbon than flying them from Africa or wherever. We only have the heating on in the evening as you know, but she makes us turn it down, so we're going round the house in coats. We're not allowed to use the dish washer and she's a vegetarian because animals fart."

"Not all animals," Laura said mildly. "And doesn't buying from

47

developing countries help their economies?"

Will had invited Marie out for a meal. The food was good and the wine plentiful, but their conversation was stilted. Marie was not sure what had made her agree to go out with this much younger man. He looked so imperturbable, sitting perched on the edge of the chair in his suit and tie, sipping his wine and looking into his glass as if to read our fortunes. *Could I fall in love again?* No, not with him and we want different things. He wants one day to retire to the country, take holidays in the UK, mmm…

Later, they somehow ended up in her bedroom. *I know it's late, but why didn't I just tell him to get a taxi?* He came out of the bathroom with his trousers off, corpse white legs ending in socks and her mistake was confirmed. Her heart had died with Arun, she didn't want this. *I've been too alone though. It's human contact, isn't it,* she told herself firmly. *He's very kind, but I don't need a lover to further complicate my life choices. I *don't want this.**

She fully lived in her body. Not like some women who carried their lovely bodies around with them as if they were borrowed. Glancing down at it, she thought sadly that the supple slimness of her youth had gone, but her figure wasn't bad for her age. *Why was he attracted to an older woman?* He was sitting on the bed with his back to her. Bent over as he undid his shoes. She jumped up and retreated into the bathroom, where she lent on the door. Already her arrangements of fragrances and oils, the feathers, draped, delicate eastern sarong sized materials and other garnishes felt defiled and intruded upon by his washbag and big blue towel. *He had assumed he was going to stay!* She creamed her face; this mirror had never hid the truth. *I look tired,* she thought. Her heavily lashed eyes, as dark as wells, were duller and sunken, her skin, papery and lined. She looked closer, *let's have a reality check Marie. This is how I look now, *every* day.* She brushed her teeth, a quick spray of perfume and unlocked the door.

He was peeling off his socks. *What had he been doing for the last five minutes?* He turned and looked up at her, appearing shyer and even younger, then got up and padded back into the bathroom. There

48

was the sound of splashing, then a crash. "It's Ok, not broken," he called. There was complete silence. What was he doing? She lay back, closed her eyes and relaxed. Only to be jerked back to reality as a draft of cold air hit her, when he lifted up the duvet and plonked down beside her.

Sometime during the night, she woke and realised she was freezing. Dragging herself out of semi-consciousness and moving her hands about, she could find nothing to cover her. She rolled over to find his sleeping form cocooned in the entire duvet...

Beth was in the kitchen, preparing a lasagne for supper. She was wondering how it would be when Jake moved out. Hugh had gone to live with Lucy and Harriet had been in Rwanda for six months and would no doubt be off somewhere else soon. There'll be no dirty clothes and dishes and there'll be silence. No more din of music playing, instrument practice or shouting. No more arguments about the content and timing of meals. I can have dinner parties without having to rush out like a taxi service...Who will I be then? All those me's that got submerged in servicing everyone...what's left?

She thought back to when she was twenty-five and had just finished her teaching certificate. James was twenty-eight, charming and confident. He seemed years older than he was. For the first eight years I struggled with babies and housework in that little flat, while he stayed at work later and later. A workaholic, it was his identity. An old fashioned man who rarely lifted a finger in the house and who became irritable and defensive if she complained. "I'm doing it for you, old girl," he would say.

Then there came that time when she had felt so overwhelmed that she thought she was heading for a breakdown. "I'm not made of elastic, I'm not coping," she warned him. "I can't be everywhere...do any more or I'll snap." For a few weeks he went to Harriet's school play and Hugh's parents evening. "Of course I want to be there for them," he had said, but soon there were more pressing matters at work again and she knew that the intrusion of family life was unwelcome.

He was retiring at Easter. What would their lives be like with him at home and no children? There he was now, the key in the door. "Hello," he called.

She didn't have to see him to know that he was shrugging off his jacket and prising off his shoes, picking up his slippers from under the hallstand and taking his cardigan from a hanger. He's walked into the lounge. She could hear the click of the drinks cabinet door and the bottles being replaced after he had poured himself a gin and tonic. He would be sitting in his leather chair now, sipping, as he picked up the folded Telegraph waiting for him on the occasional table at his elbow. She heard him sigh with pleasure.

What do I do for myself? Swimming and book group and I don't even like swimming much. Laura says, 'keep coming, you may not be able to see much weight loss, but you look so much better, glowing and toned.'

I suppose I do feel sort of energised on swimming days, but I need to get involved in something else. I've tried lino cutting, etching, jewellery, sculpture, felting, making new clothes from old, pottery, too many courses. The only class I really enjoyed was quilting. That woman in the changing room was saying the hospital needs volunteers. Perhaps I'll ring tomorrow.

It seemed to have been showery for days now. It had lashed down at daybreak, then cleared to a faint, watery sun. A mist curled familiarly round their legs as they walked, cold and thick like mayonnaise. It slowly cleared and the pale rays of the sun strengthened, so the tiles on the roofs glistened and they warmed and cheered up

Beth was eager to talk to Marie, and manoeuvred to walk with her, Laura and Terry behind. They chatted about the weather, about vitamin D and melatonin, then Beth came out with, "I know it's not fair expecting free advice from you, but can I ask you something?"

"Of course, don't be silly, never think that you can't ask me anything. I may not know the answer, but I can always help by looking it up."

"Well," Beth blushed. "I don't think I'm unusual, lots of my friends have spare knickers in their bags and I've been fine til this last few weeks. It's so uncomfortable and embarrassing." She stopped.

"Urinary leakage?" Marie asked quietly. "Apparently one third of all pads sold are for this problem. Are you just wanting to go more often, or leaking between toilet visits?"

Beth's face was hot and red. She stuttered, "We...'ll I've never g...got up in the night before." She looked up at Marie, "and I start wetting myself a little before I get there."

"Don't worry. It happens to us all. Try limiting your caffeine intake, training your bladder to wait longer and squeezing your pelvic muscles lots of times in a day, to strengthen them. If things don't improve, that's when you go and see your doctor. It might be an infection, or a symptom of something else."

They were at the pool and Laura was looking at them quizzically. "Female probs?"

Marie smiled, "Nothing that regular swimming won't improve."

When they came out the sun was stronger and the sky was clear. Terry's dry, frizzy hair seemed to be in shocked flight from her head. "Chlorine doesn't agree with my hair," she said mournfully. "Think I won't come again this week. Anyway I don't want another run in with that old guy in the slow lane. He barely moves and he spreads himself so wide, it's difficult to get past."

That evening, Terry lay in bed, unable to sleep, trying to remember when she and Leonard had been happy. Both working, a shared social life and a purpose together, to have a child and a home, was she completely happy then? Had she ever felt ecstasy? When he was made redundant, twenty-five years ago, he had become withdrawn and bitter and their life had never again been fun or intimate. She had still been young, but their relationship had become platonic and she had never really known what he was thinking. Then five years ago, her breast cancer. He was frightened, more than her. She remembered the lines on his face deepening, his fear that they would find more cancer cells on the margins. She had a mastectomy and a course of chemotherapy. Then there was the all clear...

She could not help thinking about sex. What would it feel like after so long? After the first few years of marriage it had just been mechanical, going through the motions. At sixty-six, would it hurt? She always felt so dry down there. A grey light was creeping through the gap in the curtains. She turned over towards a hunched husband. He was so cold and unreachable. Surely he wasn't happy either. Could I leave him?

She could not remember feeling this attracted to anyone, ever. At work, her hands trembled, she had hot flushes or cold sweats and her innards gurgled and flipped. Was she truly in love with him or was she flattered because he was showing an interest. Or was he? All her life she had avoided confrontation, putting herself in situations which could be difficult. But I'm leaving soon. I should confess my feelings and ask about his. How can I?

Frances had felt as if she were sleep walking since she had been forced to leave work. If only she could get that last meeting out of her head.

One or two of the younger partners had confidently taken off their jackets in the boardroom. She had a crisp blue 'Hilditch and Key' shirt underneath, taken out of its cellophane wrapper only this morning, should she do likewise? But no, Neville the Chief Executive exuded authority and coolness with his firmly on.

"I'm sure that you don't need me to confirm the fact that there must be a radical restructuring or this company will fail. You will have read the report, and the financials so can you turn to page 15 and we can discuss the recommendations? We'll go round the table. Let's start with you, Frances." Neville sank back in his chair with a professionally neutral expression and the ten other partners, all male, fastened their expectant gazes on her. She had taken a deep breath and spoken firmly, her eyes sweeping around her colleagues.

"The first two are small savings and uncontroversial. Recommendation three that we share secretariat. I suggest that we concentrate our discussion here, rather than the contentious number four. Redundancies will require a decision on the criteria for whether we look at cost centres or early retirements?"

Andrew, the youngest partner nodded. Looking around, she

knew, as one of the oldest that this would be the most popular solution and sure enough by the end of the meeting there was a majority decision to make all those over fifty-five redundant. Frances felt as if she had been punched in the solar plexus. She had tried to keep her face impassive, but her heart had thumped out of control.

For six weeks she had bought all the serious newspapers on the days they advertised jobs. She was too highly qualified for some and others were obviously targeting younger lawyers. She applied for a few, but without much hope. The days dragged by. She was isolated and depressed. She had never had friends, never having learnt to flatter, gossip or do small talk. Apart from Pauline, who had started at Raybould and Saunders at the same time as Frances, when they were in their early twenties. She had married in her forties and then frequently became tied up with her step-children.

"Sorry Fran, something's come up, have to cancel this evening. Hope you don't mind."

"Not at all," Frances would lie. "I've been so busy."

Work had filled her life. Her routines were taking her shirts to the cleaners on the way to the office and buying and eating ready meals in the evening. Perhaps I should cut back, she thought, and put them in the washing machine until I can take my pension? I'm not going to do all that ironing, though. Perhaps if I just pressed the collars and cuffs? The creased body part won't show under my jumpers.

She had started going for walks to get out every day. One route had been down the canal path, past the Victorian warehouses, now gleaming glass and steel flats. One day she had stopped and looked into the water as it swung greasily by. A logjam of beer cans, soggy cigarette packets, newspapers and plastic bags swung together in a swirl of scum. What if some lunatic running by pushed me in there? It was difficult from then on, not to think about drowning in the freezing water with the rubbish. She changed to strolls on Hampstead Heath on fine days and on wet ones took the tube to galleries. Walking in the West End, shoppers everywhere and buses flashing by like red devils. What sort of life could she lead? She knew that she was killing time.

She was on the Heath today. It was windless, the sky was

unnaturally vacant and the air was damp and chill. People were bundled up against the cold and preoccupied with their dogs or scuttled away as she approached. No one made eye contact. Then a grey haired, grey track suited jogger ran towards her with a fixed and curious gaze. She felt uncomfortable. Should she disentangle her eyes? But then, she wouldn't know if he had too. He ran past and on and she turned abruptly left and down to a pond where she leant on the railings and peered at the coots and ducks. Gulls were wheeling overhead. Were there storms at sea, or were they just after all the rubbish they could find on land? A group of children ran screaming by and disappeared. Have I ever wanted a child? Not really.

The trees were almost bare. Just a few dying leaves hung motionless on the skeletons. Walking through them she thought she felt invisible things brushing against her. Her heart started to race and when she spun around the trees seemed to retreat under her gaze while their gnarled bare roots like talons seemed to move towards her. A scattering of raindrops pricked her head and shoulders, and made muttering sounds on the fallen leaves underfoot.

She emerged and heard a crashing noise on the opposite bank and there he was staring across at her. What's happening here? Is he unaware that he's staring? Is it just a coincidence that he has appeared again? Stop being ridiculous...thinking he's following you. She turned and walked on, choosing a rutted, muddy path up to a grassy area rather than the drier, tree-lined alternative. Picking her way through the mud he was suddenly just above her. Oh no! She was myopic, but even fuzzily, without her specs he was near enough for her to see that he had pulled down his track bottoms and there was a dark mound of pubic hair against white skin and a large, reddish penis thrusting towards her. Ugh, she screamed silently, fearful thoughts racing. Don't be silly, Frances, flashers don't hurt you. They get their thrill from shocking people. She turned away and ran along the side of the field, feet sinking and sliding on the lush wet ground. Was he chasing her? Her gasping breaths filled her head. Could she hear him behind her? She dare not stop. On, into the trees and bushes, fir branches stroking her face and holly ripping at her clothes and there was a wide path and a woman with a dog walking towards her. Slowing down, gulping for

54

air, she looked behind and thought she saw him motionless, half hidden in a coppice.

The spaniel reached her and jumped up playfully, muddy paws marking her Barbour jacket.

"Rascal, get down, heel!"

Any other time and she would have been furious, but she smiled at the young woman and patted the lively animal and when they had gone the flasher had disappeared.

Back at Kenwood House, surrounded by people and voices, she put on her specs and gazed around. Was that him, standing at the bottom of the slope, staring up at her? Don't be silly, lots of people are wearing grey. He's long gone. She went into the café and treated herself to tea and a large slice of chocolate cake.

That night, she was restless, constantly jerked awake by panic, and silent screams. The nightmare terror of men coming at her, trousers down. She got up and had a glass of whisky and paced around the flat, trying to exhaust herself. Why hadn't she walked towards him and shouted, put it away, or I'll call the police? No wonder he did such a thing when women reacted as she did...

She thought of her past attempts to have a relationship with the opposite sex. Any men she had been attracted to went off with other women. She ended up with the misfits, the men who didn't quite live up to her image of 'the one.' Everyone thinks I'm a confirmed spinster, even Lydia. It was a couple of years since her sister had invited her to dinner to meet a colleague of Mark's. I was in a bad mood, no wonder she hasn't tried again. There was bound to have been something wrong with him anyway, or he wouldn't have liked me. What am I going to do with myself? I can't sleep, can't get up in the morning. I look forward all day to my glass of wine in the evening. It was ironic that she had always known what she wanted to do, had had a clear career trajectory. Unlike so many of her friends who frivolled about trying different things, but was she now the most unhappy because she had invested her life in one area.

Chapter 5. November. Tragedies

*'And een the dearest that I loved the best
Are strange - nay, rather, stranger than the rest.'*
John Clare. 'I Am.' (1793 – 1864)

Lying in her warm bed, a grey light peeping round the curtains, Laura discussed with herself. Shall I drive? It'll be quicker, but then if I walk it's more exercise. Drive, walk, walk, drive. She thought about her friends driving styles. Beth is slow and brakes a lot. Annie, Lynne and Marie drive full pelt and rather recklessly. Helen is skilful and masterful and me? I think I'm steady, but I worry I don't concentrate. Hmm. Still undecided, she reluctantly crawled out of bed and looked at the day: dull, overcast sky and soft rain dampening everything. Ok, no friends to walk with today, I'll drive.

Jo was trying to get herself to get up, but it was so warm in bed and the heating did not come on til midday, as part of her economy drive. She leant over and pressed the button to open the curtains. Ugh, dull and misty, looks cold. She snuggled down again. The phone rang and she reached over to her bedside table. It was Laura. "Tomorrow evening? Well I'll think about it, thanks for asking me. Can I pop round later, say eight thirty, after supper? Thanks. Bye now."

Spending an evening discussing books with a group of other women? Well it's nice of her to think I might be interested, but sitting there with all those dreary library faces when all I can think about is how much I crave orgasms. Masturbation and fantasising about them are all very well, but...do other women my age *have* sex? Laura might. Daniel's an artist and they're notorious. That grumpy pile of hair, Lynne doesn't for sure. She reached into the bedside drawer for her vibrator...

It was early evening and Laura's knife scythed through the apples, logs in the stove crackled and the kettle whistled importantly. She was in a dream as she weighed the sugar, ground almonds and butter. Picking up an egg, she fondled its smooth coolness and thought back to their warmth when she had collected them from the hen house as a child. Outside, the dark pressed against the windows and the smell of soup making and baking filled her with contentment.

Daisy was hanging around the kitchen in her rolled down jogging pants showing her flat, taut stomach and the downy dip in her long back. She leant against the table with her phone stuck on her ear. Laura flicked the on switch on the kettle and mimed a cup of tea, waving four boxes of different ones but Daisy was listening intently, then did a hiccupping laugh and ignored her. She suddenly said "Bye" and mooched across to the biscuit barrel on top of the units.

"Why don't you go out with Rachel, rather than chat to her on the phone for ages?"

"I'm having an efficiency drive with people I know. I'm not seeing people who don't phone me, or boring people who just seep into my life and hang around, expecting me to entertain them."

Laura wondered which category Rachel fitted into.

"Anyway, I'm sick of endless sex and fashion chat, or save the world homilies and that's all you get with her. And you have to get a round of drinks in, don't you? And you can't wear the same outfit every time. A lot of my friends are earning. Not that I care. Not going out every single night. I quite like penny pinching, making do…Anyway I'd shit myself if I got rat assed and got hooked on coke, or hung around with would-be 'slebs', cackling and honking down champagne, like some of my ex-friends."

"If you want some money just ask."

"I'm fine. If I want to go out, I can. My generation can get most things they want. It's all there for the taking. Shops offer you credit, you get flats and money if you're pregnant. We've never had to scrimp and save, like you said you did. The Labour government told us that we are entitled to a good life and we can get it on credit. Mind, I'm not like that, I might have to go and live in a Kibbutz." She slumped down in the only comfortable chair in the kitchen.

Laura had started to chop vegetables for a mixed salad, trying to control her feelings of irritation at the predictability of Daisy's responses. How wonderful life had been for the first thirteen years when they had been so close, even bathing together to chat and tell one another stories. It was such a shock when that wall had slammed down between them. Daisy locked the bathroom and her bedroom door and looked at Laura with cold alien eyes if she suggested coming in for a chat.

Daisy carried on. "I'm starting to think that I don't belong in this world. Its beliefs, codes and history are alien to me. I'm sick of meeting capitalist bastards with nothing in their heads but more money. Society is sick, hierarchical, selfish."

Laura raised her eyebrows.

"And marriage is an oppressive, patriarchal institution. We just don't have the same values. Free love and radical politics are what I'm after. I've got shining dreams which don't fit with this urban consumerist life." She bit into the carrot that Laura had handed her, picked up a 'Metro' and turned to the minor celebrity pages.

Glass of wine in hands, the two friends sat in Laura's conservatory. Jo looked with envy at the beautiful lit garden, knowing how much effort her friend had put into achieving it. Tears stung her eyes when she thought back to their last day at University. Laura had left for a holiday job, then a teaching post in Bristol. Jo had been inconsolable, having to make a new life without her best friend, her other half. It had been almost as hard as losing her mother when she was eighteen. She had realised when her life fell apart how much she had missed Laura and wanted her back in her life.

"There's never been another friend like you, Laurs, one who knows who I am, who I trust, sometimes more than I trust myself. We've got history…you're part of my DNA. I had everything I thought I wanted, with Ed, except we knew people like us: newly rich, who knew the price of everything, and the value of nothing. None of them were real friends. Over-nostrilled, underbrained, horsey people. I never had true intimacy with any of them. No-one else has ever had that 'thing.'" She had opened a window and a sudden draught whipped her hair across her face, the alcohol was keeping her warm and her cigarette glowed in the dark. "You know how impulsive and selfish I can be, but I think I'm good hearted and I never mean to cause offence, although I know I do. I'm lonely, Laurs, but just tell me if I'm taking up too much of your time and I'll back off."

"Don't worry, it's just because you haven't settled into your new life yet. You'll be spiralling off again very soon, I'm sure."

"God, how? I'm sliding into invisibility. Men don't notice me any more. It doesn't seem that long ago when they were hitting on me, saying stuff like, I prefer fit older women, they're more comfortable with themselves and more interesting."

"But we're sixty-four Jo. No-one stays looking young for ever."

"But inside I really do still feel sexy, powerful, feisty, sparkling. What's changed?"

"What happened to Anton? Wasn't that his name?"

"Oh, I don't know. He didn't have much personality. A bit of a blank canvas for me to paint dirty dreams onto. I've forgotten him."

"You'll find a raison d'etre, settle into your new life. What are you doing with yourself? Lying on the sofa wondering where your life has gone? I keep asking you to come swimming in the mornings? It'll get you up and gives you more energy for the rest of the day."

"Swimming? Getting your hair wet and being in water that hundreds of people have peed and sweated and dribbled in? All that quivering flesh and bouncing bingo wings? I didn't even go in our pool at home much. I preferred piloxing and dynamic yoga with my personal trainer."

"What's 'piloxing?'"

"Like a mix of pilates and boxing…cardio, weights in gloves, dance, flexibility and co-ordination moves. Perfect. Swimming ruins your hair and makeup."

"Come on days when your hair needs washing and don't put your makeup on til we get back. The showers are brilliant. Lynne used to come, she doesn't like leaving Betty now, but there are my other friends you'll get to know."

"Dear old Lynne? Of the wild hair, tracksuits and donkey toes sticking out of men's sandals? Is she still a heifer?"

"She's not as big as when you knew her. Anyway, swimming burns calories and helps the joints stay flexible, strengthens the muscles. You'll look younger and fitter."

"Ah, younger. That's sounding more tempting. Why do you like it so much, Laurs?"

"I think it's because of the weightless feeling, particularly when I was pregnant. It was the only time I felt normal. Apparently the density of the body is similar to that of water, so the water supports it. My whole body feels energised and toned. I remember when I was working, if I'd been swimming first thing, colleagues would look twice at me and say how healthy and fit I was. I glowed. And if you're injured or stiff, doing exercises in the water is great for rehabilitation…Gliding through the water seems to rejuvenate my body and mind. It makes me feel so good."

"Mmm, I don't know…"

"My father had type 2 diabetes, from drinking not much more than we both do. Swimming reduces the risk of getting that. Apparently it improves the cholesterol balance, the strength of the blood vessels and heart, makes you happier and more contented, because of the endorphins, so you'll sleep better." She paused for breath. "What more can you want?"

"Ok, Ok, enough proselytising. Maybe then. Shall I ask this woman called Frances who lives upstairs? She lost her job. She's morose and miserable and doesn't know who she is without work. I asked her down for a drink last week, and do you know what she said? There's no purpose in my life now. I'll probably die one of those sad deaths where nobody notices for weeks until the smell drifts into the street."

"God, she's depressed!"

"Totally. Work was all about status and having somewhere to go all day. She doesn't seem to have friends. She had the idea that there was only one way to rise to the top. Never leave the office. And her dress sense! She's still wearing bits of her power suits, with shapeless jumpers! Is it Friday you go? Just ring me when you wake up and I'll walk up to yours."

They talked about their daughters.

"I'm not sure that Daisy and Femi are skyping one another at the moment. I can't ask, she's too unhappy and bad tempered."

"Daughters don't want to talk and learn from us. They're in pre-

60

adult limbo, waiting for life to kick in, but they think they know everything. They're confused, no feminist struggle and look at their role models!"

"Who are we talking about? Kate Middleton?"

"Yeh, silent, decorative, meek. And Lady Gaga and Katy Perry, for goodness sake. Or the WAGs who've hooked a high earning footballer. Their generation is lost in a world of appearances. Trying to get it all while being perfectly groomed and airbrushed into a clone."

"You're right. Men have constructed women like that and sold it to us as empowerment. It's so depressing. I still can't believe the obsession with hairless bodies and not eating. There's so much pressure for girls to measure up. To perform as well as men at work, be yummy mummies and geishas as well."

"I'd say their generation is pretty fucked up beating themselves up to be perfect. It's candy-coated fantasy and they won't listen! I tried to warn Jess of the dangers of unprotected sex. Do you know, Laurs, the average single testicle produces around eighty-five million sperm cells a day, and there's two of them! I tried to tell her stuff, but she never wanted to hear the facts of life. 'That's gross, shut up, Mum,' was her response to any sex education. 'Youth is wasted on the young.'"

The next evening Jo knocked at Frances's door. "Would you like to come swimming tomorrow morning at eight, with an old friend, Laura?" Jo smiled.

Frances tried to smile back and shook her head. "I hate swimming. And I'm useless at it. Thanks for asking though."

"I'm not keen either. All that getting your hair wet. But we could meet some of the local women and it'll get me out of bed. Why don't you come down for a drink? You can eat with me if you like. I've bought a Waitrose meal for two."

"I've eaten, but I'll have a drink with you."

Ten minutes later and Frances was on her second glass of Rioja. "Work has been my life. Being a lawyer is tough and tiring, but I loved it and think I did well for my clients. I feel as if I've been cut off at the knees."

"Aren't you applying for other jobs?"

"The economy has shrunk. There's huge competition and I'm nearly fifty-nine now. Most lawyers retire at my age."

"You wouldn't want to do any other sort of job?"

"All I ever wanted to be was a lawyer. I remember my teachers telling me I had a good memory and no imagination, so law was perfect for me. I loved the routine of my life. Off by eight, picking up a double shot cappuccino and the Telegraph on the way to work. What am I meant to do with my life now? I typed it into Google and it came up with 12,600,000 results. Clearly I'm not alone in wondering. What can I do with myself? I'm not used to not working."

"You're on holiday – enjoy."

"Holiday?" Frances looked blank. "I don't particularly like holidays. I liked my routines. The hall and kitchen lights and the central heating are on the timer, so they'd come on before I got in. I'd warm up my M&S meal, pour a glass of wine and sit in front of the television. I loved my evenings at home. Now I'm stuck in it all day if I don't find things to do. The flat's become a trap."

"Haven't you got any family?"

"Yes, my brother met an Argentinian girl and lives there, teaching. I've got a sister in Guildford. I'm the middle one. We have never liked one another much. We probably never will…nothing in common. She married very young, had three children and didn't work. You are supposed to love your family. In my case blood is not thicker than water. We have no allegiance or depth of feeling; we just share DNA."

"How about work friends?"

Frances thought for a moment. "I used to go to the cinema or theatre with a colleague, Pauline, before she met Bill, then it all changed. That was years ago though. I'd got into the habit of working late most nights. Everyone seems to have such busy lives. I must be a sad loser. Should I fill my life with lectures, concerts, plays and classes and then tweet about them? Then everyone would know how busy and popular I am. I keep thinking, is that all there is to life? Mine seems over now."

She's so depressed and bitter, Jo thought. A couple of lines from a poem by Dorothy Parker came into her head:

> *'Her mind lives tidily, apart*
> *From cold and noise and pain,*
> *And bolts the door against her heart,*
> *Out wailing in the rain.'*

"Why don't you try swimming this once? You don't have to go again if you don't like it."

Frances was well into her third large glass of Rioja. Perhaps I should, she thought. All I do is play bridge and that's making me even more depressed. There were moments when she found herself crying, like yesterday when she could not open the plastic container round her chicken and bacon sandwich. She had lost her temper and tried to tear it off with her teeth. When that had failed she burst into tears. Time was hanging heavily, a deafening roar behind the silence

"Oh, well, just once," she agreed.

It was a cold, dark, wintry morning, the cars had their headlights on and it felt damp and slippery underfoot, with the last of the leaf-fall as they strode briskly towards the pool. Frances and Jo wishing that they had stayed in bed.

"Two newbies ready for action," Jo had said when they met up with the regulars. She was now chatting to Beth. "Miss living in the country? Ugh not. It was like being trapped in the depths of life's metaphorical handbag. I was a self-snootified city girl before I got married, with Soho House membership, girly treats at Champneys and Annabel's, and lots of designer therapy. London rocked for me. I'd never lived in the country, I'd hardly even been there, I was brought up in a Kensington mansion flat. I didn't have the right clothes or any interest in country life. I'd never met a farmer or any yoghourt weavers and I didn't want everyone knowing my business."

"Well, didn't you get to like it?"

"I didn't really make any lasting friendships. I just didn't immerse myself in local life and to be honest just wasn't a 'nice' enough person,

63

doing charity work and such. I couldn't hack a world of cupcakes, tights and pearls, where I'd be judged not for my brains, but for my brownies. I was bored comatose to sulky tears and just wanted to be up in London going around the shops. As far as I'm concerned the country is cold, dark and dull and it smells of silage and wet dog. When we split, I couldn't get back to town quickly enough."

"Did you teach, like Laura, when you left university?"

"Oh God no. I really admire people who stick at teaching, year in and year out. But the whole recycling of girls growing up to teach another generation of girls and then they do likewise is just too depressing. No, I thought I'd have a career in film and got a job as PA to a creative director at United Artists. He was useless. Hardly ever in the office. I found myself running the department. I was doing his job. Then the company got taken over. They wised up, reorganised and we were all out of there. So that was it for being a director of a studio. I realised I wasn't going to get to be a golden skirt, even though I had the boobs and the shag-me stilettos so I got a job with a new promotions company, Ed's, and the rest in history. To be honest, I found that being good looking was an asset in getting jobs as receptionists or secretaries, but climbing up the employment ladder was more difficult. I wasn't taken seriously, though attractive men are."

"What's Ed like?" Beth asked.

"Harrow, Cambridge, to the manor born and family money to set up his own business. He worked twelve-hour days and liked to play sport and have house parties at weekends. Ed's good looking, charming, well dressed, don't you think, Laurs?"

Laura, Frances and Helen had come abreast as they strolled down the wide path to the door of the Leisure Centre. "Mmm, quite a dish," Laura agreed.

"Where did you two meet?" Jo asked Laura and Beth. They looked at one another. "Wasn't it at an 'Open Gardens' day?' I said how delicious the lemon drizzle cake was, and you said you'd made it?"

"Yes, must be ten or twelve years ago? Harriet and Daisy were about fourteen."

"That's right. And you introduced me to Helen," Laura said.

They pushed open the glass doors and stood in the queue waiting for reception to enter them on the computer and let them in through the electronic gates.

"When are you off to South Africa?" Laura asked Jo.

"In two weeks. It's Vic's sixtieth on the eighteenth. She's having a two-day party. She's my sister." She added looking at the other women.

"Haven't you got a daughter? Is she going with you?" Helen asked as they went into the changing room.

Jo smiled. "Yes and then she'll be off back to the States."

Jo was a strong, stylish swimmer and swam in the fast lane with various splashing men and Helen. They stopped and chatted at the shallow end every so often, to let the most frantic splasher go past and after a while Helen invited Jo to go back to her house for breakfast and to meet Phillip.

The five showers were in a tiled ante-room, no curtains, no privacy. Frances hesitated. Would they think that she was odd if she said she was going to shower at home? Laura noticed her reluctance to strip and join them. "There are shower cubicles if you go out of the door, left and left, but you may have to queue."

"No, it's fine here. I'm just coming." She sidled self-consciously under the only free showerhead with her costume on.

"Do you live on your own?" Beth was standing next to her, rubbing shampoo into her hair.

"Mmm, yes." Frances muttered. Thinking how intrusive and impertinent Beth was.

When they came out, there was a low sun, threads of mist and a biting wind. Jo was quite glad to stop off half way to have breakfast at Helen's. On the way back, out of earshot from the others, Laura had told her a little about Helen and Phillip. "They met at Newcastle University. They've been together since. She specialised in child development and mental health in children. He was a social worker, but now he's a reputed psychotherapist and sex maniac. Watch out, we all dread being alone with him."

"Really? How does Helen cope with that?"

She told me once, "I'm so good at not minding. If I let myself mind too much I'd top myself, or him. The trick is not to mind, then you're not unhappy, you're just nothing. I love my job and I feel that I can make a difference to children's lives. What could be better than that? It keeps me sane."

"So she's an educational psychologist?"

"Yes, looking after at least fifteen schools. Phillip's very charming and beguiling but he's an opportunist. Look, don't get me wrong here. He's actually got a giving, caring nature. He would have been a great dad."

Helen and Jo were eating fresh grapefruits and drinking coffee when Phillip came in. He had been out to get croissants and a paper and took off his wide brimmed leather hat and shook loose his shoulder length, silky brown hair, streaked with grey before pulling it back into a ponytail. Jo noted with approval a black diamond stud earring. Though only medium height, he was slim and fit looking and seemed taller when he sat at the table with them and stretched out his legs, encased in tight fitting moleskin ending in snakeskin boots. She was drawn to his apparent serenity, and the way he had of fixing his soft brown eyes intently on whoever he was talking to and appearing not to blink. He admitted to being quite myopic but the effect was of rapt, sympathetic concern, which she could imagine his patients found comforting and even fascinating. She speculated that he was seemingly endlessly interested in their welfare, receiving their confidences with good intentions towards them, but wondered if he fantasised about having power and control?

He read his paper while she and Helen chatted, but then when Helen went to take a phone call, she received the full treatment. He certainly knew how to melt a woman's heart. "Jo," he murmured softly, looking at her with tender eyes and total concentration. "What do you get up to on a Friday then?" His eyes seemed to spark with bright fires and the world seemed full of colours and beauty. A dangerous man.

66

"I met Phillip this morning," she said to Laura later. "Whew, he's a handful!"

"Yes, I think Helen would quite like to retire, but work gets her mind off her situation. She said a few days ago: what am I trying to prove? That my existence is necessary? That's a fantasy, everyone is replaceable. In fact, everyone is in the process of being replaced. Why don't you then? I asked her, and she said. It's Phillip, we've always been keen on 'sharing our feelings' but now that's a minefield of suspicion, recrimination and self-justification. I couldn't bear to be around every day while he's telling women to think of our front room as a haven, a sanctuary, where they can get away from their pressured lives outside and find out what's going on in their own heads."

"Helen said he's a well thought of psychotherapist and gets a lot of patients referred by the medical profession."

"Mmm…the problem is he's been getting more patients for psychosexual therapy self-help techniques than cognitive behavioural counselling and personal growth."

"Yes? What does he do for that?"

"The mind boggles. I think it used to be breathing, meditation and yoga poses, who knows about the sex bit."

Terry was ploughing ahead bravely, making plans in her head to leave Leonard, though deeply uncertain about it.

She was sitting at the kitchen table, listing what her incomings and outgoings might be when she retired, when she heard the sound of his key in the lock. Fear clenched her stomach. She felt sick and quickly closed her notebook and shoved it into her handbag. The gravity of what she was going to do had hit her and she couldn't breathe. How could she do it? He loves me so much. His life is built around me. But can I be responsible for his life and happiness forever? What about mine?

The spaghetti was cooked. She tossed it into the bowl of artichokes, olives, tuna, anchovies, capers and tomato sauce and looked out at her beloved south facing garden, the shrubs illuminated in Leonard's clever lighting. The green salad was ready on their Italian glass dining table.

Leonard had gone straight upstairs to change. He had been to visit his sister in her sheltered flat. Coming back into the kitchen, he took the homemade elderflower cordial out of the fridge.

"Can't I have a glass of wine?" she asked. "The meal tastes so much better with wine."

"I thought you were not going to drink alcohol in the week?"

"One glass isn't much."

He diluted his cordial, put the bottle back in the fridge and went over to the wine rack. "Isn't it time you stopped going into work? Surely this chap is au fait with everything by now? We could play golf."

She ladled out two helpings of pasta and sat down heavily.

"I told you I'd been organising everything alone for so long, it would take some time to pass it all on."

He put a glass of Merlot by her plate, poured water into his glass and sat down. His eyes bored into her.

She took a deep breath. "Stop it, Leonard, don't let's go through it all again." She passed him the bowl of Parmesan and started to eat.

They were both unusually quiet for a while, then Leonard, who had been playing with his food, said, "I'm sorry, but I'm not feeling well."

"Why don't you go up to bed? Take a couple of paracetemols. You'll feel better in the morning." Terry finished her pasta then cleared the table and started to wash up. Leonard often had headaches. She could hear him above in the bathroom.

He really was feeling very strange, sort of giddy. He held on to the edge of the bathroom sink and bowed his head as a wave of nausea passed through him. Suddenly he vomited so violently that he hit his head on the mirror as he lurched forward.

Terry heard the bang and rushed upstairs.

"Feel like I'm being kicked in the back of my head...can't feel my arm, neck, what's happening to me?"

She was frightened. "I'll ring for a doctor or ambulance. Do I ring 999?" He was mumbling incoherently, something about the light. Terry helped him to bed. He seemed to be losing consciousness. She ran downstairs and phoned her nearest friend, Laura.

"Ring 999, or NHS Direct, they'll probably give you the number. I'm coming round now."

The ambulance took forty minutes and by then Leonard had lost consciousness. Terry and Laura felt so helpless. Putting cold compresses on his brow, making him comfortable, head supported, airway clear. "He's still breathing and he's got a pulse," they told the ambulance men. Terry jumped into the ambulance with Leonard. "I'll lock up and get the car and follow you," Laura called after her.

Neither the paramedics nor the doctors in the hospital could resuscitate him. He had had a ruptured cerebral aneurysm, a subarachnoid haemorrhage. He would have lost brain function if he had survived. Terry wondered if it was better that he had gone quickly. He would have been a terrible patient.

Beth had a phone call, asking her if she could go to the 'Friends Room' at the hospital, for an interview. She spent the rest of the day trying to decide what to wear.

The next morning she opened Harriet's bedroom door, usually closed, so she could not see the stained carpets and the walls with their constellation of bits of Blu Tack. Why was she creeping? Harriet was still in Rwanda and James and Jake were out. She opened drawer after drawer and surveyed the rejected clothes in messy disarray in each. "I can't take them all, Mum. Maybe I'll want them when I come back. Maybe they'll be out of fashion and I won't," Harriet had said.

If they were not really wanted, it must be all right to borrow them. I would like the person who interviews me to think I'm not totally old and boring, that I can relate to younger people. Better not wear the pink jumper again. It didn't suit me anyway. How about this yellow print top? She thought back to how Harriet looked in it. Little sleeves, neck not too low. She pulled it over her head and stood in front of the mirror, smiling expectantly and trying to see her reflection with detachment. Oh no, too tight on my tummy bulge and cutting into my fat arms. I'm old, old and flabby. I'm an overweight thin haired mouse with spreading badger stripes, who goes "Oooooagh" when getting up from chairs and who's done nothing apart from that nightmare stint teaching and running the house and bringing up three children for over thirty years. What's next, fumbling and falling?

Disconsolately she pulled the top off, replaced it, closed the wardrobe and went back to her room to find a safer option.

Sophie, Betty's cat, did not appear for breakfast. Sometimes she stayed out all night, but she was always back before Betty got up. Lynne went out into the street and found her bloodstained body in the gutter further down their road. She must have been run over.

"She won't part with her body, Laurs. I said to her, I'll dig her a grave, Mum. We'll have a funeral and invite some mourners. But she won't part with it. She's sitting there cuddling the body and saying she wants to die too and follow Sophie to wherever she's going."

"How sad. Do you want me to try and talk to her?"

"I don't think you'd get anywhere. She's in a world of her own now. I'm going to have to put her in that Home in Lauceston Road. I can't leave her on her own any more, even when I'm in the house seeing patients. She's left all the gas rings on twice and is constantly trying to get out of the front door."

"She'll hate going to a Home."

"Well, what else can I do? I can go and see her every day. At least she'll be safe."

Chapter 6. December. Sad Thoughts

'My very heart faints and my whole soul grieves
At the moist rich smell of the rotting leaves.
And the breath
Of the fading edges of box beneath,
And the last year's rose.'
Alfred Lord Tennyson 'Song: A Spirit Haunts the Year's Last Hours.'
(1809-92)

"How is Betty getting on?" Laura had rung to ask.
"She's so lonely and frightened. Do I stay here til I die?" she asked me.

"Oh, how awful!"

"Desperate…she's trying so hard to show she's independent. Shuffling purposelessly about the entrance hall, like a hamster trying to get out of its cage, repeating 'what shall I do? What shall I do?' She's trying to feed herself, and wipes her mouth fastidiously, but her hands can't grip properly so her food's cold and congealed before she's managed more than a few mouthfuls. Does she think that she can get better? That she can live on her own again? Oh god, what have I done?"

"Can I go and visit?"

"Yes, of course, but it's difficult to know what she's really registering. She's in her own little world walking up and down, and round and round, not speaking to me. Yet she cries when I leave, balling her hands into fists, jamming them into her eye sockets and howling. She's never behaved like that before. It makes me cry too. We upset one another every time. If you can stand the assault on your senses, the smell of lunch, bleach and nappies and seeing all the residents staring blankly into space or shouting 'help', yes, do go."

"I'll go this afternoon. By the way, will you both still come for Christmas?"

"Hope so. Don't want to eat school dinners in the Home."

"Why don't you start swimming again, now Betty is safe?"

"That's an idea. I need some exercise. Are you going tomorrow?"

71

The wind had howled most of the night. Trees had creaked violently and rain had pinged like bullets on the window. Laura had slept restlessly and Daniel had been up sketching for most of it. She peered through the curtains to see large and small branches and what looked like bits of slate littering the ground. The rain had stopped, but the sky was a dark grey.

The swimmers wrapped themselves up and walked along briskly to the pool.

"Is there a date for Leonard's funeral?" asked Beth.

"Are endless wakes our future social activity?" Lynne said morosely.

"I think it's a week Friday, Terry's checking that's Ok with Leonard's sister's family. "So depressing people dying," said Laura. "Deaths leave holes in our lives that can't be filled."

"What are we all going to choose? The bone orchard, the furnace or cryonics? Not so attractive if you die at the wrinkly, loose, hanging flesh, no teeth stage," said Jo cheerily.

"You're going to give me nightmares!" squeaked Beth.

"Who believes in reincarnation then?"

"Don't be ridiculous," said Lynne sharply. "When you're dead, you're dead, game over."

"Enough, enough. Oh look, there's Liz and Angela. They've finished already." interjected Helen as they reached the Leisure Centre doors. "Hi, girls."

"Too many young thrashers this morning. Gotta go. I'm lecturing at the RA. See you next week." And Liz rushed off.

"Bye," smiled Angela, following her.

"This is definitely the best time to swim. The workers and the older people who struggle to sleep queue up when the pool opens at 6.30." Laura said to Jo

"That's not us then?" asked Lynne.

"Very funny. Which changing room?"

The water was grey and churning with too many bodies. "It's like a rough sea when there's not enough water in the pool. Hate it like this." Laura said. "Think I'll just do fifteen minutes and have a nice long shower."

The others nodded and they got into their respective lanes.

After their unsatisfactory swims, they found Laura standing under the fiercest hot shower. It practically knocked one over because some of the showerhead holes were blocked. She was blissfully happy, pressing and re-pressing the push button for a powerful back massage. The other four showers were busy with two women whose gleaming skin strained against its amply burgeoning contents and two with sagging, used breasts and stomach flesh, all soaping themselves and rubbing with loofahs. "Come on out Laurs and the rest of you, there's a queue here."

"Ok. Ok."

"Two minutes."

"Nearly finished,"

The two Asian women obliviously brushed their long hair under the water.

Two others, slowly drying themselves were having a heated conversation about the ingratitude of their children. "This generation's so different from ours. I shared a bedroom with my sister, then a room at college with a girl I didn't know before and then I still shared bedrooms in flats until I was over thirty and met Adolpho!"

Laura smiled to herself, thinking about the preserved and sculpted women at the Health Clubs she used to belong to when she was working. They had been cold and unfriendly. There was always a conversation going on here, which everyone joined into. These women had accepted and embraced the ageing process, no wrestling with decisions about where to cut, what creams to use, which fad diet or how to regain their long past youth.

She opened her locker and joined in. "What about our Mum's generation? All the girls in a family shared one bedroom. My Mum and her three sisters had one small wooden wardrobe between them!"

"Yes, but it's our fault, slaving away so we could give our kids their own bedroom. They expected the same when they went to University."

"Yeh, I've always had to share, at home, college, flats, then I met Don. They hate it because we're comfortable now and they can't

73

afford to buy their own properties!"

"I'm sick of their whining. I'm not going to feel guilty for property hogging or breaking myself to help them buy flats. No-one helped me…"

Laura and Beth looked at one another, wondering where they stood on this issue…

"Where's Marie, I thought she came most days?" asked Lynne as they walked home.

"She did tell me," replied Laura. "Was it a lecture she was going to? Sorry, forgotten."

"Who is she?" asked Jo.

"A doctor and masseuse who lives in a flat in our road. She worked for 'Medicin sans Frontieres' and met another doctor, Arun a Buddhist from Burma. They set up a hospice in Mandalay, but he died a couple of years ago?" She looked at Beth.

"Yes, about that. She's trying to go off with MSF again now. She just can't settle here."

"We'll miss her. No one could be nicer. She's kind, interesting, generous, always puts others first."

Jo was thinking about her friends eulogising about Marie for most of the day. What would they say about me? She wondered. Nothing nice, in fact I don't even like myself, so why would anyone else? She shivered with shame as a catalogue of her misdemeanours flashed before her eyes. And painfully, the last time she saw Ed.

He had wanted to arrange their divorce through their solicitors, but she had wanted to see him one more time; perhaps he would change his mind?

A girl in towering heels and a tiny dress had said he was far too busy she had to make an appointment. Jo had been that girl. She had hated the job, running Ed's diary.

She had pushed past the young woman and opened the door to his office. He had always dressed immaculately. That was a beautifully tailored suit and crisp pale blue shirt. His hair had been greyer, but longer. He had looked seriously sexy. It was quite a shock to find how much she still fancied him.

He had not listened to her apologies for dropping in, but had started a rant about her unreasonableness, about all he had been to her was her money machine. He had a new life and a baby on the way. She had not been listening until then. She had been remembering how she used to pop in after a shopping spree. A caress would trigger waves of lust so that he would lock the door and she would strip off her clothes slowly so he become frantic and fucked her over his desk. She must have had a lustful look because she had seen a faint blush on his worn, handsome and so familiar face. A baby? That had been a shock. She had talked in a light bantering tone trying to control her heart flutters and could not help flirting a little. He had been business like and cold. "Why don't you get a job? I wanted to retire next year."

Same old script, she had thought. What did Oscar say? 'Arguments are to be avoided; they are always vulgar and often convincing.'*

"Why should Fiona have to live frugally, so you can live in luxury?"

Jo had not wanted to start making comparisons. She had known that Fiona was her polar opposite. She ironed his shirts, cooked every meal and probably even cleaned their home.

'Anyone who lives within their means suffers from a lack of imagination,'* she had muttered to herself. Bloody Oscar Wilde. That was the last time she had seen Ed.

She had messed about miserably all day. She should cheer herself up and go shopping, perhaps Harvey Nic's? No, somehow her heart wasn't in it. It was only 4.30, but she poured herself a drink and lay on the couch. Thinking about Ed had made her confused and upset. I still fancy him, she thought, and when Beth asked me if I had given up work when we married, I felt so shallow. What have I ever achieved? Who am I? The sponger who married her boss and gave up her career and independence. I've done nothing with my life. I'm a selfish leech. She got up, went to the kitchen and poured the untouched glass of wine into the sink.

A girl called Mel, with short, spikey hair, a stripey jacket, leggings and towering heels, had called round for Jake while the family were eating supper.

"Would you like something to eat?" Beth asked.

"No thanks, I'm doing the 5 and 2 and it's a 2 day."

"How about a glass of wine?" asked James gallantly.

"Same, thanks. Too many calories."

"Are you working, Mel?"

"Yes, Event Management. Brand awareness functions and product launches, driving sales and traffic in the retail marketing industry. Actually I've just organised some very successful Fashion, Image and Style workshops. Actually, can I use your bathroom?"

James and Beth looked at one another after she had gone to the downstairs cloakroom. They were impressed, in fact they were thrilled. She seemed quite a nice, sensible girl. "Oh jolly good Jake, a girlfriend at last," James said quietly.

"A girlfriend?" His thin, pale face was incredulous. "You're joking me? Mel? She's wasted most of the time. Female and breathing, but no bangin' babe!"

Daniel had the air of someone who was not sure why he had come into the room. Although Laura said what fun he could be, her friends did not see this side of him and felt they hardly knew him. He had a habit of looking at people intently as if enchanted by something that no one else had divined, which was quite unnerving. He saw no reason why he should say or show things to appease other people's prejudices. At dinner parties, he tended to be silent unless spoken to. He would not compete in holding the floor, but went deeper and deeper inside himself. If dinner was at their house he busied himself cooking, clearing and refilling people's glasses, but rarely engaged them in conversation.

He had never been competitive or acquisitive or the sort of person to be comfortable with the corporate flow to the top. It made him feel guilty that he earned massive amounts for doing something which seemed worthless in comparison to any jobs which directly helped people.

Getting off the tube, he spotted Beth. There was no escape. They were funnelled near to one another coming down the stairs and almost collided in the rush for the Oyster reader exits.

"Shall I carry your shopping?" he asked chivalrously, as they reached the leaf strewn, damp pavement. She had obviously been to Sainsbury's.

"No, I'm fine. How is Daisy? Haven't seen her for months."

Here we go, pointless banalities for another five hundred yards, he thought. "Seems Ok, and James?"

"Oh, fine, though he has had a very heavy cold."

"So many about."

"Yes, there's no escaping them. And of course if you've little ones. How are Daisy's children?"

She was becoming breathless, talking and hurrying, but they both knew that politeness decreed that they must not walk in silence.

"Ok, thanks. Hate it after the clocks go back. The evenings are so long and dark." He stalked along, trying to slow his long stride to her short legged, straight skirted trot.

"Yes, me too," she said emphatically, as if they had just discovered some amazing link. "Lighter in the mornings though."

"Oh, yes," he agreed in a voice flooded with relief that he had arrived at the path to his house.

Laura had just watched a programme about the financial crash in America and was eager to talk about it. "It goes right back, you know. Clinton stopped regulation. He was advised by power crazed guys gambling with ordinary people's money, selling on the risks and debts. I've become an anti-capitalist."

He smiled. "Are you going down to join the activists at St Pauls, or how about going the whole hog. Join the protesters at Wall Street?"

"I may well do. Do you know that Lehman had his own entrance and lift to the 31st floor so he never had to meet or speak to anyone."

"Didn't you know? Bankers are in their own world."

"You're telling me! Apparently some risk taker bankers use cocaine and prostitutes and write the costs off as 'computer repairs'. My eyes are opened."

The evening after the funeral, Terry stood in the kitchen, staring out at the subtly illuminated garden, one of Leonard's many successful projects. David and Rosie had gone and she was suddenly alone, for the first time in her life. Is the worst thing about losing your partner that he would be the one person one would want to discuss the day with? On the one hand she knew that he was dead; on the other though, he still seemed to be here. Her friends who said how well she was coping did not know that she could feel his presence. He hadn't had a chance to enjoy our retirement together. All those plans of outings, holidays, perhaps, in a few years, grandchildren? He couldn't miss all these. He didn't deserve to die. Why should I be fit and here when I was considering leaving him? How can one believe in a god who kills the blameless people? He's still here, I know it. The door suddenly swung open in a little gust of wind and cold air shouldered its way in. Could that be him? She stared out into the creeping dark. No, it was the wind. Nothing more. She opened the fridge. Poured herself a glass of wine, lit a cigarette and went out into the dusky garden. The sweet smell of the night air reminded her of nights past, of mown grass, tree bark, damp earth and the scents of flowers.

Leonard had been disgusted by smoking. Terry had told herself that it was not as if she was the only smoker in England. Apparently one in five people still did, though many were like her, secret smokers. She had started again, when she had been diagnosed with the breast cancer, as a coping mechanism and had managed to keep it from Leonard. She would say that she needed some air last thing at night and would go to the bottom of the garden, making sure she was wearing clothes that were about to be going into the wash or to the dry cleaners. She would tie her hair back, get her cigarettes, lighter and gardening glove from her little greenhouse and smoke quickly by taking long drags. Then she would go in straight to the bathroom and shower and brush her teeth for twice as long as usual. If he had ever smelt anything, she would blame smokers at work. Perhaps part of the pleasure she had derived from her elaborate subterfuge was the fact that it was her secret. Somehow being able to smoke without guilt made it less pleasurable. She stubbed out her half smoked cigarette and went in to replenish her glass and get one of the leftover sandwiches, which Laura had carefully wrapped in cling film and put in the fridge. In case she felt like eating later.

Annie called round to see Laura. She rung the bell and waited and waited. She was just going off back down the path, when Daniel opened the door, wearing his usual beanie hat and muscle top only instead of shorts he had on baggy track bottoms.

She should have realised that he would have been in the loft, which he had taken over as his studio as soon as he had retired. Laura had shown her his lair. It was boarded, both floor and ceiling and had large north facing curtainless windows overlooking their quiet road, and another south facing looking out at the garden. He had built shelves, cupboards and racks to stack his canvases and there was one big comfy chair next to a kettle. Mug, tea and milk on a side table. Dan was fastidiously tidy and well organised.

There was blue paint on his cheek, and irritation at the interruption in his light green eyes. "She'll be back in ten minutes or so. Do you want to come in and wait?"

She followed him into the kitchen.

"I'll make some tea, what sort?"

"Black, builders please. Aren't you a bit old to become an artist? Oh sorry, don't mean to be rude." If she had looked she would have seen Dan's face darken for a minute, but she was gazing out at the garden and busy with her own thoughts.

He turned his back on her to fill the electric kettle. "I've always painted a bit, but there's never been time before to really concentrate on it. I'm getting better, because I'm doing it more."

"It's a shame, you might have been really good."

"I'm only sixty two, Lucian Freud and Picasso were still painting in their late 80's. I've got years to improve and find my style."

"Yes but Freud painted every day, didn't he, practising reproducing skin and hair and life? He had so much experience."

"While I've got the energy I'll carry on. Perhaps I'll peak at seventy. Age depends on your health, your genes." There were sounds of the front door opening and closing.

"There'll be no need for those painterly skills by the time you get there. Technology will have taken over. Look at David Hockney."

"I take your point, but in twenty six years in the city I'd had enough of spreadsheets, valuation models, complex derivatives and leveraged buyouts. I often worked twelve hour days and sometimes through the night. And I was pond life, no integrity, respect given or real teamwork. It was all about self-preservation. I was exhausted, empty, lifeless and lived and dreamt numbers. This is a change for me." He handed her a mug of tea. "Sugar?"

"What are you two talking about?" Laura came into the kitchen, her hair still wet from swimming.

"Oh, just art. What a seriously artistic, intellectual pair you are," said Annie. "Is there any cake?"

Daniel hovered around vaguely for a few seconds, then escaped to his attic as Annie continued. "You're my only friend who reads the weekend news before the colour magazines and all the big books we're supposed to read, like 'The Goldfinch' and 'Freedom.' *And* you're a writer!" She bit into a rock cake, which she had found in the cake tin.

Laura smilingly put a plate in her hand, then poured boiling water into the teapot. She liked to use leaf green tea and china cups. "Hmm, occasionally and unpublished!"

Beth had come back from swimming to find Harriet, big brown eyes under her grown out bleached razor cut thatch, sitting at the kitchen table eating muesli and yogurt. She put on the kettle for tea.

"Shall I make a little appointment at Ray's for you? Did you bleach your hair yourself?"

Harriet smiled fondly at her. "Don't you read mags, Mum? This is fleek, the hot look!"

"Oh, I see. Well, what are you going to do next? Work wise, I mean. Are you plotting something with Nicola? You've seen her every evening since you've been back."

"That's only five days. I've only been back *five days* and she's my bessie, Mother."

Beth looked blank. "What's a Bessie?"

"Bestie, bae, you know, best friend. We've missed one another!" Harriet said witheringly. "And, we're thinking about my future. I wanna make my mark, be part of something important. Excel in an area."

"That's very nice dear."

"Mind, I'm not going to live in cities all my life. Eventually I'll live in the country. Be sustainable. Grow veg, keep chickens, a goat and pigs." She looked thoughtful. "Or then again I might do something with food."

"With food? What sort of thing?"

"Have a pop up restaurant, or a personal cookery service with Nic. We talk about healthy food all the time. But what are you going to do with *yourself* when we're all gone, Mum? I was talking to Laura coming out of the tube yesterday and she was telling me about the choir and their Christmas concert. Why don't you go to choir?"

"Oh, I don't know, it's in the evening."

"What do you do on a Monday night anyway? Nothing. You just sit, eating and watching TV."

"Well, who would cook the supper if I was gadding about every evening?" Beth answered mildly, getting a tea bag from the tea jar and taking a mug off its hook.

"Get real, Mum. We don't need the constant supply of food. I can get my own, when I'm in and it will do Dad good to have to forage for a change." As if to start foraging she opened the fridge and stared inside. "Look, there's tons of food in here. No one's going to starve if you go out occasionally. You don't have to stay in night after night!"

"Well, I'm not sure that I want to sing in a…a thingy. I haven't sung since I met your father."

"You see!" Harriet was triumphant. "You gave up your life when you got married! Life has moved on. Women don't do that anymore."

Beth was irritated. Why should she have to sing? "Why don't you go?" she asked.

"Because I'll be off again soon, and then you'll have even less to occupy you. Anyway, they're probably all old like you and Laura. You'll be more at home there."

Harriet rarely gave up. Beth watched her flicking through the newspapers on the chair, looking for the 'Style' supplement to bear off to her room. Her back spoke volumes for her determination to get her mother out of the house.

"You like music, don't you?"

"Of course, look how many classical and opera thingummy's I've got." She felt a rush of guilt at how rarely she played any of them. Except when they had guests. To create a good atmosphere.

"Listen Mum, just give it a go. You were always singing round the house. You're going to have a gap in your life when me and Jake are not around to be fussed over anymore!" She smiled, encouragingly.

"I'll think about it," Beth said with a heavy sigh. Would she really stay at home most nights with James and the cat? "Just don't keep going on about it. I probably can't sing in tune."

Later:

Harriet came into the kitchen carrying her pink jumper. "Have you been wearing this, Mum? It's got a pull. Look, and it smells different. It doesn't smell like me."

"Oh, yes, sorry love, only one little time. I needed cheering up, my clothes looked so drab!"

"You go mad when I borrow your clothes. You made me promise not to touch them again. Then as soon as I'm away for a bit, you're into my things!"

"I didn't think you wanted the ones you left behind."

Harriet rolled her eyes. "I didn't want them in York, and then Africa. I want them here. I haven't died you know. This is still my home and I don't want to feel that you're in my room, nicking my clothes!"

She grabbed a saucepan and emptied pasta shells into it. While boiling the kettle, she peered into the fridge. "Do we have any of that yum pesto from the deli?"

"It's too expensive. There's a jar of pesto on the top shelf."

"Ugh, no, that doesn't taste of anything and it's full of preservatives and colourings." She looked through the tin drawer and chose tomatoes. "I'll have this and parmesan. Why don't you buy truffle oil? Oh mi God, I spent a fortune on that at uni. And it's false economy buying cheap pesto. You don't need to have as much with the deli one."

"Funny that it doesn't last more than a day then." Beth muttered to herself.

Looking out of the window, a shimmer of frost lay over the garden, the pale morning sun giving it a ghostly glow. Laura dressed warmly and went downstairs and out of the front door. There was a low mist and she stood for a moment, looking down the road towards the railway bridge where the mist rose higher. Her breath was cloudy in the sharp air and her head was still locked into thoughts about Daisy. She loved her daughter more than anyone in the world and understood that she was prickly and ungrateful because she felt so vulnerable. She had not even started a career and she was responsible for twins...and did she love Femi? What must she feel like being left, with no reassurance that he was coming back, or was going to take any responsibility for their girls? If only they could talk about it.

Two tubes, going in opposite ways rattled and boomed over the bridge and rooks rose cawing from the bare trees. She turned and walked up the road, toward her friends' houses and the shy winter sun.

Five minutes later Marie, Helen and Beth had been gathered up and they were heading off to the swimming pool.

"I *must* find something to do." Beth said. "What am I going to do with myself, when all my little chicks have flown? I think about it constantly, but I'm old now and have been out of the job market for too long."

"I think," said Laura, thoughtfully and slowly, her head still full of Daisy's predicament. "It's very hard not to have a raison de'etre."

Beth was quiet for a few paces. "Harriet keeps telling me to join the choir. 'You like music, mother, you're always playing it and singing along. Do more for yourself. We don't *need* you to cook supper every night and Dad's virtually retired. Tell him to get his own!"

"Well, we've been asking you for years, start next term." said Laura.

"I may, though we have talked about bridge. I was really upset yesterday with Jake though."

"Why?"

"He had a little tattoo! I was absolutely horrified. He's done the one thing I've repeatedly begged him not to. It's only a tattoo, he said. I haven't made anyone pregnant." Her pale moon face was red about the eyes.

Marie looked puzzled. "Sam Cam's got something on her ankle. They're perfectly respectable, Beth."

"I read that Rihanna had fifteen, or was it twelve, and how many has David Beckham got? It wouldn't do for us though. I don't want to draw attention to my wrinkly skin. But if I was under thirty-five..." Laura said wistfully.

"He says he's been thinking about doing it for a long time and he's not going to worry about whether he likes it when he's my age. He likes it now!"

"What is it anyway?"

"Oh, I don't know, some meaningless chinesey looking thingy here on his precious little arm. All those years I was looking after his body. Making sure he ate healthy food, went to the dentist, didn't get too much sun and he's mutilated himself. He's branded himself like meat."

"Well, at least its not his current girlfriends name. It's about rebelling and being noticed. It's like their sharing of their thoughts and personal details in Twitter and Facebook. The next thing will be to write your thoughts on your body, as a talking point."

Don't go over the top with this, Laura," said Helen.

"But it's the permanence that makes me so upset. He knew I'm dead against them. It's there forever, even though you've become a different person. It can damage your career and give people something to dislike about you before you've even spoken. I couldn't stop crying all night."

Helen looked carefully at her friend. "Is this about more than a tattoo, Beth? Are you sure it's not really about the fact that he hasn't worried about your opinion when he made his decision? He's asserted his independence?"

They were standing at the entrance to the Leisure Centre. Beth looked as if she were going to burst into tears. "Come on guys. Let's get that swim," Laura said, giving her a friendly push.

The wind howled and rain beat against the window. Laura was making a chicken and mushroom pie, when a soaking wet Dan came back from getting the free 'Evening Standard' from the station. Daisy had her head in the fridge, looking for something to eat. "So you can't wait half an hour for supper?" he heard Laura saying and his irritation with Daisy rose.

"No thanks," and she was gone, bearing the remains of a quiche from the night before and an avocado.

"On one of the few occasions she's in, why shouldn't she socialise with us?"

"It's her life," muttered Laura.

"She's probably too busy being on Facebook. All these deluded young people reducing their personalities to just a few categories. My photograph, my books, my music, my friends. It's ideal for her, it's just lists like she's always loved, favourite girls' names, favourite boys etc."

"Now, now, you sound like a grumpy old man."

"Well, that's what I am!" He went off into the lounge, flicked on the outside lights and sat looking out of the french windows at the frantically dancing garden they both loved so much.

Chapter 7. Christmas

'Though some churls at our mirth repine,
Round your foreheads garlands twine,
Drown sorrows in a cup of wine,
And let us all be merry.'
George Wither, 'A Christmas Carol' (1622)

It's Carolyn's birthday, it's not just any old party, put on your navy trousers and that blue shirt I like." Laura knew Dan's sullen, pugnacious moods, when he would not look at her and he was plucking up the courage to say he was not going.

"How would I know it's her birthday party, you know I'm hopeless at remembering things like that." He admired Laura's capacity for storing such details. The threads and skeins of her friends' lives were always sorted in her head, but he hated parties and felt irritable.

Eventually he was ready and they left the house. She was feeling good in her new red 'Ted Baker' dress, but she could feel him sulking beside her as they walked. "You're not going to make me miserable and spoil it for me," she said.

Carolyn opened the door wearing a sparkly black mini dress, her face and hair glittered with silver bits and behind her a lovely Christmas tree twinkled and shone. They hugged and she took the card and flowering orchid and then greeted more people who had arrived behind them.

The kitchen was full of middle class, older people dressed in their party best. "I'll get some drinks," Laura said, knowing that Dan would not want to push through the melee. She stood patiently while Alan slowly filled glasses for himself, James and Beth. He was pontificating about something:

"What sort of world are our grandchildren being born into? An economy struggling with too many unemployed and too many huge pensions to pay out? The threat of a nuclear confrontation with North Korea? Or Iran? Cyber warfare on the Internet? Unsustainable population growth depleting resources?"

"You're being a bit of a doom-monger," said James, picking up the two full glasses and edging away. "Generally we're richer and healthier than at any time in history."

Alan was still blocking the drinks table. "Well us baby boomers are Ok. We've had the best of everything. Our mothers stayed at home to look after us. Then when we started work, we were part of a large labour force and a relatively small number of pensioners and children. And now we're silver surfers we're a financial burden to the smaller working force."

"Enough guys, this is supposed to be a party. Lighten up and pour us two red wines, please." She put the two bottles they had brought under the table packed with drinks and waited while Alan finished off one bottle into a glass for her and opened another.

Jo, looking stunning in a silver sequinned short and clinging dress, had cornered Dan to rant on about modern art. "Most non-artists only appreciate beautiful things, where they can see she the craftsmanship and feel reverential at the skill and vision. Absurd people like Tracy Emin, Damien Hirst, the Chapmans etc leave them cold." She grinned and kept her eyes fixed on his, though he found it difficult to look at her. She was swaying as she spoke, waving her glass around and her amazing tits joggled in front of him. Why did she always wear such low cut tops? It was an exercise in power and he didn't want to be mesmerised and teased.

"Looking at art is about what happens between the observer and the painting. You can't tell other people what to feel, the connection comes from who you are," he said evasively.

"What style do you paint in then?"

"Every time I start a new canvas, I try to wipe the slate clean, wipe everything from my brain and start afresh."

"Why can't you build on your last effort?"

"That's stupefying, it's stasis for me, I'm experimenting and I may as well be an automaton if I'm going to repeat and repeat."

"Plenty of famous artists have repeated and revisited."

"Yes, but I want to be open, with no single aim or meaning. I paint my feelings, so the same subject can be flat and motionless, or passionately lively. It's altered by the way I'm feeling at the time."

Jo looked at him closely, he was a good looking guy, slightly feline features, plenty of dark, slightly curly hair, streaked with grey, but he had a cloudy look as if he were not conscious of anything or anyone. He was in his own world.

"I need another drink," she said.

He smiled in an abstracted way and she wandered towards the kitchen, where most people had congregated. Why does this always happen in parties, she thought. When I have one, I'm going to keep everyone out of the kitchen, right out. Laura was emerging with Annabelle from the crush round the drinks table, carrying two drinks.

"What we think we are deciding is illusory," Annabelle was saying, impressive in her long red and black dress. "We are in fact acting out a script prescribed by genetically driven imperatives." She moved on and past, not waiting for Laura's reply.

"So if there is no self, Annabelle," Laura called after her. "If we're just automatons, that means there can be no meaningful human interaction, no reflection, no emotion. Shouldn't we die after we've brought up the next generation?"

"Nature still has a use for you, as a grandmother." Annabelle turned to smirk and then swooped into the lounge.

"She's nails," Jo muttered. "Someone needs to give her a good slap."

"She's a bit frozen faced, she always looks as if she's sucking a lemon!"

"Yeh, a grunting, self-absorbed twig with pneumatic breasts and freakin' weird cat's eyes. She's wearing a choker! Why would anyone wear a red lace choker? Unless they were mental, a Victorian prostitute, a Roma fortune-teller, or had a seriously crepey neck. She might at least try and mimic human behaviour." She put two fingers to her temple, rolled her eyes and pushed through the throng around the drinks table. Wriggling between a couple of tired looking men with receding hair and lined, pouched faces, she wondered; did I fancy any of you once at a party: where we drunk Hirondelle or from cans of party four, picked at cheese and pineapple on sticks, straddled for a shag and then rolled a joint? Getting hold of a bottle of Rioja, she

88

filled her glass, took a swig, pushed her way back to Laura, and topped up again. "Parties are much more fun than dinner parties, don't you think? No spending the evening stuck between people who bore for Britain, love it, love it, you can say disgraceful things, then bugger off. You know I've been to parties where a tray was passed round with little rows of coke and straws to sniff up your row with."

"You're kidding…doesn't it rot the membrane between your nostrils?"

"Probably. Some people get twitchy socialising without powder. Everyone's doing it, you know. But then, who wants to end up a boring, self-rotating, gibbering cokehead? I'm clean now. So healthy! I've just been talking to Dan. Guys who won't dye their hair, have piercings or tattoos and shun the cutting edge look: in my book they usually have beards? So where's his? Interesting. Anyway, you've landed on your feet with him. Self-sufficient, mends stuff and does the washing up. Lucky girl!"

Laura grinned and headed off towards him. "And he's been accosted by you and Annie and hasn't even had a drink yet!"

Jo was sipping and refilling when she saw Phillip coming towards her. "Jo!" he swept forwards, encircling her in an embrace. "You look wonderful!"

Her eyes scanned the room for rescue. Laura had nearly reached Dan and Annie, nothing doing. He took the bottle from her hands and emptied and refilled his glass in between what he presumably thought were witty and clever observations. His long hair and leather biker jacket gave him the look of an ageing hippie, a camp ageing hippie, what's more. She wondered how many leather jackets he possessed and smiled a vague damp flannel party smile as she sidled round him and the bottle and away into the lounge.

Daniel and Annie had somehow got onto the subject of communication. "I'm not interested in living my life through social media. Its for needy, attention seeking, insecure people."

"And I'd be able to get hold of you too easily," said Laura handing him his wine. "Hi Annie, it's such a scrum in there."

Helen was late, she had needed to write a report while it was still fresh in her mind. Alexis, Carolyn's partner, opened the door, greeting her effusively. She smiled, gave him her jacket and made for the kitchen, where two bearded older men she did not know were having an animated discussion. "Capitalism operates through forced oppression of workers, who conspire in their own oppression by seeing work as a way to be upwardly mobile. That's Marx and Engels."

"Yes, carrot as well as the stick." They both laughed and looked at Helen, "I'm Barry, can I get you a drink?" the shorter one asked.

"I'm Helen and thanks, a white wine please." She took it and turned away from the North London leftie talk, towards the lounge, where she hoped the conversation would be lighter. But there, in front of her she saw with fury, Phillip, in animated conversation with Jo. "Let your passion be your compass in all things," he smarmed, pushing his lips forward in a mock kiss, then smiling his admiring, 'you're so stunning smile', with which he had probably made endless conquests.

I've only just met her and already she's infiltrating every aspect of my life, the cow, she thought, opening the back door and stepping outside. She's tediously, suffocatingly materialistic and sex mad. What's she doing with Phillip? He can't be rich enough for her. The wind raced around her head and her tears were chilled on her face. She shivered and went back inside and spoke to a little black dress she didn't know. "We're going to have snow in a few days," she confided. It was obvious that the woman was not the slightest bit interested in her weather prediction, as her eyes glazed and she turned to talk to someone more interesting. Helen wandered past her into the lounge, just in time to see Phillip placing a prawn with his fork into the red full-lipped mouth of Annabelle, a purring tabby, licking herself with pleasure. The playful, lascivious act made her feel suddenly deathly faint as she realised what most of her friends had probably known for months. Annabelle was newly divorced and had regular sessions with Phillip, Jo wasn't the one, it was that bloody – people are just mirrors for her – I'm so important -Annabelle! The couch was behind her and she sat down suddenly, half upon Beth who squeaked in surprise. Phillip looked up, rushed over and asked solicitously, "is everything alright, darling?"

90

The room went quiet and the air was still and sticky. She could hear the rhythmic throb of music in the other room. To her horror, she started to cry and could feel those nearest to her moving away in embarrassment. Beth squeezed her arm consolingly.

"Helen's mother is ill," Phillip said quietly.

"And the rest," those in ear shot thought.

Jo had had enough. She had drunk too much and apart from her friends there did not seem to be anyone else worth talking to. Women with short grey or painted hair and orange skin, filling their clothes confidently, and paunchy balding men shouted at one another against a backdrop of mostly empty bottles and plates. It was after midnight. What's that Wendy Cope poem, she thought? About men being tedious because they need to show off and compete and bore you to death for hours and hours…'

A blue veined, liver spotted, silver nailed hand seized her arm. "Lovely to see you."

It was Lila, her ancient next-door neighbour whose lipstick had seeped like tendrils into her face. She had seen her this morning in Waitrose. Why is it lovely this time? Yak, Yak, let go of me, she thought sourly as Lila held her close to whisper catty comments. "There's Sabine, like a little violet in Erik's shade, reaching out desperately for some light. Who's your shrink, darleeng?"

"I don't do shrinks. Isn't therapy the ultimate self indulgence?" Jo sniffed. "Have to get another drink, excuse me."

"Everyone in the US has a shrink, darleeng. We don't make decisions without discussing it with our shrink," she heard as she moved away.

"Well, we'll soon be outsourcing decision making to India, to rows of therapists with webcams," Jo muttered to herself as she escaped into the coats room and home.

The trees were bare and grizzled with snow as Laura and Beth slid and slipped along the slushy pavements. A sombre sky hung low over the grey rooftops. "Hope it's not going to snow again."

There had been a snowfall in the night, but already there were footsteps and tyre marks everywhere. There were the sounds of trickling and plops as the melt water and soft snow capitulated to the sun.

The pool was often quite empty in bad weather. They luxuriated in the warm, calm blue water, relaxed and content.

"Let's not have Christmas this year!" a young woman called Hannah said as they towelled themselves dry after their swims. "There are so many people out of work, lost their homes, can't afford to buy presents, how can we feel jolly? We should give it a miss."

"I don't think it works like that," answered Laura. "Most people want to celebrate, even if they don't have much to spend. Though the older one gets, the more averse one is to acquiring new things."

"Yes, there's nothing I really want, I should be getting rid of half the stuff in our house, but I'm useless at de-cluttering," agreed Beth.

Suddenly a bombshell hit number 25. Laura came back from her book club and found Daniel pacing about wondering if he should apologise to Daisy. "What did you say to her?"

"She was moaning that you hadn't left her much for supper and the twins had still been up when she came home. First thing she does when she comes in is look in the fridge to choose the freshest and most expensive items. This isn't a hotel you know Daisy, I said. What is it then, a prison? It's not a home, she said. So I'm afraid I let her have it."

"What did you say?" Laura's heart sunk, she went cold and stared helplessly at Dan as he continued.

"She was feckless, acting like a typical teenager, a naive idealist not an adult. I was fed up with her expecting to be waited on: the fact that we're supporting her, she's totally selfish and treating you like an au pair and that she's a waste of space. You're not able to do the things you've dreamt about all those years when you were working and bringing her up. All the summer she hung around saying she was writing and refused that job checking pensioners' application forms for their freedom passes. Boring yes, but it would have paid for her journalism course. Now I've packed in work I can see how little time for yourself you have. And I don't want her here all the time. I want to be able to take off on walks, to see exhibitions, have holidays, with you, but she relies on you every day." He paused and blushed slightly, "And I probably said a few other home truths too."

"Oh, God, No. No. You know what she's like, so unforgiving."

The next morning Daisy was up before anyone. Laura tried to tell her that Dan didn't mean it, tried to get her to talk about it, but she would not speak, just got the children breakfast and took them to school for their last day of term. The years of resentment were too strongly embedded.

That evening, she would not listen to Laura's apologies. She was hoarse from weeping and buoyed up by martyrdom, self-righteousness and vengeance. "I'm leaving, I'll never come back while he's here. This house is dysfunctional. You and Dan are hypocrites and you don't want me around."

"Of course we do. But you have always distanced yourself from being a family unit."

"Unit? Don't make me laugh. How can a driven mother and her switched off partner ever form a unit with anyone?"

"You have never given us credit for anything. We've always been the bad guys. Remember the nice moments, Daisy!"

"The *rare* nice moments. I'm different from you. I don't want to be like you. The more I stay around, the more you influence my thoughts and ideas. I was free of you at Uni. *I don't want to be like you!* I want the story of my life to begin away from you. I'm stepping out of this life into my own."

Three days later Laura came home from tennis and Daniel from shopping and Daisy, Lily and Ruby had gone, taking most of their clothes and some toys with them. There was no forwarding address and Daisy would not answer her mobile. "How did they take so much with them? She couldn't have got on a train or a flight with all that. Which of her friends would have taken them and where?" Daisy didn't drive, it was a mystery.

It rained, quietly and kindly most of the day. The wind rattled and the rain was spitting on the glass when they got into bed. Their bodies laid down to rest, but their minds went on thinking about Daisy for some hours. Laura woke again at four, with an anxious feeling. Her mouth was dry, the heavy shadow of Daisy filling her head. Not sleeping had been normal during her menopause and for long periods every so often after. She found it difficult to switch off if something was bothering her. Her mind raced and her body twitched and wriggled. She'd been replaying endlessly Daisy at twelve, clinging to her: "It's just me and you Mum, isn't it, the rest of the world doesn't matter. When I'm old enough I'll look after you, do all the housework, cook you meals so you won't be so tired. I'll do anything for you. You're the best Mum in the world!" That shy, loving little girl, who changed when Dan moved in.

She had thought that she was teaching Daisy that she could be anything that she wanted to be, by gentle pushing, encouragement and telling her how talented, clever and strong she was. Yet Daisy had told Beth and Harriet that her mother had taken away all her confidence.

"I'm the daughter of a workhorse," she had told them. "Her stamina, drive and creativity overwhelm me. She forges ahead, never tiring, always achieving. We're just not cut from the same cloth, I could never keep up, I don't want to. She makes me feel tired!"

Laura sobbed quietly into the pillow.

The next day she was in shock. She sat in her familiar kitchen, her porridge cold and congealing. Her surroundings were suddenly foreign, the shelves in front of her with their lines of bottles of herbs, glasses and their favourite plates were strangers. Perhaps Daisy would ring soon and say she was coming back? Her mind skittered about. "You are my best friend, Mum. You are wonderful with the children," she had said only a few weeks, or was it months ago. She felt dizzy. Hold the chair, press toes into the ground, breathe deeply.

In the following days Laura was lost to her friends, buried under her pain and agony. She could not sleep, going over and over things Daisy had said and her ungiven responses. There was tension in her shoulders, deep bags under her eyes and a throbbing ache always in her head. She rushed to her computer every morning, heart pounding, torn between the desperate need to have an email from Daisy and the equally desperate need not to have a mind shattering one. She wrote long letters to Daisy, in her head and in a notebook next to the bed.

I am no doubt a deeply flawed person, and you are able to continually tell me so, with little fight back from me, because a mother will rarely tell their child his/her flaws. She wants her child to grow, stand tall and proud and be strong in who they are, so you are safe. I will never point out your faults and am trying to take on board my own. You know that you can pile all your pent up anger at anything and everything on me, because I will always take it. I will never walk away, as you won't when one day your children do it to you.

What I find difficult is that you only seem to be able to be you at the expense of me. I have felt diminished, inadequate and unconfident in your presence for five or six years now. Why does it have to be a contest? I'm dismissed, in order for you to be yourself? I love you more than anything in the world Daisy and will always be here for you. Please remember that.

Marie could hear her front door bell, is that the post? She glanced at her wall planner. Oh, it must be Laura. She had forgotten her insistence that Laura had a massage to help her with her grief at Daisy's departure. "Stress," she had told her, "can trigger cancer or other nasties we might have lurking in our bodies. I'll give you a therapeutic massage to help lessen your anxiety."

Laura had felt guilty at accepting and Dan said, "What good is a massage, why not try the sleeping pills I got you?"

"I don't want to get addicted to drugs. It's so kind of Marie to offer. It's easy to be sceptical about energy healers. I don't believe in lots of therapies, but massage, the laying on of hands, I can take completely seriously. Not many doctors believe in complementary therapies, but the fact that she knows so much and still does, makes an even stronger case for them."

They embraced and Laura followed Marie into the lounge. This flat is like a shrine to an eastern way of life, Laura thought, gazing around at statues of Buddha, handcrafted teak furniture, brassware, oriental cups, plates and jugs with gold gilding. Are our homes a critique of who we are? A little draft fluttered the curtains and the setting sun through the stained glass windows made a dazzle of fractured colour. They walked through to the conservatory with its rattan chairs, citrus trees, jasmine and bougainvillea, so Marie could show her the unusual white and pink forsythia, already in flower in the garden.

Back in the lounge, Laura lay on the massage table, being stroked and squeezed and kneaded like warm dough. She was in a strange trance-like state and the smell of smouldering herbs filled her head. "They remove the sadness and negative energy. Can you turn over, dearest?" Marie asked, maintaining Laura's modesty with skilful towel management.

An hour later, she opened her eyes to the soft half-light coming in through the almost closed wooden shutters. She felt relaxed and light headed, as if she had had a long, deep sleep.

"Take your time," Marie said softly. "Sip this water, it'll help you to feel less woozy. Then come into the kitchen for a cup of green tea. You need to look after yourself, pamper yourself more."

"And you, are you looking after yourself?" Laura asked. "You're always giving, when do you get to receive?"

Marie began to answer then her eyes welled up as her past overwhelmed her and the love she still felt, but had lost, poured out in her tears.

"Oh god, she's still suffering." Laura tentatively reached out a hand to gently rub her back in sympathy, but Marie shook herself and raised her face, forcing a radiant smile.

"Sorry, I still think of him day and night. I have to move on." She had a horror of showing her heart and always had. "But, I haven't told you because I only knew two days ago…I've got a posting, to South Sudan. I've got to leave in eight days."

"Well great if that's what you want. We'll miss you terribly though."

"I think I do, yes. And coincidentally, Suki, you know my goddaughter, and her family are having their house renovated. They can move in here for six months."

So with Marie packing and then gone and Laura listlessly moping,

96

no one went swimming. They could always find reasons not to.

After just a few weeks Betty's balance and movement had deteriorated so much that walking had become difficult. She stayed in her room, unwilling to go into a lounge full of slumped bodies with their uniform red and blue legs and elastic waisted skirts. Life was continuing outside the lounge window, but these women no longer noticed or had any involvement in it.

What was she thinking? Were memories swimming through her like dreams - glimpses of the past, her parents, school, Lynne's birth. Some days she talked as if her sister and husband were still alive. She and Lynne would sit in silence, each with their own memories. Lynne's head full of anguished thoughts about age, why it had to come to this, how painful it was to think they might never really talk again and how she may never again register how much Lynne loved her.

This particular afternoon Betty was completely absorbed in trying to move imaginary things from just in front of her to just at the side. Her lips seemed to be trying to capture the thoughts speeding through her brain, as if they were ducks in a fairground that were flying past as she aimed her rifle.

"Have you got a tissue?" She suddenly asked.

"They're in front of you, Mum. On the table."

Her shaking hand picked up a banana, and then she couldn't co-ordinate the movements to let go of it.

"The tissues are straight in front of you, Mum." Lynne said gently, but Betty picked up the banana again. Her mind was obviously playing spatial tricks. Lynne tried not to think about what was happening. Can't this blank faced mother, stripped of her dignity and intellect, see or feel anything anymore?

"Are you alright, Mum?

"I'd be alright if I could just go home and have a sleep."

"You are home," said Lynne, but Betty looked at her with betrayed discernment.

Had she done the right thing, bringing her here? Was being with and having her nappy changed by strangers, often men, an unremitting

97

nightmare? Lynne could now see patients uninterrupted, go out when she wanted and go swimming again. She was a strong swimmer and had missed the exercise. But the guilt was unbearable.

Laura had asked: "You are still bringing her here for Christmas?"

"I just don't know what to do. Her body is being toileted, washed, dressed and fed, but her mind is rarely there. It was such an interesting, perceptive mind; where does it go? Instead of the lively, whirlwind of a mother, always up to something, there's just this husk. I feel no more warmth from her. Does she think I've abandoned her? I know it's the plaques and tangles, but I don't know who or where she is any more. How would it be, could we manage her?"

"She used to love Christmas. You can't leave her there. Let's try, just for lunch?"

There was a silence. "I'm wondering if it'll make it a miserable, depressing meal. She can't feed herself properly any more, you know."

"Let's try, unless you've other plans?"

Despite Laura's pain she and Dan had still put up decorations and bought a tree, but they did not have the heart to host their annual Christmas Eve party.

Laura had bought lots of little presents for Ruby and Lily, just as she used to do for Daisy, just in case. She also made a photo album for the two girls, of all the photos of Daisy growing up. The moments of joy on Daisy's face, frozen in time, made her weep. Dan said she was mad to give herself so much pain.

For Dan, she had filled a big silver box with every sort of packet of crisps that she could find, every vegetable and every flavour. She bought him sexy boxer shorts and a really nice pair of pure cotton cords, which she knew would end up at the back of his sparsely filled cupboard, either to stay there forever, or to emerge when the shape was out of fashion. He had bought her a Kindle, some lip pencils and a lovely pen.

On Christmas Eve Laura went into Daisy's room and stood, remembering all those schooldays where she had had to wrench Daisy from indignant sleep. Her bedroom had invariably been in chaos. Plates with half eaten food, mugs with mould in them and the animal droppings from hamsters, rabbits or guinea pigs, scattered over most of the content of her drawers and wardrobe. Yet she would pick a few items of clothing off the floor, shake them and come out looking radiant. I miss her so much. If she would just come back. I wouldn't moan again. I'd be so grateful to see them all.

Further down the road, Beth had made her usual puddings and cakes. She had brought out the artificial tree and put up the decorations, ordered the turkey and bought crackers and presents for all the family.

Oxford Street was mayhem with what seemed like inebriated people doing their last minute shopping. The stores and bars were full. The shop windows and lights lifted Frances's spirits as she wandered about looking for presents to take to her sister's family.

David and Rosie had taken Terry to a hotel in Brighton for three days. Rosie had bought Terry a book on 'Mindfulness' which told her to concentrate 100 per cent on the present by doing a boring, repetitive task and doing it 'mindfully,' to block out the past and future.

Ben and his friend Nathan had arrived to spend Christmas Day and Boxing Day with Annie and Martin. They were then going to Scotland for a week before returning to the States. Annie had bought Martin a beautiful Italian bike frame. She knew he would enjoy building a bike with his own choice of handlebars, saddle and so on. He had bought her a white towelling dressing gown, thick, warm and soft. Ben had wanted money and they had bought both him and Nathan books and put cheques inside.

Jo and Jessica were lounging by the pool and going to parties in Cape Town with Vic and Cliff.

Helen had bought Phillip a smart weekend holdall from Barbour. He had bought her a sexy silk and lace negligee set. They were spending Christmas and Boxing Day at the Stirling Hotel in Reading so that Stella could come for lunch and they could take her out for drives.

Hugh was spending Christmas with Lucy's parents this year. On Christmas day, Beth was up early to put the turkey in the oven. Harriet and Jake came down at mid-day, by which time James and Beth had opened a bottle of vintage champagne and were drinking a toast.

"That's so sick!" exclaimed Jake, witnessing their happy Christmas kiss. "Pensioners snogging, it's just gross, all that saggy skin and wrinkles…like two turtles. And by the way, why'd you buy this wholemeal Cranks' shit?" He held up the loaf and made a vomiting sound. "Harriet doesn't eat gluten and you and Dad are into porridge."

Harriet was irritatingly sanctimonious. "Why are you poisoning your bodies with alcohol every day? My generation realise that we can achieve far more and feel better without alcohol. You can't fire on all cylinders if you've got a hangover."

"Don't people go to the pub after work anymore then?"

"Yes but who needs alcohol, it's a social crutch. If you're the only one not drinking and you're surrounded by champagne, you might feel like an outsider, but so many others don't drink now. You two should cut down. You probably don't know what it's like for your bodies to be alcohol free."

By the time that lunch was over, the day was feeling like an overdose of quality time. Beth struggled on, trying to whip up some Christmas cheer, insisting upon playing charades and Monopoly but by the time she suggested whist the gloves were off and any pretence at politeness had evaporated.

A month ago, she had circled a blue parka in a Lyle and Scott catalogue for James, as part of his move from formal work clothes to more casual attire for walking, shopping and being a man of leisure. James did not have casual clothes, just tailored suits, shirts and ties. Jo had said he should wear polo shirts or tee's a pair of 'Indigo' jeans or chinos.

"But what about his tummy? His jackets disguise his fat tummy."

"Not sure about that, Beth, and there are T-shirts for all sizes," Jo had replied, privately thinking that he dressed too much like who he was. A privileged old-fashioned man with his long held prejudices and assumptions intact.

Beth rang Laura later to ask how her day had gone. "I've always hoped that I'd get a beautiful piece of jewellery and a romantic card telling me how gorgeous I am, but James spotted the marked catalogue and thought *I'd* wanted a thingy, a *parka,* so he bought me a huge yellow one that makes me look like a lagged boiler or a huge fat chick."

Lynne and Laura had hoped to give Betty a normal Xmas lunch and presents. The house groaned and crackled with heat and the tinsel in every room twinkled and swayed. They dined on turkey, two kinds of stuffing, Dauphinoise potatoes, roasted vegetables, cranberry and bread sauce, sprouts, beans, broccoli and red cabbage in the big, warm kitchen. Alan had brought champagne and gave a toast: "Thanks so much for inviting us waifs and strays. To absent friends…"

Laura's heart almost stopped beating. Would she ever get over Daisy's absence? As she served everyone with vegetables, she could barely breathe, and her heart pumped as if it would burst out of her body. They were spending Boxing Day with Dan's parents, but this was the first Christmas without Daisy.

It was a miserable, fraught lunch. Betty hardly spoke and was blank faced, and disorientated. She did not want to eat all together at the table and sat grim faced like a spectre at the feast when they insisted. The present bonanza was a failure too. Betty had loved buying gifts and of course had nothing to give and her presents of nighties and chocolates must have reminded her of her reduced life, her incarceration. "It's no fun being like this you know," she said to Laura when the three of them were struggling to change her pad.

She did not remember she had been anywhere a few minutes after Lynne had taken her back to the Home. "Is it Christmas day soon?" she asked.

Chapter 8. January. Children

'Here where the rain has darkened and the sun has dried
So many times the terrace, yet is love unended.
Love has not died.'
Edna St Vincent Millay (1892-1950) 'The Hardy Gardener.'
Reprinted courtesy of Holly Peppe, Literary Executor, Millay Society.

The wind seemed to have camped in the winter garden, gusting wildly, rattling the bare twigs and redistributing the last of the old autumn leaves. It sprang like a bullying fox at the pittosporum so the grey leaves shivered in fright. Where were the birds to peck up the crumbs and bits of bacon rind Dan had left for them? Probably cowering somewhere. Laura put on her outdoor shoes and jacket and went out of the back door, the icy cold hitting the back of her throat. Down to the bottom of the garden she went, for kale and broccoli for supper. Every tree and bush stood out against the dark azure sky. She bent over the brassicas and heard a movement in the holly and there were eyes shining in the cold. Was it a cat, a fox? She picked quickly and retraced her steps.

All the unaccustomed acres of free time, which she had had since Daisy's disappearance, had been unproductive and painful. Christmas was over and she and the house had settled back down into drowsy brooding. In the long solitary hours where nothing was expected or required of her, Daisy was always in her head. Then at night she lay, trying not to thrash and wriggle, but far from sleep. She and Dan were barely speaking. He was silent with misery, fatigue and disbelief at the situation he had created. Every day for Laura began in an exhausted stupor. A swim usually revived her and gave her an adrenalin boost. Yet as the morning wore on, she would sink back into uncommunicative lethargy.

"Isn't it nice and peaceful without Daisy and the children?" her friends asked.

"Peaceful? Suppose so. It's tidier and all my stuff is where I put it, but I'm grieving, missing them terribly."

It seemed to have been raining for weeks. There were floods all over Britain. It had stopped, but the temperature had dropped. Car windows had iced up and there was a sprinkling of snow everywhere.

By the time that Laura and Helen came out of the pool, it was snowing heavily and the air was sharp and fresh. "Would you like to talk about Daisy sometime?" Helen asked.

Laura jumped at the chance and cooked supper for them both that evening.

"I'm very surprised that she left your TLC?" said Helen, a glass of Rioja in her hand, watching Laura tipping the cooked pasta into the strainer and pouring boiling water over it.

Laura paused. She seemed to be trying to keep calm. "She must have wanted to show that she didn't need us."

"After everything you've done for her, it must feel devastating?"

Laura swirled salad leaves in the dressing she had mixed earlier, while she thought about her answer. "Well, I miss them terribly of course, but it *had* become too much. My life was sucked up by her demands. Her bedroom will be tidy instead of messy mountain ranges of 'nothing to wear'. I'm not permanently baby sitting, shopping and cooking, so a tiny part of me is relieved, but ninety-nine per cent is devastated."

They helped themselves and there was a psychiatrist's silence as Helen forked in her food. She looked at Laura steadily, without expression. They chatted about the pool and Helen's work, then over the fruit salad Helen went back to the subject.

"Daisy resented Daniel coming into your lives, didn't she?"

"Yes, she's always been very imaginative. A wonderful writer, who told herself stories and loved make believe. She dreamt of a happy ever after without Daniel and rather put herself in the role of an emotionally abused child. I kept hoping that one day their relationship would improve, and there were moments, but Daisy certainly clings on to grief. She felt rejected because up to then there were just the two of us. Any boyfriends I had, she could see I didn't take them seriously. With Dan it was different and Daisy resented the change in her status as my companion and best friend. I said over and over to her: You are the most important person in the world to me Daisy, Daniel won't change the amount of love I have for you. I know it wasn't easy for her. She couldn't spend weekend mornings in bed, reading and chatting with me. *He* was there. Meals were no longer the two of us and sometimes guests. *He* was always there too."

She hid in her bedroom, reading trashy books and feeling sorry for herself. Getting them both to sit down together and play happy families rarely worked. One of them always found something more urgent to do. Her childhood suddenly seemed lonely and neglected and no matter how hard I worked at trying to get us to be a family, Daisy was having none of it."

"Did you invite Daisy to come back home to live after university?"

"Well yes. She wanted me to go up to Liverpool all the time. I tried to help her, going once a week to help her and take the girls to the pool. But though Daisy's lips said "thank you", there was resentment in her eyes. The last time I went, she had a terrible cold, she was wild eyed, wild haired in a dishevelled bed with plates of half eaten food, mugs with dregs of cold, scummy tea, half read newspapers and two naked feral children rushing to me in rapturous glee. 'Nana, Nana, look at this!' 'Can we go swimming?' 'Nana, I'm a galloping pony.' She had no money. Femi said he'd send it, but he hadn't. I couldn't turn my back on her. It's my fault, isn't it? If I hadn't always done so much for her perhaps she wouldn't have felt impelled to clamp herself to a man. Perhaps she would have stood on her own feet. I thought I'd brought her up to be independent."

"What do you think went wrong?"

"Well my aim was always to encourage her to have opinions and curiosity. I wanted to inspire her with energy and ideas, to make her into an independent, fascinating, confident person. I told her over and over how talented and clever she was, that she could be anything she wanted to be. Yet she said I took away all her confidence! Was I depriving her of who she really wanted to be? I think my aim was for her to start her life where I had struggled to arrive and she didn't want an empowered working mother. She just wanted me to be a stay-at-home mummy who made jam tarts and allowed her to make every mistake for herself."

"I'm sure you did your very best," said Helen sympathetically. "But frankly, I think Daisy's behaviour is unforgivable. She is a highly intelligent girl and had a privileged, loving upbringing. Perhaps you made her feel too special, so now she thinks that her pain is greater than yours and her feelings of injury surpass any that you might have. She seems to feel that she was so traumatised by the presence of Daniel in her life and your collusion that for evermore she is the injured party. Unfortunately, she doesn't seem to have understood that a mother doesn't stop loving their child just because a step-father comes on the scene. She seems to have no compunction whatsoever in damaging her own children, who were so close to you both. Now they don't have their Nana or Daniel in their lives. Everyone would be so much happier if she put whatever she feels was unjust or hurtful behind her and tried to do her best by you and her children. By going away, rather than discussing the situation, she's giving you no chance to make things better. Once one starts the 'labelling, blame game', it stops one letting go of hurt feelings, resulting in a severe relationship conflict. She has to let go of the idea that other people are making her feel bad. She is doing it to herself by focussing on your labels to enable her to be judgemental and angry. She can press a button called 'Mum' and all the usual stuff plays in her head, reconfirming her resentments and sense of injustice. Until those emotions change, she's not going to contact you, she's going to make you suffer. And by the way, early learning doesn't have to determine your course in life. Your neurones can re-wire." She sipped her wine.

"Remember, when children need their parents, they're close and when they're happy or have their own children they don't think about them at all. Each generation has to live with this. Try and get on with your life without her for a while."

Beth came home from food shopping into the kitchen to see her two lodgers sitting there. Neither looked up. Jake was lost in his iPhone and Harriet was thumbing her Blackberry, while both spooned muesli into their mouths. She stood, waiting for someone to notice her, wondering if she were invisible. "How about a little cup of tea?"

she asked brightly.

There was no answer from Jake.

"No thanks, Mum," from practically vegan, environment warrior Harriet.

Beth sighed. "Don't either of you do anything as revolutionary as eating your breakfast at breakfast time anymore?" she asked by way of diversion.

Jake pushed his empty bowl into the middle of the table, stood up, all staring hair, sleeveless tee and baggy hipster jeans. His iPhone started squealing and he jabbed at it with an onslaught of spewed obscenities. "Who the fuck is that? Bye." And went to his room.

"Mmm," muttered Harriet absent-mindedly, putting her bowl in the sink.

Beth wondered if she would ever be able to communicate with them again. Despite growing up in the same house they seemed to lack shared cultural references. They had become strangers to her. She felt almost intimidated by their self-confidence and the way they moved through life with such expectations and no doubts or fears.

"Have you cleared up that mess in your room?"

"Lay off, Mum, I'm working out my future. Your mind is suffocated by triviality. It doesn't matter that my bedroom's a tip. There are more important issues. Open your mind, lift it out of its obsession with trivia."

Jake thumped down the stairs, changed into tight, ripped jeans and a weird t shirt.

"I'm late. Have you seen my fleece?"

"Oh, for heaven's sake, I washed it. It's not dry yet."

"What am I supposed to wear?"

"The combat thingy on the hallstand is yours. You're not going out clubbing again tonight are you?

"Not a crime, is it?"

"Perhaps all children become little aliens sooner or later, however hard we try to prevent it," Beth said to James later. "He stays in bed, sometimes, til the afternoon and is either out half the night or in his room playing some Ninja, Birds game thingy, or tweeting on his

106

computer. Do you think it's the internet that's made him like this? He does exactly what he wants. I never know where he is. He won't talk about his future or what he's going to do with his life, even to Harriet, who at least is applying to thingies, um, you know, charities for a job. You need to talk to him, James."

James did not like confrontations. He wanted life to not make too many demands on him, and so far everything had come easily. Harrow and Oxford, then more than forty years in what had been his father's law firm, specialising in corporate and commercial law, wills, trusts and probate. When his father had retired, he and two of the four other partners had stayed on after dispersal. He was happy with his life and had never been hugely ambitious. At sixty-five, he had wound down to two days a week, he would finish at Easter. A self-satisfied, self-sufficient man, happy with his marriage and children, two of whom had been reasonably industrious and kept to their career plans. Unlike so many young people he had read about. He wondered if this were entirely due to Beth as he did not remember having that much to do with their day-to-day upbringing.

A few days later Annie witnessed Jake's rudeness and petulance when Beth had not washed his jeans because he had not picked them off his floor and given them to her.

She did not hold back, if she thought something, she always followed through. "You've become a lazy, middle class mediocrity. What happened to your digital savviness and undoubted linguistic talents? You seem to be fluent only in anger and irritation. You've never stood on your own feet, it's time you left home, grew up!"

Jake opened his mouth to make what was probably going to be a rude riposte, then closed it again, pulled his long, skinny body and spikey hair to its full height to give her a filthy look and slammed out of the door.

James at last gave way to Beth's pressure and spoke to his son. "We're having a bit of a problem coping with your lifestyle, old chap," he began. Jake glanced up from his iPhone, then looked down again with an exasperated, 'get it over with' expression. He obviously thought that half-heartedly pretending to listen would be sufficient and he could then carry on going his own merry way as he had done all his life so far.

"This house, the world does not revolve around your needs. The time when you were the centre of our universe is long gone. You're an adult, Jake, and no-one cares about selfish, run of the mill people who make little effort to be a useful, giving part of society."

Jake's expression was sneering. "There's no chance that I'm going to live like your cricket watching, golf playing, wine drinking generation who watch 'Downton Abbey', with its cosy middle class world view of life. I'm considering my options." He walked across the kitchen, cut a slice of bread and jammed it into the toaster.

James spluttered. " Your scorn for the way we live is derisory. My generation did holiday jobs. We never expected our parents to look after us after we were eighteen. You're twenty-three and have yet to grace the job market. We see no sign of you applying for jobs. You're embracing an idle culture. One that expects to receive but never gives. Life is not going to come to you. If you think that you are so extraordinary, such a special being, the voice of your generation, stop thinking, it's time for action!" James was warming to his task, faced with Jake's seeming lack of interest in what he was saying. In fact Jake had cut the bread too thickly and the toaster was emitting smoke and he was trying to poke his charred snack out with a knife.

"I hope you've put that off," James said testily. "Are you taking this in Jake? We're giving you a deadline of three months to get a job. After that you're on your own!"

"Should you have said that?" Beth asked later. "What if he runs off, like Daisy did? He's never lived away from home…The police arrest people for squatting nowadays."

Jo had decided it was time that she had a dinner party for her new friends and neighbours. 'I'll have it on my birthday, so *I* can celebrate, but I won't tell anyone, don't want them to ask my age. There's Laurs and Dan, Annie and Martin, Helen and Phillip, Frances, Pierre, Lynne. Oh and what about that friend of Laurs, Alan?" She made some phone calls and all, but Phillip could come. On the way to the pool, she realised that Beth was the only one of the swimming group she had not asked. "I hope no-one mentions it to her, Laurs."

"Why didn't you ask her and James?"

"They just didn't come into my head. She's such a poppet too. She's got the sort of guileless, straight-forward look that people trust and approach if they want directions in the street. Maybe it's the way she fixes her eyes on your face and nods understandingly when you're telling her something. She's not my usual friend type, not edgy enough, and those clothes! What *is* she wearing today? That huge shirt and cardigan must be James's. And his suits! Did he get his personality off the peg too? And that badger stripe, that awful French pleat, she doesn't look after herself. I'll have to take her in hand! Should I ask her now?"

"Yes, she'll be hurt if she's the only one left out."

Beth accepted enthusiastically.

The day before the party Jo wrote out a list, then shot out to Waitrose without it and careered around the bright aisles filling up the trolley. Was it dill and lemon or ginger and coriander? I don't know, perhaps lemon? She queued to pay. Oh Christ I've forgotten my Bag for Life again. I've got so many. I'll just have to pollute the environment. A vision of all her plastic bags swirling around in the Atlantic, choking fish and turtles, flashed through her head.

The next day, Saturday, she got the lounge ready with red and silver flowers, bowls of olives, nuts, sparkling glasses, fairy lights and tea lights. Dan made two trips in the car with extra chairs, plates, bowls and cutlery. They were going to eat soup, sea bass fillets, potatoes and a salad and then a 'Heston Blumenthal Hidden Orange Christmas pudding', which she had bought in Waitrose some months before, because everyone else seemed to be buying them.

She decided that the food would not take long to prepare, so spent the rest of the time getting dressed in her usual fashion, sluttish with designer style. A red velvet mini, tight red sequinned bustier, black lacey tights and teetering heels. Plenty of makeup, dusted off with glitter around her eyes and cheekbones and a splash of 'Christian

Dior's Poison'. 'Illusion is the first of all pleasures,'"* she said to herself.

All her guests arrived around eight as she had suggested. Dan was to pour the drinks while she cooked.

"Oh brilliant, love them," she said, taking the proffered beautifully packaged chocolate almonds, an old friend Pierre had brought. "Can't wait to open them. Pierre, this is Frances just arriving, Frances, Pierre.. Dan, can you get these two thirsty people a drink, please?" She waved them together and dashed off towards the kitchen carrying the flowers Frances had given her. Pierre was very charming and athletic looking, but after a few minutes of pleasantries he wandered after Jo into the kitchen.

"Don't come in here," shouted Jo. "I know what I'm doing. The first course is nearly ready. Help Dan with the drinks in the conservatory if you want a job."

"Ok, Ok, but do shout if you want any other help." And he back-tracked through the lounge to the drinks table.

Frances had had to force herself to come. Dan gave her a glass of white wine and left alone, she fell into her usual party depression.

The room had filled up with people she knew, but they were all chatting to one another. She stood awkwardly, self-effacingly, near the windows to the street, half looking out. A woman with a loud voice was just behind her. What's her name? I know we've met once, she's Laura's friend. Oh god, I've got a mental block about her name. I must write new people down. Does it start with S?

"Frances, come and talk to us. Persuade Annie to come back to swimming," called Laura.

Annie, that's it. "Oh, hello." Her mouth felt as if she had been chewing loft insulation. Frances hated small talk.

At nine they were still waiting to eat. Jo popped out of the kitchen occasionally and refilled her lipstick-smudged glass. Then disappeared again. By 9.30, no one wanted to drink any more, they wanted some food. Jo made a refilling appearance and Laura, seeing that she was getting increasingly flushed, followed her back into the kitchen, which was a complete tip. "Shall I lay the table, Jo?"

"Absolutely not, my guests are not allowed to help, especially you. You're always cooking for me. I want to be the *capo di tutti capi* for once. Go and relax, please!"

"But couldn't you do with a hand? Let me help you with the food then. Be your lieutenant. Everyone will be drunk if Dan opens another bottle."

"No, I'm fine, I know what I'm doing. Why do we over emote about eating? All it does is make you fat. Who was it said, 'Nothing tastes as good as skinny feels?'" She turned to open the oven and peer in. "Damn, it's all burnt on top!"

Laura was across the room and taking out the sea bass and sliced potato with lemon, garlic and spring onions in tinfoil. The juice from the food had burnt the tinfoil and the pan. Jo had put the grill on, by mistake. "The fish is par-cooked, but these potatoes are raw!"

Jo's face sagged. "Oh no."

"Let's parboil them and then fry them with the fish. Where are the vegetables?"

Jo pointed to some packets of mixed salad. "I was just going to make a lemon dressing, but I only bought one lemon."

"Have you got balsamic vinegar? Use that and where's the first course?"

"Oh God, the soup is foul, that's what taken me all this time, I keep adding things, but it just tastes like boiled sticks."

One glance in the saucepan, confirmed this. She obviously hadn't discarded the old, tough beetroot leaves. "This wasn't how I told you to make it!"

"What's going on in here?" Annie had come in and taken the situation in at one glance.

"What else have you got?" she asked.

Jo looked helpless. She was now red in the face, almost crying. "Bread, tomatoes somewhere. I know, I'm in a mess. Don't think I'm going to be opening a 'pop up' any time soon. This cooking is harder than it looks."

"Go and lay the table and tell everyone it's just coming." Not even Jo could argue with Annie's tone of authority.

The tomatoes were in the pan, potatoes on, bread ready to toast

111

and olives and anchovies found in the cupboard. Jo silently thanked Jess for stocking her so well. Within minutes there were delicious looking bruschetta ready to serve and the potatoes and sea bass were nearly ready.

It was well after midnight when Laura sank into bed with relief that Jo's party was over. Dan had been in a bad mood because he considered it a waste of an evening, hanging around serving drinks for hours. She was irritated and resentful at his switched off sulkiness. Why couldn't he make a bit of effort to talk to people as well as pour? She was exhausted from trying so hard. She wanted to feel his arms around her. His strong hands massaging her back as he did so often, but she had rolled away from him and could not bring herself to speak or move towards him. They lay in an awkward silence, side by side in their own spaces.

She felt every muscle letting go at last and she was sinking into oblivion when his hand tentatively stroked her hip and leg. Feeling guilty at her coldness she reluctantly rolled over to face him. She had accepted who he was when she fell in love. Why was she now annoyed that he found social situations difficult and trying? She patted his arm, then turned away before he could get encouraged.

As Helen drove towards Reading, she pictured her mother as the young woman of her childhood. She smelt the sweet smells of the cakes and the rich, meaty aromas of the pies she had cooked and her talcum powdery scent as she leant over Helen to kiss goodnight. Stella had been a good, old-fashioned cook for family meals and for the friends invited for dinner and games of bridge. She no longer bothered since Helen's father, Peter, had died five years ago and it had soon became obvious that she was not coping alone.

She had tried to discuss her problem with Phillip. "Well, you don't expect her to live with us?" had been his first response.

"No, no, of course not." But her tone had implied she did.

"You don't want her any more than I do," he had retorted.

But he had come to Berkshire for the weekend and they had hunted for the most suitable place for Stella. Lakeside was a large mansion, set in two acres of parkland. The lounge and dining room had long windows and elegant ceiling cornicing and she had been offered a big bedroom with an ensuite bathroom overlooking the garden. Attractive though it seemed, Helen had been consumed with guilt. "What respect am I showing for my mother by putting her in death's waiting room?" she had agonised.

Stella had tried to argue, but they could see that she had known a move was inevitable. She had taken no interest in what she was taking with her and had been sullen and mute when they had tried to involve her in the arrangements to sell her house.

There were a few still lively incumbents of Lakeside. They sat in the small lounge playing whist, whereas in the main lounge Stella and eight other women sat with glazed eyes, slumped bodies, swollen feet and useless legs, waiting, for they were of course temporary fixtures. Soon the next wave of helpless, inanimate, old people would take their places, of which one day I will be one, Helen thought, as she arrived at Stella's prison.

Annie and Martin were having supper and everything he said she had mocked and returned spiteful put-downs. Normally he would go quiet and white lipped, withdraw into himself like a pathetic, beaten cur. He would have that familiar helpless feeling as if he were locked in a cage, enduring her taunts. Then, this evening after a particularly acidic comment, he jumped up and shouted "enough!"

Pacing up and down, his shoulders hunched as if he would receive a blow for his temerity, he started. "Annie, when you're depressed I do my best to comfort you and build you up again. I listen to your accounts of your day, I support you in every way I can." Stopping and looking straight at her, he continued. "I've had enough. We were happy when we first got married, but over the years you've become more and more cutting and destructive. You treat me like a pet. Keeping me to stroke sometimes, but mainly to kick. You don't care about my problems, my interests, my ideas. You don't allow me to have any, unless you've agreed them first."

Annie looked at him with amazement, trying to make out his expression in the candlelight. What was he talking about? This

113

couldn't be happening. But he carried on.

"You're so arrogant and sadistic to me, but I've never been cruel to you. Never told you that you're a dominatrix, you can be boring, limited, petty, self-obsessed and..." Here he paused, thought, then knowing how sensitive she was about her weight, spat out... "and FAT!"

She sat in shock, staring at him as if she had never really seen him before.

He was starting to enjoy his tirade. His expression was tight and taut and his eyes were sparking with rage. "I've always tried to help you, but it's one way. We haven't had sex for years. You always look disgusted at the prospect. There is no point in us carrying on. I don't want to live any more with a sexless ball breaker who doesn't know what love is!"

He had never turned on her before.. She could not take it in. He would calm down in a minute, go back to how he normally was, but he could not be allowed to get away with it. She gathered herself and got to her feet. "Get out, go away, you make me sick," she snarled, though she was not sure that she did not mean the opposite.

"I was going anyway. I'll come back for some clothes tomorrow when you're out at your choir." He turned and went out through the door, slamming it and the front door as he left.

Where is he going? He hasn't got many friends. She felt a twinge of guilt at having been critical of those he had. So where could he go? Has he met someone else? Well who would want him? Her mind was haemorrhaging. She had not meant to push him that far. No, he would calm down, come back later, but she was in a cold sweat. What if he didn't? She began to weep with self-pity and shock. Only fifteen minutes ago she had felt herself to be popular, successful and smart. Only fifteen minutes ago she had been confidently smashing down his ideas for a buy to let in Manchester. She was the business woman, the one who made the big bucks...well, she was still all of that. But without his devoted support? What have I done? No, he'll come back, where's he going to go?

Sexless? I'll show him. Just because I don't fancy it with him. I'm an attractive woman, Phillip told me only last week. Phillip? Helen's away visiting her mother and staying with an old friend.

And before she had time to think, she was dialling Phillip on her mobile. "I've locked myself out and Martin's not back til late. Can I come round for a while?"

He agreed immediately and she rushed out of the door, oblivious of the cold sweat that had dried on her skin and her garlic breath from the chicken chausseur she and Martin had been eating.

A warm and scented draft enveloped her as Phillip opened the door. "Hi, come in."

A piano concerto was playing. The light was soft and golden from the frilly pink lampshades Helen had made.

"Red, or would you prefer white?" he asked, filling a large glass of her choice of white wine.

She took it and gulped it down quickly to give herself confidence.

"Another? Are you upset about something?" he asked, his soft brown eyes full of concern.

She was sitting on the couch by now. Phillip sat on a cushion on the floor. Annie didn't think that she was supple enough to follow suit.

"Hope you didn't mind me barging in like this?"

"Delighted to see you, Annie dear, but I hope Martin isn't too late. I'm off to Durham early in the morning and don't want to be late to bed."

She looked at her watch, ten past ten. She was beginning to feel quite muzzy, quite tired after the shock, the wine and the warmth.

"Are you feeling Ok? You don't seem yourself." His voice was gentle and sympathetic and suddenly she was crying, sobbing and sliding onto the floor in front of him. He reached over, turned her round and pulled her back against him. His hands were everywhere, rubbing up and down her body, massaging her head, then her small breasts, her chunky hips. Waves of excitement surged through her. Sexless? No, I want this. I want him. A powerful need gripped her as his hands reached down under her skirt, under her thong and...she cried out. He twisted her to face him and pulled her hands to touch his crotch. He was naked inside his loose sweatpants, naked and...tiny! His fingers weren't in quite the right place. She wriggled, angled her bottom upwards and when that still wasn't right, rubbed at his little penis and pulled it towards her. She wanted to be transported. She was sexual, sexy, she wanted sex NOW.

He was on top of her, fingers inside her and the years of unfulfilled longing were crashing, washing over her. She wanted it more than she could bear, but suddenly he shoved his tongue into her mouth. It tasted like fish. She imagined an anchovy wriggling down her throat and, oh no…she volcano vomited, on Phillip, the cushions and rugs. Retching chicken chausseur, wine and shock at what she was doing.

Phillip leapt up with a disgusted expression. "There are cloths in the kitchen," he said and disappeared. Annie rubbed vainly at the sick down her clothes with a tissue from her pocket. She could hear the shower running as she went into the kitchen to get a bowl of soapy water. He reappeared as she was finishing sponging the rug and without looking at her took the covers off the cushions. Feeling revolting, she staggered off into the night.

Terry sat in the lounge, gazing around at the oiled oak floorboards and IKEA furniture. The bookcase was crammed with an eclectic collection, reflecting Leonard's random enthusiasms. He had been obsessive about Russian nineteenth century novelists: Gorky, Chekov, Tolstoy, Dostoyevsky, everything they had written was here. Dozens of First World War books, American Presidents and then it was steam locomotives. He'd be proselytising to any friends they had to dinner, trying to enthuse them with his passions. How could a man with so many interests, so much life, now have none?

I could have a dog. It would be good for me, taking it out for walks, and company. Leonard had hated dogs and their presence on the Heath put it out of bounds to him. He had sneered at the innumerable dog walking women, deciding that they were mostly wealthy ladies on their own, who poured all their affection onto their dogs, trying to make them into what they wished their husband or children had been, cowed and following them obediently everywhere. "Look," he would say, "they talk to their dogs as if they were human and endowed with comprehension. Dogs are disgusting. Look at that

116

one over there, straining to get at that bigger one, so he can sniff its bottom. Look at it," his voice raising higher in disgust, "it's gazing covetously at that pile of poo and now it's licking its nether end."

Perhaps I'll have a spaniel…

She stared out at the wintry garden. It had been a damp day. The forecast was for snow and Arctic winds. I hope I'll have the energy and interest for it this spring. I won't be able to bear an ungardened garden. Threads of rain fell softly on the window and puckered the pond. The borders, so rampant in the summer, had sunk back to earth. Were large slugs multiplying to eat the young shoots stirring in the borders? A few sparrows hopped amongst the brown and decaying clutter. Earth to earth. The ends of the gardens would soon be loud with rustlings and screamings when the nightlife emerged.

Fran rang from the office. "How are you?"

"Oh good, good. Tell Tony, I'll be in next week."

"Well, I'm afraid he's given us all a bit of a shock."

"Oh?"

"He rang in yesterday and said he'd changed his mind. He hadn't signed a contract and he'd been offered a job he'd prefer to do in Scotland. I'm not sure he suited us anyway. He was too high powered and used a different language, like 'bringing things to the table', 'Level playing field', 'thinking outside the box'. He must have found us very dull and backward. We're looking for someone else, but if you could, come in when you're ready?"

She tossed all night and at seven found herself dressing in her work clothes, having agreed with Fran to do twelve hours a week, to tide them over, until they found someone. She must absorb herself in the work she had loved, to keep the grief away, but she still felt quite weak and was losing so much weight. She wasn't sure she was up to it. I'll get on with that grant application today she thought, letting herself into the office. No one will be in for another hour. Her desk was a mess of papers and files. Tony must have left in a hurry.

Terry finished the form and gathered up all the supporting documentation to send them off. She felt shattered. "I'm going home now," she said to the rest of the office. "I must have a virus, I'm tiring so quickly."

"Why don't you stay home til you feel better? Tell us what is urgent and we'll deal with it, or I'll come round to see you and you can tell me what needs doing." Daniella was a good and caring office manager.

"Oh no, that's not fair. I'll take the annual report statistics home with me and work on them for a couple of days."

"I'll carry them downstairs for you," Daniella insisted. She ended up carrying them round the corner to the tube.

"Thanks," Terry said. Until she got over this grief phase she was going to have to learn to accept help gracefully.

When she got home, she went out into the garden. The sun had just disappeared behind the houses and her unpruned trees and shrubs stood out in sharp relief in the softer light against the watercolour pale sky. She pulled her coat tightly against her in the cold wind. Trying to come to terms with the loss of her fantasy, because that's what it must have been. He had run away when she was free. She must have been a passing flirtation. Never destined to be part of his life. With her parents and Leonard gone, she realised that no one would ever think of her first again, would love her best of all. She was filled with such longing for Leonard, pierced with so much emotion that all control seemed to leave her body, the garden spun and she had to lean against the back door. How could I ever have considered leaving him? She was seized with an overwhelming panic at the loss of her unreal hopes. Opening the door, she reached the fridge by leaning on the sink and surfaces and poured herself a glass of white wine. A gulp and she managed to reach the sitting room and the CD player. Putting on Beethoven's violin concerto she relaxed onto the sofa, and sunk down into the music...

Some time later the music had stopped and the room felt empty. She shivered with fear and cold. I've been half a person this last few months. In a limbo of grief and guilt, too many tears, and only myself to talk to. I'll go and see one of my friends at the weekend. Laura has asked me to tea so often...

118

Chapter 9. January. Downhill

'In the bleak midwinter
Frosty wind made moan,'
Christina Rossetti. (1830 – 1894)

Jo was on the phone to Laura, while pacing around in front of her hall mirror. "I still get a buzz from pulling a man. If I'm honest I've always chosen conquest over companionship, hungered for admiration. God knows how Ed and I were together so long."

"Yes, Mr Right becomes Mr Ordinary in a very short time," said Laura with mock sarcasm.

But Jo was too deep in her thoughts to notice. "I've always preferred the chase to the potential destination, it's so much more thrilling. You know how impulsive and selfish I can be, but I think I'm good hearted and I never mean to cause offence, although I know I do. I should have lived in France, or Italy. European marriages are much more open about infidelity, it's expected and accepted. It adds spice to a marriage. Sex isn't thought of as the be-all and end-all of life, it's the spice, not the main ingredient." She pursed her lips and wondered if her neck was starting to sag.

"Mmm, think there's been a shift in attitudes though," said Laura. "Fidelity seems to have become more important than it was. Probably because the rest of life is so insecure in this economic climate."

"Well, that's no help to me. How am I going to find a sexy man? I can't hang around bars and clubs for pick-ups. It's too demoralising and embarrassing. Don't want to sit at home alone and disappear either. I feel like I'm waiting to be picked for a team, when all the best players have already gone. No dinner invitations from the couples we used to see. If I ring them I get the 'we must meet for a quick coffee' somewhere convenient for them." She had been studying the left side of her face, but turned to the right, keeping eye contact in the mirror. "Dating site? Ok, I'll try. Are you Ok, Laurs? Yes? Let's speak soon. Big kiss, bye."

Betty was losing weight rapidly. It took a little time each visit to

119

reconcile the skeleton with her mouth in the shape of a Munch scream and dead, unfocussed eyes as the image of her mother, which Lynne had carried in her head for her sixty-five years. Her arms and legs, which once were well covered and dusted with gold in sunny summers were becoming stick like. She was not interested in eating and did not care what was spooned into her mouth, but today she would not unclamp her jaw. The nurse squirted in a few mouthfuls of drink with a plastic syringe, shouting, "You won't be able to talk to your daughter with a dry mouth."

Her cold stiff hands were clenched in front of her face. Her hair was dry, straight and filthy, and she had an open wound on her bottom, so could not bath or sit in a chair.

"How do you feel, Mum?"

"I don't know. I'm going down hill. I can't do it all. I firm bits of fur," she answered. Then in the incomprehensible jumble of more words, Lynne managed to squeeze in a few spoonfuls of mashed banana, before her mouth clamped shut again.

Occasionally, it was as if some chemicals, which her neural pathways had been holding back, cascaded into her brain and she would look penetratingly at Lynne, dissecting her, before allowing her to reassemble. Lynne found this so disconcerting. Her lucidity was more shocking than her confusion. For it was not how she had become accustomed to find her. "I've got to go now, Mum. I've got a patient in half an hour."

"Wait for me then. Don't go without me. Take my hand and pull me up. I don't want to go alone."

"But Mum, you live here," Lynne said gently.

Betty looked searchingly at her. The terrible shock of self-awareness and despair in her eyes, as yet again she realised that she was not going anywhere. She was never again going to escape her room. Her visitors could come and go, yet she could have no influence on whom, when or for how long. She had to lie there, trapped in her increasingly stiff, immobile body. Impatient, hurried visits from people who could not wait to get away were the best that she would ever have again. "Am I coming with you? How am I going to get there? Will you wait for me? We may as well go together." Her dead eyes with their papery lids seemed like a mirror, reflecting back Lynne's gaze.

Lynne felt so alone. Betty was leaving her, not all at once, one moment she was here and then she was gone again. This was protracted, on-going grief. Sometimes a whole sentence would emerge, but mostly her thoughts were scrambled. She no longer searched assiduously for a word. She seemed too tired. It was all too hard.

"Who am I, Mum?" she asked.

Pale eyes focussed steadily on Lynne. She looked as if she were trying to say something comforting. Seconds passed, minutes, then lifting her left claw, she said blankly: "I think I'd like to have something up to the neck."

Lynne could feel the tears as she stood up to go.

"Can't you even wait for ten seconds? Where do I go now?" A betrayed look on Betty's gaunt, but still pretty face.

"This is your home, Mum."

"No, it isn't. I don't know it."

"I'll see you tomorrow."

"I may not be here."

Lynne walked to the door feeling as if she were abandoning her mother. I put you here, to be controlled and contained, she thought. This is my agony, which never goes away.

Betty watched her, with big, soulful puppy eyes, which seemed to stare into her soul. The guilt padded insistently behind her down the stairs and through the darkening streets where she wept bitter tears at leaving her mother behind in her hot tiny room which she had never recognised as home.

A nurse rang late that evening saying that they had had to restrain Betty with a strait jacket. "What?" Lynne was horrified. "Mum can barely move now. How can she be a danger to herself or anyone else?"

"She was screaming and fighting the staff."

After a sleepless night, Lynne cancelled her early patient and rushed to the Home, but the strait jacket had been removed and Betty remembered nothing about it.

Lynne sat looking at her inert uncommunicative body. She had shut off and turned her sagging, pallid, blotchy mask, a face no longer fitting on its underpinnings, to the wall.

Was she asleep? Her eyelids fluttering over her dreams, her breaths, little shallow puffs. It seemed from those eye movements and facial expressions that her brain was working. Are her thoughts in pictures or words? When she dies, where will her self be? One minute here, the next, where?

Is there something, someone inside her that is more than just biochemistry? Are our thoughts, feelings, our personhood, really just produced by neurons, so when they die, the person dies with them? I'm a scientist, but I want to believe that her identity, her soul maybe, is intact under her clogged, tangled and misfiring brain cells and it will soar free at death. But to go where?

She looked over Betty at the grey sky through the dusty window. There was a pause in the rush hour traffic assault on the road outside and only the ticking clock kept her company. Betty suddenly snorted and opened one eye. "Bye love, thanks for coming," she said and a glutinous softening touched the edges of her mouth, then it fell open into a Munch scream again as she sank back into sleep.

Laura suggested starting a new fitness regime. "What sort of exercise?" Jo asked suspiciously. "Isn't the odd swim enough?"

"How about coming to the gym? I go Thursday mornings, first thing?"

Jo was about to say no, when a vision of ripped, muscular men popped into her head. "Well, as long as I don't develop man biceps or Jennifer Lopez buttocks."

It had been a cold night with a snowfall then a hard frost and it was a dazzling morning. Already there were footsteps and tyre marks everywhere when Laura, bundled up against the day, set off for Jo's. The icy air hit the back of her throat. It felt pure, as if it were from fresh mountain springs. The weather forecast was for the coldest winter day. The bare trees shivered and a few snowflakes were blown in the wind.

She was taking a roundabout route to make sure Jo was up and suitably dressed. Sure enough, she had on an edgy Gucci silver tracksuit with red detail. "It's just an ordinary council gym. You'll stand out like a sore thumb. Haven't you got some leggings and a tee-shirt?"

Toned down, they strode off, gloved hands in pockets to keep warm. Jo was struggling to keep up. "Slow down, Laurs, just because you're in racehorse condition! It was only a few weeks ago when I was sunbathing by a pool. Nothing and no-one else but you would have got me out of my warm bed this morning!"

The main road was cordoned off for water company repairs, so there was unending traffic, barely moving, and the stink of exhaust fumes filled the air. Groups of uniformed children hung around the shops. Only two were allowed inside at any one time. Skeleton trees stood out against the slush coloured sky.

"What happened to us Laurs, the generation who thought they'd change the world? We were such strident feminists…"

"We withdrew from the fight to get jobs, we met our men and then we got old," Laura said wryly.

"How long have you been with Dan?" Jo asked, looking carefully, quizzically at Laura.

"Oh, ten years or so."

"Don't you ever have an urge to have sex with someone else, to feel that 'Grr' and 'Wow' just one more time?"

Laura smiled and shook her head. "I've read that most women's sex drive disappears over sixty, mine certainly has. I have to be really worked on to get interested. Sometimes I think it's a relief to no longer feel desire, but I don't feel desirable either. It's very peaceful, but I feel guilty, as Dan's still interested. There's no surge of hormones, so it hurts more and I'm too stiff to get into any positions other than lying flat on my back. Mind, I'm not sure that most people our age wouldn't rather slump in front of the TV than bother with sex."

"There's a women's Viagra on the market now that's supposed to give you intense orgasms. It probably messes with the chemistry of your brain though. I'm sure there are plenty of books you can read, like the 'Hot Sex Bible' and 'Spice Up Your Sex Life'. Why don't you get reading?"

"Mmm, they're probably full of gymnastic feats. Once you've been together for a while, you can't rely on spontaneity. We met an elderly couple at a party once, who said you had to have a dedicated sex night, not endlessly deferred good intentions, because it's the glue that holds you together. They said that you have to plan for a time and place for it to happen, like they had every Tuesday evening. This didn't spoil it. When you knew it was going to happen. It took the pressure off not on."

"Yes, you're probably right. Every couple has to invent sex to suit themselves. I don't know why, but I think my sex drive gets stronger with age and I'm much better at it than when I was young. It's just finding the partners."

"You look stunning, Jo, that never seems to have been a problem"

"Mmm, the trouble was that my sex drive was much stronger than Ed's. You know how much I loved him, but I felt ashamed always asking for sex and it felt degrading if I couldn't arouse him."

"So you had affairs?"

"I suppose I felt it was my right to have a fulfilled sex life. I needed satisfying, especially as I wasn't working and had all that time to think about it. It was at its worst in my fifties with the menopause. Hormones and chemicals roared through my body and my thermostat went bonkers. I was boiling. There was a furnace blazing inside me. My body was exploding, my nipples were flames. I felt rapacious…

Weeks went by with no sex, then months, an endless sexless Sahara. Having my phone vibrate was the nearest thing to sex for me. He didn't seem to notice how awkward the situation was. He was wrapped up in work problems, but I wasn't built for celibacy. His libido was obviously affected by the stress of his job. He bottles up stress, whereas I dump it out there. We went to psychosexual therapy, but it didn't help him to deal with his resentment and stress, or me my feelings of frustration and rejection. I know men's testosterone declines with age, but what was I supposed to do, with no sex and him

124

being irritable and putting on weight? We even tried Viagra and TRT."

"What's that?"

"Testosterone Replacement Therapy. He had injections for ten weeks."

"Did it work?"

"Well yes, briefly, but it made him incredibly competitive, aggressive and more muscular. It's a banned substance for athletes and sportsmen. And then there were dire warnings about blood clots, baldness and prostate cancer. It's a no-no long term."

"Ok, I've got the picture. But as I said, I'm the opposite. Look, this is a bit embarrassing, not only am I less interested, but I'm finding sex more and more painful, even with KY Jelly. It puts me off doing it and it's not fair on Dan. How come you haven't dried up?"

"I'm still on HRT and I'm not giving that up without a fight. Why don't you get some oestrogen pessaries or cream from your doctor? They're supposed to plump up your vaginal wall."

"Ok, I'll do that, thanks. I'm so lucky to have met Dan. I don't see many attractive, unattached males around."

Jo's brow creased at the word 'unattached', but Laura did not see. They were striding down the Leisure Centre car park towards the entrance, fine flakes of snow, the kind that intended to settle, whirling around them. "I'm so grateful for the pleasures of long term companionship, having a person one likes and trusts and have a lot in common with. That sounds so sanctimonious and self-satisfied, but you know what I mean."

And Jo did, only she had thrown her companion away. She pushed open the big glass door after clocking her trim reflection. "Women can have their best sex after menopause, without the fear of pregnancy. I'm missing out!"

An hour later and they were showering. Jo peeled off her high top trainers, shiny black jeggings and low cut pink tee, which clung like a bathing costume over her boned bra. Lifting her large breasts without puckering the skin. "It drives me mad all those guys just sitting on the machines I want to use," she complained.

"Yeh, they're doing endless sets, but I don't see why they have to rest on the machine. I say: I only do one set. Can I do it while you're resting, please."

"Did you see that gorgeous black guy I was chatting to?"

"Which one? The place was swarming with fantastic bodies."

"He showed me how to use that tricep machine. I couldn't take my eyes off him!"

Dark mornings and icy, slushy pavements are not conducive to early morning swims. Enthusiasm dwindles. The north wind was fierce and bitter, the trees thrashed about and the birds were being thrown around. More snow from the Arctic, much heavier than before, had arrived in the night. People were stuck on motorways and in their homes. Laura was scared to drive and pedestrians were skidding about on the pavements.

Beth phoned. "My New Year's resolution was more exercise and more moisturiser. Shall we walk quickly? Um, power walk or whatever it's called?"

It was fairly quiet. Four or five swimmers in each lane and in the large unlaned area half a dozen Asian men and women clung to the sides, talking.

When they walked briskly home the sun had come out and there were sounds of trickling and plops as the melt water and soft snow surrendered to the sun.

On Friday, Terry drove Laura to the pool. Helen was working and Beth was seeing Harriet and Jake off. Harriet had taken a maternity cover as Community Support Manager for Shelter in Edinburgh and had talked Jake into taking a support worker job. They had been offered a small flat.

It was a changeable day. Dark sky and rain, then harsh wind and the clouds breaking to expose a low sun, then rain again. Pigeons were already flying in pairs and gulls squawked and flapped above. The kerria and forsythia were out in the gardens they passed, splashes of cheerful yellow. A road in their usual route was closed, so they had to take a diversion. "I loved that garden centre," Terry said wistfully as they drove past the now ugly, rubbish strewn concreted area next to the railway.

Laura sighed as she thought of all the beautiful plants, which had been packed into the small space. "Yes, it had everything. There's nowhere else around here to buy the kind of things they had. It's going to be more flats. London is bulging at the seams!"

"And yet our children can't find anywhere to buy."

"Mmm. Young people have such overblown expectations now. I didn't have a house til I was in my mid thirties and my parents had to live with their parents for years until they could afford their own place." Laura had launched into one of her hobby-horses. They had had this discussion many times, Terry wondered about deflecting her.

"Yes, in Europe they don't expect to buy their own homes when they start work. Some people rent all their lives. Any news of Daisy?"

Beth was thrilled that Harriet and Jake were to be working for Shelter. Yet she had been feeling quite empty and strange, as if a piece of her had been cut off. She had a little weep after she had waved them goodbye, then went straight to do her shift on the hospital 'Friends' desk. First to the little Friends room behind the shop, where they left their coats. Then she took her seat in the busy entrance hall ready to direct people and immediately saw Terry, wandering past in a white-faced daze. She stared at her retreating back. I'm so slow, I should have called out. Mind, she looked as if she didn't want to see anyone. I wonder what's wrong with her? She watched Terry until she disappeared through the exit door, then became aware that a woman was standing in front of her, tapping her foot impatiently. "So sorry," she mumbled, "I was miles away."

After her shift, she was not looking forward to getting home to a child free house, though she knew she should be. James was listening to the news: 'economic down turn, slump in world stock markets, will the banks collapse?'

"A good day?" he muttered, following her into the kitchen to search in the wine rack. Selecting a good Cote de Rhone, he opened it. Immersed in thought he poured himself a glass, swallowed half of it, sighed with pleasure and looked towards her. She stared pointedly at the bottle.

"Oh, sorry old girl, shall I pour you one? What's for dinner?"

Annoyed by the assumption that she is in charge of the shopping, the content of the cupboards and fridge, even though she was the one who had been out since early morning, and he had been home all day. She bit her bottom lip and shot out of the kitchen, banging the door behind, rather than engage with his continual selfishness.

She thought she had got over the pain of being locked in an unsupportive relationship. "I love you old girl," he sometimes said absentmindedly. She thought he no longer understood what love meant. There was that year he had missed both her birthday and their wedding anniversary. "How could you," she had said and stormed off to their bedroom, weeping bitterly, locking the door behind her.

He had been angry with himself. A client had wanted to see him before he had left and it was complicated, so yet again it had slipped his mind.

That had been the moment when she had decided that she must get a job for herself, but look how that ended up. James complained at the drop of standard of his meals. More importantly, Jake had been going 'off the rails' and mixing with the 'wrong' boys. Discipline was a huge problem anyway. Every day in the classroom had been a nightmare for her.

It was a rare sunny day, so Lynne pushed a grumpy looking, well wrapped up mother into the garden. Her skin seemed to crumble as it met the sun. "I want to go back," she said.

Lynne tried to feed her with her favourite fruit, raspberries and point out birds and flowers around them, but Betty was getting more and more distressed, so she pushed her back to her oppressive little room. It seems the older one gets, the narrower and more confined life becomes, til it ends, in a box, she thought.

Two nights later, Lynne dreamt that Betty was lying in a boat and looked cold. She wanted to get her a coat, but found she could not move. For what seemed like hours, she kept trying and trying again to get up, while Betty shivered and grew paler. There was such a silence in this dead time of night, she strained to hear past the boundaries of herself and her bedroom. Was there someone in the house? As the first grey strands of light peeped through the chinks in the curtains, she fell into an exhausted doze.

At six o'clock, the house alarm rang out. Lynne jumped out of bed and ran downstairs to put it off, somehow sure that Betty had triggered it.

A few hours later the Home rang to say Betty had died.

"She was trying to contact me, Laurs, to say goodbye. I know she was," she said later.

"Oh Lynne, I'm so, so sorry."

"She never settled down there. You saw her at the beginning, sitting near the door all day hoping she could escape. She said to me yesterday evening, I'd be alright if I could just go home and have a sleep. You are home, Mum, I said to her. Oh god, why did I put her there? I feel so guilty!"

Laura felt a rush of tears and tried to stifle a sob. "Well, don't. She knew you loved her and it couldn't have been much fun for her, slowly losing her mind. Don't feel guilty. We all have to die sometime."

"I'm drowning in self pity and agony that I didn't do more for her."

Laura made comforting noises.

"Maybe I need to wear an armband, a long, black veil or a badge or something. Everything's getting to me. This stupid Sainsbury's checkout person asked me how I was feeling today. Feeling? I felt like screaming. My mother just died. I feel like howling at the moon, cursing the gods. How do I feel? I feel like an orphan without my best friend and champion in this cruel, silly world."

"How can I help?"

"I'm in a daze. I've got to get the death certificate, go to the undertakers, the church and the crematorium. Come and help me choose the service, the coffin and flowers? Sprays or wreaths from just me or more? You know, all these things I hoped I'd never have to decide again."

Annie had seen no one since the Martin and Phillip fiasco. She had been lying low, convalescing, and anyway she was certain he'd be back. Laura called in on Friday on the way back from the pool. Her grey eyes were still and watchful, seeming to see inside Annie's head. "Sorry I haven't been in touch. Didn't have time for tennis. Hope you haven't felt neglected?"

"Not at all," Annie lied. "I've been too busy," she added lamely. It wasn't true. Time had hung about her like a moody child. The house was silent and there was no tea in bed in the mornings. Gone were all the comforting routines that had knitted their lives together. She had said nothing to anyone, but had had a frenzy of busying herself, doing all the little jobs that Martin had done for so many years. Getting the bins and recycling ready on the right day, watering all their many plants, cooking most evenings and doing the washing up. He had fetched the free Metro and Evening Standards from the station. She rushed there one morning, but he must have gone earlier. There was no sign of any. She had her Freedom Pass, so she went onto the station to look in the bins. One had chewing gum stuck to it. A drink had spilled all over another. Not to be defeated she thought she would pick a discarded one up on the train. One pulled in and she jumped on, sharp eyes scanning the carriage. None on the windowsills or seats, ah two men reading them, perhaps one would be discarded. She sat between them, willing them to put their Metros down. A woman was deep into her book, nine others were playing with their phones. The brow of the large man on her right, gleamed sweat, and he shifted uncomfortably in his suit and tie. "Go on, put it down, you're not well enough to read," she muttered to herself. He closed his eyes, leaned into the corner, but the Metro stayed firmly on his lap and minutes later he had resumed flicking through the pages. She jumped off at the next stop and caught a tube back, having found a clean Metro in a bin.

Walking home victorious, she was determined to sit at her desk and get ahead with her weekly column. Only next week's was written. She liked to have plenty in reserve. She could always change them to react to a current trend. After years of producing copy, she could almost produce the right number of words in her sleep.

130

Unlocking the front door, she took off her jacket and opened the cupboard under the stairs to hang it up. Her heart almost stopped. Where was Martin's anorak? His jacket? His walking boots and best shoes? She was sure they had been there earlier. Trying to breathe deeply, stay calm, she raced upstairs to his wardrobe and chest of drawers. Why couldn't he have come when she was there? His case and rucksack had gone, filled with clothes. Oh god, Martin, don't do this to me.

Later at her desk, she sat and sat, moving things around, picking through her emails, deleting old ones and then looking at Jamie Witherspoon's online column. It was better than she had thought it could be, certainly better than she could write at this moment. Her brain was an empty vacuum; she had no energy, ideas or interest. The phone kept ringing and after a succession of cold calls from insurance and loft insulation companies, she unplugged it.

Why am I so tired? I haven't done much today. She made herself scrambled egg, then put her coat on and went out into the garden with a glass of Rioja. The air was cold, but calm and peaceful. Bats floated about and the skeletons of the cosmos and evening primrose were illuminated in the light from next door.

The morning of the funeral was bright, clear and cold, but Lynne could feel herself flushed and sweaty. The church was quite full. What was Betty's death to do with all these people? She had only lived in this area for a couple of years. After the crematorium, six people came back to her house for Marks & Spencer finger foods and the sandwiches Laura and Dan had made that morning.

"It seems so long ago that life was fun, we looked and felt good and had no worries," Jo said to a grey-faced Lynne, giving her a hug.

For once, Lynne was silent. The guilt feelings were consuming her, she would never again have her mother to tell everything to and the fact had hit her that it was now her turn to find the world changing so she no longer recognised things or felt a part of it.

Helen was at work when the post came in the afternoon. Phillip picked it up from the doormat and saw an envelope from Germany with writing he didn't recognise. He ripped it open. It was a letter from Frederika, another delegate he had met at a conference in the States a few weeks ago. It said, 'I think of you all the time and our night together. When shall we meet again? Shall I come to London to see you?'

Phillip was flattered. It proved that he could cast spells on women, but he was apprehensive. He certainly did not want to encourage his conquest and risk his marriage. He had to put her off.

She must have got my address from Hans. I hope she didn't tell him about us, he thought, and quickly replied saying that though he did not want to seem the sort of man who takes advantage, surely as a modern liberated woman she enjoyed the night they had had together too. They should see this interlude as a one off. The distance between them made anything else difficult. 'Let us think of our brief happy time together with gratitude,' he wrote and went out immediately to post the letter, ripped up hers and hoped that that was that.

Did he enjoy living dangerously? He had a strong need to be desired and although he loved Helen, that was not the same as fucking a new woman. There was that stranger on the train yesterday. Soft, full lips, an elegant, white, swan like neck. Her eyes were closed and she crossed her legs, put one arm onto the table, so close to his. He could never tell Helen about his desires for random women. He knew his cheating on her demeaned her in others eyes, but sometimes his greed for mindless fucks was insatiable. He saw himself as a normal man with more opportunities than most. James, whose infidelities had never strayed beyond his imagination, asked him once, after quite a lot to drink, why he did it.

"Because I can. Why do you eat delicious food? Because you can. Ok that doesn't hurt anyone, but you get the drift." Aren't all men *almost* adulterers, constrained by fear, decency, habit, lack of opportunity and also the reluctance to hurt the women they love? But the desire was still there. He often saw it in other men's eyes, the un-named secret.

"Have you ever thought, I won't do this because it will break Helen's heart?" Helen asked him after a woman he had met at a

132

conference in Helsinki had found his address and come to their house to see him. "It's because I'm old and wrinkly and you're bored with me, isn't it?"

"No, no, you're the woman I desire most, you're still gorgeous."

"Why then, why?"

According to the leaflet which Laura had given her, the 'Sing for fun' weekly session would make her relaxed, stimulate her brain, give her an endorphin rush and the enjoyment of singing with others. Frances had had to wait for weeks til the start of the new term.

This isn't the sort of street one should walk in after dark, she thought. Some young people skulked at the entrance to an alleyway. She skipped past. They ignored her. She felt slightly ashamed of her prejudices, but here was the huge, dark Gothic church, the door was open. She walked in. The temperature didn't change much, though as she passed a large radiator she could feel it pumping out heat which was sucked up to the high ceiling, through the huge stained glass windows and out into the night. One woman was standing in the front sorting out music and another was taking money. "You don't have to pay for your first week," she said as Frances approached her. "Come and see me with £5 next week." Most of the twenty or thirty people standing in the pews chatting or moving the piano and other furniture had their coats on,

"Here's what we're singing today," said the music-sorter. "If you're an alto stand over there." Frances looked to where she was pointing. Three rows of older women looked back at her. "But if you want to sing the melody, stand here in the sopranos." There seemed to be far less of them and it was the front row which was being indicated, so she stuttered, "I think I may be an alto" and shot into the fourth row, which was by now also filling up. "Have you been singing with this choir long?" she asked her large elderly neighbour.

"A year or so," she answered. "But don't ask me anything. I don't know many people. I just come and sing and go home. I don't bother with the concerts and practising."

Frances felt sick with nerves. This is ridiculous. I've managed staff and clients' cases, spoken at conferences. I can't be nervous at singing with other people. She thought back to her failed audition for the school choir, where her throat had seized up and only croaks had come out.

She still felt the humiliation of that try out, so long ago, but with only bridge and occasional swimming, her empty life had stretched before her. She had a nasty thought: would they be expected to read music? Maybe I should go now, get out, before I make a fool of myself again. As she dithered, a young man came in and stopped next to her, "Hello," he said. "I'm Mathew, I teach the class, welcome." He smiled warmly and she relaxed slightly. And they were off, warming up their voices. She looked around. There must be sixty or more, many of whom had rushed in at the last minute and were sitting behind her. Some scales and a round followed and then her row and the one behind had to sing the first line of the round. She could only wheeze and cough and was hot with embarrassment and shame.

Everyone else seemed to be singing freely, their faces soft and smiley with the pleasure of it. Scared to try because her throat was tight and the cough not far away, she whispered the familiar song, 'Swing Low, Sweet Chariot.' Why can't I do it, why am I so hopeless, she kept saying to herself, praying for the session to be over so she could go home. She could feel tears near the surface as she mimed through 'Drink to Me Only'.

At the end, she was hurrying towards the door, when Laura, who had arrived after they had started, called out: "Hang on, let's walk part of the way together. Annie's usually here and Beth is starting next week. How did you get on?"

"I was terrible, my throat closed and I could only make squeaks or whispers. All I could think of was that I wanted to go home and never come again. It was so embarrassing."

"Have you sung recently?"

She shook her head.

"Well, don't worry, it'll be more familiar the second time, you'll relax."

The next morning she was in her shower and to her surprise started singing 'Swing Low, Sweet Chariot', clearly and loudly. Why did I get so screwed up about singing? She said to herself. It's not as if it's a job. I don't have to do it at all.

The next week they did some voice warm ups and exercises, then some simple unison songs. Frances's voice was getting stronger and stronger. Even in the round she held her own comfortably. Tears of relief ran down her cheeks. She mopped them away quickly. Her neighbour smiled at her, thinking how much less pinched, earnest and uptight she suddenly looked.

Chapter 10. February. Life isn't fair!

'Why, what's the matter,
That you have such a February face,
So full of frost, of storm and cloudiness?'
William Shakespeare. 'Much Ado About Nothing', Act 5.
(1564 – 1616)

Laura came out of the pool building into the early morning sunlight and had no idea where she was. She stood still. Her brain had emptied, she felt very strange.

Gradually some clarity seeped back and she saw the familiar car park in front of her, but did she walk or bring the car? She set off purposefully towards her usual parking spot. It didn't seem to be there. She pressed her key fob and a car in the next row lit up to welcome her. She sat in the driving seat feeling as if her brain had been off somewhere else. Was it a stroke? A precursor to dementia?

Lately she had been forgetting words. They floated away, returning when she no longer needed them, so she had had to use other words to replace them. Please god, not dementia.

"Don't worry about it, I'll look after you," Dan had said.

"What when I ask you the same question a hundred times a day, don't recognise you, am incontinent and smear things with my poo?" she had asked in exasperation.

"Well, perhaps not the poo, but we'll manage somehow," he had said comfortingly.

He doesn't realise how irritating, how impossible someone with dementia can be. He'll soon lose respect and love for me, she had thought.

That night, thrashing around in bed, unable to sleep, hoping that the darkness would pull her under, she searched through her head full of frozen memories. Herself in her twenties, looking for something to believe in. Searching for who she was in different countries and by taking different jobs. Then at last alighting on feminist politics. All those years looking for an ideology, yet Daisy's generation seemed to

136

have been born complete, ready made, self-assured with no apparent inner doubts or struggle. Is my agonising, battling generation an extinct species? This is the last phase of my life. I should be relaxed and enjoying it, but I need goals, I need to be useful. I'm only doing two hours a week at Brookfield House. Shall I fill out that form I was looking at on the DfE website to be a school governor? Oh I don't know. She pushed one leg wide, just cool sheet, wider, no Dan. She jumped up and stared at the clock…3 am. Friends had said that when they couldn't sleep they got up, read, had a relaxing drink, listened to the radio, but she wriggled and thrashed round and round invariably dropping off when it was almost time to get up.

She was woken by the wind bullying the bare trees so their skeletons rattled against the window. A grey light was peeping around the curtains. Her brain was fuzzy, caught between the waking and a dream. She turned over and tried to get back into the novel she had dreamt she had written. It has beautiful description and she is unique in having found how to write interior monologue in real time and make it natural. It has fragmentary thoughts and leaps in syntax, yet it holds the readers' attention. It's brilliant. She felt a rush of pleasure, a glow of achievement, which faded with the dream…if only. What if I never achieve it? When I die what will have been my contribution to the world? How am I useful now? How, how? The room shook with the vibration of a passing train. There was the chatter of birdsong, a bark of a fox and her clock said it was nearly time to go swimming.

No one was coming today and there was the perennial question of whether to walk or drive. Drive, walk, drive, walk? Still undecided she reluctantly crawled out of her warm, cosy cocoon and looked at the day. Dull, windy and thick raindrops blurred the windows. Ugh, drive.

Days were merging seamlessly into one another. Life was rushing by with her accomplishing very little. With no babysitting she should be writing. And she would, except that today after swimming and breakfast, there was the kitchen and hall to clean, the washing up and recording that programme about Dickens that she would miss later. Oh, and the conservatory plants needed watering. Half the morning had gone by the time she got to her study. She was full of resolve, but sat dissembling for the first hour. There were nine emails to answer and then she had to look up cinema programmes for that evening.

"One from Janet, that's interesting, I'd better reply. Well I'd better let Dave and Fran know, and probably Megan and Beth. Oh, I didn't know that. Shall I order it? Perhaps I should compare prices on a few other sites first. I must start writing after this."

Then suddenly it was one thirty, and she was definitely going to start after lunch, because tomorrow there was tennis, the RHS exhibition and the Book Group.

She had a sandwich, then went back to her study to see four more emails. I'll just answer this one then I'll start. Who was it who said something about the cause of man's unhappiness is that he doesn't know how to stay quietly in his room? She typed it into her MacBook. Pascal, Blaise Pascal, wow that was the 17th century!

Reading a few lines of good prose was often inspiring. She picked a book out of the bookcases covering three walls of her study: 'beautifully wrought, wonderful writing', it said on the jacket. She read a few pages, it was turgid, boring, and banal...the phone rang...

Ending her call, she tried to refocus. There are times, she thought, when I inhabit my brain. It feels sharp and clear. I can hear, smell, feel as if I'm closer to everything. Then other times, like now, I'm trying to think through a fog, a lump of suet...I've got the opportunity to write, but I just procrastinate. Perhaps it's too late to be a writer, to concentrate on one thing? Work had been so buzzy and creative. There was the excitement and satisfaction of dreaming up new courses and getting validation, funding and customers for them. Then teaching, coaching teams to win competitions, supervising, report writing, budget control, staff development. Sitting in quiet solitude like this was the antithesis of her work life.

What did Oliver Sachs say about swimming helping writing? She did a search: 'There is something about being in water and swimming which alters the writer's mood, gets his thoughts going, as nothing else can, New Yorker Magazine,' came up. Hmm, hasn't worked for me.

I'll fill up the DfE form, then I'm definitely going to start.

Rows of dusty books jeered down at her, their bright, published covers sapping her resolve, their contents sneering at her feeble prose. "We've done that...said that before...that won't work...who'd want to read that?" they sniggered.

Yellow covered 'My Cleaner' smiled comfortingly and ruffled her pages at the others. "Shush, let her try, she has some good ideas."

There was a short silence, then: "Who'd want to read it," they chorused nastily, "Who, who, who?"

She opened the top left hand drawer of the desk, where she kept memorabilia and took out some cards she had kept. 'To the best Mummy and Nana in the world, Happy Birthday, all my love, Daisy,' she read. Gazing at it she filled up with tears and wept silently. Seeing Daisy's writing pierced her heart. There was a beautiful Valentine card from Daniel. They'd become strangers living together but skirting round one another.

It was probably time for tea.

It had been grey for days, grey and cool. It made the swimmers feel grey, inside and out and energyless. They trudged along towards the pool, Jo wondering why she had bothered getting up. Laura seeing her hunched misery thought of a topic that might spark her interest.

"I read that more and more women are buying sex toys, and quite brazenly, in places like Tesco and Superdrug. I wonder if they're our age group, or are we shyer about using them?"

"I've never thought about it. I don't think I've ever seen one, have you?" Beth looked at Jo.

"Well, how do you think I've survived this last few months with such slim pickings?"

"The article said that using a mechanical toy gives you quick and intense orgasms, so you then have to relearn how to enjoy sex with a human being. A vibrator desensitises you to a lighter touch," Laura continued.

Jo cheered up a little, thinking of what she would do when she got back home. "I've never noticed that. Yes, they're different, but I can get off on either. You should try it you two."

As the weeks had passed, Laura had started to look gaunt from lack of sleep. Her hair was dull and dry. Her skin seemed flaccid and sagging, eyes bruised and sunken, shoulders hunched and she dragged around the house not wanting to go out.

She found herself staying in four or five nights a week. Annie had not been organising her into tennis games and she could not rouse any interest in her other weekly pursuits, films, theatres and lectures. She sat knitting cardigans for Ruby and Lily, though having no idea when she would see them.

"Why don't you come and try yoga or beginners bridge with me?" Beth asked.

"I don't like yoga, it's difficult for sporting people, our joints are too stiff, and I don't want to be playing bridge, just to fill my life I know that it's supposed to be good for the brain, but why play cards to fill up the time, when there is so little of it left?"

She lay in bed, unable to sleep, scenes from the past flashing in and out of her head like a kaleidoscope. "Stop thinking about it, Laura," she would say sternly to herself. "What good is it doing you, going over and over things half the night and then chunks of the day too. Is it all my fault?" She had asked herself that so many times, and avoided the answer.

She wrote endless letters to Daisy in her head, about how much she loved her. "I'm sorry we don't get on and I don't seem to understand you. But surely you know how much I love you. I love you so much it's painful. I want you to be happy and to have the life you choose. I want you to be loved as much as I love you."

Dan didn't know how to cope with her depression. So for much of the day he shut her out and was in his own world, deaf and blind to her. Sometimes it drove her mad and she wanted to scream and scream her anger, her loneliness out.

Sometimes he tried to talk, like this evening. He got into bed, wafting cold air at her as he lifted the duvet. "Are you ill?" he asked, gently stroking her leg. She rolled away from him and buried her face in her pillow. "I'm just tired," she said. There was a silence and then he too rolled away and a few minutes later she could hear his gentle sleep breathing.

The next morning was Wednesday, their day in the week when

they tried to have an excursion together.

They took the tube to Southwark, wandered around the Tate and then headed down the embankment towards Waterloo. It was a cold, clear morning, so they strode along briskly to keep warm. Were they talking about Daisy again?

"If you hadn't."

"If I hadn't what?

"You know very well, you told Daisy to grow up and stop leaning on me. You told her to go."

He paled. "I wanted her to give you a life," he looked at her intently. "You're so determined that it was my fault, it's always there, hanging between us. She couldn't have stayed indefinitely. We were all unhappy. Are you going to forgive me? Do you still love me? Are we Ok?"

"Of course we are." She felt as if she were in dangerous territory. She must stop feeling resentful, she must shut up about it before it destroyed their relationship. It's done now. He has probably been just as unhappy, knowing what it has done to me. There are always some things better not said. Her heart filled up when she looked at him. What would she do without his support, his affection? They were passing a pizza place. She linked her arm through his and tried to smile. "Let's have lunch?" She suggested, before she said something irrevocable.

Terry stood at her bedroom window, staring out at the wintry garden. The first quarter was decking and paving, but she had insisted on gardening the rest and it felt like an extension of herself. Leonard had helped by doing the hard digging and high pruning but she had been wondering whether, with so little energy, she could get out the ladder and do the pruning herself, when an ad had come through the door for 'All Gardening Jobs.' She had rung the number and Ivan assured her that he was experienced and could come the next day.

I must get stronger, get over this grief, she thought. Threads of rain fell softly on the window and puckered the pond. The borders, so rampant in the summer, had sunk back to earth. The room had become quite dark when she turned from the window.

141

She had almost fallen in the street today and coming down stairs, just before the last step she had tripped. With a grab at the banister and newel post, she had regained her balance, but found herself shaking with shock at what could have happened. Going into the kitchen she leant on the dresser. "I must be more careful." Her mother's plates rattled a warning behind her.

All those dreams of being independent and free, rather than living under Leonard's dictatorship. Why was I so afraid of what others might think, of hurting Leonard and David? Now I've got my dream state I no longer want it.

Terry showed Ivan which shrubs and trees to prune and fixed up the electric pruner, but when she went out to check, he had cut back a camellia. She was horrified: "I didn't ask you to prune the camellias, they're about to flower, you've cut off all the buds!'

"Yes, yes, sorry Miss, not camellias."

"Don't do any bush or tree without asking me. I've already told you to only prune the euonymus, the myrtle, the golden box and these roses." She pointed at each one. "*Nothing* else, thank-you."

"Yes Miss, I make garden good." He wandered away unrepentantly towards the euonymus and roses on the arch. She was sick at heart at being deprived of seeing the beautiful double red camellias this year. Feeling cold and powerless, she went back into the house and looked out of the lounge window to see him cutting her other camellia, the prolific pink. A red haze of fury blinded her as she fumbled for the window catch, to open it and scream at him, when the doorbell and then the phone rang together.

Laura called for Terry to go swimming. They walked slowly, but she was exhausted when they got there and she did little more than lie in the water and then have a shower. To her relief, Cynthia offered them a lift back. Terry sat in the front with Cynthia who said her husband had died ten years ago.

"If it's any help," she said, "one gradually gets used to the pain. In the end, you learn the triggers and avoid them."

Terry was thinking more or less the same thing. She was bottling

142

up the guilt, unable to tell anyone that when he died she had been considering leaving him. "Yes," she replied, "A partner becomes one's best friend and he did so much to support us. I've got close women friends, but they're all part of a couple, and David's too busy. He rather shut me out when he met Rosie. It's having someone around to talk to that I miss."

Frances was now relaxed and singing out at choir, enjoying herself. Happy to feel her lungs fill and her diaphragm lifting. They finished with 'Keep Young and Beautiful, if you want to be loved.' What rubbish, she thought, but sang along with gusto and could not get the tune out of her head. When she got home, she was in such a good mood that she picked up the phone and rang her sister, which she was not in the habit of doing. Lydia would probably launch into how selfish she was, how she had had a privileged upbringing and never gave anything back, particularly to her parents when they were ill and dying. 'I had to force you to even come and see them!' She could hear Lydia shouting this at her, fifteen years ago, as she dialled the number.

"How nice to hear from you. Is this a social call, or do you want something? Are you seeing someone?" Lydia asked.

She had to bite her lip not to snap back 'I'm too old for that nonsense!' and instead asked: "I thought I'd see what you were doing?"

"Well darling, same old, same old. Vic is working hard for her finals. My arthritis is worse, Theo retired and plays golf all day, so how about you?"

Frances wanted so much to say how lonely and bored she was, but found herself talking about the singing and asking if she could visit.

The next morning Frances got in her car to go for a walk on Hampstead Heath and after a short distance realised that there was something wrong with the steering. I nearly hit the kerb. There's something badly wrong with this car. She kept going slowly and limped into the public car park, stepping out into the icy air to look at

143

the tyre. It was completely flat. I don't know how to change a tyre. Have I even got one? I hate February. It's freezing and miserable. I'll walk for a bit and think what to do.

She picked her way over the frosty grass. Clouds of rooks rattled out of skeleton trees, cawing and flapping their big wings low in front of her. The cold wind stung her face and the frozen ground was turning her feet into unfeeling blocks. The sky was not clearing. Perhaps it's going to snow? All she could think of was why me? What did I do to deserve all this misery? The puncture was the last straw, but she could not seem to think about it, her brain was back in the office. Was it the Deacon account? Did the MD complain about me? Why is that person looking at me like that? She stared angrily back and glared at a family just passing, then at another older woman talking on her mobile phone. Who *are* all these people not speaking English, they're *immigrants*. How dare they give *me* strange looks. Then she wondered if she had been carrying on the conversation, which she had never had with the partners, out loud. I must stop this, she told herself.

"Hello, Frances."

She turned and for a moment, though he was familiar, had no idea who he was. Slight build, thinning and receding hair, prominent eyes and ears, mild of manner.

He smiled. "Are you out for a walk?"

Oh, it's Martin, Annie's husband. We met at Jo's party. "Yes."

"I was just thinking of having a cup of coffee to warm me up. Do you feel like accompanying me?"

They were standing almost outside the café. "Er, well, why not."

Twenty minutes later, feeling warmer and more relaxed, they were walking towards the car park.

"I can't forget how undignifying, how unfair losing my job was. I'm still so angry." She had taken off her gloves and Martin saw her knuckles whitening as she balled her hands into tight fists. "My career was my life. If I hadn't cared so much, losing it might be easier. I thought I was making a difference, being a valuable employee, building my status, but it was all illusory. I was naïve. No-one actually cared!" Her wounded expression touched his heart.

144

Then she remembered her tyre. "I've got a puncture and I haven't the faintest idea what to do."

He looked at her resignedly.

"Can't you ring up the AA or something?"

She had stopped her membership, trying to save on her outgoings, until she could take her pension at sixty. "No, I'm not in it now."

Right, he thought, trying to swallow his irritation at her helplessness. I'm cornered. Annie was right. I'm too accommodating. "Well, I was going to try and catch the bank, but…"

"I'm so sorry, please go if you have to."

He felt guilty at his reluctance." It's not a problem," he said. "Changing it won't take a minute."

They had reached her car. "Open the boot. Let's see if the spare tyre and jack are here? Yes, yes, and the spanner. Just give me two ticks."

She had never lifted the floor of the boot before. "It's flat," she said despairingly.

"It is now," he said patiently. "I've got a foot pump. Don't worry."

He jacked up the car expertly, loosened the nuts. Frances felt helpless, cold and depressed and couldn't think of anything else to say. He worked and she hung about in silence. "There you are, you'd better take your tyre for repair. This one is only meant for emergencies."

"I'm so grateful. Thank you so much."

"It's Ok. I like tinkering and helping damsels in distress. And if you give me your address I'll pop round and stop the dripping tap you were on about earlier."

She blushed, damsel? And scribbled her details on a scrap of paper from her bag.

"Wednesday?"

She nodded and he was gone.

In bed, Annie often found herself talking to Martin, telling him about her day as she had always done. It often ended by her getting heated with accusations and questions about his whereabouts. She would work herself into an agitated state and mouth streams of venom and have to get up and take a sleeping pill. Next day she would have a thick head and be unable to concentrate. She had TV on all day to keep her company and in the evening sat mindlessly in front of endless cooking programmes, soaps and sitcoms, police and hospital series, where no scene lasted more than thirty seconds. Invariably she became infuriated and had to turn them off. She had cancelled all her regular tennis games and refused two radio spots and what would have been a well-paid lecture. She felt a wreck. If only he were here. He would hug and rock me if I had had a bad day. We would lie on the couch in front of the TV and he would rub my tense, tired feet and legs, back and shoulders, patiently kneading and stroking. He could always make me feel better.

The next morning there was an email from Julia, the new Home and Leisure editor.

'Hi Annie, I'm so sorry, but now that I have taken over, we've decided to change the look of the Home and Leisure Supplement and won't be including your 'Fifteen Minute Supper Dishes' column after next week.

As you know, so many of our younger readers buy ready prepared dinner dishes for two plus wine, for £10 in any of the major supermarkets. They're not interested in spending the time sourcing the ingredients for your menus. Times have changed and so must we.

We will be inviting guest celebrity chefs to supply copy for the revamped pages, starting with Jamie Witherspoon.

Thank you for your wonderful column over the last fifteen years. We hope that you will use the time to put a new book together, which we're sure will be very successful.

Best, Julia.'

Annie was totally still, her mind and body paralysed. Unable to accept that she no longer had an income from the 'Daily News'. Sacked! I'll never get a book published without my column. Julia didn't even suggest inviting my input for the revamped section! She stared blankly at the window, her face in her hands. Then her disbelief changed to fury. Jamie Witherspoon! Hot raging blood coursed through her and she screamed and screamed. Jamie Witherspoon, even his name was a joke. He slapped unlikely ingredients together and said little more than "Yeh, terrific." She wondered about going on to Twitter and letting his followers know how ignorant he was. But what if I get found out?

I'm a serious food writer. He can barely put a sentence together. He's not even a chef. Just a talentless celebrity with blonde sticking up hair. She took her hands away from her hot face and tears of frustration and self-pity poured out. Where was Martin? He knew how to calm her down. Huge sobs wracked her body as she took a bottle of wine upstairs and collapsed onto her bed.

Rain spattered against the window of the box room in Ray's flat. Martin had finished re-tiling the splash-back in the kitchen and was listening to Mozart's Piano Concert No. 21, on Ray's tiny ancient radio. He was musing about what had happened between Annie and himself. Was there any way back? For over thirty years he had done everything he could to make her happy, but she had gone too far this time. Although all he wanted to do was hear her voice, he was not going to phone her.

He had been shopping and wondered if he should cook supper for Ray too. Their sharing arrangements were informal. He knelt on the carpet to do his daily fifty press-ups. He was strict with himself about maintaining his fitness, even standing up on the tube when there were seats. His reasoning was that invariably a woman would get on at the next stop, so he would have to get up anyway. It was easier to stand so then he could play his game of not holding on. He would try to maintain his balance with his knees slightly bent, feet pressed downwards, upper body alert for violent movement. It was about mastery, improving proprioception.

It was a gloomy wintry day, there were patches of ice on the pavements to avoid and a bitter wind. Laura and Beth walked quickly without talking much. They had perfunctory swims, hot showers and then Laura went food shopping.

When Beth got home, she made herself a cup of tea and a piece of toast and settled down with her pad and pen to make a menu and a list of what she needed to buy for Sunday lunch with Patricia, Gerry and Rae. The children mocked her for her dinner parties. It felt like a criticism of her life, as if it were shallow and valueless. Antipasto for the first course is always popular, takes time to eat and feels healthy. Or is it too boring? Creating a balanced visually beautiful meal, a feast of all the senses, is a work of art. Then choosing the participants, enabling everyone to contribute to the conversation, keeping it harmonious is like putting on a little play. She was good at it. It's a skill, not valueless, even if its participants didn't fully appreciate her special abilities.

Pigeons were shuffling, pushing and pecking up and down the roof of the little conservatory off the lounge. Their droppings were impossible to keep up with, the roof was disgusting. "I must get those spikes," she said to herself for the fiftieth time.

James wandered into the kitchen, peered over her shoulder and looked at her with fond amusement. "Another list, old girl?"

"Stop calling me that. You make me feel so ancient and useless!" It was true that she ran the house and chose everything in it, but James ran the business side of their lives. He paid the big bills and decided how they would save or invest, never consulting her. She did not have a clue where their money was or indeed how much they had. It was no wonder she felt so demeaned some times.

It was Sunday afternoon and Terry determinedly left her house to call on Laura, who was out. I can't go back home without speaking to anyone. Come on, Terry force yourself to go and see someone else. How about Beth?

James answered the door. "Come in, do come in. We're just finishing lunch."

Terry followed him into the rather cold house, which seemed to have been immune to change since they moved in. Blue or beige wall paper, lino or brown carpet, bright overhead lighting, wheezing, clanking radiators not often on and there was a pervasive smell of cooking. It was Edwardian, yet featureless with a kind of deafness and blindness to interior fashion. A triumph of comfort over style.

Into the dining room with its heavy, old fashioned brown furniture, where she saw Patricia and a flushed looking couple she did not know. Beth was busily clearing up plates with remnants of chocolate pudding on them.

"How nice to see you, Terry, white or red?" Beth asked. "Terry, let me introduce Rae and Gerry. Would you like some chocolate soufflé?"

Embarrassed, Terry demurred. "I was passing and wondered if you knew of a reliable builder. There are a couple of little jobs I need doing," she said lamely.

"Oh, stay and have a drink now you're here. It's white isn't it?" Beth filled a glass. "Yes, of course, most people we know use Michal. He's Polish and his little team don't overcharge and work so hard! Nine hour days with no break. They're thoughtful and unobtrusive, wonderful. We've all been ripped off so many times by British builders. I hope they're getting their just deserts now. We were just discussing Russian novelists and how many of us have read Dostoevsky. I can't even think what he wrote, I've drunk too much."

"Oh, you know, 'Crime and Punishment', and 'The Idiot'. I never finished either," the woman called Rae laughed.

The last of the sun glinted in through the open patio doors and the air was scented from the yellow azalea in a pot just outside. The conversation resumed and ebbed and flowed around Terry. Patricia was confessing to have found 'The Brothers Karamazov' too heavy, but Terry was thinking how strange it was that they should be discussing Leonard's specialism. Every room in their house existed as a collation of memories and smells of him, the streets were full of phantom resemblances, nothing seemed to matter now, certainly not what she thought of Dostoevsky. Her brain felt slow and sludgy. She tried to concentrate on what Rae was saying, but the pain of it all was suddenly so overwhelming that she felt that she was going to sink to the floor and be unable to move. She put her half finished glass down and pushed herself to her feet. "Sorry, I must get on. Just dropped by for a minute. I'll see you at swimming?" Somehow she got to the door and, with Beth looking at her strangely, she forced herself to hurry off in the opposite direction to home.

James played golf on Saturdays. He and Hugh had played a round the weekend before. Well wrapped up against the cold, they had come back exhilarated by the exercise, the beauty of the frosted trees and the nutty crack of the hit and sometimes the distant thud and tinkle of ice. Now the golf course was too wet and was closed. James had no alternative way of exercising. He was in a mood of sour gloom.

"Shall we go to a beginners session at the bridge school up the road?" Beth asked.

James shook his head. "It's exercise I need not sitting doing bridge, anyway I used to play for my school. I'm hardly a beginner."

She had already asked Laura. She tried Helen. "Sorry Beth, I'm just not interested in card games of any sort. I don't have time to read much or do all the things I want to do as it is."

So Beth knew she would have to go alone. She had been having that dream again recently. The one where she was in front of a class with no idea what she should be teaching them. The students were all smirking and talking, ignoring her. She tried to shout over their noise, but they just shouted louder. She banged on the desk and on the whiteboard, stood on the chair and threatened dire punishments, but they started walking out and then she had woken up feeling humiliated and panicky, realising she had been shouting in her sleep. James was luckily a heavy sleeper. She was wide-awake now, and lay there remembering how unsuccessful she had been as a teacher. Mostly she had felt inadequate and miserable. It had been a supply job, taken when all the children had been in secondary school. After a term of purgatory, the teacher she had been replacing decided not to return, so she was offered a contract. She had lasted two more terms, then given in her notice.

Chapter 11. February. Avoidances and Depression

'All nature seems at work. The slugs leave their lair
The bees are stirring – birds are on the wing
And Winter, slumbering in the open air,
Wears on his smiling face a dream of Spring!'
Samuel Taylor Coleridge. 'Work Without Hope.' (1772 – 1834)

H i, hello," Martin's voice came over the intercom. Frances pressed the buzzer to open the downstairs door, thinking what a nice voice he had. Gentle and relaxed. She opened her flat door and felt the heat in her cheeks as she stared mindlessly at him. He shuffled his feet on the doormat, hunched his shoulders. He was carrying a bag of tools.

"You were meant to come tomorrow. Not today."

"Oh, well," he said. "I was in the area."

"Come in then," she said rather ungraciously. She hated surprises.

He was looking around at everything. Her black and chrome kitchen becoming unhomely and covered in smears and finger prints in the bright light of his gaze.

"Would you like a drink? I've got tea, coffee, wine..."

He seemed puzzled that she should be so nervous and unprepared for him to just drop in. "Shall I go, and see you tomorrow?"

"No, no, sorry. I just have to put something off. There's the kettle. The wine is in the fridge and this is the tap. I won't be a moment." In her bathroom, she pulled a comb through her hair and quickly cleaned her teeth. She had done neither all day. All the while her mind was racing with astonishment that he was here.

He had made himself a coffee, switched off the water supply and taken the top off the tap. "Couldn't find the milk? It's Ok, though, I can drink it black."

Oh god, he's looked in the fridge. Seen how lazy I am. How I don't cook or clean. Nothing but the bare minimum. Did he see all

151

the ready meals in the freezer? He's looking at me, smiling.

"So what are your plans for the afternoon?"

"Um," she could not tell him she was going to play internet bridge. "A walk," she said. "I was thinking of going for a walk."

"Let's go then? After I've finished the tap?"

She was shocked by his assumption. He was talking as if they were old friends. As if this sort of thing happened to her frequently. Perhaps he feels sorry for me, losing my job, living on my own, and he's lonely without Annie. He was waiting for a response. Why am I making such a big deal out of such a simple choice? She realised that she was not ready for slipping easily into a friendship with him. It was happening too fast. From no one to someone two days running was too much for her. She wanted him to go now. Why hadn't he come tomorrow as arranged? "Oh sorry, I've arranged to meet a friend today."

He turned away from her and looked out of the window so she could not see his expression. "Ok, I'll just finish this. Have fun, shall I meet you in 'Roses' at two tomorrow and we'll go for a walk?"

Frances sat in the corner of the café, pretending to read the paper. She hated waiting, and even more, being kept waiting. The coffee was foul: bitter, murky, slimy. She felt self-conscious sitting alone reading. Are people looking at me, feeling sorry for me? Why doesn't he come? Did I say that out loud? I must stop talking to myself.

He was at the door, looking nervously around. She waved and he gratefully walked towards her. "Don't have the coffee," she said, "unless you like gravy browning."

"Shall I order tea for both of us then? They can't ruin a teabag can they?"

It came, together with a teacake each and she took out a tissue and wiped it around her cup. She always had to inspect cups and plates, tilting them into the light. He wondered if this habit would enrage him after a while.

They set off for a walk around the park. Spring was on the way. He could almost smell it. There was a pale sun and the twigs were swollen at their tips. The beds had hellebores, pansies and primula and underneath some trees were snowdrops and even a few crocuses. She wasn't used to walking with anyone. He seemed different. *Have I just not looked at him properly? I just don't know him. He's walking too quickly. Can't he see I'm struggling to keep up?*

He turned and looked at her, trying to take her in. *She wasn't unattractive. Her hair was cut in rather a short, mannish style, but the pale sun lit its indeterminate colour to gold. She looked sort of old worldly, uninterested in clothes, so different from Annie. Was that a Barbour jacket?* "You seem as if you were very committed to your work. What did you do for leisure?"

"The same as most single people I suppose," she said defensively, not wanting to seem boring, but wracking her brains for a spark to show she had some imagination. "I went to the theatre, films and galleries sometimes. I played bridge and watched TV. Same as I do now, only I've added weekly swimming and I've just started singing."

"Have you? Where do you do that?"

"In the St Joseph's church hall?"

"That's where Annie and Laura sing. On Monday nights?"

"Yes."

Frances had not seen Annie there and did not know whether she should encourage him to talk about her or not. But she was not very good at emotions, so started to tell him about her walking holiday in Tuscany last year.

They had only had tea and the teacake, but she felt pleasantly relaxed and in a warm cocoon of friendliness. He was a good listener and apparently enjoyed walking.

"I was dreading having to retire one day, because I haven't had time for many friends or interests. My job has been my life. I thought I'd be a lonely old woman rattling round in my flat looking for things to do."

"Yes, it must have been a shock having to leave before you were ready to, but you're a clever girl, healthy and must have enough money to have a good retirement. The world's your oyster."

The sun was lower and their shadows long and pale behind them when they realised that they were almost back to where they had started. She looked at her watch. "Oh, I'm playing bridge at the Acol. I've got to go."

"What time do you finish?" he asked.

"About nine," she said hesitantly.

"I'll meet you after for supper." He fished in his top pocket and handed her a card, smiling into her eyes. "I'll be in 'The Red Lion' just down the road from the club. If you're late there's my mobile number." He turned and walked briskly away without waiting for her reply.

"What a cheek," Frances thought. "He has just assumed that I've got nothing to do later."

As she hurried to catch her bus she took out her Blackberry and texted him. *Sorry can't do tonight, Frances.*

Laura went to the DfE for an interview, then called to see Lynne. "Why do you never ring me? How about coming to a comedy at the 'Arcola'? It'll be fun."

"I don't want fun, and it wouldn't be fun for me. I'm getting a bit deaf, so I miss a lot. I'd rather stay home with the cats."

"For goodness sake Lynne. We've all got to get old and die and it's sad, but that's the way it is. Betty had her life. She wasn't five years old."

"I need time alone in my space. I enjoy my own company. I've got my gardening, art lectures and photography classes to go to. Plenty of pastimes if I want them. I don't want a whirlwind of displacement activity at the moment. I miss Mum. And I'm tired. In fact exhausted and depressed. I don't want to see patients and I can't be bothered to cook for myself. Even deciding what to wear and washing my clothes feel like an enormous effort. I'm swamped with grief. 'Don't ever put me in a Home, shoot me first!' she said to me. And I put her in one. I thought I had to and I can't forgive myself. My mind goes round and round it, over and over again."

She did not mention that it had brought back memories of Ken. It had been seven years since he died. But in the endless black expanse of the night, she would often wake and her mind would go back to the things she and Ken had done together and inevitably the last few

154

weeks, when he had become so thin that the duvet looked as if he had no body. It was so flat. "Hold my hand," he had said. "You are life." She would hear his whispering, rustling breathing and smelt not him, but the decay of death. His papery skin was drawn so tightly over his skeletal frame; she had wondered why his sharp bones had not punctured it. What had he been thinking? Did he want to go or stay? His living corpse, shrivelled and mute, could no longer tell her. She had held him. Held his dry, stick like claw, until touching him hurt him too much.

She still missed the companionship and his hugs. They had both been very tactile. She knew that she must guard against those feelings now that she was older, more forgetful and so stressed and upset over Betty's death. She had passed a mannequin in John Lewis wearing a very similar linen suit to the one Ken wore so often and she had heard herself sigh and her arms had stretched out to cuddle him. Luckily, she had come to her senses and pulled her hands back before they reached the polystyrene model. It appeared that nobody had noticed, but was she going mad? She must be more careful.

Laura took a mug of tea and a piece of bara brith up to Dan. "I'm so surprised that Lynne is taking it like this. She's always been strong and capable. I'd never have thought she'd be this vulnerable."

"Give her time."

"She doesn't call anyone. She's not seeing her patients. Do you know what she said?"

Dan had looked back at his canvas. "Go on," He muttered.

"I dream I'm making parmigiana, a simple Jamie Witherspoon recipe. Putting salt on aubergines so the bitter juices come out, and I do it to me, but I don't get nicer and happier, I get more sour and miserable."

"Mmm," said Dan. "Give her time."

"I'll go back and have another go on Friday."

Jo had been brought up to be frugal. Her mother had worked as a librarian and her father had been a programmer in a city bank. He had died of a heart attack at forty-one. So they had had to live modestly.

She could not wait to grow up and get some of the high life.

She liked to clothes shop alone, rather than have someone else distracting her who might try on clothes too, or want to go to different shops or get bored waiting for her to decide. She did not need anyone else's opinion. Drifting where the mood took her, often with no preconceived notion of what she might look for or how much she could spend, screening out all distractions to concentrate on finding the perfect item. Designer clothes shops were reverential, like churches. All energies could be concentrated on the quest. The clothes usually had no price tags, the few items displayed said, 'wear me, I am for the rich and powerful.' Shop assistants could see that she was an experienced shopper and kept away until they saw that she had chosen.

Disappointingly, today she had found nothing she liked enough to squander her allowance on. Drifting down South Molton Street, turning the corner into brightly lit Oxford Street, teeming with the usual cast of Londoners: homo sapiens in different guises, hijabs, burqas, work suits, bargain hunters carrying 'Primark' carrier bags. She sang Ralph Mctell's 'Streets of London,' in the privacy of her head, before slipping into Bond Street station and squeezing into a tube packed with countless people with empty faces, going home from work.

It was starting to sleet when she emerged from her station. The 'Coach and Horses' looked warm and welcoming and only an evening of television watching was ahead. Her fashionable two toned riding boots felt seriously uncomfortable. What was that poem? Something like: 'firm, well-hammer'd soles protect thy feet. Thro' freezing snows and rains and soaking sleet'. * Nothing about comfort. She went into the pub, bought herself a glass of Merlot and, carrying it to an empty table, pulled off the boots. Sipping her wine she listened to the football conversation and dirty jokes told by three sharp suited, banker type men who were leaning on the bar. She wondered if they had exhausted wives waiting at home with their evening meals. A short grey haired older man came in, glanced at Jo, bought a pint and came to sit at the next table, walking bow legged, as if his balls were in

156

the way. He got an Evening Standard out of his rather battered briefcase and began to flick through it. She studied his profile. Not bad looking and a compact powerful body. Would he be interested? Or am I too old or too tall, he hasn't looked up again. Oh, give up, Jo. She pushed her feet back into her boots, walked to the door and almost collided with Phillip, who put his arm around her shoulders and guided her back inside. "What luck to have bumped into you. Please stay. What would you like to drink?"

Sitting back at her table, she studied him at the bar. Nice cream cashmere polo and leather jacket, brown hair pulled back…does he dye it? Moleskin chinos, leather Chelsea boots with a little heel. Why do I run into this sex surrogate so randomly and regularly? 'You again?' at St Pancras station; 'What you?' on Oxford Street. 'Not again?' in Waitrose.

He returned, offered her a crisp, then sat eating steadily through the packet, gulping his pint. He seemed thirsty. He had fixed his soft, warm eyes on her. She had allowed him into her eyes, but he pushed further, right in, so she felt stirred and on edge. She looked away, avoiding the collusive look with which he hoped to bind them together. I can resist anything except temptation. No, I'm not going to get in trouble with my new neighbours, she told herself sternly. It would be a quick fuck to me, but if Helen found out…He's probably got a dinky little lady wand anyway. No, *no*.

She gulped down her wine. "I must go. I'm meeting a friend and I'll be late." She felt happier already at the lie.

"Ok, I'm in a rush too. Just fancied a quick drink."

Outside on the pavement, she stood awkwardly. One normally kissed friends, mwa, mwa, hello and goodbye. He moved towards her. A bit shorter than me, she was thinking and suddenly he was kissing her on the mouth, his hand on her bottom, pressing her to him. Oh God, nice if I was an ancient virgin or erotically desolate, but…

"Bye," she stammered and hurried awkwardly off up the street, hoping no one had seen them.

It was an overcast day with a brisk wind and no sign of birds, other than a few fat pigeons guzzling the grain someone leaves for them on the pavement at the corner of Laura's street.

Jo, Laura and Beth arrived at the pool to find that there were adult lessons in one lane, but luckily there were less swimmers than usual, so the remaining three lanes were not overcrowded. The water was cold and Jo had soon had enough. "Perhaps I've got a bug, I don't feel great. I'll wait for you in the coffee shop...don't rush," she said.

Laura had been making herself swim crawl every fourth length, for the past few months. Today, her arms and legs felt strong, her spine lengthened, back muscles tightened, her breathing had improved, so she did whole lengths of three then four arm strokes before breathing. Waves of energy flooded her body as if the water was recharging her. Standing in the hot shower after, she was so happy to be alive. Swimming gets rid of the aches and creaks, sort of lubricates the body and lifts the spirits, she thought.

When they emerged from the centre, the clouds had cleared, the wind had died down and the sun was shining. The bare twigs and branches had little swellings where the leaves will be and birds were singing despite the very cold temperature. As they walked down the sheltered parade of shops, Beth stood for a moment gazing into the window of the one selling wedding dresses. "Do you watch the Oscars, Jo?"

"Not if I can help it. All those acres of bare flesh or galleon gowns. Boring."

"And fake teeth and faces," Laura added. "It's sad, not glamorous."

"I've always rather enjoyed it," Beth looked crest fallen.

"On a more important subject, what shall we do about Lynne? She's in a trough of misery, eating tons of rubbish and can't seem to get over Betty," Laura asked.

"Don't expect she'd take much notice of us," said Jo. "Take her round a glass of valium and a bar of soap and get her to shake off those cat hairs and step back into life."

"Yes, I don't know her well enough. She needs to find some little interests, like fighting to keep the libraries open," said Beth. "Tell her to come and join a group of women I've met at the hospital. We're lobbying the council. You don't see them cutting their huge salaries and perks to keep a library going. Or what about her volunteering to teach something in the new community hall? I'm going to do that. Did you get that email about it?"

"No. Is that the one that used to be part of the church in Brook Lane? Some of the buildings have been made into flats?"

"Yes, it's going to be brilliant. There are a couple of classrooms, a canteen and a multi-purpose hall. They've got a grant to fund a full time worker. I'm thinking of volunteering to teach a little bit of adult literacy and speaking and listening skills."

"What about ESOL?"

"Perhaps I should get a qualification to teach that or Life in the UK and Citizenship?"

"Mmm, I'm just getting to grips with my writing though."

"You could just do one little session a week. You can teach so much."

Laura looked thoughtful. "Well, I suppose I could take an exercise class for older, unfit people who haven't the confidence or money to go to a health club. It would keep me fitter having to practise the lesson. But it's so committing. How can we go on holidays?"

"Perhaps you could make that clear when you start. That if you're going away, there won't be a class. Come to the meeting anyway."

Beth was flushed with enthusiasm. Teaching would be with small groups of adults. She could surely manage that and banish her nightmares.

"Do you want to come to the meeting, Jo?"

"Maybe...maybe," said Jo to her friend's surprise.

Annie had sunk into a dazed inertia, which could not be penetrated. "No thank you. Not at the moment," was her answer to all social and appearance requests. She could not summon the interest or energy to look for job projects, play tennis or go to choir and the concert and theatre tickets she had booked months ago, were wasted. Days and nights merged into one another. She was barely eating and her rule of rarely drinking alcohol in daylight had long since lapsed.

How could he just walk out like that? She sat dull eyed in front of her laptop, writing nothing, or lay in bed, sobbing into the pillow. She slept and slept, but never felt refreshed. When she woke, she was disorientated, sluggish and exhausted. She felt old and unlovable and was incapable of directly asking anyone for help or even admitting that she needed it. Laura could see that she was in a poor state and, judging by the empty bottles outside, was drinking too much, but had reluctantly given up trying to get her to talk. "I haven't seen Martin for a while, he must be really fed up with her. Perhaps she's in one of those dormouse phases, where she hibernates, recharges and then she's off again?" She said to Dan.

"Sounds a bit more than that this time. Why don't you ask her?"

Annie was lapsing in and out of a sleep punctuated by nausea and misery. The bedroom was flooded with morning light. It was warm in her nest of single duvets. At some point in the night she had dragged Martin's over her too. She pulled it close and lay, listening to the blood pounding through her head and staring at the frost flowers on the windows, her breath like smoke. Moving her eyes to the ceiling she followed its circular patterns, spinning, spiralling out. She felt unclear about her edges, where she stopped. Was she seeping into her bed? Dissolving away? He was in her head and heart every minute of the day, as he had never been when he was living with her. The smallest reminder made her seize up with pain. He lay in wait for her with his books, the smell of him on his old coats in the lobby, his glass he would raise to their future. She could not escape the memories.

The blue carpet looked like a river, running past her bed, smoothly out of the door, cascading down the staircase. Pale by day and dark blue in the evening. An empty wine bottle fell to the floor as she struggled out of bed. "Damn. My head!" She moved slowly into the bathroom, as if wading through water and lent on the wash hand basin, staring into the mirror. She looked old and defeated. Grey, ghostlike, crepey skinned, deep lines between her brows and around her mouth. Too many nights crying and too much alcohol. I'm a failure and unlovable. Am I having a break down? She had had cramp earlier and was stiff and achy. She wondered about suicide, but her brain was too muzzy to think properly. After a wee she staggered back to bed.

One morning through the grey fog of sleep the familiar sound of the doorbell penetrated. It was probably Laura wanting her to go swimming. She would soon go away. But then she never rang the bell if the bedroom curtains were drawn. Who was it then? She groaned and rolled over to peer at the clock. Ten past eleven? Well it definitely wasn't Laura. Oh god, why don't you all leave me alone? She dragged herself out of bed and crossed to the window. A man she recognised as the courier from her publishers stood there holding a parcel. She often did reviews for them. Should she run down, or at least open the window and ask him to wait a minute? But what would he think of her, looking like this, in her dressing gown, refusing to open the door for so long? She hid behind the curtain as he looked around and then went back to his motorbike. She went back to bed.

Next day the courier tried again and this time she was up, sitting at the kitchen table, drinking black coffee and eating a tin of beans with a spoon. They tasted like sawdust. I'm going to have to go out to get food and drink. The thought was frightening. I'll order it on the internet. She turned on her laptop. Oh, an email from Ben. The first since Christmas and that awkward, embarrassed two days he and Nathan had spent here. I shouldn't have given them separate rooms, but who was I to make assumptions? She cringed at the memory of his barely concealed anger. He's living his own life in Chicago that he tells me nothing about. Ben, that dear, longed for little baby, sweet little child. He's so ungrateful. Is he being sarcastic? 'Thanks for Christmas, Mum and Dad, x Ben.' Thirty-four years and that's all he can write…

Six emails from Laura. Each one becoming more worried. Why doesn't everyone leave me alone? They've got their own busy lives and partners. I don't feel like doing anything or speaking to anyone. I just want to curl up in a ball and sleep.

She wondered who had written a book this time and after a while picked up the package and pulled it open. Jamie Witherspoon's! How dare they send me his rubbish. How insulting. He's so tirelessly self-

161

promoting! She threw the book across the room and dust rose to meet it. "Vegetarian food? I was the one who made it fashionable in the first place."

She opened her book file and tried to write, but tears blurred her vision and the familiar room seemed cold, empty and strange. She forced herself to write a paragraph. It was clumsy and lifeless. *What's wrong with me? I've got to come up with something special, fight off competition…*Wandering over to the bread bin, she cut the mouldy crusts off the last slice of bread, toasted it, then didn't feel like eating it. She lent on the work surface and put her forehead against the cool cupboard above. *Marriage, however flawed, was better than this. And at least Martin understood what life as a freelancer is like. Oh God, what am I going to do with myself? Are microwaved meals for one and single supplement holidays all I have to look forward to? I've got to pull myself together…*

Beth came out of the Scissors Salon with a new look. Her thin, straggly shoulder length hair had been cut to her chin line and brown and fair streaks merged in with the grey. Instead of it being pulled back and fastened with a slide, which accentuated her rather heavy podgy face, it had been blow-dried loosely so it looked thicker and wavier than it was. She floated out of the salon feeling upbeat, glamorous and younger. *I must start thinking about what I can wear…not my blue dress again,* she thought. *I wore it to Barry's retirement dinner and did I wear it to David's as well? I'll have to have something special for James's last hurrah.* She had always been grateful that it was not often that wives were expected to accompany their husbands to social events, certainly never to their Christmas dinner. And unlike larger law firms there had not been all the charity bashes and the corporate event calendar of Test matches, Wimbledon, Ascot, etc. to have to sit through. Just that awful day at Glyndebourne years ago when the firm changed hands. She went hot with shame remembering it.

Richard, the new Chief Executive, and his wife Claudia had ordered a Fortnum and Masons hamper: oak-smoked-trout quenelles, pheasant goujons, acorn-fed Iberico ham and much more, complete with champagne and polycarbonate glasses. James had been instructed to bring two folding chairs for them. He puffed and complained at the distance he had to carry their ancient heavy wooden ones, which were all they had. Everyone else bounced along with modern, lightweight chrome. Beth followed the party. Past the lawns, lakes, ha ha's, beautiful borders and overdressed people with their collective sense of entitlement who were milling everywhere looking for the best picnic spots. Snatches of braying conversations floated towards her as she trudged along, heels sinking into wet grass, her teeth chattering. It was an extremely cold day and she had been completely inappropriately dressed in a light frock and cotton jacket and after half an hour it poured with rain and they were the only couple without an umbrella. She had felt like a drowned rat and had had to sit shivering all through the concert.

But for James's farewell dinner in the Court Dining Room at the Fishmongers Hall she wanted to look special. Well, as special as she could, at sixty-two and overweight. She had looked it up on the internet. It was an imposing building on the riverside, with high moulded ceilings and huge crystal chandeliers. Lovely.

Next morning, they were walking to the pool. Jo's hair gleamed gold and perfect. She had on straight leg jeans, a biker jacket and Uggs. "You always look so good." Beth felt a rush of helpless envy. "I'm an eclectic rag bag. I wish I had your taste. Will you come shopping with me?" she asked impulsively. "I hate shopping, but perhaps with you…"

"So you want a makeover? Fine with me. Is it for something special, a turbo megabash?"

"Yes. All my clothes are old and boring. I need to look special for James's leaving dinner and then my cousin's daughter's wedding. Let's have lunch and get a little bit tiddly, then I'll be more inclined to be daring."

"You might regret it later."

"I can always take them back."

"Not if you give all your boring possibilities to a charity shop. Then you'll have to wear what you buy."

"I don't think I could go that far. You never know when I might

163

need them."

They agreed on the following Tuesday, but later, Beth feeling demoralised and in a turmoil, rang to cry off. "I bullied you into it, and I'm quite happy with my clothes really. Let's forget it."

"You'll regret it Beth. We'll go with a view to not getting stuck on the styles you liked years ago. Not buying anything just because it's useful and making sure it's advertising your best bits."

"Well, I haven't got any of those. I'm so overweight. I just can't come."

"Why?"

"I've got some things to do…"

In the end though she gave in and the date was back on.

It was Friday and Laura had gone back to Lynne's. "This staying at home day after day, eating junk food and watching daytime TV can't go on, Lynne. You're not even seeing your regular patients!"

"No?" she asked, pouring boiling water into two mugs and then opening a box and lifting out a chocolate cheesecake. "What difference does it make to anyone else? Anyway I haven't got time to see patients. By the time I've waited hours in a queue to speak to someone at Betty's bank or building society or the Registrars, suffering dozens of stalling tactics and holding patterns or endlessly retyping account details, sort codes and password into menu after menu. Then at last getting through to someone in India who only has stock responses, I've wasted half the day and I'm in a fuzz of incontinent fury."

"We hardly see you and are you trying to double in size?"

Lynne gave Laura a cold look. She didn't doubt that her friend was concerned, but it was her life, she could do what she liked with it.

"You were such a good and healthy cook." Laura went over to the bin. "It's full of takeaway containers. Why?"

Lynne looked at her beseechingly. "Eating eases the pain. I can't stop thinking how unkind I was to Betty. Cooking for one is a waste of time."

Laura brushed cat hairs off a chair, sat down and stirred her tea. "She didn't stop loving you. She'd be horrified to see you like this and

I can't stand to see you so depressed."

Lynne closed her eyes and sighed deeply. Her voice was quiet and toneless. "I know you're being caring. I know I'm depressed, but I don't want to take pills or buck up. Just get off my back will you. Give me time to get over it all." Then feeling as if she had been too rude, she got out of her chair and put her arm around Laura's shoulders. "I need to grieve. Think about our lives together. Make sense of it all for a bit longer. I'll move on when I'm ready to."

"But going to a Memory Clinic. What's that about? You'll talk yourself into having dementia if you're not careful. Your mother didn't start losing it until she was in her eighties, you're only sixty-six."

"My aunt and grandmother had it."

"Didn't her stay in hospital with her fractured femur set off your Aunt Violet's dementia?"

"Yes, the anti-psychotic drugs made her into a zombie. By the time I'd managed to get her off them, a part of who she was had been lost and never came back. Look, half my family have ended up with it. I want to make sure I'm diagnosed early to get the right drugs. I've got some signs already, like agitation, hand rubbing, paranoia, mood swings and obsessive reorganisation of my cupboards. Sleeping and waking are not as distinct as they were. And I only had twenty-eight in the MMSE last week."

"What's that?"

"Oh, you know, the Mini Mental State Examination. I suddenly couldn't remember two of the words they tell you. I kept thinking of the three from the time before."

"You just need to get your mind onto something else. How about an evening out with Jo and me? Just the three of us like old times?"

"I don't want to go out, I'd rather stay home with the cats. Look Laura, if I'm getting dementia like Mum, I need to know what to do and how I'm going to live the rest of my life, but I have to do it alone." A wave of nausea washed over her and she almost stopped breathing, trying to thwart a gas bubble creeping upwards. It seeped slowly into her throat. Laura was looking at her questioningly. "You know, what misery's ahead? If only we had a crystal ball. I don't want to be a bitter, resentful, powerless old lady in a Home, weak,

165

dependent and embarrassed at myself."

"You're in a state, Lynne. You're suffering from grief. Who's told you you've got dementia?"

"No-one yet, but they haven't told me I haven't got it either. Dying is the last thing I'll do, so I want it to go well. I'm not dragging it out in hospital and old people's homes like Mum and Aunt Violet. I gave instructions for them not to be resuscitated and I'll want the same for me. None of this lying there with intravenous drips and nasal and tracheal tubes. That's not living, it's dehumanising. And I'm off to Dignitas before that stage anyway."

"How will you know when to go to Dignitas? You're so practical, so unsentimental. Does death have to be such a brutish act? You're worn out so you'll bump yourself off, like you do with your cats. Old and suffering, so off to the vet, get a new one. I hate you talking like this!"

Lynne looked out of the window at her new kitten, Sophie 2 with her caramel coloured fur, white whiskers, rosebud pink nose and pads, crouching, in front of the hebe at the far end of the lawn.

"Death is a fact we all have to face," she said drily. Just because hospitals and funeral parlours do everything for you and people call it 'passed on', 'gone to heaven', 'resting' and such rubbish, the reality is we all die and rot and I want to be in control of the coup de grace and go out and meet it. I want to be a person at the end, not a patient, a degraded vegetable. What fun is that?"

"I don't think we realise how humans cling on to life, however reduced, until we're there. My Mum was trapped in bed for the last few years, in pain and bored, but she still didn't want to die, she said she was Ok, she'd got used to her reduced circumstances."

"Hmm. When should we finish supporting life? When is a person dead? When brain function has gone, or when breathing, blood circulation and heartbeat have ended? I want responsible, controlled euthanasia for me. If I'm no longer human, if my life isn't worth living, it's a vegetative existence. If it's unethical, so be it. I'm mature enough to make this choice." She reached over to the table and cut another piece of cheesecake. "For you?"

"No thanks. Why are we talking about this? Don't keep worrying about death and dementia. You're not going to stop it happening if it's going to. You've got us and Jo to help look after you."

"For how long, when I'm asking you the same question a hundred times a day, can't dress myself, when I'm incontinent, can't clean my own teeth. You'll soon get tired of me then." The prospect of her friend's inevitable irritation and loss of respect was an unbearable thought as was that of having to cope alone.

"What should be preoccupying you is how do you live your life when you retire? We spend the first part striving to become something, then the next part doing it and then there's the last part. As far as I'm concerned this is the biggest challenge, how to make a useful contribution, how to be happy, that's what you should be thinking about. It's as if you're preparing for death."

"Lynne Kennedy to see Dr Williams." Lynne walked down the corridor to his room, as if going to her fate.

"Hello, Mrs Kennedy." Dr Williams looked up from what were presumably his notes. "How have you been feeling?"

"I can't remember things, I'm anxious and depressed, I definitely think I'm getting dementia."

He took her through the same tests, for her memory, spotting anomalies in drawings of shapes, doing mental arithmetic; she had never been good at that. Today she couldn't concentrate, she knew she was doing badly and was close to tears. At the end she had scored twenty-six.

"You see; I'm going down each time. It's those three words. They go straight out of my head. I've deteriorated, haven't I?" she shot out.

He looked puzzled. "Your concentration was not as good, but that could be that there are other things you're thinking about, and your mother only died a month or so ago..."

"Thanks." She tried to force a smile, then took out her handkerchief to stem her tears.

"You're suffering from grief, which can affect everything including your ability to process information and your confidence. It will take time to get back to normal."

"Will it?" She blew her nose. "But what if my lack of confidence

167

is due to dementia, not grief?"

"That is not my diagnosis. You are not exhibiting the symptoms I would expect from someone with a form of dementia," he said gently.

Gratitude surged through her. Everything could be blamed on grief, her up and down moods, her lethargy, she felt almost cheerful.

"If you're still not remembering the words in a year's time, then we'll take it seriously. Go home, eat good food, go for long walks, have a holiday, live healthily and forget about dementia for six months."

She looked at his solid, sincere face and felt a rush of relief. All her bingeing and putting on weight, her crying and inability to concentrate…it was grief and it would pass. I will get over it.

Chapter 12. March. Spring

'Strangely apart, yet strangely together,
Silence between them like a thread to hold
And not wind in.'
Elizabeth Jennings 'One Flesh.' (1926 – 2001)

The nights had been frosty, but today it was cloudless and bright. Laura opened her bedroom window and breathed in the soft, mild, sweet air. The sun had coaxed the buds and shoots to come out of their winter sleep, yellow and purple crocuses, daffodils and primroses were beginning to flower and birds were flying around in pairs. Dressed in her comfortable 'going swimming' clothes, she opened the front door and was thrilled to find Lynne waiting outside. "You've emerged at last. I'm so pleased to see you."

"I'm not a pretty sight with my clothes off. I've got flaky skin, hairy legs and horny, crabby feet."

"Oh come on. No one looks at anyone. I don't shave my legs til I'm forced by the heat to wear a skirt for tennis."

They walked down the road admiring the blossom on the horse chestnut just beginning to uncurl and found Beth sitting outside on her wall. After remarking on the perfect morning and the bluebells in her garden, her brow creased and she launched into something, which had obviously been worrying her.

"I wonder if Jo should expose her bosoms quite so much? Perhaps it gives the wrong impression? They're a little bit too much on show, don't you think? It's not really appropriate for someone her age, is it?"

Lynne sniffed. "Perhaps we're just a teeny bit jealous?"

Laura smiled at Beth. "They're rather magnificent, aren't they? I don't think she's crossed the line into looking ancient and desperate, has she? Older women are hanging on to their sexy clothes and going on dates far more than in the past."

"Well, I was thinking a little bit the 'mutton' phrase."

"Mmm, well I can see that if you dress conservatively, seeing Jo flaunting herself must seem a bit insane. But if she wants to hide her

169

white hair and wrinkles, that's Ok by me. It doesn't make me feel insecure or anything. Life has changed from the world of our mums, the world of 'Excellent Women', that Barbara Pym book we're reading this month. That was your choice wasn't it, Beth?"

"Yes, well said Laurs. Sorry Beth, I haven't any objections myself. Why should older women's bodies be hidden and forbidden? Jo's doing the right thing for the sisterhood. Unfortunately I've never had anything worth putting on display." Lynne grinned and looked down at her modest boobs.

For a change, the pool water was up level with the floor, so it was smooth and calm, like blue glass and surprisingly it was not crowded. A welcome return for Lynne. They swam for an extra five minutes. Their usual twenty did not seem long enough.

"Why isn't it always like this?" said Laura as they got their towels and shampoos out of their lockers and went into the shower area together

"I feel like two people today, the stiff, aching, cross old lady who got out of bed, then this one under the shower, all little creaks and pains washed away," said Beth. She dressed hurriedly and went off in the opposite direction. To B&Q.

"So there's a chink of light into your dark depression? About time too," Laura said happily to Lynne.

"I've begun to feel human instead of useless and wretched."

"We're having some friends for dinner on Friday. Can you come?"

"Ugh, no thanks. Hate dinner parties. They're usually a parade of ego and self-righteousness, boasting, vanity and showing off. No one is actually interested in anyone else. Guests just fight for air time."

"Thanks a bunch. Who says my friends are like that?"

"Yes, sorry, I shouldn't have said that, but anyway I'd prefer not to."

"Do you want to come to the cinema tonight then? We're going to see 'Trishna'."

"Um, can't. Sorry."

"Is this a secret?"

170

Lynne looked uncomfortable. "Not exactly. No. It's just someone I used to chat to in 'Rainbow Court', Robert was visiting his father. We've had a coffee together a couple of times. He lives in Brighton."

"Oh ho, you're a dark horse! What's he like?"

"A bit posh and buttoned up, but pleasant. Open, unlined face, perceptive, amused eyes and old world manners and charm. About my height: grey, wavy hair, loves cats and is a good bridge player. Think I'll take it up again. His wife died a couple of years ago. He was an accountant. He's well into his seventies so just does occasional troubleshooting for IPAC, looking at failing companies. Just a few months work every year. The rest of the time he keeps a grip on his investments."

A sudden image of their last meeting shot into her head. He had lent over and kissed her gently on the cheek. She had almost jumped away as he got within range, her mind full of how fat she was at the moment. How he might be repulsed by her body.

Laura was thrilled for her. She was grinning from ear to ear. "Are you coming for a walk this Sunday then? We're thinking of starting the London Loop. Dan's got a really interesting guidebook. Robert could come too."

"He doesn't like walking and actually I'm booked in for another walk with Ramblers."

"Where? Perhaps we'll come on that."

"It's near Brighton. Robert is picking me up at the end of it. I'm going to his place for supper."

"Well, well, well. Who was that person who was telling me a few weeks ago how completely defended against love they were, how their life was even and organised and just how they liked it?"

"Look at that disgusting dog, pooing everywhere!" Lynne had had enough of that subject. "Having said that though, Thira has been peeing all over the house. I had to take her to the vet."

"What's wrong with her?"

"You're not going to believe this, 'cystitis'."

"I thought that was stress related?"

"Yes, well cats can be stressed, like people."

"What from? She just lies about all day. Are you serious? Does she have panic attacks as well?"

"The vet said perhaps she's afraid of something. She's got a course of Prozac," Lynne said hurriedly. "Animals suffer from the same diseases and psychological problems as humans you know."

Laura looked sceptical. She wasn't fond of cats, the way they licked their bottoms and stared at you with a cold, uninterested gaze.

"Research shows that animals get cancer and even insects have tumours. Fish can faint from fear and birds can pull out all their feathers. When Betty went into hospital, when she had pneumonia that time, Sophie started biting off her fur."

"So what did the vet prescribe for her?"

"He put her on Valium. I didn't give her the whole course though. I didn't want her to be addicted." Lynne had taken a cigarette out of her swimming bag and lit up. "I've taken up smoking again. I haven't smoked since I was in my twenties. I've craved a fag to stop me eating, take my mind off things, to help me think about my life. Betty would kill me if she saw me now. I don't smoke the whole thing though," she said, seeing Laura's bemused face.

They had reached the corner where their paths divided and Lynne carried on to her street. When she arrived outside her house, she took a last drag and put a mint into her mouth before going in to await her first patient of the day.

That afternoon Lynne went to the gym at David Lloyd Leisure which she had joined that week. She changed and went upstairs and to her surprise Martin was in front of her on the treadmill.

"Hi Martin, didn't know you were a gym bunny?"

"This gym must be my favourite charity. I've been a member for three months and only come four times."

"I promised Laura I'd come, but no amount of press ups and the cabbage diet is going to work on me. I crave sweet, sticky things or fatty, salty ones. I actually like feeling stuffed and glassy eyed. I don't like being hungry. What's the point of feeling miserable and starving all the time, we're all going to die."

"Well at least if we're fit we may put off having to spend the next part of our lives in wheelchairs." He had been walking to cool down, stopped the machine, picked up his towel and joined her on the carpeted floor in front of the banks of bikes, rowers and treadmills.

"What's your aim then?"

"Let's face it, I'm never going to look like a ripped underpants model or a rugby player. Bulbous shoulders, huge chests and cantilevered thighs are out of my reach and I don't want to spend huge chunks of every day exercising. I thought I ought to try and ward off diabetes and heart disease, tone up, get fitter."

"You're slim though. No pallid paunches or flabby moobs on you." Lynne looked around. "Gyms are such nostalgic places. We all want to be how we like to think we used to be. Before we led sedentary, hunched, over eating lives. People in gyms have a fanatical, desperate look as they try to push back the years."

"Wish there weren't all these mirrors everywhere. There's a whole wall of them in the changing room!"

"Yes, I can successfully think of myself as looking not too bad, then there's this horrible shock when I catch sight of a hunched, fat, grey, blotchy and droopy skinned stranger and realise it's me!"

They grinned ruefully at one another and got on with their workouts.

Helen was lying in bed. Cars swept up and down the road outside, their headlights sending sabres of light through the crack in the curtains and across the bedroom ceiling. Trains passed intermittently at the bottom of the garden and the house shuddered as it always did. She had been woken up at the sound of voices, the front door closing and then the click of the hall light switch. She had been tired and had drunk more cabernet sauvignon than she had meant to, so had gone to bed before nine and fallen into a deep sleep. Phillip had had two appointments this evening. They must have gone by now. What time is it? She reached her arm out and flicked on her bedside lamp. Ten-thirty, she had not slept for long. Perhaps she would go down and get some camomile tea. It might help to get her back to sleep. Barefooted she went down the stairs. There was a dim light coming from under the door of his practice room, the murmur of Phillip and his patients' voices and she could smell the incense.

173

Then there was silence. They must be meditating or in a long pose. It was quite a comforting silence. She pottered into the kitchen and put on the kettle.

A cup of herb tea and a paracetemol in her hand, she again passed the door. The quiet seemed to have been going on rather a long time. What was happening in there?

Going closer she heard some quiet moans and oh, god, a little scream! She flung open the door to see Phillip, sitting on the rug in his sarong, sucking a beautiful black breast.

Her heart began to beat so hard that she could only see a red haze. Phillip had turned. His face went white and saggy and he indicated to his patient to cover herself up.

"I can't go on like this." Helen's voice was high and trembling. "I can't stand all these betrayals, in my own house! It's making me ill. I feel like I'm going mad."

The woman had edged around behind her and was trying to get through the door. Helen would have pushed her through if she hadn't been so quick. The outside door banged.

There was a tremor in his voice. "It was a treatment. I'm sorry, it wasn't for pleasure."

His shoulders had slumped, his neck had come forward, his skin was grey. He looked like an old, tired dog. All the fight drained out of Helen and her limbs were cold and weak.

He knew he had gone too far again, but should there be boundaries when helping a patient to heal? "Emotions are a powerful expression of energy. We all have a positive, a negative and a neutral mind. Can't you aim for a neutral mind as I have? Take control of your mind and your energy, don't let negativity take over, let's meditate together."

She looked at him with narrowed eyes and an expression of utter contempt and bitterness. Loathing him for making her so powerless and humiliated.

Their bed was king sized and there was a big space between them. He could hear her sobbing gently into the pillow and put out his hand to stroke her. She knocked it away and moved to the very edge. How was he going to get out of this one? He lay pondering. Their marriage can't be over? He felt a fierce surge of possessiveness. She was the only woman he had ever really loved. "What I do for my patients doesn't affect the fact that I love you only and that you're my soul mate." There was no answer. Perhaps he had tried that too many times.

"I don't want to hear any more lies from you. I've had enough." A muffled plea from the other side of the bed.

"Are you twitchy and can't sleep? Let me help you clear your mind and energy field. If you're blocked, you've lost the connection to your deeper self. Let's do some relaxation exercises together, then I'll give you a massage."

"Shut up and don't touch me. You disgust me." Though really a massage was so tempting. Oh to be back in the time when I was overwhelmed with love and so was he, she thought. "I carry you in me like a part of myself," he had said. He was as much a part of me as my blood. We knew all the creases and odours of one another's' bodies, but most of the time now there is a wall between us, or perhaps a pane of glass. I see him, I tap on the glass, but he is in his own world. We're apart. Sharing the house but not what is in our heads.

Jo found that she was keen not to miss the gym, even without Laura who had a dental appointment. She and Antony had exchanged names and the odd greeting. The time went so quickly as she admired his strength, his gleaming healthy skin, his slouching athletic walk, like a tiger. She made sure that they got into conversation when he was doing his cool down and he asked her to go for coffee in the café. To her relief, he was only ten years younger than her and, although he had three children, he lived alone. He ran a youth club and worked out on his evening off, Monday, as well as Thursday mornings.

The following Monday she went 'training' and offered him a lift home when they coincidentally were leaving at the same time. She drove him to a four-storied block with a communal garden in front and clean, fresh smelling corridors and stairs. No push-chairs, graffiti or lurking youths, she thought with relief.

His flat was modern, and very tidy. There was one wall of books, mostly classics, and another of CD's. She followed him into his kitchen. Marble effect floor and oak effect cabinets. Why was she assuming that they weren't the real thing? And what was she expecting? A scruffy pad with well thumbed copies of 'Nuts' and 'Zoo' lying around everywhere? He was opening a bottle of Chilean Shiraz, filling a little bowl with mixed nuts and putting on a CD. She thought it might be Beethoven. They discussed a few current films, which she hadn't seen, but had read the reviews and then he asked her about her husband. "He's gone," she said flippantly.

"Gone where?"

"Oh, just gone off with his PA. We're divorcing."

"Your relationship broke down?"

She felt a twinge of guilt. "I took him for granted I suppose and overstepped the mark."

"Did you know he'd met someone else?"

"Not really, I just thought he was leaning on her. I was too wrapped up in my own life. He's not the two timing type. I just went too far once too often."

"How have you been?"

"Ok, fine," she lied. "Busy, busy. Starting up a new life."

She was warm and comfortable, so slipped off her 'Marni' biker jacket. He lent over to refill her glass and she felt the fringes of his breath raising the hairs on her arm. She heard a rushing sound, which was probably the blood in her head and there was a trembling, melting feeling inside her.

"Let's go to bed," he said. "No strings, just for the enjoyment."

She took a deep breath. 'The only way to get rid of temptation is to yield to it.'* A man after her own heart.

"Great," said Mathew. "That sounded great. Let's try the 'Rutter' next. Hands up those who need a copy of the music. I'll sing the soprano part through to remind you, then we'll break it down and practise."

The choir was improving and, thanks to their new website, they had been joined by some younger, better singers. Their repertoire had become more classical and they had been practising part of Handel's

176

Messiah for the Easter concert. It's so beautiful. Even if we sing it badly, it's still inspiring, Frances thought. The first time they sang it all the way through, despite the mistakes, they were lost in the glory of it. Their eyes alight.

"Well done, we're getting there. Keep the joy, the vitality. Tone it down a bit bases, it's not a drinking song. Sopranos, a bit more confidence please and altos, lighten up, it's a bit flat and dreary. How many people have practised with their midi files?"

Six people put their hands up.

"By next week, you have to know every word and every note. Try and practise every day, and get together with other singers."

Daniel sat up in bed and saw Laura's dark head on the pillow in the little pool of light through the curtains. There was a rustle as she turned in her sleep. She was not thrashing, wriggling about and sighing. The agony inside her must be seeping out. He had become used to being able to drop off with Laura moving around but now guilt often kept him awake. Daisy would still be here if he had not opened his mouth…

Laura woke suddenly. What time was it? She lifted her head to find Dan sitting on the bed, the sleeves of his painting shirt rolled up and the front buttons absent-mindedly left undone, showing his taut abdomen. He was sketching her in the light that came in from the landing. She was un-nerved. Conscious that she was lying on her back, naked and cold, hipbones sticking out like bookends and diminutive breasts splayed under her armpits. What was he seeing? She knew that the years had nibbled away at the contours of her face and it had blurred into soft sagginess, so when she lay down it slid downwards as if formless jelly. "No, No, don't!" she cried, rolling off the bed and pulling on her dressing gown.

A visual image of a Freud painting flashed into her mind and his promiscuous lifestyle with it. "I don't want to be exhibited on a wall. I don't want you to do a portrait of me. And don't get obsessed with painting nudes. For all sorts of reasons. What time is it?" She picked up her clock from the bedside table. "Five o'clock! I'm getting some

177

sleepy tea and going back to sleep."

When Dan had retired he had begun by trying to paint still life, then experimented with finding new ways of seeing objects. He had flirted with surrealism and cubism in bright colours and reduced objects to three solid shapes: cube, sphere and cone. Chunky abstracts had been followed by dark, brooding symbolism. Then it was Jackson Pollock's paint drips and splatters, followed by reductionism, where he took the colour and content from the work. Now he wanted a complete change, to try portraits.

Later, they had finished tea and Laura was standing framed against the window, the early evening sun burnishing her brown hair to gold. He could not really see her expression, but thought it was probably the usual anguished, haunted one she had adopted since Daisy left. She looked beautiful, but he did not say. It would seem frivolous if she were mourning Daisy.

"How am I going to see if I can do life drawings then? I've got to practise on someone," he said quietly.

"I don't want to sit for you. I'm too hideous and you might make me worse. I don't want you staring at me with your head on one side, screwing up your eyes, measuring me with your brush held up, like they do in films. I'll feel stupid! *And* life's too short to sit around doing nothing. Oh god, don't make me feel guilty. Well...just start for half an hour now. I'll try and think about a short story I'm trying to write."

She settled down in the kitchen in a sitting pose, staring at the window as directed. He started to sketch, a workmanlike frown on his face. She could hear the scratch of the charcoal and his steady breathing. Her back started to ache. She wanted to write something down, rub her head, blow her nose. She could feel panic rising. To distract herself, she started to think about a plot for a novel. "People are mysteries, even those who're close to you, don't you think?"

"Mmm," he grunted absent mindedly.

"You never really know what people are thinking and feeling, do you? We never really understand others. Just ourselves and perhaps not that much then. Perhaps I could write a novel to help us

178

understand one another. Showing how people think and act in certain situations. Perhaps a group of newly retired women. That would be worthwhile, wouldn't it?" She turned to look at him.

He sighed and put down his pad. "You can go if you want to, you're obviously going to wriggle and fret, you're hopeless."

It was another shining, perfect spring morning, with balmy air, flawless blue sky and birds carrying twigs for their nests. The patch of green on the corner before the shops was a mass of daffodils, some trampled by children and dogs.

"I read an article in 'The Sunday Times' yesterday, about how infections caught from pools have rocketed, particularly through some nasty intestinal parasite, and bacteria such as E. coli. Why are we doing this?" asked Jo.

"Hmm, I bet it didn't say that swimming is the best activity for mind, body and spirit. How it helps stress and perks you up when you're tired. It's probably better than Prozac, which doctors dish out too often, did it?" Laura said crossly.

"And it's the most popular sport," said Beth. "Or is that fishing...or...or football?"

Jo had been thumbing her iPhone. "Look, here it is. The parasite is called cryptosporidium and it says that there are particles of faeces, urine and waterborne viruses such as hepatitis A, and even threadworm! Too many people are allowed access to the pool and when big classes of children have swimming lessons, they are swimming in a sea of contaminants and murky water from all the dead skin cells. Disgusting!"

"Well, we have to keep fit somehow. Would you prefer to sit at home getting older, stiffer, deafer, your teeth falling out...losing your memory? The days merging into one another, as you rush towards your end?"

"Oh for goodness sake Laurs, pack it in. At least she wouldn't be lonely, she's got her iPhone." Lynne said sarcastically.

"Don't get her on social media." Jo groaned.

Undaunted Lynne carried on: "Us humans have never shared so much, so publicly. We're tweeting, Instagramming, Facebooking,

179

Snapchatting, taking selfies,, sending emojis. But we don't tell the truth. It's just boasting about our perfect glossy lifestyles, not mentioning the bad and boring bits. We don't tell the truth, yet we believe what other people write. It's just relentless boasting for one-upmanship. No wonder there's so much depression around!"

Daniel didn't really comment either way to suggestions of Laura's for their social life. He often did not seem to hear. There would be a silence and then he would carry on with whatever had been in his head, as if she had never spoken. She bought tickets for plays and films and invited friends to supper and he would look surprised, but went along with it. If it were a large theatre and a long play, his heart would sink. The warmth and darkness of the auditorium and the slowness of some of the plays made his eyelids droop. Every few minutes his head would loll forward and he would jerk it up as a reflex action. Laura would stick her elbow into him and he would wonder if he had snored. She would often regale friends with the time when he and his close friend Garry were sitting a few rows behind Laura and Pria and had both snored so loudly that an attendant had asked them to leave if they could not stay awake.

But then often he would make a perceptive rejoinder to something she had said or suggested some days before, as if there had been no interval. He had obviously been mulling it over. She was used to this, as she was when he went off on solitary walks for the day or weekend. He had said: "I need space. I've never explored the possibilities inside myself. I don't know my shape; I haven't yet grown edges…"

"Wha…aat?"

"Art is about the journey to find out who you are…letting your inside come out."

She was pretty sure he loved her, but sometimes he felt cramped and oppressed by her. This had been fine when Daisy was around, they had enjoyed mother and daughter time, but now…

Laura lengthened her stride as the first heavy drops thumped down onto her uncovered head. "Should have brought my mac,

180

should have driven today," she muttered to herself. "Why do I always think I should walk instead of ride?" The March morning had looked brilliant through the bedroom window, but the sun had gone. She turned the corner and a vicious wind snatched her breath away and blasted her with sheets of stinging rain. Cold droplets trickled down her neck.

Head down she marched on, cars sailing past carrying warm, dry people. "Haven't they got legs?" she thought bitterly. "Hey, look where you're driving."

The pool was calm and blue. Only quiet swimmers who did not disturb the water glided up and down. Her arms and legs felt powerful as they arrowed into the water. Pulling it towards and behind, smoothly, no splashes. After twenty minutes, she floated on her back, her knees to one side, arms to the other. She was rejuvenated and suffused with peace and calm.

Her shower gave her that clean, aerated, relaxed feeling, mixed with the virtuousness of having got up early and done her exercise for the day. Perhaps she should be grateful to Dan. There was no more baby-sitting and the rest of Wednesday lay before her.

On the way home she stopped off at Annie's house and determinedly rang the bell. "What's up with you, you've become a hermit?"

Annie stared at her friend, aware that she looked wrecked, with red-rimmed eyes and greasy hair. People would have to know some time. She took a deep breath and plunged on with bravado. "I've lost my weekly column and Martin left me. I'm having trouble believing it, but no lawyer has been in touch, so perhaps he's sulking somewhere."

Laura felt tears rising. When she got home, she rushed to tell Dan.

"I could never have imagined Annie not being in control and going to pieces like this. She won't come out, even for a walk and rarely answers her phone, emails or texts. She trampled all over poor Martin, used him as her whipping boy and, now she's driven him out, she misses his support. It's tragic. I love Annie, but she has treated Martin terribly. I'm surprised he didn't walk out before. I told her that. She constantly demeaned him. What matters more than love in the long run is respect. Caring how the other one feels. Wanting to know what they think and finding it interesting and important. Contempt is a killer."

Dan was always the placator. "We don't know the whole story. We just know what we see from the outside. Which may well be wrong. We don't really know what went on or how they came to split up. Don't jump to conclusions. Perhaps their relationship was only bad in public." He thought for a moment. "Though it does seem as if he's been suppressing his anger and frustration for years. Just to keep the peace."

"Yeh, I suppose she had it coming. Always goading him."

"People get ill and die from all that suppressed anger. I don't know why you put up with her. She's a pain."

"You know why. We've played tennis and been mates for years. In some things we're very different, but in others we're so similar. We've both got a big appetite for life. We complement one another. And she cares about me."

"Hmm," Dan looked unconvinced, but decided not to pursue his thoughts and turned and went off upstairs

Annie had lost the habit of regular meals and anyway her back hurt, her legs were stiff and her hands didn't seem to belong to her. After Laura left, she felt really rough. Perhaps a drink, she hadn't been drinking much lately. No wine in the rack. What's in the drinks cupboard? Whisky, ugh. She fumbled with the top of the whisky bottle, managed to pour herself a glass and dragged herself to bed with it.

Waking, in some timeless expanse of the night, she was on fire, covered in sweat and her heart was pounding. "I'm going to be sick." She carefully slid out of bed and blundered towards the bathroom, throwing up in the bidet, as the nearest receptacle. Pulling on the light cord she fell against the sink and saw herself, a greenish, ancient ghost in the mirror above. Sipping at some water in the tooth-mug, she staggered back to bed, wanting Martin more than ever.

Before dawn she was sick again and realised she had a raging temperature. Lying there all day, she floated through a fever. In and out of fitful sleep. Was it the whisky? Was there something wrong with the whisky?

On the second day her temperature seemed to be even higher. She had sipped water, but eaten nothing. She thought she had heard the phone and doorbell, but she could have imagined them. Her heart was beating too hard. She could not breathe. There seemed to be holes in her head and the world was pouring in. Her ears were bursting with the noise of her blood. That afternoon she grew wings and soared through the ceiling and out over the houses and gardens. She saw Laura walking towards her house and suddenly her friend was bending over her.

"I know you said I wasn't to use your key, but I've been ringing and ringing. You look awful!"

Her tongue had become loft insulation and her lips swollen and cracked. "Ill," she managed to croak.

Laura gently wiped her face, her arms, her chest with a cool flannel. "How long have you been like this?"

Annie had no idea.

"You're not on drugs or anything are you?"

She shook her head.

"Can you manage some soup?" And she was on the phone, instructing Dan to bring soup and bread. Then speaking to their doctor and doing all the things that Martin would have done. Her heart filled with gratitude that someone cared, that it was going to be Ok. "I love you, Laurs," she whispered.

Laura was getting ready for an old friend, Janet, to come to tea. She loved getting out the bone china, linen napkins, silver teapot and jugs, doilies and cake stand. Oh, and the special cake knife. She was smearing lemon curd on the tops of the courgette cakes, when a scene from five years or so ago flooded into her head.

Dan had gone off to walk around the Isle of Wight for the weekend. She had dithered until she heard the weather forecast and then decided not to do a route march in the rain.

Daisy had rung to say that she was in London. Weren't her exams in two weeks? The doorbell rang, and here she was. They stared at one another, analysing clothes, hair, expressions, looking for the alter egos of old. Laura put out her arms and they embraced awkwardly. Daisy was strangely stiff and pulled back quickly. She turned away and walked ahead to the kitchen, her familiar proud swagger bringing tears to Laura's eyes.

"This is a nice surprise. I love your dress."

She looked back with a strained smile and guarded eyes.

They made polite conversation while Laura made tea, then they went into the conservatory where Daisy stood looking at the garden and there was an uncomfortable silence. Laura cut the still warm walnut and banana cake. What has happened to make us such strangers, she thought. Then suddenly Daisy blurted out: "Mum, I'm pregnant!"

Pregnant, pregnant, pregnant, the word reverberated round the room. Was that scream my voice? Pregnant? Icicles formed deep inside Laura and swelled and mounted up, up. She felt as if her heart had stopped. Ice broke out on her clammy skin. She stared at Daisy. At her soft vulnerability.

"Why, Daisy, why?" She could not help her horror. Daisy hadn't started her adult life yet. "Who?"

She shook her head, she wasn't telling.

"How long have you known?"

She admitted that she was four months gone and had known for two. Laura could not stop the recriminations tumbling out.

"You've got another year at university. You're only a baby yourself. How do you think you're going to live? Why didn't you tell me before? Is the father pleased?"

"I haven't told him yet," she admitted.

"Will he want a child?"

Daisy's features bunched together. Her lower lip trembled for a second, then hardened defiantly. "I don't know. I'll have to discuss it with him. I'll live with him or something. I don't know yet."

Laura felt desperate. It was just the wrong time in Daisy's life.

"You got pregnant with me," she said accusingly.

"Yeh, but I was so much older with a house and a job. I could support you."

184

Laura threw practicalities at her, which she clearly didn't want to think about. How had she become this strange, separate entity? So impenetrable, incomprehensible her head down concentrating on twisting her napkin and playing with her cake. She stared at her daughter realising that they were not inhabiting the same world. Hers is the one that I have grown out of, lost through becoming old, but in any case it has irrevocably altered since I was young. I love her so much, but for all our past closeness, I can't fathom what is going on in her head. She searched in vain through the layers of her experiences for a common chord, any tiny bedraggled experience that she could offer as something they had in common, so she could say: Yes, I felt that, did that…But she could think of nothing. Laura did not know how to communicate with her daughter.

"What do you want to do? Do you want to come home?"

Her face was expressionless, stony eyed, like a defiant child. "I'll work it out. Be happy for me. That's what I want."

"I'm here for you always. Don't struggle on your own," Laura said as Daisy got up to leave.

Pregnant! The word went round and round in Laura's head, the letters undoing and dancing around in an incoherent jumble. How will she manage? She found herself in the kitchen, without knowing how she got there, or why she came. I should have been more restrained, more supportive. She is obviously harbouring grudges from her childhood and I confirmed her prejudices.

Daisy, that tiny, clinging child who always wanted to learn. The shy but composed teenager with her vast inner life…this chaotically untidy, unemployed pregnant young woman. How will she cope with her finals and supporting herself?

We used to discuss everything, listing the advantages and disadvantages, so we could work out what was best. Or was it what I thought was best? I often ended up doing things for her; she knew I would if she didn't bother. Was this symptomatic? Oh God it was my fault. I've made her into a dependent person who relies on others to get her through life.

She shook the memories out of her head and screwed the top back onto the lemon curd and put it back in the fridge.

185

Chapter 13. March. New Beginnings?

'And frosts are slain and flowers begotten,
And in green underwood and cover
Blossom by blossom the Spring begins.'
Algernon Charles Swinburne 'Atalanta in Calydon.' (1837-1909)

It had been a whole week of shining weather. Laura had been waking to each fresh new day with a blackbird's song outside her window.

The walk to the pool was in the morning mist and back under blue, cloudless skies. Their spirits were lifted in these perfect spring days, warm air and blossom everywhere. The silver swimmers were in full force. Unfortunately, so were all the other regulars and more. The sun brought everyone out, with thoughts of getting fitter and toning up for summer. Beth was feeling grumpy as there were far too many new people in her lane, who were not giving way at either end to faster swimmers, and some were dangerously stopping and standing up, mid length.

"Did you see that biggish woman in the blue costume, swimming in my lane?" she asked as they walked home.

"Mmm, yes, why?"

"She was thrashing all over the place, hitting us, she couldn't swim straight and she looked like a gorilla, black hair everywhere, not just her legs and armpits."

"Poor thing, but perhaps it's a feminist statement? I stopped shaving my armpits years ago. Three cheers for her right to be *au naturel*? Two fingers to you body fascists?" Lynne said irritatedly.

"Agreed, it's gendered bullshit. The media are responsible for the smooth hair-free look." Laura said. "I was so mad at Daisy, when after I'd given her all the reasons why she shouldn't start shaving her little golden hairs off, she succumbed to pressure from her friends and had a nothing-left-behind Brazilian."

"I suppose that's true," agreed Beth.

"So shouldn't the sisterhood let the hairy lady do what she likes without censure? Waxing is a tyranny. If we want the full bush, we should have choice and not give a damn, I say. Bye, guys." Lynne peeled off at the corner and headed towards Tesco.

"What about older women wearing little bikinis then?" Beth continued. "You'd think that other lady in my lane would be embarrassed with that crinkly, sagging stomach and the stretchmark's everywhere." She turned to Jo and Helen, walking behind. "What do you think about large ladies wearing bikini's, Jo?"

"Annoying, if we're talking about Rosa. We introduced ourselves when she swum into the lane divider and me today, with her pounding thighs and rear of a tank, but for all I care, she could go commando. We're not the style police."

Beth ignored her sarcasm and continued. "Would you wear a bikini then?"

"My skin's no longer sumptuous, I've got the odd wrinkle and sag, but, on a hot summer's day, if I'd had a Brazilian, well, yes, sure. Who cares? There's all shapes and sizes in that pool."

Most of the retired population of north London seemed to be at Tesco's. Big trollies and grey heads blocked every 3 for 2 offer. Lynne waited, seething as Mr retired-and-there's-no-rush, examined every single packet of tuna twice, before deciding on one and moving out of the way. They all seemed oblivious of other shoppers, shrink wrapped in their shrunken, smug, fussy worlds. Is this *me* now, lingering over the soap powders, comparing sizes and product claims, intent on saving a few pence? Am I part of the ten million, grey, affluent, bored pensioners whose routine is to shop in the morning rather than the evening grab and dash? Shuffling around, examining every item. Spinning out the time before lunch. Agh!

Later the other swimmers went shopping, though to different places. Laura took the tube to Oxford Street as soon as the shops opened, to buy Ruby and Lily a birthday present or two, in case there was a miracle and Daisy contacted her. Helen did a tour of the local high street charity shops where she bought a blouse, a colander, two plates and three books.

And Jo went with Beth to buy something to wear to a cousin's daughter's wedding and James's retirement dinner.

Beth was feeling nervous, her stomach in knots. She stared desperately into her wardrobe, as if something new and exciting could have materialised inside it. It's only going shopping, she kept saying to herself, but the thought of spending time choosing clothes at West End shops with Jo was exciting but also a nerve wracking prospect. Going swimming with her was different. Laura and sometimes Helen, Frances or Lynne were there and there were so many other women chatting and laughing in the changing rooms. She had never been actually alone with Jo before.

Jo was wearing a Prada black trouser suit, a red printed silk top and her Manolos. Beth had resorted to jeans and her purple fleece. She zipped it up, sighing at the sight of her arthritic knuckles.

They walked down towards the tube station in silence.

"You're quiet?" Jo remarked

"I've never done anything much, so don't have a lot that's interesting to say and you all told me off about criticising those women at swimming," Beth sighed.

"You were just cheesed off with their swimming etiquette. You must have noticed that people like talking to you, because you're interested. You're a good listener. Most conversations take the form of alternating acts of self-assertion, statements of opinion. The other person waits until the speaker finishes, but they've rarely listened, they've been preparing their next opinion. Most people don't know how to communicate. You do."

"Thanks. That sounds cynical. What's the point of talking to anyone then? Anyway, I hate shopping. I'm forced to look at myself in mirrors. I don't want to see that dreary spreading woman, with lines around her eyes, a badger stripe in her hair and comfortable clothes."

"You are funny," Jo smiled. "You're an attractive woman. You know I dye my hair too and none of us look like we did when we were young. The amount of maintenance involving hair is so time consuming and expensive. Older women look so much younger than they used to and its not through better living or diet or exercise. It's because of hair dye! Sometimes I think that the advantage of death is that one wouldn't have to worry about ones hair any more. Come on, we're here."

Beth puffed along behind Jo out of the tube and into Oxford Street. "I'm ashamed. I let myself go when I was a full time mother. I never had the time or interest in my appearance. I feel like Les Dawson. My feet have spread. Do you know I used to wear five now it's six. That Trinny and Suzannah tell us to wear heels all the time. What a joke, I'd be on crutches after fifteen minutes. I tried a bit when I was teaching, but soon went back to flats. Where has that passionate, flashing-eyed young woman gone, full of conviction about what to wear and where I was going? These sturdy legs and doughy fat round my hips have to squeeze into my size sixteen jeans. I look in the mirror and everything is drooping down towards my feet. I feel like a runaway hippo which has blundered into a washing line. What happened to me?"

"You just need to pay a bit more attention to your appearance, as does James. Tell him that the best way to hide a guy gut is not in Billy Bunter outfits, but darker colours and nothing clingy. Most men need steering. So come on, you're an attractive woman. Be confident. Where do you want to go first? 'Donna Karan,' 'Nicole Fahri?' You can never be overdressed."

"Oh no, not designer shops. I don't know, anywhere. How about John Lewis? Then Debenhams and House of Fraser?"

Jo was starting to despair. Beth was a hopeless shopper. She gravitated to every sale rail with grey or black, high necked, capacious cover-ups. She tried a few on, but looked like a walking tent. They went to have a coffee in a side street and there opposite was a small shop with 'Closing Down Sale' plastered all over its windows. They finished their lattes "Come on, we may as well look in here," Jo said.

Beth reluctantly followed her across and inside, then stood helplessly gazing around. "There's nothing suitable," she said.

"Just try something on. How about this?" Jo fished an emerald green silk jersey dress with a wrap over top off a crowded rail.

Beth held it against herself. "I need to lose some weight first. This'll cling and make me look like an elephant."

"No it won't. You can wear a rollon and a good bra. That neckline will show off your cleavage and it's cut so well. Try it on and you'll see."

"I shouldn't be buying any clothes, not until I lose weight anyway. I'm much too fat for this."

"Don't be ridiculous. I've told you, you're a beautiful woman. It'll take pounds off you."

Beth squirrelled this comment away to examine it later. Not many people tell you anything about yourself and she was unused to being flattered. "But it's green. I don't know if I can wear green."

"What colour do you want? Minimum risk magnolia? Tweed? Rusk? Green's the new black. It'll look tasteful and sophisticated."

Beth peeled off her jeans, past legs covered in dark hairs that she had ignored for weeks. It didn't seem to matter at swimming. She piled her clothes on the red velvet stool, afraid to look in the bright mirror.

"Let me do the zip up for you. See I told you!" Jo was triumphant.

She dared to look and was startled. "It's a flattering mirror. It's taken pounds off me!" She stood on tiptoes as if she were wearing heels and saw a flash of the slim, vivacious girl she once was.

"You can wear it with a jacket for the wedding. There are some perfect ones in Warehouse and it can be your party dress with a pashmina for James's leaving bash and it's only £99! Right, let's get you a decent bra now."

They came out of the shop and onto Oxford Street, where Jo turned left.

"Shouldn't we be going right? Marks & Spencers is towards Marble Arch."

"No, we're going to a proper shop, where you'll be fitted."

"There's nothing wrong with M&S. I always buy my bras there."

"You wait til you see the difference." And down New Bond Street they went.

It was busy but Beth found herself being steered towards the only empty fitting room.

"This shop will be far too expensive," she whispered.

"Shhh! Do you want a great shape or not?" Jo hissed back.

Beth sat, considering whether it was worth possibly losing Jo's friendship and running off, but a fitter was approaching. "Good Morning, madam. I'm Chantelle. What would you like today?"

"A bra and latex knickers, please," said Jo quickly.

"I've got a perfectly good pair of control pants. Just the bra please." Beth countered.

Chantelle closed the curtain of the fitting room and indicated for Beth to take off her jumper. She stood studying her upper body, flesh bulging over the top and out of the sides of her rather old bra. She was hot, sweaty and deeply ashamed feeling like a white whale. A lump of blubber.

"This bra is the wrong size and shape for you, madam. It's not comfortable, is it?"

Beth thought, "Well no, I don't think I've ever had a truly comfortable one. My breasts are so heavy. See?" And she lifted her shoulder strap to expose deep red weals underneath.

"It gives you no support and look at this." She pointed to her puckered, wrinkled cleavage, then measured Beth's cup size and distance between her breasts. Slipping a tape measure around her back she said, "You'll see what a good fitting bra can do," and off she went.

"You wait til you see the transformation." Jo sat on the plush silver chair, looking pleased with herself.

Chantelle reappeared with two beautiful little silver bags each containing a bra. "Let's try the 'Fantasie' first." She carefully opened one and told Beth to lean over so her breasts dangled into the cups, while she fastened the back then expertly eased them into the black satin. Beth looked in the mirror, and saw a miracle. There were no wrinkles, no puckers. Her breasts rose gently above the lace edge, looking smooth and young looking. A wave of excitement and pride flowed through her. Within minutes she had succumbed to a pair of high waisted support pants, with legs ending above the knee, to reduce her thighs and a strong panel in the front.

"Do I have to wear high heels? I've never been able to walk properly in them." Beth looked fearfully down at Jo's four-inch spikes.

"You're right. The omnipotent Trinny and Suzannah tell us to wear heels at all times, even with jeans. But, don't worry, mid heels are the hottest shoe height. I'm just in love with my stripper Louboutins

191

and Manolos. Get a hand sized clutch, sheer black tights, not too much bling and red lippy and you'll look fab."

Jo wanted to 'just have a look' down South Molton Street, so Beth set off home, elatedly clutching her packages. The late afternoon sun had come out and she felt like dancing and singing. As the tube reached her stop her wave of euphoria drained away. Perhaps they had been trick mirrors and she had spent all that money to look ridiculous.

Do new clothes always seem like a new beginning? By wearing them our lives could be different? But there were other more pressing questions: what would she cook for James for supper? Did he let Michal in to fit a new lock on the side gate? The shopping trip slid to the back of her mind.

The clocks went forward today. Under the dull, grey sky the trees had dressed in their spring green and danced and thrashed about in the cold north-east wind and flurries of rain. It was chilly and Laura felt old and stiff.

"I actually did some writing yesterday," she confided to Jo as they walked to the gym. "It's so sort of inspiring when it goes well."

"What were you writing? Chick lit?"

"Hardly."

"Nothing wrong with chick lit, Ok, some's awful, like Jackie Collins, but there's also Jilly Cooper and Jane Austen! The industry's powered by women. You could do worse."

"Mmm, perhaps it's going to be 'granny lit'."

It was only a week until James's leaving party. Beth thought she would model the dress for him, in case he did not approve. After dinner she put on her tights, new bra and pantie girdle and a pair of earrings, which looked good with the dress and holding her pashmina, paraded up and down the lounge. "You look beautiful," he said. "An excellent choice."

"You really like it?" she asked, smoothing the material down over her hips. "Really?"

"You look wonderful," he said, but he was already reaching for

192

his glass of wine and 'The Telegraph' and his attention on her was over. Her initial thrill seeped away. She wanted so much to bask in it for a little while longer. She was so unused to being admired.

The air was warm and soft with the faint scent of apple and cherry in bloom. Rich, dark, pale and shiny greens and flowers everywhere. A heron flapped lazily, high above them and Laura wished she had remembered to put the cover on their pond. They were cleaned out of frogs last year. The new goldfish stood no chance.

It had rained overnight and Terry had found her shoots of lupins and delphiniums, bitten off at the tips. She was completely despondent. The slugs and snails must have been out in force in Laura's garden too. Why isn't she depressed? Is it because I've never controlled much in my life, so I expect the plants at least to do what I expect them to do? Or am I being silly?

She breast stroked down one length, then returned slowly on her back, legs only, exulting in the blue sky and water and the blue of the lavender in the raised flower bed outside. The rhythmic movements free from the downward pull of gravity were meditative. It had taken so long to feel normal, to get a foothold on a normal life. My head is getting better. I'm calmer, can think more clearly, but when is my energy going to come back and this annoying cough go. Two more lengths and she was shattered. "I'm going to have a very long shower. Don't get out," she called to Laura.

The hot water made her feel a little better, but she was tired and her back and shoulders hurt.

"How do you feel?" asked Laura, when she joined her under the shower.

"Ok now, thanks. I've been getting bronchitis twice a year for some years. It's really dragging on this time and I was short of breath. I enjoyed it though, but I'm just not fit."

"How are you managing on your own?"

"Not bad, I suppose. I used to think that those people who said, 'Not a day goes by that I don't think of him,' were exaggerating. Using quaint hyperbole, but now I know that it's true." She did not add how she still heard the sounds of his feet on the stairs, his occasional snorts as he slept next to her and the rattling, clinking noises as he washed up every evening.

"Come on Friday again then. You just need to build up slowly."

Frances had a text. "Sculpt exhib RA 2morrow 11? Martin."

Why not? They had talked about it and he was a Royal Academy member...

She was early, so went into the ladies and checked her face and hair. I don't look too bad for nearly fifty-nine, but then who cared what she looked like? Why am I doing this? There was a nervous flutter in her stomach and a slightly sick feeling. He's probably just being friendly and wants someone to discuss the exhibition with. She went out into the foyer and there he was. Near the door. He was losing his hair at the back. Is he mid-sixties? Then he turned and smiled and she forgot about his age as he kissed her cheek and shepherded her into the gallery with old-fashioned courtesy.

Lunch was very pleasant, the fish delicious and she even relaxed her rule of not drinking in the day time and had a couple of glasses of Muscadet.

An ex-colleague of Martin's joined them. He loved the Epstein, Hepworth and Moore sculptures, which Frances found incomprehensible. "They're like those smooth pebbles you find on the beach," Martin said. "You want to run your hands over them, but as to their meaning?"

Neither man liked Adam or Queen Victoria or the athlete struggling with a python, that Frances preferred. After her second glass of wine she started to feel warm and prickly and quite attracted to Martin. Go away now, Paul, she thought. I want Martin to talk to me now, just me. I haven't thought like this about a man since I was in university. Am I desirable? She couldn't imagine so. She was conscious of her 'sensible' clothes, her no nonsense short haircut, her complete inexperience with men. Why should he be interested? He's still married. He's probably lonely and I'm a substitute companion to go to galleries and lunch with. Is he flirting with me, or just being kind and friendly? He seems interested in my life, what I do with my time.

Perhaps Paul was telepathic, because he stood up and said he had to go.

To Frances' surprise, Martin then talked to her honestly about the breakdown of his marriage.

"She treated me like a punch bag. I couldn't go on with so little tenderness and support. I needed to be loved, to be cared for, just occasionally. We never talked, I just got shouted at."

"Well, don't most long marriages get into a rut? If you both try, couldn't you go back to how it was?"

He shook his head. "I tried often enough. It's just gone too far. There is no love or desire left. Perhaps it's my fault. I've been too compliant. Though the person in my head is so different from the person I am in the world. I wish my inner person would come out more often but I can't help trying to please."

He put his hand over hers. It was cool and smooth and his nails were clean and manicured.

"Shall we walk down to the embankment? I don't feel like going back to my little room just yet."

Her heart gave a little lurch and she felt like a giddy teenager. They wandered through Green Park, dog walkers everywhere. How many dogs were they allowed now? Young men in their tribal casual gear pushing strollers or playing with small children, yummy mummies trailing behind, their mobiles clamped to their ears. Two old homeless men sat on a bench, drinking cider.

They worked their way down to the South Bank. The cafes and restaurants were busy and the riverside was packed with sauntering people. Across the dark grey river was Somerset House, and Charing Cross Bridge. Youths showed off their skills, skate-boarding in their concrete undercroft. Outside the National Theatre a reggae band was playing and tables were heaving with second hand books.

They reached the Tate Modern and looked around for a while, then bought fish and chips and some cans of lager and sat on a bench looking at the glittering river, the bright buildings and the boats passing.

"Are you in a relationship?" Martin asked.

She gave a wry smile. "I decided long ago that romance and love are not my forte. I've worked with plenty of men, but I was wedded to work. From as long as I can remember I hated my mother's unwaged status and her servitude, her everlasting domesticity, though she always said she was happy with her lot. It's never been for me though."

They found that they remembered the words of many of the Beatles songs and wandered over Charing Cross Bridge lightheaded with alcohol softly singing "When I get older, losing my hair..." Into the tube station and he gave her hand a squeeze, kissed her cheek and waved as she went towards the north travelling line, while he went off into the west corridor.

Her world had suddenly become upbeat, suffused with light. Could she fall in love, after all these years?

It was Friday. The damp morning air smelled fresh, sharp and expectant. The fecund earth stirred with green shoots. Was it Spring?

Terry felt rather weak, but was meeting the others, so determinedly dressed and went out when Laura rang the bell. Before they got to the end of the road she was panting and feeling rather faint. She sat on a garden wall as the world drifted about.

"Shall I go back and get the car? We don't *have* to walk," said Beth.

"No, no, I'll be fine in a minute when I get my breath back," Terry insisted.

In the pool she managed two lengths and a long shower, then Bruna offered them a lift home. Terry was hugely relieved.

"Why don't you go and see your doctor? That cough doesn't sound good," Lynne advised.

In the next few days she had chest pains, shortness of breath and even coughed up a trace of blood. "You've lost rather a lot of weight," her doctor observed when she walked into his surgery.

Within a week, she had had a chest x-ray and an appointment with a consultant.

"Tell me everything," Terry said to the serious looking middle aged lady, Dr Errani.

"It is by no means certain that this dark area here on the x ray is

196

malignant and there is no evidence of metastasis. We need to do a bronchoscopy and biopsy. Any tiredness or dizziness?"

Describing her own symptoms sent a tremor of shock through her. Did she have secondary tumours in her lungs?

"But I was given the all clear…"

Laura had been approached by a pre-school centre to join the governors. She had been pondering the offer for a few days. Dan could never understand why she made decisions so tortuous. "You applied to be one, you need something to get your teeth into, what's the problem?"

"The children are only there for a year. The parents won't be interested in getting involved in such a short time. And they're *four* year olds!"

He looked puzzled. "So?"

"I'll be thinking about Lily and Ruby even more!"

Dan sighed and turned away.

After Annie had told Laura about Martin, she began to feel better. The huge burden felt lighter, she felt immensely relieved to have told someone. She wondered if she would feel even better if she told everyone. She picked up the phone and rung Helen. "Can you come round for a drink tonight? About eight thirty? Yes? Great, see you then.

Helen listened to a tirade about how Martin had gone off, Annie did not know where and how useless and spineless he was and ungrateful, and how she lost her job to a half-wit, Helen took a deep breath and started. "Annie, excuse me saying, but you're stuck in your old habits and patterns, it's called character sclerosis. When your circumstances change you have to, or slide downhill. You're making yourself miserable by only seeing the worst of every situation. A little self-reflection would be good here. Don't you think there is a tendency for you to see yourself as right and the rest of the world as wrong? Retract those claws. Lighten up and allow yourself to be happy. Laugh. Don't cling on to your misery, let it go. You're a clever, attractive woman, who is at a crisis point. Don't become a bitter old lady."

Annie opened her mouth to retort, then thought better of it.

"If you want to see an experienced counsellor, I can recommend a few. Too many people think that they can handle things themselves, but struggling alone can make things worse. You can move on, but it's very hard on your own, playing the same thing over and over in your head. Certain things are probably imprinted indelibly in your mind by now. The stain of them will stay there until you get help to remove them. You have to accept that most things are not in your control. We are all vulnerable. Don't be afraid of your vulnerability. And anti-depressants really could help you know." She refilled their glasses. "Let's drink to the new positive, happier Annie."

Next morning Annie got up, went into the bathroom and studied her jowly face in the mirror. *What am I doing to myself? I'm a respected food editor and I've been eating nothing or filling up with rubbish convenience food. I couldn't even be bothered to put a pizza in the oven on Sunday. I just ate chocolate. How dare I write 'Suppers for Slimmers' in 'Women's World.' They'll be sacking me too if they see me like this. When did I last play tennis or swim? Why don't I just take the quick way out and jump under a train...*

She went downstairs and into the kitchen. The sun streamed through the window, showing up all the bird poo and grime on the outside. Balls of dust drifted around gracefully. The water muttered in the pipes. Annie put her head in her hands. "The boiler has become temperamental, the drain and the washing machine are partly clogged, three knobs have come off drawers in the kitchen. I'm in a mess without you, Martin."

Laura dropped in after swimming and was pleased to see her up and dressed. "I was beginning to think that you'd never get out of that dressing gown!"

Annie sat her down and put the kettle on. "I haven't wanted to know before. I was afraid to actually find out." She poured boiling water onto the green tea bags and handed Laura a mug. "I suppose you know," she said.

"Know what?"

"Where Martin lives and if he's seeing someone?"

Laura felt a sinking feeling. "What's it matter?" she said evasively, concentrating on fishing out her tea bag.

"I'm ready to cope with knowing now. I want to know Laura. Who is it?" The words tumbled out as if they had been waiting for too long.

Laura looked beseechingly at her.

"Come on, who is it?"

"Well...he doesn't live with her. He's sharing a flat with that guy he used to work with, you know, Ray." There was a pause. "Are you sure you want to know?"

"Yes, who? Do I know her?"

"You met her in January at Jo's party. That girl who was a solicitor and was made redundant. She lives in the flat above Jo?"

Annie went cold. All colour drained from her skin and she could feel herself starting to shake, to choke, to sob. So he *is* with another woman! She stared out of the window at the garden, turning wild without Martin to contain it. "Her!" She said venomously. "Her! She's not even attractive."

That night she sat at the kitchen table, unable to eat or drink. She felt numb, veering between panic and disbelief and in a world she didn't recognise, where nothing was as she thought it should be. She imagined Martin was there. "You're not serious about Frances, are you? You wouldn't do anything to hurt me, would you?" She stood up and sudden terror pushed itself up into her throat from deep inside and she clung to the sink, sick with fear. How was she going to live her life now?

Chapter 14. April. Health shocks

'I am the master of my fate:
I am the captain of my soul.'
W.E. Henley. 'Invictus.' (1849 – 1903)

A vicious east wind kept most of the silver swimmers at home. The daffodils had withered and some of the trees were unseasonably bare, waiting for some warmth to unfurl their leaves. Only the hawthorn has dared to start. There were racing clouds and intermittent sun and a blizzard of early plum blossom like snow in the blustering wind as Laura and Beth walked to the pool.

"I had a letter yesterday inviting me to be a Governor at Highfield."

Beth smiled. "Oh good, that's nice and near and you know some of the teachers from choir."

"Yes, If Ruby and Lily were here, that's where they'd go." She sighed and they walked the rest of the way deep in their own thoughts.

It was crowded and the water was cool, so they swam briskly around the standing and the slow. After fifteen minutes, they still felt cold, so retired to the showers.

Terry had an appointment with her consultant. Dr Errani was explaining the results of her tests: "I'm afraid that the tests show that the cancer has spread. There are metastatic, secondary tumours in your lungs."

Terry's brain stopped. She stared at Dr Errani's shiny black, Mont Blanc pen, which she was twisting round and round in her hand. She started to shake, "What?"

"We will try and control the growth of the tumours and relieve the symptoms."

"How?" she swallowed. She could barely speak.

"Surgery and chemotherapy."

I can't take any more. Why can't I just die now, she thought. She knew that there were dozens of questions she should be asking, but her mind was blank and she could feel the tears coming, and there they were, pouring down her face. A box of tissues was pushed towards her. "Does everyone cry?"

"No, but you have had to cope with rather a lot recently. Apart from this shock, you're suffering from grief, which intensifies your moods, concentration and emotions."

Dr Errani was so gentle and solicitous, that Terry, excusing herself for a minute, locked herself in the toilet and sobbed. By the time she returned, she knew that she did not want any more treatment. "If I do nothing, how long will I live?" she asked.

Dr Errani looked surprised. "That is your prerogative, but you would be foolish to refuse treatment. And speculating about your future would be foolish until we operate. There is no way of knowing before."

"My parents and my brother died in their fifties. Cancer is common in my family." She thought of her brother suffering horribly with chemotherapy and dying anyway. "I want to think about all this. I'll let you know what I want to do." She almost ran out of the room.

She walked down the stairs to the entrance hall in a daze.

"I'm so glad to catch you."

Beth's voice...there was no escape.

"I was worried when I saw you here again. It's my break. Shall we have a cup of coffee?" She indicated the café behind her.

Terry was trapped, pinned down.

"Come on, you look so pale."

Caring and concern shone out from Beth. She seemed to have lived unaware of spitefulness, bitterness and hatred. She had a naïveté, an unworldliness about her. Although Terry recognised that she and Beth were similar, in that they had both lived their lives, doing what was expected of them, she was not the one Terry felt she could unburden herself to. She had always been loathe to discuss her illnesses anyway. Her mother had been unloving and unsympathetic and taught her to be stoical. If she told anyone it would be Laura, she would know what she should do. Somehow she had no confidence that Beth could do more than sympathise.

"It's the bronchitis," she said abruptly to Beth's questioning look.

"Oh dear. What have you been advised to do?"

"As we said, I must get fitter," she answered in desperation.

"Why don't you come swimming more often? Come tomorrow." Terry found herself agreeing.

Black clouds had massed by the time Terry reached home, and she shivered in the cold dark hall. They had not allowed themselves to have the heating on in the day, just a few hours from six til nine. Thick jumpers until then. She looked at her watch, only four fifteen. Why be abstemious? I don't have to be cold all the time. I can at least be warm, for my last few years, or months. She switched on the heating, recklessly turning up the thermostat and made herself a sandwich.

She had just finished it when the phone rang. "Hi, are you Ok?" Laura's voice.

"Yes of course, why not?"

"Well, Beth said you seemed shell shocked in the Royal Free. We were worried."

Terry's mind raced. Should she tell her? "I'm fine," she said, "just fine."

"You don't want to pop down for tea do you? I'm just about to cut a large slice of fruit cake for myself."

Part of her wanted to snuggle into bed and sob, but when was she going to tell someone? I'm not ready to talk about it. "I've just finished my late lunch. Can I have a rain-check on that," she said.

Laura had had an early hospital appointment for a bone scan. So having missed her morning swim, she decided to go at 2.45, just before the last school vacated the water and the pool got busy with lessons for the public. It was a dismal, damp day so she drove, changed and went into the pool. It smelt like a urinal. Twenty or so teenage boys were racing up and down in two thirds of the pool and the stress of competing had obviously made them empty their bladders. What a stink. Oh well. She got in, noticing another woman turning tail behind her. Didn't Rebecca Adlington say that all swimmers when they were training urinated into the pools, that it was impossible, over a long training session, not to. Urine hadn't killed her to this date, so, get on with it, Laura.

A short swim and a long shower later, she went home and surfed the web. "Oh God, Dan, the pool smelt and tasted like urine. I've just found that chlorinated pools increase cancer risk by inducing DNA damage. Apparently chlorine, urine, sweat, sunscreen and dirty bodies form a toxic mix of chemicals which can increase the risk of asthma and bladder cancer by mutating the genes. The dirtier the pool, the greater the risk and it was disgusting today. The lifeguards never check if people have showered before getting in the water. I think everyone should have to wear caps and teachers should get kids to go to the toilet before getting in."

"It sounds vile. Are you going to stop swimming then?"

"No, it says don't stop swimming. The benefits are greater than the risk for most people."

Beth was on her knees planting wallflowers in the front bed. "Yoohoo," called Laura. Beth tried to get up to greet her friend, tugging at her clothes, the way plump women do. She felt so stiff and ungainly. I was never supple and springy, but I wasn't this lumbering and couldn't even heave myself up from all fours, she thought.

"Just passing, thought I'd drop off the review of the play at the Arcola. It looks good." Laura couldn't help noticing Beth's lumpy, dimpled thighs in what looked like old khaki shorts and a work shirt of James's. Not flattering, she thought, but all Beth was concerned with was getting through her jobs. Her rather large face held her usual mild, slightly baffled look, as if everything in life came as a huge surprise.

"Oh thanks. Will you have a little cup of tea?"

Laura was keen to get home. She had thought of a good twist to a story she was writing, but Beth seemed to need to talk, so she smiled and followed her inside.

Pouring boiling water into the mugs, Beth looked out at the featureless garden remembering when tricycles, prams and tents were on the lawn, most rooms were littered with toys and the cork pinboard in the kitchen was covered with drawings rather than hospital and optician appointments. Laura wondered what was bothering her friend. It soon came out.

"I feel so boring compared with most of you. You juggled all the balls, while I've just managed to be a little housewife and mother. You've got successful careers to look back on."

Laura smiled. So this was it. "Don't judge yourself by other people's lives Beth. You've done what's important to you and done it very well. You chose to be yourself and many people would envy what you've achieved. Anyway, once one retires it doesn't matter what you did. No one is interested. We're all just the same, grey geriatrics. And we all get our crisis – who are we? Is this it?"

Beth smiled. "Thanks for that," she sighed. "I think sometimes that I made my life into a prison for myself, but now they've gone I miss the mess everywhere and worrying about them coming home late." She looked perplexed. "Perhaps being a housewife wasn't too bad. Being able to do everything in my own time, the sort of queen of my home, even though they've taken it all for granted. It's just that I keep wondering where has my life gone?" She thought for a minute, "and I thought I'd feel less anxious when I had less responsibilities, but I'm just the same."

"Really?" Laura was surprised. "I probably did when I was teaching and organising a department, bringing up Daisy and trying to maintain a social life and fitness regime. But now? If we're healthy what's there to be anxious about?"

"Well, I know it's irrational, but it's little things like, will the electrician turn up. Are the children Ok? What can I wear to something? All sorts of thingummy's. I can worry about anything. I'm permanently, chronically anxious. I let James think that I gave up the teaching job for him, but I wasn't coping, I was having panic attacks at the thought of facing particular classes. I couldn't have carried on!" She shuddered. "But it doesn't have to be about anything. It can well up from nowhere. I can just be watching TV and my breathing gets tight and I feel I'm not in control, panicky, perhaps it's hormones, perhaps I shouldn't have a little drink every night."

"I wouldn't go that far. You don't drink much. A lot more people

204

than one realises rely on valium and anti-depressants because of anxiety and insecurity, especially now when money is tight. Helen says that some people have Cognitive Behavioural Therapy for years. You're just missing Hugh, Harriet and Jake."

"Yes, I was so looking forwards to the quiet and watching the TV programmes I've chosen in my tidy house. But all that's happened is I've realised that society doesn't value stay-at–home mums, I've lived other people's lives for too long and now I don't know what do with my own."

"But you enjoyed your life as mother hen?"

"I'm not sure now. I was always desperately tired and struggling and juggling with four other people's demands. Every day was a nightmare of me urging them to hurry up, get ready, go somewhere and now they have. It was always: get me this, can I have that, as if I'm a machine, someone to do their bidding. I read a quote somewhere which could be on my gravestone…about not being afraid that your life will end, but worrying that it will never begin. My job has just been 'being' which isn't a job at all."

"But they love you and need you, Beth."

"Love what I do for them more like. And they just need me to be alive: out of the way in the background somewhere, so they can use this house as a hotel when they need to. The awful thing is that I miss their noise, their continual needs and being at the centre of their lives."

"Well, you brought them up to be confident, independent adults who can make lives and friends of their own. You wouldn't want them to be any other way would you?"

"No, but why am I so needy? So anxious and unsettled? I'm an observer, a supporter of other people's lives. They move on purposefully while I pretend I've got a life, but I'm really going nowhere. When they were young I was too busy to worry about the meaning of life and where I was going. Then suddenly they don't need you. I don't have to service anyone any more, except James of course and now he's going to be around all day, so he can jolly well lend a hand. Long, empty years loom in front of me. If we're on earth for a purpose, what is mine?"

Laura was quite stunned at Beth's unaccustomed eloquence and was wondering how to reply, but she rushed on. "In most ways I'm privileged, never having had to make my own way, but I despise myself for the fact that I probably never could have. I was an ineffectual teacher. I've never excelled at anything."

"Beth, Beth, you're a wonderful mother and friend. Those are important roles. And, by the way you have wonderful dinner parties!"

"Mmm." Beth was quiet for a moment. "But even if I manage to create a successful, stimulating evening, the guests go away and everyone forgets about it. So why bother? If I wrote a book like you're doing, it would go on library shelves and be sold in bookshops and the internet. It would last longer than an evening, and Dan can get his paintings displayed in galleries."

"Beth, you've said how much you enjoy quilting. Why aren't you doing that then?"

The sky was a beautiful blue and there was the faint scent of apple and cherry in bloom. A soft, shining day with the lightest of zephyrs, lifting the spikey fans of Laura and Dan's 'fox bush' which they had bought to stand up to the foxes' scratching attentions as their pampas had never been able to. The birds were busy, beaks full of nest material. Walking to the pool, there were gardens with mauve and white, pendulous bunches of wisteria on the bare stems, and splashes of blue on the ground as bluebells uncurled. So much colour and all shades of green trees.

The pool was like a rough sea with too many violently thrashing bodies fighting with the water. Only the non-laned area had room, as the Asian women stood chatting in the shallow end. They all piled into that and started swimming up and down, avoiding one another.

Lynne was finding Beth irritating. On the way home, she and Laura were walking together, while Helen and Beth had stopped to buy a paper and were some way behind: "Sorry, Laus, but when I'm talking to her, I can feel my eyes glazing over and I have to say stuff like wow and fascinating to keep myself awake. She rabbits on and on so I'm desperate to get away or else praying for death's sweet release!"

"That's mean. It's cruel, Lynne."

"Well, you have to admit, she's hardly wildly entertaining. Our conversations are hardly Socratic debate…She's perfectly 'nice', but so serious, so plodding, so stonkingly boring and such a goody two shoes wifey! I bet she doesn't nag or criticise, is super-grateful and ignores James's faults."

"Enough, you're just too cynical. She's a nice person and a good and loyal friend!"

"Nice is the default position of the coward and self-hater, but yeh, sorry. Robert says my wisecracking sophistry and cruel tongue need to be reined in. I'll try and keep my trap shut and be kinder."

It was the last week of term and a tanned and fit looking Bob and Yvonne had come to choir for the first time since the Christmas concert. Laura and Yvonne being tall, stood at the back of the sopranos. They were chatting quietly while the other parts were practicing, "We've been on two walking holidays, spending Bob's pension lump sum. Can't wait to go again."

"You didn't miss us then," Laura whispered.

"Yes, of course, but we're also hoping that our daughters will have made alternative babysitting arrangements because we weren't around."

Laura remembered that they had three daughters and five grandchildren, but Mathew was looking at them warningly. "Sopranos and tenors this time please."

When the last note had been sung, Yvonne explained. "I'd gone from being a busy, youthful person to becoming 'granny' and prematurely aged. As soon as I retired I was no longer supposed to be clever or interesting, just available and reliable. I was stuck with my grandchildren every day. I couldn't say I'm not ready, give me a few years of freedom, come back later. I felt press-ganged."

"Yeh, granny duties can suck up one's life," said Laura sympathetically, though wishing with all her heart that she could still look after Lily and Ruby.

"It's not as if we don't love them to bits, but my life seemed grey and downhill. I'm not ready to be granny. It just happened. I wasn't asked if I wanted the role, it was assumed that this would be what I

207

wanted more than anything, and there's nothing one can say! I was so busy being tactful, diplomatic and keeping my wits about me, I felt as if I was on trial. It seemed as if Danni particularly had harboured grudges from her childhood and was watching me, waiting for her prejudices to be confirmed. I had to get away from it."

"Really? I thought you and Danni, Julie and Lea were so close."

She nodded vigorously so that her tight, grey curls, sprouting from her angry head bounced impatiently. "Yes, yes we are, but the dynamics in a relationship change when one's children have children. You're no longer the authority figure. They're now the master race and we're expected to step aside. We're old, old fashioned. They don't want to know what we think or feel. Having an opinion is *interfering*. They call the shots. It's a horrible shock to be pushed to the edge of what was a cosy family, to be expected to hover uncertainly on the edges of their lives, like visiting spirits. Not quite part of anything that's going on, yet having to be there when needed. And the grandchildren just accept that you'll do anything to please them. They don't see you really. It's as if you'd sprung into life old. Bob wanted to put space between us all. We're buying a flat in Portugal."

Beth and Frances were waiting to go and Bob had finished putting the chairs away. They wandered towards them. "So you won't be here much in the future then?"

"No. Wish we could take the choir and our friends, but there seem to be a lot of friendly people in the development. You'll have to come and stay. There's an enormous heated pool."

Laura went straight from swimming to see her doctor for the results of her bone scan.

Annie wanted to find out more about Martin and Frances, so had called at Laura's.

"She's gone to her doctor's," said Daniel. He felt uncomfortable with Annie. She often had a set, cold face with a staring expression, which seemed incapable of showing surprise or pleasure. She made him feel nervous.

"What do you think about Martin and Frances? He can't like someone like her. Could he?" she suddenly burst out.

Daniel shifted uncomfortably from foot to foot. He and Martin had always got on very well. "I expect she makes him happy," he said and picked up one of his shopping lists and started grouping the items into shops and areas of the shop where he would find them. "I don't think Laura will be back for a while." Annie felt dismissed. "Tell her to ring me," she said and left.

"You have osteopenia," Laura's doctor said. "Don't take risks. You won't be able to have hip replacements. I'll prescribe you some calcium tablets with added vitamin D."

"What? After all the exercise I've always done and my healthy diet?" Laura was stunned and rushed home to look on the internet.

"Mum had osteoporosis. I realized that it was genetic, having low levels of minerals in your bones, but the fact that the calcium goes into the blood vessels and makes them crunchy, puts me off taking 'Adcol'" she said to Dan.

"What else could you be doing?" he asked in concern.

She made a sad face. "Taking Vitamin D. Cutting back on alcohol and salt. They increase calcium loss. Though if that's the case, I don't know why Gwyneth Paltrow has it, because she has the perfect diet and apparently doesn't often drink alcohol."

"Mmm, perhaps stress hasn't helped," he said guiltily.

Laura wandered upstairs and into Daisy's bedroom. Remembering how in her late teens she would emerge from the mess, looking breathtakingly stunning, wearing clothes that had lain under discarded piles and had never seen an iron. She smiled to herself picturing the rabbit that had lived undetected in her room for weeks, until they had run out of mugs and plates and opening Daisy's bedroom door to look for them, the animal had rushed past her. The shock had been heart stopping, especially as the heaps of clothes and bedding on the carpet were liberally sprinkled with little balls of poo.

She sat in front of Daisy's mirror and examined her face, conscious of how rarely she did more than glance at it from a distance. 'Lived in' was probably the correct description. Deeply lined from endless hours sun bathing, playing sport or gardening. Thin skin, sunken into hollows beneath the cheekbones. Those big, dark circles acquired in adolescence from reading under the bedclothes were now criss-crossed with tiny lines. Her saggy neck and dull, faded grey, pink-rimmed eyes gave her an unpleasant shock.

She felt unsettled, unsure how to live her life now she suddenly had all this freedom. I know I'm driven and perhaps too serious. I don't do things outside my comfort zone but I do always try to do what I do to the best of my ability. Though that seemed to infuriate Daisy.

She smiled into the mirror and her wrinkles were lost in the smile lines. Her neck tautened. It depends on *me*, whether my life is good...*me*! I'm Ok with being invisible, but my energy and vitality can only diminish. I *must* write more, now I've got the chance.

She sank down onto the carpet by the basket of soft toys, some of which had belonged to Daisy and others bought new for the twins. Pulling them out one by one, she put them in rows. Fluffy ones, knitted ones, the loved ones, which had names and were almost bare, they had been sucked and chewed so much. Then there were the pristine, unloved, nameless ones. She felt tears welling up as she held a once orange duck, Daisy's favourite, to her breast.

The pool was crowded and the changing room floor a mess of black hair and dirty footmarks. They dressed and left quickly to find they had just missed a heavy shower, which had spoiled much of the blossom. It lay on the pavements and as they passed under the trees, a little wind whipped it into a blizzard of wet pink and white around them. The swifts were swooping about very high up and the clouds were building for another downpour, as they walked quickly home.

Laura cleared her throat and looked out at the sea of people in the lecture theatre. She had been asked over a year ago to present a paper on her PhD subject, 'Representations of Dementia in Contemporary Literature', at the annual humanities conference and had agreed, thinking that it would keep her sharp and focussed. Why did she feel so fragile today? Picking up the glass of water on the table in front of her, she sipped, and trying not to seem exasperated, directed her gaze at the questioner, who was looking triumphant.

"Thank you for your interesting question and observations. If you don't mind, we can talk about it further after this session. There are other people with their hands up. We need to move on." He was saying something, but the stewards had handed the microphone to a middle-aged woman and she drowned him out. Phew. Why were some men so point-scoring? She would try to disarm him, neutralise him after by asking him questions and congratulating him. What am I doing this for anyway? To keep my brain working? Previous jollies to conferences in Thailand, Istanbul and Vancouver flashed through her head before she turned her attention to the next questioner.

The shushing sea below echoed the sound of the wind in the trees above her. Lynne was happy. How could she not be, when she was walking through a landscape of yellow: daffodils, primroses, celandines and cowslips. The sky was a beautiful blue and as she entered a copse, so were the bluebells and dog violets. Out of the trees, the grassy banks were bursting with wild garlic. It was impossibly beautiful and the smells were overpowering.

The leader had been setting a cracking pace and the group were straggling behind. She was walking with Kay, a powerful looking woman in her seventies, who seemed to have been on every Ramblers holiday offered. The leader had stopped, so they chatted until everyone caught up, before going through the arched gates of an estate and down a drive flanked with towering beeches. There were oaks, elms and chestnuts in the distance, then they turned and walked between the high hawthorn hedges of a secretive, shadowy lane with blind curves and narrow passing places. Kay knew every plant and every bird, from their call or flight. Lynne wondered if fascination with the natural world was a sign of incipient decay...

At the end of the walk she called Robert before having a quick pub drink with the other Ramblers. The sun was setting when they pulled into his drive in front of a detached cottage overlooking the downs. In the hall, golden shafts of light were pouring through the stained glass in the door, a grandfather clock ticked and the delicious aroma of lamb tagine hung in the air. As he led her inside, her eyes roamed down his back, from his powerful shoulders and well shaped buttocks to his Lobb brogues. She felt sweaty and stiff from her long day and welcomed his suggestion that he pour her a glass of wine which she could drink in a hot bath.

"I'm not sure what I can offer you to wear though," he mused. "You're six inches taller than Hilary was and definitely slimmer."

She settled for his denim shirt over her own leggings and emerged from the bathroom feeling wonderful.

His face was flushed from cooking. He smiled and adjusted his shirt. "That fits well." Lynne was unsettled by his touch and she could feel her heart pounding as he handed her the refilled glass.

"I'd better not drink this, I'll be wasted."

"You can always stay the night," he said, putting his arms around her tentatively. She felt his body pressing against her various points. Chest against breasts, thighs together, the gentle bulge in his groin pushing through his trousers. He pulled her nearer, with his hands around her buttocks.

She stood still, unsure, unease slithering inside her. "No, I can't do that. I've got the cats to think about," and wriggled away from him.

He shrugged and bent towards her, turning her to face him again. She trembled as he pulled her closer. "I'm nervous too. You're so beautiful," he said. She could smell his aftershave and as their lips met, taste the strong fruitiness of the Rioja. How long has it been since I kissed a man? She wondered as raw lust rose through her. "No," she said. "No, I'm not ready for this," and pushed him away.

"Right," he said, reaching out to tuck a stray strand of hair back behind her ear. It was familiar. An ownership gesture and she felt faint, off balance. When did I last feel like this, she asked herself, as she walked away from him to keep her composure. Even pretending to look at his books in the bookcase, her back tingled and her knickers felt wet.

After a delicious dinner, they sat on the floral, loose covered sofa and he switched on the TV. "Isn't Downton entirely predictable, silly and just one outlandish plot after another?"

"Well, I'm enjoying it. But I am recording it at home, so if you'd rather talk? Remember my train is at ten thirty."

"Yes of course and you watch it. That's quite all right," he said.

His face was so close, she found that she wanted to press her mouth on his. "I've drunk too much," she thought. Then suddenly they were kissing. He groaned as he drew back. A tiny nerve was beating in his jaw. She slid her hands under his shirt feeling the warm, smooth skin. It had been so long. An exultant feeling surged through her, "I want this man. I want him," filled her head.

She was flooded with so much pleasure that she wanted it never to end. Her body had come alive after years of torpor.

But it must. She had to go. She made herself look at her watch...Help!

"It's nearly ten. I've got to get the last train." She pulled him to his feet and rushed around throwing on her clothes and collecting her things. Within minutes they were in the car. He turned on the ignition, then paused for a minute. "Are you sure you have to go?"

"The cats," said Lynne tersely, edgily. "Drive please, quickly."

He had impeccable manners, so silently let out the clutch and drove off. She glanced sideways and by the set of his neck and the tension in his body, she could tell he was irritated. They did not speak again until they arrived at the station.

"Well thanks for a lovely evening, and the lift," she said airily, hopping out of the car, banging the door and running for her train. That's probably the last I see of him, she thought. Oh well, it was good while it lasted.

It was a warm day, 18 centigrade and the smells of blossom and bright spring flowers everywhere. "Did you see that programme about bees last night?" Beth asked.

Helen, Laura and Lynne shook their heads. "It takes a bee to visit 1,500 flowers before it can produce one drop of honey, you know." They looked suitably impressed. "And ten million foraging trips to make one pot of honey! I'll feel guilty eating it now, though apparently a lot of makes of honey have added sugar and water."

"There was a programme about the West in the Middle East, on at the same time," said Laura.

"Yes, why don't we learn lessons from Iraq. All this trying to force secular western democracy on strict eastern theocracies. It's so arrogant!" Lynne said heatedly.

"Fear of radical Islamists winning power, I suppose…why can't we have more dialogue and attempts at understanding?" Muttered Laura as they arrived at the pool.

Jessica had come home for Easter to find that Jo had been wearing her clothes. "You're sixty-four and wearing little girl clothes. Are you going clubbing or something? And you're thinner and look like you've had botox again. You'll end up looking like a freak!"

Jo laughed. "I've got a seriously skilful guy in Harley Street." She held her face nearer her daughter's for examination.

"What have you had already?"

"Oh, only a tummy tuck, an eye lift and chin lift."

"Why don't you just act your age?"

"Why? Some people are old at eighteen and some young at ninety. I don't want to hide in the shadows, be invisible, or rejected. Anyway, I've got a new man, he's seriously hot," she grinned.

"You're seriously sad, Mum."

"I thought you'd left my apron strings. Had set up on your own? Love your wowser trousers and flatform shoes, by the way."

Jess grimaced. "What apron strings? You've never worn an apron. You can't even cook. I've fended for myself as long as I can remember."

Jo felt a stab of guilt. It was true that she was a hopeless homemaker. If it wasn't for Antony's visits twice a week, the flat would have been in a state and the fridge would have been empty.

"That Indian man with a nappy."

"Er, Ghandhi?"

"Yeh, him. He said there's more to life than increasing its speed. When are you going to slow down, Mum? You're such a slut!" Jess put her arms around her mother and Jo felt a wave of warmth replacing defensive irritation. It had been like this since Jess was four. She had always been the tidy, practical one, who had had to act as the adult in their house.

"I haven't left for good, you know. I still need to have a home in the UK. I'm not sure how long I'm going to stay in New York."

"Darling, I'm sorry, I shouldn't have gone in your room. I've been a hopeless mother."

"There's a certain age when wearing young women's clothes, tight jeans and low cut tops isn't appropriate. Why don't you do some more serious things? Go to gallery talks, join a book club? You're stuck in your rut. You don't read any more. You always told me that reading takes you out of your world. You learn things, extend yourself, become a more interesting person. Who said it was better to be the heroine of your life than the victim?"

"Nora Ephron," said Jo.

"You see, Mum, you've got so much knowledge in that head." She tapped it, lovingly. Let's see you using it. Be my heroine too!" She gave her a hug.

Chapter 15. April. Rifts

'And after April, when May follows,
And the whitethroat builds and all the swallows.'
Robert Browning. 'Home Thoughts From Abroad.' (1812 – 1889)

The seasons seem to have gone into reverse. The wind was arctic. It was grey and trying to rain. All the fault of that jet stream again. The group of three walked along, shoulders hunched against the gale. Lynne was ranting on about Berenice who swam most days.

"That's pretty cruel, Lynne. Why the poison dwarf?" asked Beth.

"She never stops moaning. Just endless moans on and on and if you're new she's all nicey-nicey and tries to get you to complain about something, and if you don't do it, she ignores you, talks across you as if you didn't exist!"

Laura looked thoughtful. "Isn't that generally a British trait, the default position, to be cynical and moany?"

"True. That's what you get from newspapers: politicians are crooks, newspaper hacks are amoral freaks, successful women are hard and neglect their children. It's easier to write nasty things and find fault than be cheerful and positive. Anyway, people like her depress me. It's Ok to be fed up sometimes, but knee jerk cynicism and moaning are the pits, and so is she."

There was a silence.

"Well, I think we've covered that one," said Laura breezily. "Who's up for coming to the Picasso and British Modern Art exhibition at the Tate?"

The next morning the sun shone into Annie's bedroom and the copper beech had ruptured into leaf. The breeze through the open window swirled the curtains as if they were alive. Her spirits lightened. She got dressed, went out to the car and drove to Hampstead Heath to join the dog walkers, joggers and perambulator pushers who appeared, then minutes later disappeared down hidden side paths. She wandered around for a while until she found herself on a bridge over a pond. Leaning on the railings to watch the pairs of ducks and swans below, a huge involuntary sigh and a wave of grief washed over her. All those years of pretending I was independent, that I didn't need Martin. He was my backstop. Always there for me. I'm no good at being alone, no-one knowing or caring what I do. He was so supportive. He made me think that I was important, successful, beautiful…

And it was his fault, being so retiring and letting me take centre stage. I got too big headed. Loneliness flooded through her, permeating her every cell. I should be liberated. I can go anywhere, do anything now. I can disappear for weeks and no one would object, or notice. She looked down at her newly almost flat stomach, her thinner legs encased in skinny jeans. I must have lost a stone or two. You'd be so proud and its just because I'm grieving for you. Wondering what you're doing. She suddenly felt extremely hungry.

In truth, Martin had been agonising about the way he had behaved in his marriage. Perhaps I wasn't manly enough, he thought for the thousandth time. Perhaps I should have made up opinions about clothes and food and what to do on a Saturday night? I never thought that those sort of decisions were important. Whatever she wanted was fine by me. I thought I was pleasing her going along with her choices, but maybe it was putting too much pressure on her. I'm too accommodating. Not strong enough for her. And how could she be proud of me? I was never promoted. "Your quality is that people trust you. You reassure people. You're too good on the ground. You would be wasted in a desk job," Duncan Phillips said when I asked him if I could be considered for Senior Manager. I've felt like a ghost sometimes. I'm a loser. No wonder she didn't respect me. I take the easy way out mostly and don't fight for things, I let Annie push us forward. He walked past the hall mirror on the way to the door and caught a glimpse of his reflection. Pale face, small grey eyes, receding hair line, nothing distinguishing. Why should anyone fancy me?

He caught a bus to the Heath and walked the same route that Annie had trodden only minutes before. She had by now gone to the café for a latte and roasted vegetable panini. He lent on the same railings and thought how he missed his shed. Sitting at his bench, listening to his radio. Looking out at the garden, the wall of shelves with all his tools behind him. Something to mend in front of him.

Fortified after her snack, Annie went back outside and decided to ring Martin's mobile.

"Annie?"

"Yes, the woman you are married to."

"What do you want?"

Her mouth felt as if she were chewing razor blades. She was hoping their split was like people overthrowing their governments, getting rid of the dictator and then perhaps finding that what they had had hadn't been that bad after all. "Can we talk?"

"I'm just on my way somewhere."

"A few minutes?"

"I guess so."

"I want you back," she swallowed. "I miss you." Came out in a rush. She could hear her voice vibrating with anxiety. There was silence.

"You know why I can't live with you, Annie. My life is much calmer now."

Her surge of happiness at the lovely day and her desire to share it with no one but him deflated. "I'm different. I've learnt my lesson. I'll be a better wife to you. I promise."

"For how long? Till something goes wrong or someone crosses you and you have to take it out on someone? No, Annie, I've left you because I'm better off without you. I'm sorry if that doesn't suit you, but you'll find someone else to bully and demean I'm sure."

The cruelty of his words left her gasping. She had barely functioned since she had found out about his affair. F off, she thought, but the new Annie was more conciliatory.

"Don't you want to pop round and get some of your things? You didn't take much with you."

"No thanks. They remind me of our life, which started off so well." There was a pause. "Are you Ok?"

There was something about that question and the real concern in it. She felt a huge wave of sadness and emotion engulf her and tried to blink back the rush of tears. She swallowed, tried to open her eyes

218

wide. Don't let him think I'm crying. "Yes fine. Lost my job with the Daily News and feeling really old, but I'm fighting back and have lost a couple of stones."

"I'm sure you look great and you'll easily get other jobs." He could feel his resolve weakening. All he wanted was to give her a cuddle. Stroke her to take the pain away. He must get off the phone. "Look after yourself. Bye."

They walked in opposite directions.

The morning crept flirtatiously through the curtains with intimations of impending warmth. The house was still and breathless. Laura got out of bed, opened the window to let in the fresh spring air, and dressed in her costume and 'going swimming' clothes. Brookfield House, the Care Home at which she had volunteered to help with 'activities' for a couple of hours a week, was only a short bus ride away, so she swam first. Out into the street. It was sunny and bright. Clouds had swept the sky clean and sunlight flickered through the poplar branches above. Jo was hurrying up the road with Lynne. They carried on together to call for Beth and Helen.

"I'm re-reading the 'The Golden Notebook'. It seems so old fashioned now. Do you remember when it was such an exhilarating read?" Jo said to the group.

"Yes and 'The Second Sex' and 'Women in Love'. Starting us thinking about politics and feminism." Laura smiled at the memory.

"Ah the sixties. It seems like a golden age now, the time when everything was possible," added Helen.

"Hardly, I couldn't have a mortgage without a man's signature and the banks were so sexist! The counter staff checked every woman's account before they paid out. Whereas they didn't check men's! Infuriating," Lynne said heatedly.

"Yes, I got mad and kept challenging them about it, but it was pointless," Laura agreed.

Beth was looking puzzled.

Lynne turned on her. "You wouldn't know. You were wrapped up in motherhood. Making jam tarts and reading Enid Blyton to your kids. You weren't out in the work place fighting for equal pay and recognition!"

Beth knew she was out of her depth. "Well, I'm reading a book by a biologist. Is his name Wilson? It's about how it's in our genes to form groups and then defend them. He says no other species show such blind devotion to their tribe."

"And I thought we spent time together because we enjoyed each other's company!" Lynne had calmed down.

"Whether we come every time, or some times, it's because we're comfortable with one another. We're similar aren't we?" said Laura.

"Are we?" asked Beth.

"Middle class, older?. We might vote differently and have different views about the monarchy, but at heart we're pretty similar."

"Anyway," said Beth, "it's James's book and not sure I'm going on with it."

Phillip was going on a weekend course and was being especially fastidious in his morning ablutions. After shaving, showering, washing and conditioning his hair, he put on a hydrating facemask of avocado and macadamias, trimmed his nose hair, rubbed artichoke body cream into his arms and legs and finished with a crème de la mer toner. Helen asked him what the course was about and he muttered something about 'meditation' and then was rather evasive.

A few days later while eating a sandwich at her work desk, she flicked on to his website and in addition to *physical release therapy which works with specific muscles, pressure points and the lymphatic system to release the blocked emotions and memories'*, he was advertising himself as a sex therapist, an orgasm guru…

His therapy sessions now could include not only *'yoga postures, relaxation and self help techniques, discussion and meditation,'* but *'phase four is sensual awakening massage which can help women understand their primal fears and reach new heights of sexual pleasure.'*

Helen went cold. So now he would be touching women in the name of therapy? He was out, so she raced home early, went in to his treatment room and searched through his desk until she found a pamphlet. Was this the 'meditation course' he had spent the weekend at Bendale Hall doing?

220

Psychosexual Therapy: A therapy to help women who have issues with sex and intimacy,' she read. *The blocks to orgasm are psychological rather than physiological. Sensual awakening through therapeutically assisted orgasm. Learn massage of the yoni (Sanskrit for a woman's genitals or 'sacred place'),'* what? *Inter-vaginal massage releases tension, stress and bad memories. Experience as much pleasure as you can take.'*

So while she had been at work and visiting her mother, he had been 'massaging' women's vaginas! I'll kill him! Or was that what he had taken last September and last weekend he had gone to this one?

'Advanced tantric practices: A certificated course to enable the practitioner to teach men who have premature ejaculation, inability to reach orgasm and loss of libido to have greater sexual excitement, including 'lingam massage' – the manipulation of sensory points around the penis. The Taoist purpose for men is controlling their ejaculation, so that they can use that saved energy for spiritual and healing purposes in their bodies. You have more energy, less anxiety and physical ailments improve. Help couples achieve euphoric bliss.'

Men as well! I can't bear it!

"I knew you'd be angry," he admitted later, trying to hold onto his smile, though his face was stiff with the effort. "How can I develop as a psychosexual therapist if I'm not open to learning new practices? Sexual healing is the buzzword in psychotherapy. I see very vulnerable people. I've always told you that it's entirely appropriate with psychological therapies to have physical contact with the client."

"Go and do it in a hospital or clinic then. We learnt in our code of ethics that sexual contact is never Ok. It's exploitative! Don't the BASRT have an ethical code? You've just said it. Your patients are referred to you because they're in a vulnerable state. They want your help with painful unresolved problems. You may be adding to their suffering and you're setting yourself up to be sued. Understand this. I don't want you giving women – or men - orgasms in my house!"

"Let me show you what I do?" he wheedled. "Only I'll do it to you with love. Not as a clinical treatment. I want to help women love their bodies and feel sexy. In fact, I want to start using my healing and Taoist practices to become a tantric practitioner. I could sustain my orgasm for hours then and give you multiple orgasms."

221

"Don't come near me, don't speak to me and if you have to stay in this house, sleep in the guest room. You disgust me. You're depraved!" She felt sick and sank onto the settee, her head in her hands.

He stood, not knowing what to say or do. He could understand that she thought he had gone too far. Yet he felt innocent. A therapist needs to develop into new areas. He felt that he had had no evil intent. Why should marriage mean that one can never touch another woman to give her treatment? What about doctors, masseurs, osteopaths, physios? What's the difference between them and me?

An image came into his head of a golden moment at Sheffield, when he had been waiting outside the library for her. She had come bounding down the steps, stylish, lithe, the sun's rays setting alight her long tawny hair, her orange blouse. When she saw him, her face lit up with such joy and happiness that he thought his heart would burst open. Now he felt it lurch and a sigh came out from a deep sad place inside him.

How often had they made love that wonderful summer? Deep into being young. With their flowing clothes, guitars, the sweet smell of marijuana, singing and dancing til dawn. Then, with guilt, he remembered his client from last night. His penis had been in the ready position for nearly an hour. To keep it keen, he regulated his breathing and ground his pelvic muscles and imagined the air travelling down his front, rolling across his sexual organs, while he clenched his perineum. He could increase his arousal through this exercise and even more with aggressive, quicker breaths. With this method he hoped he could delay ejaculation and keep an extended sensation of orgasm for hours. Not with a client, of course. That was absolutely taboo. Helen would be grateful when he had gained complete control.

This had been Ms Bates's sixth appointment. She sat cross-legged opposite him while they did the breathing and meditation exercises together. Without touching, she went through the relaxation and exploration exercises, her self-help techniques for vaginismus. After half an hour she confessed to being in a warm, sensory bliss. Phillip decided it was time for some gentle yoni massage. Within ten minutes she could hold back no longer and reaching out, pulled up his sarong and guided his penis into her...

Helen lifted her head, pale and shattered looking. She's going to tell me she's leaving me. A stabbing pain of physical anguish winded him. "I've learned my lesson this time, honestly. If you don't want me to treat people with sexual problems. I won't, I love you. There's never been anyone else for me. You're everything to me."

She stared at him wearily, helplessly. "Love me? You only know how to lie to me, to degrade me. I've never refused you sex, never looked at another man. Why do you need to do sex therapy? Why can't you stick to counselling?" She pushed a strand of hair away from her eyes, "Don't talk to me. Get out of my sight."

For days they avoided one another. He slept in the guest room and she got up early and went out. Presumably to work. He did not know where she was or what she was doing, but he hoped that she was calming down and would forgive him again. They were in limbo. The house was a sort of cold waiting room where language was suspended and there seemed no answers.

In bed, she missed his closeness and found herself thinking about those snatched, urgent, shuddery couplings in the backs of people's cars when they first met at university and the dreamy, orgasmic hours in bed when they moved in together. Could she ever feel desire for him again? She tried to remember for how many years sleep had been more important than orgasm. Was it her fault? Was that why he sought solace with other women? He was still attractive. Occasionally desire flared in her loins. I suppose that's why I keep forgiving him, she thought. For the first ten years of their marriage when they were in bed, he would read poetry to her in his rich, melodious voice. She imagined him next to her, reading and the nostalgia for that intimacy was painful. Sometimes she would get out of bed and look down the corridor at the light from under his door. If only...

Laura had been to her first Governors' meeting. She came home to find that Dan had made a meat pie for their supper.

"Not too much for me. There were tons of sandwiches and cakes. I suppose some people and the teachers are coming straight from work."

"How was it?"

"Pretty awful really. I was a bit taken aback at first, the Head and I seemed to be the only non-Muslims. I mean I'm used to being in a minority at swimming and the gym, but I was wondering if people's views would be informed by their faith? Then at the tea break, a woman called Kadiza said she was glad I'd joined them, because she and Aamira were the only women apart from the Head. And not to worry that she'd be pushing the brown message, they want to uphold British values and traditions. The meeting was totally uninvolving though. It's obvious that the Chair, Head and Deputy Head just talk at everyone and don't want any interference. They don't even send all the papers out beforehand. Shocking really. We'll be agreeing budgets next time, so I've asked to see the targets and objectives for this year and last."

"You'll be popular then."

"Mmm. I can't stride in there and make enemies. But if I'm going to do the job, there'll have to be a few changes."

It was the monthly meeting of the Book Club.

"This is Jo, everyone. We met at university and she moved into the area last summer."

Jo smiled and looked around. Apparently not everyone was there. Just one man, Laura and five other women. She remembered Laura's words: Beth and Heather read slowly so not one word is missed. They mark beautiful passages for rereading and pointing out to the group. Irene tends to read into the small hours the night before the meeting. Annie and probably Alan are wanton, greedy readers. Galloping through and fast forwarding to see what happened. Saira and Isobel rarely finish the books and we don't see much of Nomusa. I tend to dislike the books at first and have to force myself to read onwards, and then I often get hooked and write notes and check their reviews on the Internet.

Alan had taken charge and was listing the books they had read recently. "'Rodinskey's Room', 'Anna Karenina' 'Tess of the Durbevilles', 'Wuthering Heights', 'Madame Bovary'…"

Jo's ears pricked up at the last four. "Are you majoring on

hapless women who were taken advantage of and ended up dead?

Some of the women sniggered. Alan looked rather put out. "You get to choose your own title once or twice a year. Shall we discuss the Graham Greene?"

On the way to the pool, Beth told Lynne about starting quilting again and was surprised when Lynne said:

"I made a quilt when I was in my thirties. I've still got a quilter's stash, which I often add to, thinking I'll make another one day. Why don't you come for tea on Sunday and drool over my Fat Quarters?"

"That would be nice. Yes, please."

"Remind me, what's a fat quarter?" Laura asked.

"Oh, it's half a metre cut in half. I should try and stick to similar patterns and hues, but I can't resist buying more when I see them."

Laura gave Lynne a hug after they had dropped off Beth at her house.

Lynne looked sheepish, but pleased. "Yes, Ok. I shouldn't have been such a bitch about her."

That Sunday, James had been hoping for a walk in Kew Gardens with tea in the Orangery, but Beth was excitedly going off to see Lynne. James had had colleagues, but no particular best friends. He wondered if this was a failure on his part. Beth seemed to have plenty. It had always amazed him that she still had girlfriends she had met in school and teacher training college. Then there were the friends from her first baby-sitting circle; mothers of the children's friends, couples they had met on holidays and neighbours from the three places they had lived in. When the telephone rang it was invariably for Beth, but then it was she who remembered birthdays and asked after other people's children. Even though Beth said they were his friends too, if they came for tea and he walked into the room they were immediately, awkwardly silent. "What do you talk about all the time?" he asked.

James wondered what would be next in Beth's period of growing independence. In the past year she had taken up swimming, book club, bridge, choir and volunteering at the hospital. She was talking about having her own work space and enrolling in a Narrative Quilt making and Family Stories quilting class. With hindsight, perhaps he should have thought about Beth's life more. Perhaps she would have had a far better life with someone else? She had not seemed to mind not having a career. There was that short period of teaching, but she had given it up, seemingly happily when Jake was going off the rails. He had never really thought to ask her. She's a clever girl, but when we met she didn't question my paradigm of conventional roles for our marriage. Perhaps if I had not been packed off to school at seven it might not have been so important to me to have my wife dedicate herself so completely to bringing up our children. They are happy and well-adjusted mostly due to Beth, but has she paid the price?

James was proud of having bought their valuable North London five bedroomed house at the right time. It had wonderful mouldings, solid doors, original hall floor tiles and lead-paned windows. It had been a prescient, clever action, investing in their home so many years ago. Yet without the children, they seemed to operate in different areas of it. He felt that she was spiralling away from him, with all her interests. They didn't even have the same tastes in books; she read novels and he non-fiction, mainly history. He was starting to feel quite lonely. He spent some time thinking about sharing more time together and came up with the history of quilting. It dated back to medieval times, one of his special interests. He bought Beth a book, which he started to read parts of to her when she was preparing their supper. "Do you know that some patterns have evolved over centuries? Such as the Sampler quilt, Wedding Ring, Joseph's Coat, Ninepatch, Rail Fence, Bears Paw, Grandmother's Favourite, or Flower Basket to name just a few," he read.

Frances and Martin were seeing one another three or four times a week. He had started to stay overnight and had been very affectionate and patient at her inexperience. But after years of being alone, she was finding having a partner difficult. She had no experience of being the centre of someone's life: of nesting, of sharing. Being in control and morose when she felt fed up was the only way she had known. It was true that his attentions had given her self-esteem, but she was not sure that she would not prefer to just have a friend. I'll have to try not to be so independent, she thought. Like yesterday, making tea and forgetting he was there. And buying enough food for one, without thinking about his tastes and needs. I must stop being selfish.

She found sleep difficult with someone in her bed. He woke her in the night by joggling his legs and thrashing about as if he were break dancing in his sleep. It was very disturbing, but when she mentioned it to him, apparently she snored?

Having to think about someone else and stay cheerful was not what she had ever done before. It made her vulnerable; too thin skinned, I could easily be hurt, she thought. She wondered if he would ever be free of Annie? He had said he could never be himself with her. He was always the person she wanted him to be. Does he think about her?

Frances was obsessive about doing crosswords and quizzes at weekends, when she had not brought work home with her. She had evolved a series of rules for herself when doing quizzes, which she detailed to the reluctant participant, Martin. They took it in turns to read out entries from a book of quiz questions. Awarding one point for a right answer and half a point if the reader of the clue had to give a second clue to describe the same answer. Martin felt that Frances enjoyed winning and making him feel stupid, so he often made the excuse after a while that he had the meal to cook.

This evening over the salmon en croute with salad and new potatoes she was still trying to make him get the answer to what she said was "incredibly easy, child's-play in fact. Shall I give you a third clue? I'll really laugh if you don't get it after this!"

"Can we leave it now?" he asked. "Let's finish the evening watching the BBC News with the last of the chardonnay?"

She was miffed. I wish he'd go home, she thought. Being in her flat all day and all night was far too much for her. She willed him to say that he was going.

"Shall we go to bed after the news? I'm pretty tired," he asked, oblivious of her thoughts.

It was a sunny, balmy day. Jo and Frances had been swimming and had said goodbye to the others and were walking back to their house. Jo looked at Frances in her shapeless trousers and suit jacket.

"Frances, I'm pretty good at doing makeovers. How about if we go out and buy you a new wardrobe?"

"I don't *need* new clothes thank-you. I've got tons."

"Believe me; you *do* need new clothes. You're not working any more. Why are you wearing parts of suits all the time?"

"They're perfectly good. I don't want any more things sorry. I'm just not interested in clothes. I don't *want* to go shopping."

"Now you're going out with Martin."

"No!"

Terry had started to talk to Leonard. "I love you, I miss you. Why did you leave me to face this!" She put her head in her hands and pressed her lips tight together, surprised by the act of talking to herself. Thoughts came pouring out of their own volition. "We could have had such fun when you retired. If you hadn't been so penny pinching: so set in your ways, so blind to my needs, so hell bent on moulding me into what you wanted me to be."

Telling Leonard what she had never dared say before made her feel braver, less alone, even euphoric. I should have said this to him before, but perhaps he can hear me now? "I can talk to you anytime I want, can't I? No-one but you can hear me." She looked out at her mangled garden and it seemed suffused with light. Walking out into the balmy evening air, she felt comforted and part of nature, part of a bigger, eternal life force. "Immortal, invisible, God only wise," she sang and felt calmer than she had in weeks.

Beth enrolled for the quilting class advertised by the University of the Third Age. She went along and found that she was the only new student. It was a social club really.

"I've been coming for over twenty years," said the woman she sat next to, "and I'll be here as long as eyes and hands hold out."

Everyone was helpful and friendly and she brushed up on accurately cutting and piecing fabrics for the first week. They told her where to find the specialist quilters shops to buy materials and that Friday she joined them on a trip to a Quilt Show at the NEC in

Birmingham. She marvelled at the beautiful quilts and the scores of stalls selling fabrics and all the paraphernalia associated with quilting.

Having seen Daniel's artist studio, she decided to get on with making a workroom for herself in part of the loft. Moth, spider and mouse had thrived. She set to work with the vacuum cleaner, mouse poison and moth traps. The last owners of the house had boarded the joists and rafters and put large dormer windows into the west facing, garden side, so it was a bright, light place to work. Hugh and Harriet had seen the loft as their storage facility for furniture and boxes brought back from university. Will they ever want these things again? She moved them all to the dark end where her father-in-law's forgotten huge Victorian partner's desk stood. How on earth did we get this up here? She cleaned it up, manoeuvred it to the light end and gave the oak a polish.

Her new quilting frame went against one wall. The dresser which had belonged to her parents was brought from the laundry room by Michal and his brothers and was gradually filling up with sewing things: sketches, patterns, paints and small frames. Under the large window was the desk covered with her tools: her rotary cutters, rulers and cutting mats and of course her Bernina sewing machine. A radio hung off one beam, so she could listen to Radio 4 and a spider plant in a macramé holder hung from another. The loft room became truly a room of her own.

For over thirty years on six days a week, Beth had been wrenched out of her deep sleep by her alarm clock. She had put on her dressing gown and gone downstairs to make porridge for the family and to lay the table with orange juice: butter, marmalade, honey, yoghourt and fruit to add to the porridge. Now there was just James, who was in no rush to get up, she could put on her bathing costume and comfortable clothes and leave the breakfast until she came back.

She had been up for half an hour; doing little jobs while she waited for Laura's knock. Perhaps she could spend a few hours on her quilt this afternoon. There were only a few months till her class quilt competition, but chopping vegetables for tonight's casserole would have to be done first and a dust and vacuum of the lounge and hall.

The bedrooms could wait until tomorrow. The size of their house was beginning to oppress her. On some days she dreamt of a small two bedroomed house with a studio for her quilting and a study for James and just a courtyard outside, for a few pots.

She took a cup of tea to James. "I'm off in a minute," she said, lifting the duvet, which was covering his head. "So early?" he mumbled, slowly opening his eyes and pulling her towards him. He smelt of warm sheet, unbrushed teeth and was that a waft of faecal matter? "Come on get up, James. Sunil's coming to service the boiler. You said you were going to take some interest in how it works."

He pulled her closer, so she was half kneeling on the bed. "Are you spurning me?"

"Drink your tea. There's no time. Laura will be here any minute."

"You're looking very beautiful this morning. Is this jumper new?"

"You've seen it hundreds of times before." But he was lifting it over her head and reaching round to unhook her bra.

She was half protesting as she always did in this game of theirs where he flattered and pursued and she feigned reluctance, then allowed herself to be won over. He was murmuring "Beautiful, my love." Her breath quickened as he sucked a nipple slowly. She was on her back, her trousers around her ankles when she heard Laura knocking, but she was powerless to answer.

Chapter 16. May. Conversations

'For me, degenerate modern wretch
Though in the genial month of May
My dripping limbs I faintly stretch
And think I've done a feat today.'
Lord Byron.
'Written After Swimming from Sestos to Abydos.' (1788 – 1824)

There had been no let up in the showers. Wild purple and black clouds chased one another making dark shadows, then shafts of sunlight. Birds were washing themselves in puddles, when they were not being buffeted about. More crushed and dying blossom was underfoot and the gardens had turned blue with cornflowers, hyacinths and heather as Laura, Helen, Frances, Lynne and Beth walked to the pool.

"Are there any results yet?" asked Beth.

"Nothing on the radio, though all the polls have put Boris in the lead. I'll leave London if that Ken gets in," said Frances.

"Really? That's a bit drastic," said Helen.

"The trouble is," continued Frances, "In some areas forty-five per cent of votes are postal, and you can bet a large percentage of those are fraudulent. The Electoral Commission needs to get a grip. Cut out all postal votes I say. Unless a doctor confirms that a person is too disabled to get to the polling station."

"Why isn't there a woman candidate? I read in the Standard last night that over three quarters of MP's and council leaders are men!" said Laura.

"Yeh, the corridors of power are full of male buddy-buddying. Should we have an all women party, go back to fighting the feminist cause?" Lynne had a glint in her eyes.

"As long as it doesn't mean trampling on men. I'm not sure I'm a feminist."

"Oh Beth! Unless you actually think women can't be equal, we're all feminists. What about the huge pay disparity and how women are treated socially and culturally in all countries. You sound like that awful Mary Berry! Mary Wollstonecraft said she wanted women to have power over themselves, not over men," said Jo.

"Well I think Mary Berry is wonderful. She had polio when she was a child, you know."

Lynne spluttered. "That explains why she's anti-feminist, does it?"

They had reached a narrower part of the pavement, where children were rushing past on their way to school. Frances, Lynne and Beth went ahead, continuing their conversation and Helen asked Laura if she had heard anything from Daisy.

"No, nothing. It's as if she's disappeared into some sort of sect."

"Could well be," Helen suggested.

Laura raised her eyebrows quizzically.

"Well, some cults do tell you that you must 'disconnect' from your parents, never see or communicate with them again. And even if she was having doubts, she'd be scared to leave, because then they'd turn their backs on her. They'll have pinpointed someone in her life who causes her difficulties such as Daniel. So your connection with him means you have to be disconnected too."

"How do you know all this, Helen?"

"We have to make it our business to know about cults. Families are routinely torn apart when one member enters such organisations."

The others joined up with them again and heard Helen's words.

"But you don't know where she is, Laura. She may be with Femi or her father. It's only been a few months. She'll be back," Beth said comfortingly.

Laura asked Jo if she would sit for Dan. "I can't sit still for long enough, could you?"

"Probably, I'm pretty lazy. Tell him I'll come over tomorrow afternoon."

Dan was excited. His first proper portrait. They climbed up into his studio. There were jars of brushes, vivid smears of paint on palates, the acrid smell of solvent and canvases stacked against the walls.

He sat her down, not expecting her to take on an uncomfortable pose. She made him think of gardenias, white and waxy, cool and perfect with their unforgettable perfume. He decided to paint her dressed in rich greens in future. To frame her loveliness.

"I'm not sure I can sit around for hours. I'll do an hour now and one tomorrow and Friday. That'll have to be enough. What style are you into anyway?"

"I'm trying to find my own way of seeing things. A particular movement or style is limiting. I want to interpret a subject for myself. Art is about communication. I'm expressing whatever is significant to me. Looking with my fresh eyes and interpreting, experimenting with techniques. Postmodern, perhaps?" He was silent for a few minutes, in his own world. "The point of postmodern art is that it can contain aspects of futurism, cubism, surrealism or expressionism. Observers interpret it for themselves. Can you keep that pose, please?"

She sat in the chair. Desperately trying not to change position and wondering if he fancied her? Artists were supposed to be highly sexed. She wondered if she fancied him. In any case he was Laura's and he was concentrating, moving as quickly as he could, sketching initially in charcoal. Seemingly indifferent to her.

At least he hadn't asked to draw her front bottom and nipples, like Tracy Emin.

After the three sessions, she demanded to see her portrait. She was shocked. It was crude and she looked like a caricature.

"I wanted to portray your real, natural beauty. Portraits of older women aren't what we're used to seeing. Without artifice they're the map of the person's life."

The more she looked, the more she could see the life and character shining out. "It's actually very good." she said.

"It's not exactly what I wanted it to be. I wanted to emphasise the beauty of age. But then, that's the whole problem, trying to make what you see and feel come out onto the canvas."

"I'm not flattered, but there is something powerful…and sort of joyful about it. Not like Bacon and Freud. They seem to just paint their pain. Unfathomable. Hurtful and ugly, ugly pain. They seem to

233

have seen only the unhappiness in people."

The sun was shining again at last on the new leaves, turning them gaudy green and the mayflower garden hedges were releasing their sweet perfume. Swifts swooped and swerved in delight above them as they walked to the pool.

"I've been reading that shagfest: 'Fifty Shades of Grey'. Shall I make it my book group choice?" Jo looked cheekily at Laura and Beth.

"Is that about older women?" the latter asked.

Jo laughed. "Mmm, more about bondage, sadism, masochism and how erotic pain is. Don't look so shocked! Ms James has written three novels about this mucky stuff and they're the best seller and third and fourth on Amazon. Over three million sales. Anyway, it's just Tess of the D'Urbevilles with more dirty bits. The XY chromosome is back to its' biological destiny with an arsehole billionaire male character. Eat your hearts out, Greer and Steinem. I'm thinking of going to S & M classes, or even a club."

"You're mad, Jo. At least they've hooked people who don't usually read, though they're not well written are they? Did you read about that spanking teacher in the Evening Standard. She gets thirty people a time in her classes. I find that incomprehensible!" Laura said.

Jo grinned. "Why? Are you not open to spicing up your sex life?"

James was fully retired now. It had been five weeks since his leaving dinner, and he had only twice popped in to his old chambers to talk about an on-going case. Beth wondered if he was thinking about how he would live the rest of his life. She watched him wandering round the house, or sitting reading, his few plumes of fine white hair nodding as he dropped off to sleep and his shiny bald pate and head with large pink ears falling forward. He was still wearing his beautiful shirts without the old fashioned attached collar and with the cuffs rolled up and an old knitted waistcoat.

Perhaps he was not thinking about it at all. Perhaps he would spend it, as he had weekends; playing golf, reading and resting. Beth thought she would discuss it with him over dinner that evening.

She had cleared away the pudding and they were relaxing with the rest of the bottle of Sancerre. Beth thought, this is nice, we used to sit and talk after a meal quite often when we were younger. She was imagining her idyllic life in the future, with time for quilting and James having more time for her, when he reached over and placed his hand over hers. "Well, my dear," he said.

She felt a twinge of alarm. Has he met someone else? What's he going to tell me?

"I rang Sybil this morning and she sounded quite confused. I'm sure she's not eating much. I don't think she should be living on her own. Perhaps she should come and live with us, we've plenty of room now."

Beth was suddenly sweating and there were flashes in front of her eyes. She pulled her hand away from his. "No. Not your Mother, not here. Not living here!"

The immediate utter fury, almost hysteria, which had erupted in Beth shocked her, but she would be trapped and responsible for that awful woman, day after day. "No, absolutely NO," she said resolutely. "I don't know how you can even ask!"

James looked a little taken aback. "She could live her own life. Play bridge at your club, go for walks. She can look after herself, but we could keep an eye on her."

"Sybil has never shown the slightest interest in anyone but herself. She is barely civil to me. I WON'T have her living here."

He looked paler. 'I know I haven't helped much in the past, but I've more time now. I'll be responsible for her."

"You don't know how to boil an egg! Will you be changing her sheets? Getting her meals, washing her clothes, changing her nappy one day?"

A cold, stubborn look came over his face.

She felt as if her heart had stopped. Oh, no…"You've told her, haven't you?" She dropped her head onto her arms on the table. "No, no, no…"

They were on the way to Sussex to see Sybil. Crawling along in the usual Camberwell traffic jam. Beth was thinking how tender and conciliatory he had been to her for the last few days. It was the "I

235

need you, Beth" which had crept under her defences.

"Have we really thought this through?" she asked miserably as they reached the large detached houses of the stockbroker belt near Egham. "Should we be rushing into this? Can't we discuss it a little bit longer?" A ripple of panic shot through her. "You're asking too much of me."

"I feel I have to offer her this," he said quietly.

"But will you help? Will you be the one to mainly look after her?" He drove into 'The Laurels' drive. "I've promised."

A young man was strimming the edges of the beds, which were overgrown with weeds. Such a shocking comparison to last spring. Sybil and Tom had been excellent gardeners. James felt a wave of guilt and remorse at how little he had done to help since his father had died. He put his key in the lock and pushed open the door into the darkly decorated hall of his childhood home. "Sybil? Mother?" he called. "We're here."

Sybil came out of the lounge, as ever, beautifully dressed. Her grey slacks and off-white cashmere jumper looked as new and her makeup and hair were immaculate. But as she came into the light they could see that she had a large bruise on her cheek and forehead, which she had tried to cover with powder. She seemed a little flustered.

"I thought you'd have been here long ago. We could have gone out to lunch."

James's tone was firm. "I did tell you it would be after lunch, mother. Haven't you eaten anything?"

"Yes, of course." They had walked through to the bespoke oak kitchen. "I'll make you tea." She opened the fridge for the milk and Beth saw the empty shelves. She looked more closely at Sybil and saw that her hair was not clean and her expensive clothes were hanging on her.

"You've lost a lot of weight, Sybil."

"Yes, good isn't it," she said airily. "No biscuits, I'm afraid. I seem to have eaten them all."

James carried the tray into the elegant lounge, it looked as usual, but then she had a cleaner. He put the tray down and as if starting as he meant to go on, laid out the cups and started to pour the tea.

236

"Have you thought about my proposition, Mother?"

"Yes and I think it's a no. I can manage perfectly well myself. I've got Mrs Othen coming in twice a week to clean for me, and she'll shop on her way here if I need anything. The gardening is covered now, by her nephew and I've still got a few friends who pop in for tea and bridge. So I'm fine, thank you."

"Why not come for a few weeks holiday and we can see how you get on? You could play bridge with people we know. We could make sure you're eating properly and there wouldn't be all these worries you seem to have about leaking taps, the boiler and the roof."

"Dorothy comes for coffee twice a week. I'd miss her, and Ruth. I visit her sometimes."

"Why not try it with us for a few weeks?" James persisted.

Beth felt as if the water was closing over her head. Sybil looked out of the window. "Perhaps I could have a car. I could pop back to see them then."

Sybil had not driven for thirty years. "We'll see," said James quickly.

Sybil slumped in her chair and suddenly looked very old and defeated. "Being old is no joke. Why did Tom have to die?"

James, true to his word, helped clear Hugh's room and told him that his things would be stored in the attic, and he had phoned Michal to come and freshen up the paintwork. A screw had worked loose on the window catch. Beth fetched a screwdriver and tightened it. James watched her. "Sorry I've never taken to DIY. You've always been the practical one." She didn't tell him that necessity had been her teacher. James was obviously proud of his clearing efforts and he had unprecedentedly offered to go with her to choose the paint colour. She envisaged a shade of blue, reminiscent of their last holiday, sightseeing, sun and sand; graceful yachts on a calm, turquoise sea.

"Will we ever be able to have a holiday again, with Sybil here?" she asked.

The clocks had gone forward and the evenings are long. There are voices in the street til late: cars honking, people playing music, but it is cold and lonely in Annie's house and she was still grieving for her old life. She felt as if she were navigating uncharted territory. What should she do now?

On her way to Waitrose, Beth decided to ring her bell. "How are you, Annie?"

Annie stared at her. "Fine, thanks."

"You've lost a lot of weight?"

"Yes, alcohol is supposed to be so fattening, but I've lost a stone and a half. Though that may have had something to do with the fact I wasn't eating!"

"Anyway, you look good. Have you stopped drinking now?"

"Definitely. The sight of alcohol makes me feel sick. It was certainly a good way to go off social drinking."

Beth wondered why Annie was not inviting her in. This was feeling awkward. "I never thought you and Martin would break up."

Annie was embarrassed at the mess the house was in and why hadn't Beth called to see her before? Did she think depression was catching?

"Anyway, I'm sorry, I was just going out. Nice of you to call."

"Oh, right. We must get together soon. Supper? Tea?"

Annie had been hunting through her iPhotos to choose some for her book. She had scanned in quite a few from her childhood. Here's Daddy. He looks so young. Always on the edge of groups, drowned out by his wife's and two daughters' strident voices. The smell of alcohol and anchovy paste, my main memory. Such a gentle, yielding nature, is that why I chose Martin?

There's the day I went off to college. Blue bri-nylon, permanently pleated dress, white nylon cardigan and white plastic shoes. Mum's choice. What about this one? The silky, beaded dress, hot from the hippie trail. I was so proud of it. We wore bells and rings on our legs and toes, so pretty. Wonder what I did with it all?

Here's one with my flatmates, in my pink mini skirt and plastic thigh boots, getting wolf whistles from builders and white van men no doubt. What fun! Though we just wanted to get married. We never thought how we were giving up our independence, taking on the man's name, we fell for it. So long ago…this age thing is depressing.

It had started to rain. She stood up and looked out into the overgrown garden, which she and Martin had tended so assiduously. Back to nature. Just like life's impermanence she mused.

Rain spattered against the window of Ray's tiny lounge. Martin was watching the Proms, half listening to a Verdi aria from 'The Masked Ball.' He was only half concentrating because he was yet again pondering about what had happened to his marriage. Perhaps I'm a failure and unlovable? I'm a shadow without Annie's abrasive, insistent presence. Is there any way back?

"Are you still lost and unhappy at being retired?" Jo and Frances had just left the other swimmers at the corner and were heading home.

Frances thought about it, deciding to be honest. "No, I've cheered up a lot since I met Martin. He's really helped me appreciate my life. It's not completely empty without work. There's so much more I can do now. I'm going to look around for voluntary jobs. He's been very encouraging."

"Are you in love with him?" asked Jo.

"I really don't know," Frances frowned. "Having someone to do things with for the first time in my life has been good. But then I've really had to bite my lips when he's around too much. I'm just not used to it and I can't imagine living all the time with anyone. I'm certainly not ready for that. I've had a lifetime of making my own decisions and I'm not used to considering anyone else…cooking for them, ministering when they're ill…"

"So you're not going to move in together?"

Frances looked shocked. "Absolutely not. I want to stay as we are."

"But apparently the guy only has a tiny bedroom to live in and you've got your big flat. Are you worried that he'll go back to Annie?"

"That's a risk I'll have to take. I'm aware that I'm the novelty, and Annie was his 'til death do us part'." She wondered to herself if in any case she would ever be wife material.

The next day Frances and Martin went to West Wales for two days walking. The coast path was steep. Sheep grazed between rocks which burst out of the springy turf, and the biting wind coming off the sea cut through their clothes and made their noses run and eyes sting. There were the sounds of unseen birds and of a stream falling into the silence of the valley below.

They reached the top and stood on the cliff, watching the cloud shadows racing across the sea. The wind lifted Frances's thin hair away from her bony face and had polished her nose red. A drip gathered itself at the end. Martin wondered if he really fancied her and if he would feel unattracted to Annie with a dripping nose. How trivial and superficial I am, he thought. He watched a tractor and plough making a long, straight groove, soil rearing and crumbling like a wave breaking. Seagulls streamed behind, swooping with their cruel razor beaks into the turned over dark earth before it dried out in the wind.

"Shall we plan a holiday somewhere warmer?" she asked suddenly. Her words lay like small, cold stones between them. Not like the joyful fountain spray she had anticipated.

After an old fashioned pub dinner, where the menu consisted of meaty things and chips or other meaty things and mash, Martin went out for a stroll. Frances was looking forward to reading her 'Telegraph' in bed.

The moon was full. So even without street lights, he could see his way up the hill behind the pub. His heart and brain swelled at the beauty of the night. He took a deep breath of the fresh, sweet night air. It felt like a magic draught. A bat swooped silently, like a ghost above him. After a few hundred yards, the trees crowded around and his little torch could not penetrate the blackness. The silence was almost tangible. It wrapped itself around him. He was gripped by a deep loneliness and he dropped his head back and felt strangely giddy as he gazed up at the stars through the branches of the oaks and chestnuts. An owl hooted and a fox howled in the distance. Nature was elemental, spell binding. How temporary and vulnerable we are, he thought.

The second day Frances did not want to do a long walk, her legs ached and her heels were sore. She wanted to potter. They were sitting at breakfast and Martin was reading the local guide and walk book.

"What are you planning for today?" she asked. "Look here at the weather forecast. Not good," and she waved the local newspaper at his balding crown, bent over the books. There was a silence.

"This is a good walk. Shall we leave in ten minutes?" He said as if he had not heard.

A mist rolled in as they started off. Tentative and wispy at first, but becoming thicker as they climbed, obscuring the views and swiftly enveloping them, as if with a purpose. They luckily managed to retrace their steps and had an early lunch while hoping for it to disperse. Then the sun came out and Martin decided to do quite a long walk to a ruined castle. Frances thought that when she finished her newspaper she would walk along the beach to the next village and back.

The sea was gleaming, shushing and merging into the low cloud on the horizon, so peaceful and beautiful. The beach was rocky. She stepped up onto a boulder and jumped to another, feeling it moving beneath her feet. She swayed, bent her knees and reached out her hand to the wet, mussel encrusted surface. Dozens of pairs of nesting seagulls cawed warningly and shifted uneasily on the cliff above. Crablike she circumnavigated the rocky outcrop back to the hard sand. This is ridiculous. I'm so stiff and unbalanced now. Her phone rang and her lonely soul leapt. Was it Martin? It was a message from Orange. She switched it off. Pointless being in a lovely place and not absorbing its atmosphere. Martin hated people being on their phones when they were out for walks.

A dog ran past her, weaving from side to side down the beach, sniffling and snuffling, pulled by smells, but never lingering, hoping for a more enticing one further along. In his zigzag route he stopped and looked back at her every few yards, to check she was still following behind. She called him, "Doggie, Doggie," and he came springing back, ears pricked. When she said nothing, he turned and ran on and was soon out of sight. I couldn't have a dog, too much fuss, she said to herself.

It was four o'clock and the shops were shut by the time that she arrived. She went into the only pub and ordered a coffee. The sun was sinking below the horizon when she emerged, so she set off quickly down the path to the beach and onto the dunes, shivering in the breeze. Her feet sank into the soft sand and in her haste she slid and slithered, gripping handfuls of marram grass to stop herself falling down the slope.

Ahead was a light from a fire. She could hear murmuring voices and laughter. Head down, shoving her hands into the pockets of her Barbour jacket, she strode quickly away from the fire towards the receding sea and the rhythmic suck and crash of the little waves.

The last rays of light were caught in their foam and the sand at her feet twinkled silver, but she felt a shiver of nerves at the empty, darkening beach ahead, her feet sinking deeper in the wet sand.

After fifteen minutes, she looked up and stopped suddenly, her breath sticking in her throat. Standing on a rock was a dark, shadowy person, outlined against the twilight sky. A flasher?

"Hello," she called. "Hello."

Whoever it was did not answer, but jumped off the rock and started walking towards her.

"Speak to me. Tell me who you are. Stop or I'll scream!" she shrieked.

The figure stopped.

"Who are you?" she shouted again.

"It's me. Couldn't you tell? I'm sorry, I didn't mean to scare you."

"Well you absolutely did…" Blood was pounding in her head and she was shaking.

London was grey, taupe, the Thames the colour of the expresso Martin had bought at Paddington station as they returned from their short break. They stood in the middle of the busy concourse saying goodbye. He was taking a bus, while she was going to get the tube. It felt awkward, as if this were the end. Then suddenly she found herself saying impulsively, "are we having that holiday in France you talked about?"

There was a silence. Did I sound too eager, too naive and needy, she wondered. He had reddened and was checking his watch, not looking at her. Then he did and smiled.

"Ok," he said. "I do love the south of France. There are wonderful walks in the mountains and of course sandy beaches to walk down to. Shall we book for three or four days?"

Terry was in the garden, standing under the magnolia tree. There was a gentle rustle from above. The leaves looked fresh and damp, still crumpled from their buds. The prunus in the middle of the lawn was shedding its blossom, pink and white petals covering the grass around it. Did she have the energy to mow? Weeds had sprung up everywhere. I can't control them anymore. There were fresh shoots of bindweed showing above the soil, ready to twine up plants and squeeze them to death. She had never managed to eradicate it entirely. Just a fragment of white root left in the soil grew into long green snakes in weeks.

She had been trying to pretend that she could live normally. Perhaps this horrible cancer will go away. Perhaps it was all a big mistake.

The spring flowers had finished apart from the yellow irises, standing proudly at the edge of the pond. 'Albertine' which had been the Queen Mother's favourite rose, would be out soon. Would she still be here to see the fuscias, abutilon and penstemons, just in front of the window?

Walking very far was becoming difficult. She was forgetting words and sleeping more. She no longer took the tube. She was not confident of her balance and leg strength. She drove everywhere, smooth and fast. Instead of her clumsy, awkward and breathless walking motion, she could stamp her foot down and fly along. One evening, she went for a drive, cocooned in the car, the headlights holding a bright bubble of space in front of her. Speeding round the North Circular past Leatherland, Hoo Hing Oriental foods, Sofaland, huge storage places and a recycling centre. She felt like an astronaut, travelling through space. Her real life had retreated a million miles.

She was forcing herself to go swimming, driving there and meeting her friends. They could all see what an effort it was for her and it was obvious she didn't enjoy it much.

"If you don't like swimming, you don't have to do it, Terry," Beth said one day.

"Why do anything then?" Terry asked. "We have to do some things not because we enjoy doing them, but because they're good for us. Life isn't just about doing enjoyable things."

"Mmm," said Beth thoughtfully.

Olive, who had taken on Terry's job had come to see her a few times, but concentrating for a few hours had exhausted her. She had begun having dizzy spells, headaches and blurred vision. Was this shock, or was something even worse happening to her? Sometimes there was a rushing sound in her ears and she felt as if she were falling. Falling into nothing. She tried to catch the air as she fell, but it slithered through her fingers.

Dr Errani's secretary had rung, insisting that there were things to discuss now that she had had time to consider the options. "I don't want any more treatment," she said. "Come and discuss it," said Priti.

Terry drove through the drizzle. It was a grey day. All the colour seemed to have drained from her world. Everything was monochrome.

She sat in the Consultants waiting room with a cross section of Londoners as the large clock on the opposite wall munched up the minutes. Two youngish people were listening to music on their iPods or MP3 players while thumbing their phones. A large man was trying to pacify his testy mother in her wheelchair and two women in hijabs were talking incomprehensively to one another.

Having described her latest symptoms, Dr Errani rang her the next day. "I've arranged your MRI scan for Friday. Come in at ten." Her voice was gentle.

Chapter 17. May. Relationships

'Make the most of life you may,
Life is short and wears away.'
William Oldys.
'On a Fly Drinking Out of His Cup.' (1696 – 1761)

Heavy purply-black rain clouds were massing over the blue sky as Annie waited on the pavement outside her house, but she could hardly contain her disappointment when only Laura, Jo, Beth and Lynne came down the road through the shafts of sunlight and dark shadows to meet her. "No Frances?" she asked in what she hoped was a casual, neutral sounding voice.

"She's gone to the south of France," Laura said as they crossed the road.

"On her own?"

"No Annie, with Martin," said Lynne firmly.

Annie felt sick. "They'll just be walking I expect. He's always loved walking between villages above Menton,. He says he's immersing himself in the familiar, rather than skimming the world."

"I'm sorry, Annie, but who goes to the most shagadelic place and doesn't have sex? Face it, woman."

"You're such a bitch, Lynne."

"Now that you're retired, you can go off on your own sort of holidays. You don't have to consider anyone else, isn't that great?"

"I'm *not* retired," Annie retorted. "I'm not *retiring*! I'm refocusing…rebalancing…re-engaging. Just because I've lost one job, I've still got another and I'm freelancing and writing my book." She felt a little guilty. She had not really written for months.

The water in the pool was cooler today and the water level was low, so it was rough. Annie stood in the unlaned part for a while before she ducked in and rolled round and round acclimatising, then front crawled powerfully to the other end. Swimming back, she had to weave her way round non-swimmers and beginners standing talking or trying a few strokes. She dived under the lane divider to join the six men in the fast lane.

Before they got out, rain was pounding on the roof.

"Add lustre to your pubic hair with fresh fruit cream rinse?" Jo read out the label and offered it round the open plan shower area. "Did anyone read that excerpt in the Sunday Times from Tom Bower's book about Simon Cowell?"

Laura had. "What the one about his lovers? They go to bed, but don't wake up together. He doesn't want to be seen with 'bedhead' or see them before they're properly groomed?"

"Perfect! I meant the regular blood tests and vitamin injections he apparently has every week and the buckets of supplements. Even I might baulk at them *and* the colonic irrigation! He says it makes his eyes shine brighter."

"Revolting!" Beth said with a shudder.

"Come on, guys, he's not alone. I've read that millions of men crash their cars, ogling at themselves in their rear view mirrors," said Lynne.

"Wish I had his money to have all the surgical enhancements though."

"Jo! Do you want a trout pout and a stiff face? Or a lumpy body after those risky fillers or liposuction have gone wrong?"

"It can go wrong if you buy stuff on the internet and go to a quack. Something like forty thousand women had it last year in the UK."

"*Forty thousand?* Who are all these people?"

Annie had finished dressing and was sitting down on the bench. "There are quite a few at the tennis club. Haven't you noticed, Laurs?"

"Really?" Laura looked intrigued. "I think you're mad Jo, but what are you thinking of having?"

"I'll pass on the lamb foetus into the bum, but I've been looking at human growth hormone injections. Apparently it turns your body back to as it was twenty years ago and I'm definitely having CO_2 injected into these lines, here and here. And perhaps some fillers to plump out my cheeks and botox in my lower face, to stop the lower jaw and neck sag." She pulled at the sides of her mouth and her forehead. "CO_2 injections have been around since the thirties."

"For goodness sake. What do you think that does?" Lynne was waiting impatiently near the door.

"It stimulates the circulation to make more collagen, so the skin's more elastic?"

"Oh yes?"

"Hmm," said Beth disbelievingly. "I can hardly see your little wrinkles and you don't know the long term effects of injections of hormones. I want my own face. I don't want to look the same as all those plastic people. We can't stay young forever. Let's grow old gracefully!"

Lynne looked at Jo with a smiley cat's face in place. "Well, I think that plastic surgery is the evidence by which we can identify the most desperate age deniers."

Jo ignored her. "'A man's face is his autobiography. A woman's face is her work of fiction.'* Gracefully? Disgracefully is my motto. I've been saving up. You wait til you see the difference!"

By the time that they emerged there was a dazzling sun and they immediately felt in brighter moods.

It was a Governors' day for Laura, and she was a member of the panel interviewing for a new Head. Ms Barber was taking early retirement. She made a piece of toast and tea and went upstairs to take off her swimming uniform of jeans and fleece and put on her grey pencil skirt and pale pink jumper. Standing in front of her full-length mirror, she looked disconsolately at her puffy knees, varicose veins and collapsed skin on her thighs. Withered arms and a face that life had travelled across, there didn't seem to have been a transition between admiration in people's eyes at her slim athletic build and invisibility. Now, the occasional compliment felt shocking, because it was so unexpected. Like that friend of Antony's who had asked her out when they met in the gym. She had told him that she was sixty-four, but it only made him even more admiring. He had looked at her with shining eyes, "Very good body. Lovely woman."

"You've had a great life. Laura, she told herself. I'm so lucky to be fit, to live in the UK with a pension, the NHS, wonderful travel freedom passes, cheaper entry tickets for things and Dan and friends.

Life is brilliant. Appreciate it more!

After swimming Annie spent the morning pacing about the garden, thinking round and round in circles. Her skin felt tauter, her mind clear and waves of pure energy flooded her body. I know nothing is forever, she concluded. You get a job, get married, have a child, get old…so wasn't it the wrong time of life to split up? Everything here reminds me of him. He's there in the greenhouse and conservatory he built, my ensuite bathroom and, of course, his shed. And the garden! Everything's gone mad, I've neglected it. She went inside and looked around at the comfortable lounge they had furnished together; cream carpets, the Persian rug, pale green walls, Martin's piano and our sound system.

No, nothing is forever. We're mortal. Things change, but I'm not doing very well without him. I'll have to sell up and move. Get a new life. I probably won't get another job, the internet has killed off so many periodicals. Who am I now? Half a couple, half a person? Who was I? She phoned an old school friend now living in Scotland. Wanting her to explain who she had been before she had become a part of someone else. Paula did not understand and was not very sympathetic. I suppose her Reg dying was worse. Though it might be easier if Martin had died. I'd have the memory of us together. But he's not dead. He's very much alive to Frances. It's too painful.

Laura and Daniel went to the cinema to see 'The Artist.' Laura was in ecstasy. "That was the most perfect film. I didn't notice after a few minutes that it was black and white and silent, did you?

"How couldn't you keep noticing? It was all mime. The dog was the best part."

"Whaat? It was exquisite, so eloquent, wonderful acting!" She tried to enthuse him but he could not understand what she saw in it.

"Just overacted melodrama."

"We're so different, we don't communicate!"

They walked home in silence. She went upstairs for a shower and he cooked their supper, giving her the paper to read and a glass of Malbec in front of the television, when she came down. "You can't always expect people to understand your views, or have the same opinions as you," he said. "I try to tell you how I feel, otherwise there could be misunderstandings, but I'm not good at explaining. And you make me feel really insecure when you patronise me."

Laura knew she was in the wrong, but somehow could not apologise. There was an uncomfortable silence and he went back into the kitchen.

"Magnificent!" breathed Martin, looking down at Monaco and Roque St Bruin below. Pale buildings densely packed, clinging to the cliffs above the deep blue sea. Frances sprayed her arms with more factor 50 and waited. After a few minutes he consulted his map again and they set off single file along the rocky terraced ridge. "Don't these miles of dry stone walls and stone paths that people have built with their bare hands make you feel humble?" he asked.

"Why humble?"

"Think of how many thousands of hours it took. Carting the rocks about and choosing the exact fit. Incredibly hard work! Then having to subsist on what you can grow on inhospitable stony terraces and living in one of these." He pointed at a ruined small stone cottage above them. "No-one would work or live like that now."

"Why would you when you get paid to not work?" she said cynically.

He was striding in front of her, talking and asking rhetorical questions about wayside flowers. She had already said that she didn't know any, but they were continually stopping as he noticed new varieties or wanted to take in a view.

"Look, they're growing next to one another here. This is oxalis and this is wood anemone. Can you see the difference now?"

Frances barely glanced. She was bored and tired. She looked at her watch. "How much further?" she asked and as an afterthought, "Did Annie do walks like this with you?" She couldn't visualise such a sophisticated, dominating woman trailing along after Martin. She was fed up and it was only their first day.

"Annie? She wouldn't work out the route or read the map, but yes she enjoys a good walk and she's pretty good on the names of the flowers."

She wondered if that were a reproach.

By the time that they had reached the next village, she had had enough. It was hot: her feet hurt, she was puce with exertion and her back was stiff. She was glad to take up the option of a bus back to their start point.

The next day in the bright sunlight he noticed hairs on Frances's chin and thought about her peevish, not interested in things behaviour the day before. It had begun to grate how her life was all rules and routines and the fact that she only liked plain food, which she separated into piles on her plate, tilting her head as she concentrated. Then ate one at a time following her own strict plan.

Frances found that she had started to get irritated by the speed at which he ate, not to mention the amount. However, much they were served, or they made when at home, he would finish it all. Yet he was whippet thin. Sitting opposite him, she could not help noticing again the bare patches on his head as he pored over the map, working out the day's walk. What exactly was Martin offering? Not permanence as he's still married. Does he love me? Does he still love Annie? "This could work out for us," he had said. Permanently? He was always on her home turf. How would she feel if they shared a house? She had been on her own for so long. Could she share? She was not sure. She was not ready to make up her mind. She wanted more courtship: more time, more explanation of how their future could be. She realised that they never went out with friends. He had made excuses not to meet her sister or take her to lunch with his old work colleagues. Why is our relationship under wraps? She wondered.

As for Martin, he just wanted a peaceful life. He did not want to move in with Frances, because that would mean an overwhelming closeness, which would commit them to each other. He was a coward and his instincts were not to burn his boats irrevocably with Annie.

Jo had been seeing Antony two or three times a week since March and he had come to her flat as usual after the gym on Sunday. She had made a casserole and had bought a tarte au citron from M&S. They did not talk much over the meal. Her mind was elsewhere, so

250

she barely noticed that he looked serious and upset. When they had eaten, he cleared the table, loaded the machine and made them both coffee, as he usually did. They sat in the comfortable chairs at the other end of her large lounge/diner and he stirred in a teaspoon of sugar, then lent back, looked hard at her, as if into her soul and asked: "So who was the guy I saw you with in 'Le Paradis,' on Friday?"

A frisson of shock went through her. "Oh, he's just an old friend. He's gone back to France now."

"I need you to be truthful with me. We said we'd have an open relationship. Not tie each other down, but that was at the beginning. I thought we'd moved beyond that."

Jo sipped her coffee and thought hard. The truth or be evasive, mmm...

He held her gaze until she looked down and sipped again. 'A little sincerity is a dangerous thing and a great deal of it is absolutely fatal,'* she thought and had another gulp of coffee. She had never been able to resist the excitement of juggling two or three lovers, but was this being truthful going to lose the best one she had perhaps ever had? "Only the odd fling."

His face registered shock and hurt. "So you've been having casual sex all the time you've been seeing me?" His voice was flat and trembled slightly. "Even though we were having such a passionate affair, you were also screwing around?" Disgust was the prominent emotion now.

"I'm sorry." She suddenly wanted to cry. "Haven't you seen anyone else?"

His face was hard. "No."

She was shocked. "Well, we weren't heading for marriage. You didn't want to settle down with me. I thought we were just in it for a good time."

"For some reason I didn't expect this."

She looked down at the dregs of her coffee. "What happened to our open relationship idea? Shall we start again?"

He slumped in his chair, deflated. "I don't think so. I've obviously been made a fool of by someone who isn't worth caring about." Tossing the key to her flat onto the table he pushed back his chair, said "I'll see you around," and went.

Her heart almost stopped in shock. Why do I do this? She asked herself. Destroying every worthwhile relationship.

She lay awake that night. After a few hours of tossing and twitching, she got out of bed. Her feet were cold on the bare floorboards. She had taken up the carpet meaning to strip them. Another job she had not got done. She pulled open the heavy mane of her curtains, and could see nothing. Just her face floating, ghostly in the darkness. The wind was howling and the air in her bedroom felt thick and heavy. She crept back to bed and curled up tightly like she did as a child. I'm too old for that deathly quadrille of conventional courtship. Life's too short for all those rules like no sex on the first date. That's for kids. What's wrong with being polyamorous? I never boast or tweet about my conquests. I just need sex. Men always want to be a woman's first love, or only lover. Isn't that vanity? They're 'Lotharios' and 'legends' for sleeping around, we're 'loose', 'scrubbers', 'sluts' and even 'whores'. Men say they want someone feisty to challenge them. But do they? They end up with needy types.

I'm always 'too' something: 'too flirtatious', 'too extravagant', 'too unreliable', 'too selfish'. Tears were flowing freely. I don't need men to discuss the merits of Keynesian economics or particle physics. I just want a man to lie in bed with, who's up for it. Antony was a five star lover. Did he really think of me as wife material, or was it just his ego? She screamed into the turgid air and after a few more restless hours, got up and put on her rollers and plastic moisturising suit.

The doorbell rang and Lynne went to answer it. "How about some gardening before we go out?" She asked brightly.

Robert had been hoping for late a 'luncheon' at The Tate, but was becoming used to these Sunday suggestions. He obediently went to the car to get his gardening clothes, which he left in the boot for such eventualities.

Suitably attired, he came out of the downstairs shower room and stood to attention, waiting for her command. The viburnam and ceonothus needed pruning, the potatoes need earthing up, and…and…but I can only trust him with simple tasks. He's got no interest in learning which are weeds or valued plants.

"How about you dead head these roses, like this and this. Then clip the edges of the lawn. Trimming only grass. Don't cut the overhanging plants like these." She lifted the sweet william, and alchemilla mollis, to show him.

On her kneeler to weed a nearby bed, she found it impossible not to keep checking what he was doing. His efforts were so cursory that the edges would have to be cut again. Within fifteen minutes he had fetched some cushions from the conservatory and was sitting on her wooden bench with his Sunday Telegraph and a packet of biscuits, oblivious of the beauty around him.

Lynne weeded and seethed. How can I have a partner so uninterested in nature? We're too different! He's so arrogant and patronising. Calling people 'the great unwashed!' But he's also very kind: loyal, entertaining, cultured and old fashionedly polite…and always has good ideas about where to go. More to the point, why does he see me? I'm continually deriding his snobbishness and rich person's lifestyle.

He was looking pointedly at his watch. "The gallery closes at six o'clock."

She went in to have a quick shower and change, wondering if it was ridiculous to be judging people by their attitude to gardening. Why should everyone be interested in the same things? But then, delighting in nature is so important to me. Is someone who thinks that salad leaves grow in packets and never gets their hands dirty the man for me? Do I only want someone who appreciates nature? What were those lines on the birthday card from Laura? 'And when your back stops aching and your hands begin to harden, you will find yourself a partner in the Glory of the Garden.'* I wish.

Laura came out of her front door into the chill air and headed down the road to the station. Gillian was standing at the corner, staring at a concreted over garden where four cars were parked.

"See that front," said Gillian. "That's a planning violation. They're supposed to leave one third as garden. *And* they've taken

253

down the original front wall!"

Gillian had set up their local residents association and their choir. She organised the concerts and sometimes sang solos in her powerful mezzo-soprano voice.

"Are you on the planning committee?"

"Yes, we're hoping not to have to go to court on this one."

They parted at the next corner and Laura watched her go, flopping heavily along. Badly dressed and lonely. Filling her life with voluntary work and acting as carer and baby sitter for her mother and married sister. A solid citizen. The poem 'Not Waving but Drowning' by Stevie Smith came into her head.

Hmm. She was lost in thought on the tube and then a different problem consumed her on the train. What would she find when she got to Dan's parents' house in Lincoln? They had become so frail and confused. Still living in the house where Dan had been brought up, with its big garden and wilderness at the bottom in which Dan had played his life preparation games, they were now not coping.

They had been a handsome couple. Tall, slim and fit looking, both with the dark curly hair that Dan had inherited. Their main interest in life had been golf. They had played, watched or socialised with friends from the club and had never been much interested in homely pursuits. Their house had been just a place to live, meals, plain and unimaginative.

Laura had become quite emotional at seeing how run down their home now was. She would clean the bedrooms and wash the kitchen floor or the fridge, throwing out all the rotten food. "You wouldn't have eaten these smelly chops and mouldy ham, would you?" she would ask despairingly.

"They're only a few days old. We bought them on Thursday," her mother-in-law would beseech.

"Which Thursday?" Laura would think.

Now that they were too stiff and arthritic to play golf they had lost touch with their golfing friends and despite huge efforts from Laura to get them to go to bowls, elderly keep fit, swimming or bridge, they had always found an excuse not to go a second or third time. They lived in solitude behind a door with five locks, watching TV or looking at newspapers for most of the day. Laura wondered when they had last had a bath or shower and changed their clothes.

Yet when they sat down for the meal that she had prepared, they would ask about Daisy and their step (though Laura and Dan were not married) great grandchildren and listen raptly to Laura's made up accounts. She could not bear to upset them by telling them what had happened.

If Laura occasionally said she was not able to come for three weeks, rather than two, they would say "Don't worry, we mustn't be selfish." Which made Laura want to shout: "Please DO be selfish, don't give me such a burden of guilt. I'm not doing enough for you!" The truth was that Laura felt frustrated at not only her inability to dedicate herself to a writing life, but was beginning to worry about her own life running out.

When she got back home, she rushed up to the attic to see Dan. "We must do something about your parents. Something more than just one of us visiting once a week. Their lives are reduced to getting up, eating and going to bed. Their house is falling down around them. The garden's a jungle. We've got to do more and get them some help! Your father shouldn't be driving at ninety-two. He keeps forgetting where he parked the car."

"I'll interfere when they ask me to. I've offered, but they say they don't need help. I can't stop them from getting old, or demean them by telling them they can't cope."

"But we can't just leave them. Their house is filthy. They don't wash themselves or cut their nails. They're too weak to do more than hang around the house in the same clothes they went to bed in and it takes five minutes for them to come to the door when we visit and then another five to open all the locks. *And* they're living on cuppa soup, cups of tea and digestive biscuits. They're on their last legs. Their home has become their prison. Getting older is so hard. We all want our lives to go on forever and hang on to what we know. Then it all gets too much." She started weeping.

"This is stupid, Laura. Don't make such a drama out of it. I've asked them before. They don't want help, except in the garden and

255

Neil goes every so often. You're feeling sorry for yourself and projecting it onto them, seeing problems where they don't yet exist. Calm down." He went back to his still life sketch and Laura, feeling dismissed, went downstairs to sit with a glass of wine in the conservatory.

She stared out at the darkening garden, packed with an undisciplined profusion of plants, which she could not control, thinking that it reflected her life and herself. There is no room for everyone and everything and no time to look after all that I plant or all the people I mean to keep in touch with. Why do I grow all those plants from seed? Waste hours pricking them out and planting them as food for all the slugs and snails in the neighbourhood? Every year I'm seduced by plant catalogues and I'm quite unable to keep away from plant stalls, or to continue the analogy, interesting new people to add to my email address book, in the vain hope that I can keep up with them. Why do I need all these friends and plants?

Yet regal white foxgloves, showy tree paeonies, velvety pansies and delicious beans and tomatoes. They give me so much pleasure. I'm too ambitious wanting so much…Is knowing me akin to some sort of assault course, where only the strongest survive? She remembered the phrase she had read in a magazine when she was a painfully shy teenager: 'You only exist as a reflection in other people's eyes.' Have those words shaped me into a person only happy when receiving attention from a large number of people? She sat agonising until it was quite dark.

James fetched Sybil, beautifully dressed in a cream linen suit, and locked up her house. She brought her TV and had already sent an armchair, a large walnut wardrobe and matching chest of drawers for her bedroom, which she immediately said were in the wrong places.

Beth knew that this was the only way everything fitted. "Believe me, Sybil, I've measured everything and this is the only way your…"

Sybil cut in, as if Beth wasn't speaking. "James please move the bed to here and the wardrobe here. I'll be downstairs."

So this is how it's going to be, Beth seethed to herself. Daily lashes from that woman as we fight for James attention. "I'll make a little pot of tea, Sybil, and then I'll help you unpack."

Ten minutes later when James and their odd job man, Michal, had proved that Beth was right, Sybil subsided into her armchair grumbling. "I can't live here with the bed and the television in that position. This really won't do."

That night they were woken by screaming and shouts of "Help, help."

James struggled out of bed. "Mother what's wrong?"

"What are *you* doing here?"

"I live here, Mother. You're staying in London in our house."

She was pale and confused. "Where?"

"I'll make you some tea." When he came back with it, she still looked frightened and upset. He explained again where she was and why. She had never been a tactile, affectionate mother. His instinct was to hug and comfort her, as he would Beth, but her stiff, dignified bearing forbore him offering that kind of reassurance.

Sybil was reading the 'Metro', which Beth had picked up on her way back from food shopping. "Who are all these people?" She jabbed crossly at the pages. "I've never heard of any of them. What are they doing in a newspaper?"

"You'll be glad to know that we have never heard of them either. They're probably people snatching a few little months of fame for something, who'll disappear as quickly as they arrived. Would you like to come to tea at Laura's and Dan's?" Beth asked brightly.

"Who are they? I don't know them. I don't need to know them."

"You've met them Sybil. She's my close friend from down the road. You know, the tall one with a daughter and twin grandchildren."

Sybil sniffed. "This weather is shocking. I'm not going out in that wind and anyway I'm not feeling well today."

"Well, the walk will do you good."

"Walk? Why can't we drive?"

"Because we both need some exercise before we tuck into cakes."

"What was her name again?"

Beth complained to James a few days later, "She's so bossy. A little control freak. She has to know where we both are all the time and she goes out without telling us where she's going. Doesn't she realise we worry about her too?"

"She's just not used to not being in control. She'll settle down."

Lynne had started going to Hampstead Ladies pond. "It's well known that chlorinated pools cause DNA damage, so you're more likely to get cancer at the Leisure Centre. And it's so dirty most of the time."

"Hmm, yes, well I'll give you dirty. There's far too many bodies in it most days, but at least you can see what's below the surface."

"The water's fine. It's clear and sweet and I love being out of doors. Surrounded by overhanging trees, waving in the breeze. It gets a bit crowded on sunny days, but on others it's just the regulars: the coots, ducks, moorhens, swans, gulls and swifts and martins high above. There's nothing more uplifting. I'll swim there for the summer."

"Oh, shame. Half the fun of swimming is seeing one's friends."

"You could all come there?"

"Not me. Don't like the mud: the vegetation, the ducks and pike. And it's cold."

"It's not too bad. That's why the regulars are such tough, no-nonsense women. There's some great characters there, you know. Anyway, I'll see how it goes."

"Mmm, just hope you don't get addicted. Like Al Alvarez. He wrote a book about swimming in the mixed pond all the year."

"Can't see me breaking the ice."

It was Sunday morning and Phillip was up a ladder, pruning 'Kathleen Harrop,' their climbing rose. Did he have a stroke? Maybe. Something made him fall forward like a stone and hit his head on the birdbath. Helen in her study upstairs overlooking the garden, heard a thud and looked out to see him face down in the cosmos, penstemon and phlox, his legs splayed out. She rushed down. Had he knocked himself out? Was he joshing? He was very still. She heaved and rolled him over. There was blood on his temples, seeping out on the flower bed. A thread of it coming from his ear. His eyes were open, blind and pale as the early evening sky. She put out her hand to the carotid on his neck, then his wrist. There was nothing. He was warm but had no pulse. It started to rain. Onto the blood on his head and his open eyes. His dead face accepting it without a flicker. It started to rain harder, the wind making wet whips of the trees. She was shivering with shock. "I can't leave you like this, dead in the flower bed. Dead… dead…foxes might come, cats, birds and peck out those eyes. I should shut them, but I can't, can't touch the eyes of my husband I lay next to for more than forty years? Phillip, wake up, say it's a joke! Oh God, please, please Phillip. Is that the phone? I can't leave him…"

Chapter 18. June. Celebrations and Commiserations

'Gather ye Rosebuds while ye may.
Old time is still a-flying:
And this same flower that smiles today
Tomorrow will be dying.'
Robert Herrick.
'To the Virgins, to make much of time.' (1591 – 1674)

Laura was putting on her jacket, picking up her swimming bag, when the doorbell rang. It was Lynne. "Surprise, surprise. Not going to the ponds this morning?"

"It's shut. Too much algae. It was like swimming in cold minestrone."

They walked up the road to pick up Beth. It was a cool, dark day with spots of rain blown in the wind.

There was usually a little wait for Beth and she eventually emerged in her big yellow down anorak. "It's so cold for June. I've got this thingy out again," she said in explanation.

"Yes, it's a lousy summer so far."

"Hope it perks up by tomorrow."

"Why tomorrow?" asked Lynne.

"We've got a street party. Well, a couple of streets actually. Everyone has to take red, white and blue food and wear a tiara or a crown. You know it's the Queen's Diamond Jubilee celebration."

"Well I won't be celebrating. I'm a republican," retorted Lynne.

Beth was almost speechless. "The Queen is…is wonderful," she spluttered.

"It's archaic. Ridiculous. Why should someone be so privileged?"

"Doesn't every country need a figurehead?" said Laura. And the Queen is inoffensive, and non-political."

"Why should this family and all their hangers on have unearned inherited wealth and privilege?"

"Oh, well that's another argument. Most supporters like the

permanence of the monarchy, how it holds us together as a nation. When our lives are difficult it's reassuring to have a queen in bright clothes, hats and handbags, waving, shaking hands and cutting ribbons. Loosen up."

"We're not going to agree. They really get up my nose. The whole lot of them. What food are you taking then, Beth?"

"I really can't see how you can object to people like the Queen, the Duke of Edinburgh and Anne. They work harder than anyone I know." She was red in the face with supressed anger. "Little blueberry muffins and tomato tart."

They arrived at the pool and changed in silence, not wanting to rekindle their opposed feelings. The pool was busy and the water slopped against the sides with the dozens of swimmers thrashing up and down. It was not enjoyable, so they got out early and had an extra long time in the shower. By the time that they emerged the sun was coming and going and a large group of runners were pounding past with serious sweating faces. Which gave them something to talk about to take their minds off royalty.

Saturday was pouring with rain and forecast not to stop. So instead of standing outside on Rachel and Pete's large lawn, dozens of children were playing about in one of the two tents they had hired. The majority of adults huddled in front of televisions in the house, watching the flotilla of one thousand ships on the Thames. Jo had taken over the bar tent and was mixing some lethal cocktails, suspending her new rule to drink only from Wednesdays to Friday, so her liver enzymes got some time to regroup.

"You're not going to make everyone drunk with those, are you?" Beth said doubtfully when, red, white and blue umbrella in hand, she went to get a drink.

"This is the sophisticated cocktail era. Cocktail bars are the places to be now. How about a fruity one? This is Passion Mare and I can make you a Strawberry Jive?"

"Mmm, I'll just have a little sip of that one then. Where do you go to cocktail bars?"

"There's one in the Langham. The Connaught and the Savoy opened again not long ago."

Beth tasted the red concoction dubiously. "It's nice, but can I have a non-alcoholic one?"

Laura had spotted Gillian. She wondered why she had missed so many choir evenings this term.

"I've been very busy," Gillian said, blushing. Her short, thin hair was tucked behind her ears and her eyes were focussed, but tiny behind narrow glasses.

"What project are you grappling with now?" Laura asked, glad that she had just replenished her glass of wine and expecting a boring diatribe about some local issue. Gillian did not answer at first. She looked embarrassed and even shifty.

"Oh, things. This and that."

Laura looked more closely at her. "What sort of things?"

"Have you heard of Second Life?" Gillian blurted out.

"What's second life?"

"It's this virtual world. I go dancing, paragliding, deep sea diving and chat with friends."

"So who are these friends? Can you see them?"

"Yes, we have avatars. Mine's called Dina and she's tall and slim with long chestnut hair. I've got a handsome lover, Jon. We're going to a Dire Straits concert on an island later."

"How long have you been doing this?"

"Oh, six months, more. Yes more. Jon and I bought some land and built a house last Easter. You have to pay real money to do this, so we're quite committed. Second Life is my social life. My real life."

Laura was staggered. That was why Gillian had not been around as much. She had been crouched over her computer. "Are you ever going to meet Jon?"

Gillian blushed again. "No idea. He lives in the States. He's asked me to marry him."

"Do you know anything about him? Like his age: if he's married, what he looks like?"

"I'm not sure I want to. I'm enjoying my life as Dina too much." Gillian lifted her glass to show it was empty and shambled off to the drinks tent.

"I'm sorry Laura, I thought I'd ring and tell you that Phillip's funeral is going to be just family at the crematorium."

"Oh, Ok, whatever you want, Helen. Do you need any help?"

"No thanks. Phillip's sister came down the day after he died. Her children, their uncle and aunt and my younger brother and his children. That's all we'll be. Thanks for your card and the flowers. We'll speak next week."

"Ok. But if there's anything I can do, just let me know."

"Thanks. I can't think at the moment. I'm so tired I might crumble to ash like Phillip will be. If he had died twenty years ago, I might have thrown myself into the furnace after him…do suttee or sati, whatever it is. Like good Hindu wives. Oh, what am I going to do? I've never been good at letting go. Saying goodbye."

Laura could hear the choke in her voice, then a sob. "You've been there for all of us, Helen. When we needed you. Please just ask if we can be of any use."

There was another louder sob. "Bye."

Beth rang ten minutes later. "So we're not allowed to say good bye to Phillip. Don't you think that's strange?"

"I suppose it's all she can cope with."

"It did cross my mind that she couldn't bear any of his patients turning up."

"Yes, mine too."

Outside the modern stained glass windows, the sky was black and as the last prayer was said and Phillip's favourite music was played, the coffin was enclosed by the curtains and a deluge started outside. Helen stayed seated for a few minutes, hoping to find the shining peace the vicar had promised, but all she could feel was shock and disbelief. Phillip's sister Suzanne put her arm around her and leaving Phillip to the incinerator they went out into the storm.

Laura was on her way to her 'gamesmaker' training when she saw

263

Ed. He was walking towards her wearing a beautiful, tailored suit. Still attractive. He had seen her. "Hi, Ed."

"Hi, Laura. How are you?"

"Oh fine, and you?" They looked at one another long and hard. His hair was greyer and thinner. There were deeper lines around his eyes. Poor Ed.

"I did everything for her, you know, Laura. Worked as hard as I could. I loved them so much, but I couldn't take the betrayals any more. It was like knives turning in my chest. Then that last time…"

Laura nodded, "I know. She just couldn't help herself."

"I was exhausted with the emotional roller coaster. I'm seventy-one and I want a peaceful retirement."

Laura could feel his anguish. Seeing her had brought it all up again. She nodded. "It's nice to see you. Have a happy life."

At last, another summer's day. It had rained yesterday, but today the sky was blue and it was warm. Laura was joined by Jo, Lynne and Beth as they swung along to the pool, admiring the bright colours of azaleas and rhododendrons in the gardens they passed. To their disappointment, when they came out it had clouded over and the sky was darkening. The trees looked dark green and though they could hear the birds there were none in sight.

"Shall I come with you to visit Sybil?" Laura volunteered as they increased their pace, hoping to miss the impending rain.

"That's kind of you. She's probably making the staff's lives hell," said Beth. "Can you come today? Visiting time starts at two."

Jo had not been swimming for a few weeks, but this morning the sun had been shining through the gap she had carelessly left in her curtains when she had pulled them across the night before. It had filled the room with light. She could get up and shut it out, or… some camaraderie would be nice. I haven't much to do for the rest of the day, she had thought.

She hadn't heard about Sybil. "What's she in hospital for?"

"She fractured her femur, but we never really got to the bottom of how. She'd gone out shopping to Knightsbridge without telling us. Perhaps she tripped on a kerb, or had a little stroke. She didn't remember. She was taken to the Marsden. It isn't easy for visiting, but it's a good hospital. It's so peaceful without her."

The friends were eager to find out how Jo had got on in a date she had told them about last time.

"Dreary, hideous, emetic. He reminded me of Eeyore. At dinner I heard about his prostate: his gastrointestinal problems, how work was getting him down. He was dull, dull, dull."

"What about his looks?"

"Hmm. At first I thought, well, he isn't repulsive, but after an hour looking at his miserable puzzled beaver face I'd say he made the word nondescript a superlative!"

They giggled.

"Perhaps the next one will be more exciting. Have you got any others lined up?" asked Beth.

"No, but I saw another one on Sunday," Jo said reluctantly.

"Tell, tell," said Laura.

Jo grimaced at the thought. "He was ringing, pestering and flattering me the whole week, but he just wanted a fuck. I'm starting to feel it's a meat market out there, unloving and unsafe! The men are lonely, flabby fuckers who are too mean to pay for hot sugar babes. Dating sites are cheaper. He picked me up in his BMW. A big man. Not bad looking, quality tailored suit. We had a quick cocktail in The Soho Hotel bar. Not even a meal. Then he said, 'Let's go back to your place, it's too noisy here.' I got him a drink and sat down and he was on top of me. Dragging my tights down. I wasn't wearing a thong and he was so strong and heavy and hell bent on getting his way. I was shouting stop, stop, but he just pushed his lady wand into me. So violently! A few thrusts and he came. It was rape! Then he got up, zipped up his trousers and walked out. He said nothing to me and hasn't contacted me again. Pumped and dumped! I was so angry I could have set fire to him, just by looking. But he'd gone. I felt like shit."

There was a shocked silence. What could anyone say?

Laura took a bite of her freshly baked rock cake, crunched the nuts and chewed and savoured the cranberries, apricots and raisins.

Bees drowsed in the lavender bushes, birds sang early evening songs and she thought back to her mother and grandmother's rock cakes, in which one had to search for fruit and nuts were unheard of.

"The line stops here," she said aloud. Daisy favoured chocolatey, spongey concoctions and Ruby and Lily won't be able to remember the rock cakes they had loved as little children by the time they grow up. They won't remember me, their Nana.

How could this have happened? We were so close. Oppressively close at times. But somehow all the things I longed to do when I was endlessly baby minding for her now don't seem at all attractive or compelling. I feel as if I'm in limbo, waiting.

She fetched the watering can. It had been stiflingly hot all day. She must put the tomato and basil plants out. They were getting leggy. They were like her friends. She watered them, checked for pests and patted their heads morning and evening. She had read that the patting kept them more compact. She always had wonderful crops.

Sitting down again, she gazed out at the kerria, honesty and clematis all in flower, nursing her aches and dreams. "She's not going to relent, for a while," her various friends had advised. "It's desperately sad, but get on with enjoying your life, it's not your fault, don't beat yourself up."

She knew that a small part of her agony was no longer being the centre, the lynchpin of the family and her job. Daniel was so self-sufficient. She had to get used to not being needed by anyone.

Later, she was combing her hair in the bathroom. Leaning closer to the mirror, she noticed a strand of white forking through the brown. A little ray of age, which had lain hidden under her scalp but had burst out to remind me that life is passing, she thought. She had noticed a hair on her face when she had been standing by her sunny bedroom window earlier, applying her lipstick. She flipped the side mirror over to the magnification side and horrors. There were long hairs sprouting from her chin. Why hasn't anyone pointed them out? Have they been wondering if I was growing a beard? She went to get her tweezers. After pulling out a few, she heard Daniel's key in the lock and the front door opening. There was a silence while he took off his shoes and then a tinkle as he threw his keys onto the hall table. She imagined him taking off his coat and hanging it up before he opened the kitchen door. Is this love, knowing one's partner's movements she wondered?

But this sex thing, I feel permanently guilty.

In bed the night before she had been asking him to trim the front hedge. One of his usual jobs. "So will you...in the morning?"

She knew that she had made her voice soft and persuasive and that he had wanted to spend the day finishing a painting.

"Then I'll..." She had been talking to herself, listing her jobs for the following day and she felt him waiting for silence. He had reached out to stroke the arm and shoulder turned away from him and she had tensed. She could feel that he'd wanted to say, tell me what to do. How to make it up to you? I can't carry all this guilt from making you unhappy any more. But he did not. He had been afraid to hear what was inside her and she had not trusted herself not to speak resentfully. They had lain next to one another but so apart. She knew that it should be she who built the bridge away from this clumsy, cruel silence. Why didn't she just forgive him? Was this the curse of a long-term relationship? There was always tomorrow?

"Night, night," she had said sleepily, guiltily, but her body had felt heavy and inert and tiredness engulfed her. It was not that she was no longer turned on by him, but she rarely felt the urge in the abstract. It was easier not to bother. Sometimes when she had felt the urgency of his desire, it had activated her own and with patience her tension melted and she could respond. But since Daisy, there was this unsaid...was it resentment? And she was floating into sleep. Frustrated, he had rolled over into his favourite position and all was quiet.

At the weekend they went to South Wales to do some coast path walking. It had been cold and grey all day and a stiff wind was exciting the water, so it thrashed and boiled onto the rocks and roared into caves below. On the horizon, ribbons of silver light were tussling with the black clouds and seemed to be winning. By late afternoon they had walked eight miles. The wind had softened to a light breeze

267

and the sun was warming Laura's head and the backs of her legs. She sighed and felt her spirits lift, at last. Determinedly shutting out all her miserable thoughts, she breathed in the coconut perfume from the vivid yellow gorse and feasted her eyes on the brown and orange lichens on the rocks, bursting through the grass like broken bones and the soft, blue blur of woods in the distance. Brambles overhung the fences, berries swollen and green after the endless rain in May and June. "Perhaps they'll be ripe for us to pick by September?" she said to Dan.

At last they reached the café in a boathouse on the cliff, near which they could catch a bus back to their village. Dan went into the building to get cream teas, while Laura looked around for a table. The sun was shining its last gasp so there were none free in the shade. All the places under the trees had been taken. People sat in the dappled shadows looking out from their safety as if guarding against attack.

Then a couple picked up their things and headed off. So they sat, sheltered and warm against a wall, absorbing the tranquillity and munching their way through huge, rather dry scones and mingy amounts of jam and cream until the sun started to disappear behind the distant hills. Laura was filled with longing again for Daisy and her grandchildren. She had no idea what Daniel was thinking.

Martin usually cooked supper while Frances was at choir. He had bought pans, dishes and scales, as Frances wasn't interested in cooking or, indeed in her flat. So different from Annie, who had always had ideas for improvements, to keep Martin and the Polish builder, Piotr, busy.

He was meticulous in his preparation and organisation, measuring the ingredients accurately and never deviating from the recipe. Beef Stroganoff was one of his specialities and when she arrived back, the table was laid, the wine uncorked, the salad dressing made and a delicious smell pervaded the flat. He poured her a glass of wine. "Sit down, it's all ready."

They had sung continuously for the two hours. She was surprised how tired she felt. The strong, fruity tannin hit her throat like a magic potion and she felt her body relax. Having a partner who looked after one was very pleasant.

After supper he tried on his 'games maker' uniform, which he had collected earlier.

"You were given all that?" Frances asked in surprise.

"Two pairs of trousers, socks and tops, this bag and a Swatch watch." He waved his wrist at her.

"That's actually a nice watch and it's all good quality. How did you get this job?"

"I saw it somewhere, the Standard? It must have been two years ago and my interview was a year last January. There are something like seventy thousand of us, but they don't expect us to work that much. I'm just doing eight shifts in two weeks time. Before the actual Olympics start."

For ten days it had been cold, sometimes rainy and always cloudy and dull.

Then at last, they got up one morning to find it warmer. It was still overcast and rather dark, but more like a summer temperature.

"You don't have to tell us about your dates," Laura said to Jo, as they walked to the pool.

"I'm very comfortable with you girls. It's fine. You have to try out a lot of frogs to find your prince." Jo found that she enjoyed regaling her friends with her dating exploits and she had adventures to report. "Yeh, I got into a new site. Look," with a few touches on her iPhone screen she was into her Tinder profile and flicking through photos of men. "All you have to do is 'like' someone and if they 'like' you back, you can be having sex that day. Sweaty, sexy, sex." She grinned at her friends who were trying not to look shocked. "Before that I tried a new dating agency, for the more mature person. The first guy, Ralph, seemed like he might be Ok. We spoke on the phone and agreed to meet at Livebait in Waterloo. He said he'd book a table under the name 'Jones' so whoever got there first could sit at it. I was a bit late and a plump faced, balding, unattractive man was sitting there when the maître d' showed me to the table. I wouldn't have recognised him from his photo and he was looking past me at the door, so he hadn't recognised me either. He looked like a rotweiller

269

chewing a wasp when I said hello". She stopped.

"What happened then?"

Jo flushed. "Not a lot. He was so rude, said I'd lured him there under false pretences. I wasn't gorgeous, and ten years older than I'd admitted. So I said he must have used someone else's photo. He was a fat jerk and stormed off. It was so embarrassing. He could have been polite!"

"How awful. How old did you say you were?"

She flushed again. "Forty-eight. Look, girls, I'm gagging for it. I don't want to be choosing wheelchairs for old men in their sixties or seventies. I want a younger, virile guy who's lustful and always up for it."

There was a silence as the three others wondered if they were unnatural, needing 'it' so infrequently. "Are there other sites?" Laura asked.

"Oh yeh. Did you know that there are more dating websites in the UK than anywhere in Europe?" The others shook their heads. "There's ones for sugar daddies: for ugly people, Tories, people in uniform, people who just want a shag, they're endless. Anyway, back to Tinder. I spent an evening going through men's photos and eventually found one in his fifties who didn't look too bad and sounded crazy, ridiculous interests, so I thought, I've gotta meet him. He liked my photo, so we agreed I'd go to his house and shag him."

"Oh my god, did you?"

"Yup. It was great. He's about five feet nine, my height. Shaved head, thespian beardlet, thin and strong, a coke-nosher, makes short films and is mad as a box of frogs. He wants to give me a vintage car."

"What? Is he rich?"

"Don't know. It's only been a few days. He doesn't seem poor, and he's keen, like a greyhound out of a trap. You see if I meet a man and spend some time with him, I can charm him by being well-informed, smutty, flirtatious and flattering. We can have fun. I don't want to be judged on first impressions. I hope this'll last for a while."

"What if you catch something from these men? You don't know where they've been!" Beth said worriedly.

"Hey ho," said Jo and fell silent, focussing her thoughts on the night before and how much fun it was being a bad girl and taking risks.

"Dan!" Laura called. He was standing by the door, wheezing and sweaty from his run. "A terrible thing. I'm going to Helen's. It's her Mum. She's had a stroke. She's dead. Poor, poor Helen."

Chapter 19. June. Life isn't Over

'I must enter, and leave, alone,
I know not how.'
Edward Thomas. 'Lights Out.' (1878 – 1917)

Robert had bought Lynne an expensive watch, for her birthday that she had not intended celebrating. She stretched out her arm, admiring its elegance, the thinness of the gold bracelet. When had she ever felt a buzz from wearing an expensive present before? The house was full of beautiful flowers. Bouquets from Laura and Jo and four from her regular patients. She smiled to herself. How exciting her life had become.

Annie had managed to get timed tickets for the Damien Hirst exhibition at the Tate Modern and was taking Dan and Laura after the two women had been clothes shopping.

"You can ring Dan and tell him if we're going to be a bit late," Annie said.

"I won't be at home, though. I'll wait," said Dan.

"Take your mobile."

"My mobile? Are you joking? You know what I think about them."

"I thought you may have dragged yourself into the twenty-first century by now?"

"Look, Annie. I'm not interested in the constant wall of noise and distraction that comes with having an iPhone, a Blackberry, a Smart phone, being on Twitter, Facebook, Linked In or taking selfies all the time. It's so narcissistic. I want peace, serenity and not being constantly connected. You're all permanently switched on. Switch off for a while. Find out who you are, be creative!"

Annie had never heard him speak so passionately. She was speechless with surprise.

"He's hopeless," Laura shrugged. "It's so frustrating. Dan, we'll meet you outside at two thirty."

Laura was going to the exhibition reluctantly, prejudiced against it before she started. She stared at the pickled animal carcasses and giant ashtray, with her usual bewilderment and then anger that this should be called artistic. More like emperor's new clothes! Annie zipped around, classifying, pronouncing and tutting. "That's so ugly!"

Dan spent the longest time. "What do you want art to be? Dull, safe pastoral scenes? It's conceptual. The swirling shapes draw the eye, it's aesthetically pleasing. Beauty and ugliness are not opposites, you know. They're very close to one another."

"I don't want to feel inadequate and stupid at my responses to it," Laura said.

Later, when they went into the shop and saw plastic skulls daubed with gloss paint for £36,800 and the butterfly wall paper for £700 a roll, he said: "I do admit this is more like a business."

Helen was talking to Laura on the phone. "I just haven't felt like swimming, like doing anything much. I've had to clear Mum's room in her Home. At least we'd got rid of her flat so I wasn't clearing that on my own. But you know how hard it is with things that your parents bought, loved, dusted and displayed for all their married lives. Bundling it all off to a charity shop seems so disrespectful. I'll go back to work next week."

"Is there anything I can tempt you with? Dinner, theatre, a gallery?"

"No, it's Ok. I'm fine. It's really much sort of easier without Phillip and Mum." To her horror, she began to cry and could not stop. Big, choking sobs.

"I'm coming round," Laura said firmly and put down the phone.

It was a perfect summer's day. Laura, woken by the birdsong, leapt up early and went out into her garden, to revel in the flowers and the blue, blue sky with only a few cream puff clouds and two streaks, as if someone had skated across it in their joy to be alive, wow.

Too many others had the same idea, the pool was crowded and whichever lane they tried to swim in, there were holdups and it was not safe to do more than a few strokes of back crawl, in case there were collisions.

Laura had played cricket and netball, but now, only tennis. She felt slower and stiffer…well, what could she expect at sixty-four, she asked herself. Very occasionally, her strokes free from the shackles of the will had the perfection of automatic motion, without nerves and the demands of decision-making. She would play as if in a trance, lost in the pleasure of rhythmic movement and her involuntary brilliance. For these moments, though increasingly more rare, she loved the game.

With no Annie, Laura was drawn into practice games with keen younger players. The captain asked her to make up a four at the weekend, so they could try out some new members. Their glowing health, speed and heavy hitting made her feel ancient, weak and definitely past it. Balls whistled past her at the net. She who had been such a good volleyer. Her no longer powerful serve was returned with interest.

"I felt so demeaned," she told Daniel later. "Jane had told them that I used to be one of the best players in the club. I probably had submissive, apologising-for-being-there body language, so there was no mercy. My reactions are so much slower now. And talking to them after over a drink was painful. We seemed to have nothing in common. Age is so divisive."

Annie could feel the waves of misery and pain receding. Life was not over. Everything passes and she was cutting back on the fluoxetine Prozac, which had been regulating her peaks and troughs.

She was glad she had resisted going over to Clarendon Road to spy on Frances and Martin. It would have been too embarrassing if they or Jo had seen her, sitting there in her distinctive mini convertible Mercedes sports car.

I'm stuck in my old habits and patterns and scared to change, she told herself. I only know how to push myself, compete. Life is a precarious balancing act. I've got to be happier, find things I enjoy which aren't involving winning.

Since her energy and interest in life were returning, she had begun to throw herself into writing her book, Pilates, gym with a personal trainer, some swimming and she and Laura were resuming their games of tennis. She barely had time to eat. She was slimmer than she had ever been, and wished that Martin could see her now.

Observing this frantic activity, Laura said: "You don't think that you might have gone a bit manic do you?"

"I'm making up for doing nothing for five months. Why am I so self-destructive, Laurs? I'm aggressive and selfish, why? Are these normal human traits? I deserve to be alone."

"You can be those things, but you are also clever, talented in so many areas and a great friend, or we wouldn't still be here for you."

They were sitting in Laura's lovely garden. Surrounded by flowers and shrubs, bees buzzing, the little waterfall in the pond trickling and the distant sound of trains. Annie put her mug of tea and plate of Bara brith down on the grass beside her chair and gave Laura a hug.

"I've been pulled down a peg or two, haven't I? For the past few years, ever since my weekly show finished and it was obvious that I wasn't getting another series, I think I've been struggling with insecurity and the loss of status, so I've been bitchily criticising everyone else. When you're thought to be too old to do what you've learnt to do well, what can you do then for the rest of your life? I feel such a failure now. Is that it? Will I never work in my field again?"

"It's always sounded so dog eat dog. I know it's glamorous, but do you really want to keep fighting for your place in such a cruel, lonely world?"

Annie looked thoughtful. "I've certainly been treated to its harsh reality and lack of loyalty. I've always looked out for my back and known that it's survival of the fittest, and that you survive at the expense of others. But you're right. There are no real friendships. You survive or fall alone."

"Look for something better for yourself, Annie. You've had being a star."

"Suppose you're right. I'm sixty-seven now and I've had my day in the sun. To survive today you've got to be on all the different platforms, facebook, twitter, blogs, cooking sites and constantly come up with new ideas to promote. I've been a vain, selfish achiever and now I'm a has-been, with no status, ruined pride and a vast silence from those who courted me so assiduously."

"Poetic words. Use your talent and energy in a different challenge."

They sat in silence each with their thoughts, until Laura went inside for wine and nibbles. The late afternoon had become a perfect summer evening, soft and warm with lengthening shadows and mysterious pools of shade collecting under trees and bushes. The butterflies in the buddleia and the dragonflies on the pond had found hiding places for the night and the tobacco plants were giving out their beautiful scent. Annie sipped her Chardonnay and watched the evening primrose becoming brighter and more luminous and each new flower opening with a swift twirl. Life would be good again.

She continued to feel so full of energy that instead of sleeping, she started playing video games late at night. Bejeweled and Skyrim, then getting hooked on Farmville. Some of her Facebook friends would pop over to help her with harvesting or milking. The joy of games for her was that for a while she could be someone else, in a different world, pootling around a landscape chatting to her new friends. But she had started to wonder about sex. Her personal trainer's powerful body, muscular arms, white teeth and soft lips, kept intruding into her thoughts. During their hour, he concentrated utterly on her, was very 'touchy feely' and flirtatious. She wondered what he would be like in bed. Then one day she saw him with his arm around a beautiful girl, fully forty years younger than herself. They did not notice her passing in the street. She was thankful that she had not made a fool of herself by propositioning him.

That evening she saw Mark Barnes's name on the credits of a programme she was watching. Mark? He had been the consumer affairs producer on a series she was involved in a few years ago. He was ten years younger, but was always paying her compliments and flirting with her. Shall I phone him? No, I'll never get through. I'll be put in a queue with all those stalling tactics and holding patterns. Have I still got his email address? There it is. Just a friendly email.

'Hi Mark, congrats on a great programme last week, that was

really a scoop! If you ever want anyone to use as a sounding board for your series on food prices in supermarkets, I'd be happy to meet up. I've got some free time at the moment. Annie.'

She pressed 'send' before she could change her mind, then sat thinking about the programmes they had made together. She could have had some fun if she had taken him up on his invitations.

Later that evening she could not resist turning on her computer. No reply. She was not sure if she did not feel slightly relieved as well as disappointed.

The next morning to her surprise there was a reply from Mark. She trembled as she read it. Picturing his mop of dark hair with the distinguished grey at the edges, his very white teeth, strong body and the teasing, intimate looks he had given her.

'Hi Annie, Back from holiday to a pleasant surprise! Yes of course we must meet up. How about the Aura in St James at 18.30 tomorrow? Mark.'

What would Martin say if he knew? He had never taken to Mark, too shallow and flamboyant. Well this would serve him right. Boring old unimaginative Martin. She was starting to feel nervous already. What would she wear? Lots of her clothes were now too big. I'll go shopping in the morning after swimming and then I'll have my hair done.

After a quick, successful trip to Bond Street, she lay on her sun lounger, her body down to the tops of her legs in the shade of the umbrella that was stored in their shed. Well, Martin's shed anyway. He had built it with the worktable and the shelves of jars and boxes with their neat labels in 'Comic Sans MS.' She was relaxed and actually happy. Swinging her toasted legs onto the warm bricks of the patio, she padded inside to get her nail kit

An hour later: "Let's go for a full bleach," she told Justin her hair-dresser.

"Yes, why not. A new look. You need a lift."

She was thrilled when she saw the result after blow-drying: "I love it. It's like Cornish dairy ice cream!"

Justin looked proud. "I try to help my customers feel more

confident of their sexual attractiveness. You've got it made now, babe!"

The 'drink' seemed to fly by as they exchanged news. Mark was enthusiastic about her thirty minute dinner party dishes ideas. "Email me some of the menus tomorrow. We'll incorporate a slot in my new series. I'm so pleased we've met up again. We work so well together." He gave her a hug and special smile. She was walking on air.

It was such a lovely, warm, blue morning that Laura decided to go for a swim on a non-swimming day. She rung her friends and to her surprise Beth and Jo were keen to come with her. They wandered along, chatting in the sun...

"My skin's getting so dry and wrinkly and I'm always coughing. Do you think it's the chlorine? Beth asked.

"More likely to be air pollution from all the traffic in London." Laura said. "Perhaps that's why you haven't got our problem Jo, after 20 years of living in the country?"

"No doubt the pollutants shellacked onto my skin in the past few months will catch up with me some time soon. But I do cleanse deeply every night and use anti-oxidant night creams. Come round any time and I'll show you what I use."

The water was rough and cold and heaving with swimmers so they did not swim for long. The changing rooms were busy and dirty. "How does that cleaner get all this long black hair off the wet floor?" Beth whispered to Jo.

"God knows, there's always tons of it, but at least it doesn't smell. I used to do a yoga class in a club near work in Covent Garden and the stink of sweat and farts was overpowering."

"I tried yoga once, but there were mirrors everywhere and I didn't like seeing my every move."

"Yeh. Mirrors are a problem. You get all these withered, orange, weirdos doing head stands and splits in front of them and fat, stiff, normal people cowering behind."

Terry found that she had tumours in her brain. "I don't want any more chemotherapy or radiotherapy. No more scans. I've had enough!" she told Doctor Errani.

"If you refuse treatment then you only have perhaps a year, perhaps less and it is now dangerous for you to drive. If you are determined not to have treatment, I will tell you that we work as a palliative care team here to help you. My secretary will be able to make arrangements with the District Nurse. Have you told your son?"

She shook her head.

"A friend or relative? Someone has to know."

"I'm not ready to tell anyone." Tears blinded her. "I want to enjoy my last few months. I don't want to be dragged down by other people's fears and pity. I've had enough pity with Leonard's death. I want people to feel comfortable with me, not avoid me because they don't know what to say. And even if I had treatment, there's no hope in the long term, is there?" she blurted out.

"I wouldn't say that, Terry. There is always hope. Many people have remissions and I'm surprised that you feel as well as you do at the moment. Cancer is always surprising."

On the way to the tube, her footsteps drummed like a chant on the pavement and her thoughts pounded in unison in her head. "Die, die, I'm going to die."

Sitting on the train she saw nothing, heard nothing. She had no feelings. Her body had betrayed her. She closed her eyes, to shut everything out, and when she opened them, she had gone two stops past hers. Dragging herself up and off, she headed over to the other side of the platform, where a train was about to leave. She jumped on and sat down heavily. Across the aisle her dull eyes fixed on a poem, part of the 'poems in the Underground series.'

'Knowing
we have been spared
to lift our faces up
for one more day,
into one more sunrise.'
'Carving' by Imtiaz Dharker*
"One more day, one more sunrise," she repeated over and over.

The train stopped and she got off and looked up to the sky and thanked God for this day and every other she might live through.

Arriving home, she put on Vivaldi's 6 cello sonatas, poured herself a glass of sauvignon blanc and sunk onto the sofa. Tosca jumped onto her lap, purring loudly. She relaxed into the music and the beauty of the creamy, Madame Alfred Carriere rambling rose intertwining with the pink flowered abelia just outside the window. She could feel herself sinking lower and lower. Then the music finished and she shivered with cold and fear. "I'll have to tell David and Rosie and Bella and Laura. How can I not be a burden and die happily?" The weight of the large house full of all her and Leonard's possessions, the big garden and sorting out all their affairs pressed down and tears rolled down her cheeks. Why is this happening to me?

At least my death will leave only a slight indentation. Not the drama and shock if Leonard were still alive. She went to the window. It had started to rain. A wet robin on the magnolia was fluffing out his damp feathers and a drip fell relentlessly from the leaking gutter above her.

She had always felt happy in her body, but now it seemed that there was no room in it for her. Something powerful had taken it over and was controlling it, destroying it.

I don't want to do anything, go out any more, the world's a howling wilderness.

She made a sandwich and sat down in front of the TV. She must have slept because suddenly 'Newsnight' was finishing. It's late, I must keep up my routines. Go to bed when it's bedtime. Switching off the TV, she moved wearily round the house checking that the doors were locked and putting off lights. Preparations for bed are like preparations for death, she thought. One by one lights out and then darkness.

The sun was high but the buffeting easterly wind made Laura, Frances and Jo shiver as they walked up the road towards Beth's house. They rang the bell and waited by the gate, under the birch tree rising up as cool and slim as a ghost. The wind rustled through its branches, blowing up the pale undersides of the leaves. The soft, pastel sky above was scarred with rosy welts and birds rode the wind, flapping occasionally to alter direction. The door opened. "Sorry, couldn't find my keys," said Beth and they were off, walking briskly to keep warm.

Wind makes one feel tetchy and cross. After a relaxing swim in a tranquil, quiet pool they felt rejuvenated, cleaned and suffused with peace and calm.

"Have you finished 'The Golden Notebook?'" Laura asked Jo.

"Yes and what a powerful book. You know it's fifty years since it was published? Fifty years! Her style is dated and even a bit clumsy by today's standards, but it said so much about how it was to be a woman. Brilliant," Jo said, waiting at the door ready to go.

Laura was sitting on the bench in front of the lockers, putting on her shoes. "Yes, agreed. Doris Lessing was a great thinker and fearless writer. A bit of a seer. Years ahead of her time."

Frances rarely read novels so carried on packing her bag, but Beth was stung into replying. "I haven't read many. She always seemed to be experimenting and they were clumsy and unreal. Not innovative. Just silly."

"What?" Laura was aghast. "You may not have enjoyed some of her experiments Beth, but she has always pushed boundaries. Look at my favourite, 'The Summer Before the Dark,' confronting the terrors of old age and death. And then 'The Good Terrorist' about the glamour of nihilists."

"Oh yes. Murderous public action because of their blinkered, self-righteous rage. So frightening. Wanting to smash the society they lived in. Like ISIS now," said Jo. "It wasn't an easy read. You've probably read her less successful experiments Beth. Come on, guys. Upsticks. Let's get going."

It was a Wednesday and Dan had chosen a walk out in Metroland. He loved to walk in the country. Little traffic or human voices. Just the sounds that do not spoil the silence, but make it more profound.

There was a fine, pale mist, which was drying in the sun, when they arrived. Out of the station, left up the road and down an alley between the fifties-style houses with their tidy, unadventurous gardens. Through a sports ground and into a field, still damp underfoot, lush and scented with vetch and wild thyme, the home for butterflies, grasshoppers and other flying and creeping creatures. Into a lane fringed with nettles, cow parsley and bladder campion with a small wood ahead. They walked in silence. She shivered. The trees were close together, so the light had disappeared and it was creepily quiet. Then they were out and going up a thigh aching, sheep-nibbled grassy slope past the glitter and murmur of tiny streams tumbling downwards. There was a cold little wind, so she trod in his footsteps, sheltering behind his body as if it were a coat, feeling her heart racing with the effort of the climb. Her face had been whipped by the wind into different shades of rose and red. He imagined it as a background wash for a sky.

Over the top and they could see tree rimmed pastures and houses sprinkled messily over the valley below. A track reached a five-barred gate at the entrance to a meadow. They lent on it, looking down at the river in the distance. Like a shimmering watercolour. It was warmer now so they sat to share an apple. Dan lay on his back, looking sideways through the tangle of grasses, clover and buttercups at a group of walkers heading towards them. If he made the sky into sea, they would be standing on their heads and waving their legs at one another.

Laura found the rhythm of walking made her feel dreamlike. She started off chatty, but gradually became silent. This always made Dan worry that she was unhappy. "What's wrong?" he asked.

She was puzzled. "Nothing."

"What have I done?"

"Nothing."

"What are you thinking about?"

"Nothing particularly."

He did not believe her.

They had almost completed the circuit and it was darkening. An owl coasted low in the valley below, looking for prey. They watched it and feeling guilty at her silence she put her arms around him. Feeling the warmth of the day still on his skin. The field in front of them was a rippling wave of a tall cereal, swaying in the breeze. Dan looked quizzical. His face soft and gentle. So very dear.

"I've been thinking," she said.

He smiled and her heart contracted. I can't bring it up again, can't keep on and on about Daisy. Ashamed that she had almost spoilt the day for him, she reached out for his hand. "Oh, if we should ask Lynne and Robert for a barbecue," she said hurriedly. She wondered when she would stop worrying it round and round every day and especially every night. The pain never receded.

"Help, I need help."

Beth was gardening and James was in his study, which was nearest to Sybil. He went to her. "Yes, Mother, what do you want?"

"I've been sitting here for hours all by myself."

"You could watch television. Shall I put it on?"

His mother had never been a television watcher. "No," she said testily, "I want to go out for a drive."

"I'm too busy today, Mother. Why don't you get up and practise getting around with your walker." He sounded resigned. He had asked her to do that every day, but she did not seem inclined to move without a great deal of help.

Sybil pressed her hands on the chair arms, pretending to push. "You don't seem to understand what it's like when your joints are stiff and painful. You don't seem to care."

James thought guiltily that she was probably right. Sybil was not a good patient and refused to help herself. "You need to get about more, I keep telling you. You'll get weaker and stiffer if you don't get out of that chair!"

"What makes you such an expert? You're not my Consultant. Mr Robinson told me to rest. Help me get up." He took her arm and helped her to her feet so she could lean on her walker. She moved slowly, groaning and complaining towards the kitchen. Stopping if he eased his hold around her waist.

"Come on, Mother. You don't need me to support you."

"Trying to go off again, are you? I need a cup of tea and to get to the toilet. I can't do it on my own. Put the kettle on for me."

"You can do that for yourself. You can't keep relying on us to do everything for you."

He felt himself going from irritated to angry. "If you're not going to try and get stronger and more independent, you're going to have to go into a home. We can't be at your beck and call all day and night!"

A frightened, betrayed look came into her face, which pierced his heart. She might be bitter and lazy, but she was his mother.

"I'll be back in ten minutes when you've made your tea," he said more kindly.

Laura, Beth and Lynne were on their way to the pool.

"Sybil came home three days ago. She's driving us mad. She won't do anything for herself. The physio says she has to keep on practising her walking and do her exercises, but all she does is shout out for us!"

"Why don't you bring her to me for half an hour every day this week. I'll make sure she does her exercises."

"That's so kind of you, Lynne. Really, very kind. I'll suggest that to James. What time would be best for you?"

Chapter 20. July. Togetherness

'Enough of Science and of Art;
Close up those barren leaves;
Come forth and bring with you a heart
That watches and receives.'
William Wordsworth. 'The Tables Turned.' (1770 – 1850)

In some countries in Europe, it was over thirty degrees but Lynne and Beth were wearing their fleeces to keep out the keen wind on this grey, overcast day. As they walked, a team of swifts did acrobatics high above them.

The pool was almost empty. Only nine people ploughed up and down and none in the non-laned area. No sign of the Asian women who usually clung onto the side, chatting.

The water for once felt soft and fresh. They smiled at one another in delight, quickly got in and luxuriated for an extra five minutes.

Daniel and Laura were on a five-day holiday at Lake Como. He wanted peace, tranquil scenery, and the mountain rimmed lake to sketch. Laura was looking forward to stunning gardens and walking between picturesque villages. But it was so hot. She could not get used to the heat. It was airless.

They visited a garden in the morning, then the sun baked the afternoon into stillness. The heat was heavy as a blanket. Nothing seemed to move. Not on the lake or around the villas with their lovely gardens, or the three-storey period houses on the oleander lined promenades. Unmoving curtains hung at wide-open windows. Even the leaves seemed tired. A shimmer of heat rose from the road. Everything looked gilded. The town was an oven.

She had loved the sun when young but her body no longer coped with it, she could barely breathe. Large patches of sweat were spreading from under her arms. "Will it be cooler on the lake?"

They rowed gently out towards the slow silence at the centre. She shifted her weight on the hard wooden seat and the boat rolled,

285

disturbing the dark, still turquoise water, so it slapped at the sides. It was indeed cooler here. They sat, she with her Kindle and he with his own thoughts until the sun began to sink. Does the gap widen between couples as they become more familiar? They notice less, talk less and take more for granted? Do they live in their own worlds, she wondered? But can we ever know one another really well? Or do we just cling to the picture we have made of each other and then do not look any more. Would their relationship ever recover after Daisy?

She stripped and slipped into the water. It was freezing. Like submerging herself into a container of broken glass. Her hot skin prickled and stung and her throat closed up. She kicked and thrashed her arms furiously, but the pain of the icy water was so intense her muscles no longer seemed to belong to her. She must get out. Then suddenly her body cooled down, relaxed and her panic subsided. She swam steadily, at one with the water, feeling euphorically happy and alive.

Getting back in the boat was more difficult. It rocked madly as she heaved herself up and in, while Dan struggled to help her and counterbalance her weight.

She covered her shoulders with her towel and without speaking they began to pull at the oars. Swish, slop, swish, slop until there was once again the murmur of voices. The whine of scooters had started up again as they glided up to the jetty.

Later, they ate outside on a veranda by the lake. Delicious soft, plump cushions of ricotta and spinach ravioli with ruccola, together with glasses of cool, citrusy, creamy Buriano. The moon made a glittering pathway in the black and mysterious lapping water.

They wandered back to their albergo, conscious that there was still something between them, something that was never said. Laura undressed, pulled back the cover and snuggled into bed. She could hear Dan in the shower and picked up her new William Nicholson novel. She was on page twenty-two by the time he joined her. I've got to stop blaming him. I'm so lucky, she thought sleepily, as he gently took her book and straightened the sheet around her. My caring, thoughtful, loving man. They drowsed together, fitting into one another, feeling as if their heartbeats matched. She felt as if she could almost read his dreams, get under and into his skin. He hoping that all their awkwardness had at last melted away, gently massaged her back and pelvis. She slipped her hand down over his soft hair and stroked his penis, which bucked and lengthened at her touch.

Next day, map in hand they set out for a circular walk. The town rose gently from the lake, its soft apricot walls changing shade with the position of the sun. They walked on the cobbles, through the narrow, twisting medieval streets, up into the rosemary and potentilla covered hills, dangled their feet in clear brooks and picked purple plums, swollen and silvery with dusty bloom.

They still did not mention Daisy but, instead of her being there between them, they had come together in their thoughts of wanting to see her and support her in any way they could.

"Shall I move in with you for the next year while you wind down your practice? We'd see more of one another. I could drop in on father more often and we could go to Brighton at weekends and perhaps retire there one day?"

Lynne looked at Robert and took a gulp of her Merlot. "Mmm, I'll think about that," she answered, and studied her fish pie, so he would not see the shock in her eyes. Later, after he had gone, she let herself consider the suggestion.

Do I want to live with Robert for the last part of my life? If he moved in, it would certainly test our relationship. We could play more bridge, he loves the cats and I'm very fond of him, but having him here all the time? He's ten years older and very set in his ways. I don't want to end up looking after anyone again. I don't know, I'm confused. Am I too old to start compromising with a partner? I like my life as it is. With my routines and habits. I'm fine as I am. Do I want to change my life? That's the question.

After Jo had met Ethan the dawn chorus was so different. Blackbirds sung beautiful melodies and the pigeons had only words of love. She was completely besotted. Now when she got up, instead of staggering down to the kitchen for a coffee, and sitting with it for half the morning at the kitchen table, she would jump up and take time over showering, applying cream to her face and body and blow-drying her hair.

Sex was mind-blowing with Ethan. "Mouth, tits, cunt," he would murmur in a rhythm. She had never heard that before, but she found it strangely exciting.

This morning she had set her alarm to wake up and ring Frances. "Not swimming today. Much too tired. Was at 5 Hertford Street til two thirty. Trinny Woodall was there. God, she's thin. Magnificent, but sort of brittle. Trudie Styler, Nancy Dell'Olio, Rula Lenska. All those liberated, sassy girls were up when the disco played 'It's Raining Men'. Ethan said they're often on the dance floor til the early hours. It's like 'golden oldies' time at some of these clubs after midnight. The young things can't keep up."

"They've probably got breakfast meetings and heavy work days." Frances wondered if she still missed that life.

"Well, it really cheered me up. I know I dress well and am a good dancer, so it's great to feel comfortable on a dance floor surrounded by other OAP fraggles. Going back to sleep now. Enjoy your swim."

Later that day her phone chirruped. It was a text from him 'Where are you? I'm waiting.' 'On my way,' she texted back, peeling on her skin-tight jeans, tee, numinously beautiful Acne pistol boots and fantasy fur jacket. A fashionable, attractive woman looked back at her from the mirror. What was it that Oscar Wilde said? 'Illusion is the first of all pleasures'? And then there's 'Gather ye rosebuds while ye may', only that was Shakespeare. She stepped out of the warm hug from her mirror, into the exciting possibilities of another evening with Ethan.

Annie was sitting at a corner table in the Ledbury, having invited her neighbours Laura, Helen and Beth to lunch, to say thanks and goodbye. She was feeling good. The maître d' had fawned over her. It had been some time since she had written a review of the restaurant, but he would not know that she no longer worked for the Daily

News.

She could see her reflection in the mirror opposite. Glossy, stylishly cut hair, subtle, expensive makeup, the sweetheart neckline of her Moschino fine boucle dress flattering her heart-shaped face. I look as if I'm a successful businesswoman in my forties, not sixties. When my book comes out and I get the slot on Mark's show I can do lecture tours. Martin would be shocked if he could see me now. Perhaps he will, on TV. The sun reached the window and its rays shone in on her. I'll be a star. I'm going upwards. Watch me rise. "Waiter, can you bring a bottle of champagne please and four flutes."

Her old friends arrived together. Full of exclamations and compliments at her transformation. "You look stunning, Annie, like a butterfly emerged from a chrysalis. What have you been doing these past months?"

"Gorgeous! Love the dress. Have you had offers for the house?"

The waiter had filled their glasses. Annie lifted hers. "Thanks for coming, girls. I'm sorry I've been unavailable to you recently, but I've got some news for you. This may be a goodbye. I've accepted an offer and hopefully I'll soon be off to Manchester. I'm buying two large terraced houses there. I'll rent out one of them and you can always come to stay with me in the other. There are three guest bedrooms. Your health!"

The women stared at her in shock. Eventually Beth said; "You were brought up in Manchester, weren't you?"

"Yes, I knew I'd go back one day. If I get good sales of my book, I'll buy another house. There's good money in renting."

The maître d' appeared at her elbow. "The champagne is with our complements, madam, and please accept these." He laid a plate of delicious looking canapés in the middle of the table.

Her friends were impressed. "Do you always get this kind of treatment?"

"Often, when I was writing my column. But that was months ago. They just haven't realised I'm no longer doing it." She bit into a roll of smoked salmon stuffed with cream cheese, coriander and lemon. "Delicious, ten out of ten, shame for them, no-one will know."

Beth nibbled guiltily at a chilli prawn. She had lost two kilos but was aiming for twice that.

The next day, after more than two weeks of no response to her emails, Annie dressed in her new Diane von Furstenberg coral and white dress and went to the television studios to try to catch Mark after his programme aired. The doorman recognised her and let her in. "Just into the entrance hall, Mrs Lancaster. He should be coming out in ten minutes or so."

The lobby was alive with the chatter from groups of beautiful young people, elegantly dressed. She threaded her way between them looking for a seat. No one glanced at her or registered her existence. She stood against a wall, feeling invisible; no longer part of this world, reminding herself how no one here had her experience, her savvy. After ten minutes she panicked. She should not be here. What if he was annoyed at her turning up like this? She saw a gorgeous, leggy young lovely tossing her long brown mane and laughing with a corpulent, be-suited older man, confirming the rampant sexism in TV, radio and journalism. Women had been treated as playthings or accused of being lesbians. Cookery had been the only area where it had been just about Ok to be a woman. Hurrying out of the glass doors she sidled past the doorman schmoozing someone getting out of a Mercedes. Reaching the corner, she looked back at the building, a Victorian church next to it, looking out of place like her, in this street of glass.

Mark never responded to the ideas she sent him and did not answer her calls. At first she was furious. Then by the time she told Laura about it, she had become philosophical: "I wasn't exactly a global mega star, capturing the zeitgeist. In fact, I'm rather old and I did rather throw myself at him. I can't wait to get out of London."

Beth was going to the last choir for the term. They were having a concert among themselves and Beth was singing a duet with Naomi so she had to be there, even though Harriet had come to London for an interview and was coming for supper and staying the night. Since James had retired he had taken to watching cooking programmes, though he had never even tried to boil an egg.

She had written clear instructions that morning. Plus, a list of the relevant page numbers in the Delia Smith's 'How to Cook' manuals. "Don't forget, bake the potatoes and make a salad and dressing please, ready to eat with the salmon. I'll grill it when I come back."

"Tonight, tonight won't be just any night," she sang as she arrived back home. She could not get it out of her head. Feeling elated at having performed reasonably well, she called out, "hello," happily.

Sybil called from the sitting room, "I'm not hungry. I don't want to hang around down here any longer. Where *is* everyone? I want help to go upstairs. Can someone please *come*!"

James called from the kitchen. "Where is the mustard, Beth? Why aren't the potatoes cooked?"

Beth's good mood at the thought of seeing Harriet and of the supper being almost ready evaporated. She stormed into the kitchen. James had washed the salad ingredients and put potatoes in the oven, but they were nowhere near cooked and where was the dressing?

"You've had over two hours. Why do I have to do *everything*!"

James had been watching a programme about trains until fifteen minutes ago. He felt immediately guilty. "Sorry, Beth." He moved towards her to give her a hug.

"Leave me alone! You're too selfish. I'll manage without you. See to Sybil." Beth had unusually lost her temper. She stood rigid, clenching and unclenching her hands, too furious to trust herself to speak. Sybil's constant demands made her want to scream at her, slap her. "Deal with your mother. I'll deal with the supper," she snapped.

The phone rang and Dan answered it. "Marie? It's Marie, Laura!"

"Marie, where are you?" she shouted, grabbing the phone.

"Outside your door. Shall I ring the bell?"

But Laura had rushed to open it. They stood. Staring at one another searchingly, hunting out any changes.

Marie was wearing a heavily embroidered salwar kameez. Her undyed, almost completely grey hair rested on her dupatta. They hugged and Laura, pulling Marie in over the doorstep and into the cool lounge, bombarded her with: "Have you just arrived? How long

291

are you staying?"

"We came last night. Suki's house was ready so they moved out a few weeks ago. It seemed a good time to come back and see you all. Tell me the news."

Laura zipped through seven months of happenings, while she made tea and cut some fruit cake. She ended with her worry about Terry's continual illness.

A few minutes later it was Marie's turn. "Imran has come back with me. He's a doctor too. From Pakistan, in case you're wondering."

"Is he Muslim?"

"Yes, a Sufi," she grinned. "I've converted. It's the hardest thing I've ever done. Having to fit in five daily prayers in the direction of Mecca. Keep my dress and food and drink Islamic. No alcohol and fast in Ramadan."

"At least you're not wearing a burqa! How was Sudan?"

"There's so much to tell you, but it'll have to wait. I've got to show Imran round and find some tenants before I go back. He's only here for two days for a conference. I feel so calm and inspired now. I love the ritual prayers. I miss bacon and alcohol, but hey, I find the Islamic philosophy and spiritual practice such a support. I feel less pressured, strong and serene. Not empty as I was feeling here."

Later Laura and Daniel went to David Hockney's exhibition at the Royal Academy. Daniel was bowled over, Laura less so. "Not keen on the massive ones and there's too much repetition. What about that video? People were sitting there as if they were being enlightened by a strange religion. And some paintings were crude, with strange perspectives, and so violently brightly coloured. Loved the water colours, though."

"Mmm, it's very Fauvist. He's in his mid-seventies, but what appreciation of the world around him. What vibrant colours! And I'm fascinated by the way he's always into new technologies."

"So are you keen to get an iPad now? Woohoo!"

"Mmm. Maybe."

Chapter 21. July. Thoughts on ageing

'When I have fears that I may cease to be
Before my pen has gleaned my teeming brain.'
John Keats (1795 – 1821)

What strange weather they were having. Laura's vegetables had remained stubbornly small as they waited for the sun. She was usually giving away ripe tomatoes in July, but there had been so few bees there were hardly even any green ones. There were no courgettes, just male flowers and the beans were half the normal height.

Martin had started work at the Olympic Park. "No I can't see you tonight Frances. Sorry, I'm pretty exhausted. I'm looking after teams from different countries. Then I lead them into the welcoming ceremony, carrying a placard with their name on. We had Tessa Jowell or Sebastian Coe making speeches and the National Youth Theatre dancing each time. It's quite impressive."

"Tomorrow?"

"Let's see how I feel. I'll ring you. It's only eight days. I finish on Friday."

It was a lonely week. True to his word, he rang every day, though they seemed to have less and less to say to one another. Then he took on extra shifts, games makering gave him a sense of mission and purpose.

Laura had started too. She was pleasantly surprised by how well the uniform fitted and was thrilled with the Swatch watch. She was taking her team leader role very seriously, reading all the information and watching the videos on the internet while making pages of notes. On her first day, she revised as she sat on the tube. Within an hour of being there she had learnt everyone's name in her group and was working at building a great team spirit. Their shift was a few days before the athletes arrived, so they had time to find their way around.

At the first meeting with Henri, the man who was to manage her, she felt uncomfortable. "I will be watching you all today, to see which job I think you would be suitable for. If you have a bad back and can't stand, your team can look after the locker area."

He looked pointedly at her, so she felt she had to say: "You appear to be looking at me and I don't have a bad back." She shook her head in disbelief at him, knowing that she was destined for the subterranean, airless, dark, basement changing rooms. He then went on about shyness and lack of personality and looked at someone else. What happened to the 'only be positive, encourage, inspire and engage', she wondered. This is more like 'divide and rule'!

The next morning at the meeting with Henri, he asked their ages. "You don't ask ladies' ages,' said the only other team leader who was over twenty-five. Henri looked at Laura. "Your age?" he said.

Laura had not found age differences a problem with the seven leaders. They were all there to make the games as well run as they could, and suddenly she was being highlighted as different. "Sixty-four," she said. "Why is age important?" All day she felt demeaned and as if she should not be there. She had been defined by her age. She was an old person. She was no longer one of a group. He had pushed her outside it. She went home depressed and feeling foolish. Should she have volunteered? The athletes are young. Most of the games makers are young. I don't fit in, I'm too old to be of use.

"I feel criticised for daring to think that I could be a games maker," she said to Dan that evening.

She thrashed about restlessly all night. Who am I? Is my life worth anything? Am I filling my days with valueless activities? Is volunteering at my age a doomed attempt to recreate my youth? Should I be going up onto the hillside to die?

When Daisy and my Department needed me, I was too busy to worry about the purpose of my life. What is it? What are my goals, my reasons for being?

At seven the phone rang. It was Harry. Muriel had died.

Four days later, they had organised the funeral found Harry a Nursing Home he liked and were starting to empty his house, ready to sell up to pay for his keep. She had resigned from being a Games maker, though she knew that she should have confronted Henri.

Helen sat alone in Phillip's shadowy study with the curtains closed. A trembling mess. The salty taste of tears in her throat and her digestive tract loose and gurgling. She was holding the photograph of them on the beach in Ios. They were sitting in front of the pebbles and driftwood barbecue Phillip had built to cook the fish they had caught. She was wearing her white cheesecloth dress. Her hair long and wet. His arm was around her. His hand on her breast. We look as if we belong to one another.

Phillip had been skilful at gutting fish. A quick slice with his knife and the glistening innards were on the fire, hissing on the stones. She remembered how delicious it had tasted, firm and meaty. They gorged then washed off the oiliness in the sea. It was warm and quiet, the waves collapsing softly onto the beach. They stripped off, swam and made love in the dunes.

So long ago. She put it on the desk, face down and breathed in deep drafts of his absence. The strange peace of it. Why did I come in here? She asked herself. What did I come in here *for*? She looked around vaguely for a clue then turned and wandered towards the kitchen. His winter gardening jacket was still on the back of the kitchen door. She lifted it gingerly, respectfully, the cells of Phillip were all over it, and carried it to the spare room where all his clothes were bagged for a charity shop.

A silent scream tore through her head for her mocked life. All these years of pain Phillip had given her. Sometimes when she had found him out he had been hating and hostile or self-justifying and truculent. "These things happen," he would mutter.

She would be filled with molten, explosive fury. "Do they?" she would scream. "Really? One minute you're minding your own business, then suddenly you're shagging someone?" Her mouth had been full of ashes. She remembered vomit pulsing up into it.

Then the pleading: the presents, the promises that it would never happen again. Over the years her heart had become as cold as stone. Their life had become contaminated and rotten with his deceptions.

Into the bathroom with its pink, beribboned satin toilet seat cover and matching pedestal mat. She opened the cupboard under the marble counter basin and swept his shelf of toiletries into a black dustbin bag. Then she strode through the silent house to the lounge windows and pulled up the blinds so that the sun poured in. Opening the window, the air smelt fresh and new.

Laura bumped into Martin in Sainsbury's. "How are you, Martin? Haven't seen you for ages. Are you still at Roy's?"

"Yes, still there. I've been pretty busy at the Olympics. Aren't you a games maker too?"

"Yes, it didn't work out. Muriel died. But anyway, I couldn't spend time with a sexist, ageist manager."

"Oh, pity. I'm having such a good time." He frowned and ran his hand across his sweating brow and sparse hair. "I had to leave, Laura. You've no idea how cutting and cruel Annie can be."

"I think I do, Martin. She was devastated though. She had a breakdown. I don't think she realised how much she loved and depended on you."

Martin had been wondering if he was incapable of having long term relationships. He had failed with Annie and now Frances. Was it him? He was finding her irritating, especially the way she ate. He would get mesmerised by the whole routine, like watching a horror movie and being unable to tear one's eyes away. Even peeling fruit, concentrating to get all the skin off in one long strip. It had been sweet and funny at first. He had wondered if she was a frustrated surgeon or taxidermist. And did she enjoy sex? Or just not with me...had she ever thought what I might like? Such thoughts ran round and round in his head.

But to Laura he said: "I don't understand all this myself. It never occurred to me that I'd meet anyone else. Life is much calmer with Frances, but I made my vows to Annie." He looked deflated as if his brief bid for freedom was over.

"If you're happier now, just say so. Give Annie a chance to make a new life."

"To be honest, Laura, I'm confused. I think I still love Annie. I think I always will."

The schools had broken up and one third of the pool and the learning pool were given over to children's lessons. The water churned soupily and the noise was deafening. Jo, Laura and Beth did not stay long. As they walked back, dense clouds massed. It was building up for a storm.

"Where's Marie?" asked Jo.

"Doing something at the bank and estate agents. I think she's let her flat. She'll be off again in a few days."

"Lovely girl, but hasn't she heard of not accessorising denim with felt. The war was over when she was born."

"I don't think she's interested in current fashion. She wears things she likes. And anyway she's mostly wearing abaya's and hijabs now."

"Yeh, we're poles apart. My Louboutin high heels versus her MBT high horses. My Tropez tan versus her covered up alabaster. We couldn't be much more different, but she's secure in who she is. She's a top girl!"

"True. I can't imagine you wearing a salwar kameez or niqab or putting up with the life she's leading!"

"You're right. Living in the country was boring enough."

Laura had written two short stories and entered them in four competitions. She had also started writing a novel about a group of older women and had sent the first three chapters off to agents and 'indie' publishers. Some wrote or emailed their 'No thank you' response immediately. After five rejections, a small independent publisher replied. She held the envelope above her head and wished. This time, this time. She made a cup of tea and took it out into the garden. If the datura is out it will be a yes. It was almost out, a yellow sheath soon to unfurl. A blackbird sang on the mountain ash and pigeons shuffled, pushing and pecking up and down next door's bedroom windowsills.

Ok. Now.

'Thank you. Interesting subject....doubtful of commercial success...best of luck elsewhere...Room for improvement in your writing...Have you read 'On Writing' by Stephen King?...'

297

Jo dressed with special care. Her Erdem black flowered silk crepe pencil skirt and cardigan and Manolos. She was looking forward to a romantic evening with Ethan. Perhaps tonight she would lock this thing down. Perhaps move in with him?

"I'll meet you in the coffee bar in the Royal Garden Hotel. I'm up to my eyes, so expect me when you see me. Probably around seven," he had said.

She arrived full of pleasant anticipation, but was starting to feel irritated after forty-five minutes had passed. She flicked on her Blackberry. Nothing. Time was when he had sent her thirty texts or emails a day. How had people managed to make themselves look busy before the invention of personal technology? It pulsated. "Sorry babe. Be another half an hour."

Her stomach growled. The bar was covered with snacks: croissants, cup cakes, little quiches, fruit and nut cereal cakes. Should she eat something, or would they be having dinner?

At eight fifteen, he was suddenly there. "We had to keep retaking, and I'm still not happy. We're having a quick break."

'Consistency is the last refuge of the unimaginative', she thought. And 'the very essence of romance is uncertainty'.* She was feeling really hungry. "Shall we reconvene for supper tomorrow?" she asked, lightly and casually.

"Tomorrow? Sorry, babe. Busy." Her mind started racing. She took a deep breath, trying to keep her thoughts and emotions in check. Trying to talk about something, anything, but she could not help herself. She really needed to know what he was doing. "Busy working?" she almost squeaked.

"Mmm. Anyway, gotta rush now." He got up and gave her a casual embrace. Then walked off out of her life.

Annie and Martin had spoken in stilted fashion on the phone a few times to discuss the house sale and she had embarrassed herself by writing to him in a moment of nostalgia. *'You made me feel so safe. You were the calm in my life and understood the drama I brought to yours. We are so different in many ways. When I'm choosing you a present I know to pick the one I like least as that's the one you'll love, but our relationship worked and not just for me. You loved me once. You make me laugh. You have the driest sense of humour, which most people don't get. You've been my best friend for thirty-four years. I'm so lonely without you, and no-one else will do.'*

I wish I hadn't sent that stupid, demeaning letter she thought, but if I hadn't? Oh, what the hell. She phoned him again. They made polite noises, then she plunged in with: "I've accepted an offer on the house. It's going through. You'll get half on completion." Then she said humbly: "I'm so sorry that we didn't work out. It was all my fault. You were the perfect husband."

"Maybe we never should have got together. You needed someone stronger. I've never been decisive and manly enough for you."

Annie was starting to panic, as if she were groping through a field of brambles in the dark. Her next utterance could be one of the most important she had ever made. She must speak slowly, sound calm. "I'm packing up your things. Perhaps you can arrange to get them soon? And," she paused to gain courage. "Why not come to Manchester this weekend to see the houses I've made offers on? You wouldn't want me to buy something not structurally sound would you?" There was a long silence. She could imagine him shifting from foot to foot and rubbing his chin.

He muttered, "Well, it can't do any harm. At least I can check them out and see you settled."

"Great." Annie felt almost giddy. The low sun threw its last rays into the garden and it looked golden, beautiful. Not the untidy, overgrown, sad place that she had felt so guilty about a few minutes ago. He had been so proud of *our* garden and she should have been prouder of him. *Did I ever tell him how beautiful it was, I wonder?*

Next day, Martin set out full of trepidation to pick up his possessions from his ex-home and look at the details of Annie's prospective properties. The sun was high in the sky. It was so hot that he was sweating before he had reached the end of his road. The rage and powerlessness he had felt towards her when he had walked out on her had been replaced by curiosity and excitement. His first shock was seeing the front garden. It was a mess of unpruned shrubs and weeds. What had happened to the white and pink floxes and the two coloured penstemon? They must be buried under the hypericum and that japanese anemone which had gone mad. He let himself in and walked through to the kitchen. He could see Annie on the sheltered terrace at the bottom of the garden. She was sunbathing, her laptop on the little wooden table next to her. He reined in his gaze to take in the garden and mentally mowed the lawn, pruned the shrubs and weeded the beds.

Opening the door of the sitting room, he sighed. It was just a big bare space. Nothing but the cream carpet and wonderful Edwardian fire grate. The cream suite, fashionable lighting, occasional tables and Persian carpets, their joint choices had presumably gone into storage. In the dining room there were six big packing cases with his name on them and she had said she had not touched his shed. He turned and went upstairs feeling rather hollow and upset. The three bedrooms on the first floor were empty of movable furniture. There were marks on the carpet where they had stood and patches of stronger colour on the walls where pictures and mirrors had hung. He carried on upstairs to the master bedroom. Just a camp bed. He thought nostalgically of their queen sized bed where they had made love so often until the last five years, or was it longer ago that it had petered out? This huge room, with its luxurious ensuite that he had designed and built, felt familiar, yet strangely no longer his. It was like a stage set, waiting for its next production. He sighed and retraced his steps to the kitchen where he made tea. There were only two mugs, two plates and no food in the fridge, just milk. He took a packet of Marks and Spencer eccles cakes out of his rucksack and, balancing them on top of one of the hot mugs of tea, went down the garden to talk to Annie.

She was lying on their old sun lounger, her olive skin evenly tanned. She looked trimmer, slim in fact. That was a new bikini. His heart raced. "Annie? You're looking good."

She opened her eyes and for a moment someone younger and kinder than he remembered looked out, but then they became veiled and cold.

"Thanks." She reached down and lifted up a file. "Here are the particulars of the houses. Will Frances mind if you come to Manchester?"

"Mmm. Maybe," he mumbled.

"Are you really going to be happy with her?"

He furrowed his brow. "Who can tell? It's obviously a risk."

This did not seem to be the response of a man completely sure about throwing away their marital status for a lover. She felt a twinge of satisfaction from his lacklustre tone.

"How lucky you can just dismiss our thirty-four years of marriage for someone you hardly know."

He shrugged, sipped his tea and offered her an eccles cake. "I was hoping we could be friends. Part in a civilised way. Specially if you're asking me to go to Manchester for you."

"You can't come this weekend *with* me?" she asked.

There was a pause. "Maybe Sunday. It's my last games maker day on Saturday."

She could not help the life and hope creeping back into her eyes.

Since Terry had known she had only a short time to live, she knew that she had become inert. What was the point of struggling with golf, swimming, buying anything, going anywhere and she would never see the results of planting seeds. She realized that she was already out of the world of caring about anything very much. Driving to Waitrose, she climbed out of the car stiffly and staggered a little before she found her balance. She should not be driving.

Some mornings she sat in front of the mirror in their ensuite bathroom, trying to make sense of it. Searching for the face of the old healthy Terry. The person who had always been there before. But there was only ever a haggard stranger with a lifeless grey frizz. A cloud of fuse wire. Whose body had been taken over by alien cells.

She hoped it would be peaceful and not too painful. Though at times she was full of an ugly fear, a terrified expectancy. She was thinner than she had ever been and her speech was deteriorating fast. Her arms and legs were painful, so walking was even more difficult. She had to wear incontinence pads and her expression was alternately frightened or blank.

It was time to tell Laura the truth. She had been fobbing her off with the virus story for too long. She asked if she would call round after swimming.

When Terry answered the door and led her friend into the kitchen, she was leaning on a stick, tap, step, tap, step. She put on the kettle, then turned and plunged into: "Tests have shown that I have an out of control cancer. I've only a few months to live."

There was a shocked silence. "Oh no. Oh no. Oh God, no!" She hugged her friend, her hot tears falling into Terry's hair. "Are you absolutely sure?"

"Yes." The muffled word was stark and final. "I'll be going to the Marie Curie Hospice when I can't cope here any more. Would you take me if for some reason David or Rosie were not here?"

"Of course, absolutely. But they know, don't they?"

"Yes, it's hard for him. He's thirty and he's only just found a job he likes. He's worrying about transport costs, NI contributions, pensions, taxes, innumerable bills. It's all a struggle, and I'm not going to be around to help him. He's losing both of us in a year."

"You're not dead yet. What treatment are you having?"

"I'm having no treatment. None." The last word hung in the air between them.

"What? Why not?"

"I made a choice not to have the tumours in my lungs operated on. Then within weeks I knew it had been the right decision, because it had already spread to my brain. Doctors try and fix you, whatever the improbability, the damage and the extended suffering they inflict. As I said the cancer is out of control. Nothing more can be done."

Laura's diaphragm lifted and fell and a sob broke out. A soft wail shuddered to a halt as she struggled to control herself. She mopped her face, "Sorry Terry...this is devastating. Why didn't you tell me before? I was hoping that you had some sort of virus, which would pass. You can't live here on your own. Let me help look after you."

"It's Ok. Either David or Rosie have started coming every evening. Sometimes both of them, and they sleep here too. They'll carry on til the Macmillan palliative team takes over. The District Nurse has arranged for them to help me until its time to go to the Hospice."

She smiled to herself as she thought of how different her son and his girlfriend were.

David would be cleaning fastidiously: putting things away, making appetising little meals. While Rosie was slapdash and banged and crashed around in the kitchen, had the radio up loud and slept so heavily that Terry could not wake her when she needed help to get up to go to the toilet. "I'm so sorry. Did I sleep through again? Oh thank goodness you managed to use the commode. I'll just empty it." Terry felt ashamed and demeaned filling the commode. But it looked as if this were the only option when Rosie was here and, to be fair, she never seemed to mind and was gentle and loving when she helped her to wash.

"You must tell your friends, Terry. They will be devastated not to have known that you were dying. Not to have been able to offer support or say goodbye."

"I don't want people telling me I should be drinking gallons of vegetable juice to kick-start my liver into fighting back. Or walking barefoot in dew, smearing myself in iodine or any other cranky supposed cure. None of it works. It's false hope. And talking used to be such fun. Now it is such a struggle. It's such an effort to talk, to walk. I'm losing everything, losing it all, Laura. I can't even read very well. I've forgotten most of what I knew and I can't count. Food tastes of nothing. I can't smell. I've got appalling headaches, shortness of breath and muscle spasms. I want to sleep most of the time. I'm panicky, terrified. Ready to go now."

Laura had read a review of Philip Gould's book: 'When I die: Lessons from the death Zone.' When he knew he was dying he decided that his last weeks and months should be happier, more meaningful and revelatory than any in his life. Death, being so imminent, gave every hour a brilliant intensity. He looked forward to every day and felt that nothing could be better than the delights of being alive and deepening his relationship with those he loved. She bought the book and offered it to Terry to read.

She started it immediately. Those I loved? Leonard was the core of my life. She resolved to try and talk to David more, to help him understand who his parents had been. And to let her friends visit when they asked to. She had yet to tell Bella.

303

Daniel had noticed that Laura was talking a lot about dying. "Everyone dies," he said to her. "There's no point getting obsessed about it."

"But when it's your family or your contemporaries, it's like a part of yourself has been torn away. They can't be replaced, they leave holes."

"We all have to live our own lives and die our own deaths. Get on with living yours, appreciating it more."

"I'm reading Julian Barnes, the one that won the Booker. I don't usually like his writing. His women characters are not rounded and realistic, but there's lots of bits that make me think. Yes! Like we all suffer damage one way or another. It's inevitable, unless one's family, friends, neighbours etc are perfect. Then the crunch thing is, how we deal with it and how it affects our dealings with others."

"That's a huge question and probably why 'therapists' have so much work."

"I often wonder why I don't blame my parents for their faults and for not helping me when I was so scared of that neighbour who kept trying to rape me. But I don't."

"You were better at dealing with the damage?"

"The other thing he says that struck me, was that the character wondered if the purpose of life was to reconcile us to death whenever it occurs. By showing us that life isn't that great. Depressing, hey?"

"Mmm."

"Its not mmm. It's really depressing. I mean, however strong and vital one has been. Old age is all doctors and hospitals, tests for heart, lungs, glaucoma, dementia, count backwards in sevens and what's the Prime Minister's name?"

"Ok, Ok, Laura. Enough!"

But she carried on. "And being told you're bloody marvellous just for being still alive! When does all this misery begin I want to know!"

"I give up. I'm sick of you being unhappy and negative."

Helen was waiting outside her house for the swimming group. "Are you coming? Great," they said. "How are you?"

"If I keep breathing in and out, I'll get over all this. I can be happy again, I know I can."

"Any thoughts or plans yet?"

"I'm getting there," she said noncommittally.

Further on, the pavement narrowed and they were unable to walk four abreast. Laura and Marie went in front and Beth hung back with Helen. "You've always been our positive, supportive friend. We've all lent on you for years. I hate to see you so devastated and alone. Can't we help?"

"You can't make me young again." A half smile briefly lit up Helen's face. "I can replace my clothes, my house, even my friends, but I can never look and feel young again. I regret all those years of being submerged in work and supporting Mum and Phillip. I want to remember and revisit all those dreams I had while I still have the energy. I want a new start, a new life. I feel as if I've earned it."

"How are you going to live?"

"I don't need much. I'm retiring and taking my pension and lump sum. I'm letting my house to an American family. Too many memories," she said defiantly. "I've never had a chance to sow wild oats, make my own decisions, travel alone. Remember, I met Phillip in my first year at university. Getting on for fifty years ago! And now I've got dodgy eyes and knees and what else is round the corner? I've got to get on with my life. Maybe I'll find a new name. One will come to me suddenly and when it does it'll be my cloak of invisibility. So if one day someone sees me and calls "Helen," I won't even break my stride, because that won't be my name."

"Oh, Helen," Beth sighed.

"Always look forward, never back because no moment in time lasts, my mother used to say. I realise now, even though I've had an absorbing and stimulating career, I was actually lost and constrained in Phillip's life. I didn't want to know what he was getting up to, but when someone works from home you're inevitably sucked in. Marriage can be a cage, in which you watch your life go by."

"So where are you going to go. What are you going to do?"

"I want to be free to decide on a whim. Actually if there's a disaster anywhere in the world, I might head for it. A friend was holidaying in Thailand when the Tsunami struck and she helped for

305

months with counselling victims' relatives. Or I might be a dish pig, or pick fruit, or…or…"

"I suppose you're still quite fit and healthy."

"Yes, this may be my last few years of being fit enough to travel before I'm huddling in a room with other desperate people. Breathing raggedly, waiting to die."

"You've got years yet!"

"And, I'm not waiting until I'm too infirm to move out of my home like my mother. When I come back from wherever, I'll sell up and down size."

"That's a big step."

"I'm Ok with it, Beth, honest. There's a life change glimmering on the horizon. A new dawn for me. Things don't always turn out as we expect. Exciting solutions get thrown up by the unexpected. I've always had a job where I worked with the same colleagues, looked smart and worried if my pension would be enough to live on. I'm ditching stability and my familiar routines, to travel and maybe pick up the sort of jobs I didn't do when I was that kid who fell in love and married Phillip. Soon I'll be old and decrepit…if I'm ever going to be happy again, it had better be now!"

Chapter 22. August. Coming to terms

'There is a pleasure in the pathless woods,
There is a rapture on the lonely shore.'
Lord Byron.
'Childe Harold's Pilgimage.' (1788 – 1824)

Martin sat in his small bedroom, staring at the white wall opposite. What am I supposed to do for the rest of my life, however long that is? Has the best of it gone? Nothing to aim for? There's always been something to look forward to. How happy he had been: finding Ms Right, a house, the perfect job, a child, in whatever order. What is ahead now? An image of a frail old person sitting in an awful Nursing Home, reliving their past, flashed into his head, followed by the song 'Always look on the bright side of life.' He had been singing it in his head ever since Eric Idle had sung it in the Olympics Closing Ceremony. But he could not think of one single thing to really look forward to. Was the last phase of life to be depressing and increasingly painful? He was alive and healthy and had enough pension to live reasonably. There was more to be discovered and enjoyed: 'Always look on the bright side of life.'

He was steeling himself to tell Frances that he wanted to cool their relationship, but had volunteered for more and more Paralympic shifts instead of facing her. He wanted to tell her. He was desperate to tell her. He did not want to seem a monster. When was there ever a good time to say this sort of thing? He knew that he had always been a coward and gone along with the easy option.

After he had finished his duties, he had made excuses not to see her. Pretending he was still working. It felt deceitful and cruel. The need to confess was consuming him, he could think of little else, but he still prevaricated and put off meeting up with her.

Daniel had been invited by a friend of a friend to exhibit in a small gallery in Camden for two weeks as part of a new art show to encourage local painters. He was going through his canvases and making lists of the people he wanted to invite to the opening.

"Haven't got any patrons. Don't know any journalists in the arts. I could write to Brian Sewell, Searle and Januszczuk, I suppose. But there are so many small galleries and we've only got fifteen invites each." He flicked through the photos of his canvases, remembering what he had been trying to achieve with each one. "That's what keeps one painting. The fact that one rarely achieves the picture in one's head."

"Presumably that's why Monet repeated waterlilies," Laura mused.

Some of Daniel's paintings disturbed the air. These three. Their bright, vibrating Hockney colours, the coarse brushstrokes, the grooves and ridges of paint demanded attention. Marie stood for a long time, just looking, the colours seemed to swirl around her, until she felt she was cracking open like an egg. Then suddenly the gallery was full of noise as a group swept in from the street. She shook her head to clear it and moved over to the table containing glasses of wine, where Laura had been talking to someone. "What are you writing about at the moment?" she asked her.

"I haven't written for a couple of weeks. There's always so much to fill the day. Got rejection blues…Actually I had an idea for a story a few weeks ago, but now looking back, I can see that it was just one thought amongst all the millions floating like dust motes through my cluttered mind. Sitting down and getting on with it is the problem."

"You've got imagination and empathy and you really want to write. I'm sure you'll be brilliant. Specially if you do it more often."

They smiled at one another, both wondering when they would meet again. Marie was leaving in two days.

Helen and Laura were drying their hair after an unsatisfying swim in an overcrowded pool.

"How come your hair hasn't gone grey Laura? Are you tinting it?" Helen was raking through her greying hair with her fingers.

"No, of course I'm not. It's the genes. My Father never went grey either."

"If I'm going to go travelling, I can't be grey. It's synonymous with old. Not the vibrant, energetic, resourceful person I want to be."

"You were telling me that grey was the new blonde a few months ago?"

"That was before I bumped into Harriet and her friend coming up from the tube one day and the friend asked if I was her grandmother! She thought I was Sybil!"

"That's ridiculous."

"I know I haven't kept up with the tinting lately, but to say that was depressing would be an understatement!"

"She was just one silly girl."

"Well, it made me cry. Then I got angry. Angry that my hair colour could affect the way I think about myself. I've been used to people enjoying being with me and taking my advice because of who I am. What was in my head, not on it. If being grey shows I'm past it to some people, I'll dye it back to my tawny colour until I'm ready to be judged by a hair colour frame of reference."

Martin had woken up this morning with the knowledge and clarity that today was the day. There could be no more prevarication. He bought some pink roses on the way to Frances's flat. It had been six weeks since they had last met. She opened the door and they stood staring at one another. He thrust the roses forward. She stared at them, seemingly frozen to the spot. Neither of them spoke. After what seemed like minutes, though it was probably seconds, she pulled herself together and they walked up the stairs and into her kitchen, where she busied herself with the kettle and mugs.

Having spoken so often on the phone there did not seem a lot to say. There was the weather and another dripping bathroom tap. She handed him a coffee and they went into the lounge and sat at the table looking out at next-door's garden. The room which had seemed warm and bright a few hours ago felt cold and empty. She was apprehensive and uneasy.

Martin had a rabbit in the headlights expression and was shifting nervously in his seat. Eventually he could hold back no longer and blurted out: "Annie has sold our house and is buying two in Manchester. I went to see them last weekend. They're a good buy and

309

she wants me to go with her. I'm sorry, Frances, but she seems to have changed and I did make my marriage vows. I can't see you again. I don't think an open relationship would work for any of us."

Although, after waiting so long to see him, she had been almost sure that Martin was wanting to end their affair, she felt the blood draining from her face. Her voice seemed to be coming from far away. "I suppose we've never talked about a future, but did you care about me? Was it me you wanted? Or did you just need a stop gap?"

Martin was pale and scared. This was not going well.

"Of course it was you. I can't imagine that anyone else would have attracted me. We've had a good time, haven't we?"

She thought of how lonely she had been before they had met. Had they been deceiving one another to mitigate their lonely lives? "I know you've never made any promises, but the fact that you can just walk away from me now shows me that we never really knew one another and that you never really cared."

"Don't say that. I've felt remarkably close to you, considering it's only been a few months."

She suddenly felt tears welling up. She was howling inside. Her life with a partner had had meaning, and now?

"I'm sorry Frances. I don't know what I was thinking when we started our relationship. Maybe it could have been permanent, but I didn't think about the future when we met. I was attracted to you. I hope I haven't messed up your life?"

She had started to cry. He jumped up, knelt by her chair and put his arms around her. "You'll meet someone else. I'm sure of it. Let's look back at our months together as special fun."

She pushed him away and almost ran back through the kitchen. "I'll see you out."

Martin's expression was stricken. "Please, can't we be friends?"

"Friends? With a married man who's been cheating on his wife and lying to me?"

"Forgive me," he said. Frances followed him down the stairs and slammed the door after him as he stepped outside.

Laura and Beth were walking back from the pool in the sun.

"That was a perfect swim!"

"Yes, I couldn't believe it when all those people just got out. One after the other."

"I was wondering if they knew something, or if we were all going to be asked to go."

"There's nothing better than the pool being calm and having a lane to yourself."

"You know Harriet's maternity cover is finished and she's coming back to London on Friday. She's got that job as a Programme Manager for Jamie Witherspoon's 'Good Food For All Foundation'."

"Oh great. That's good news. Is she going to live at home?"

"Only while she's looking for a flat share. What's good is that Jake has been promoted and is staying in Edinburgh for now. And Harriet and Sybil get on so well. They've always talked a lot, particularly about fashion. Sybil has given her most of her old designer clothes. Apparently they're vintage and Harriet loves to hear about Sybil's past life. They respect one another. Sybil behaves like a human being when Harriet's around."

"You must be hoping she doesn't find a flat for a while then."

"Mmm, indeed."

Frances had told no one about Martin's return to Annie. Though of course everyone could see what had happened.

Jo knocked at her door one evening. "Are you Ok, Frances? Do you want to come down for a drink and a chat?"

Professional, competent, single women don't make emotional demands or make mistakes by saying out loud what they are really thinking, Frances thought. "Thanks, but I'm a bit busy at the moment."

"Oh come on. You must be feeling down. Just one quick drink?"

Reluctantly Frances followed Jo down to her flat. They made small talk and then Jo mentioned Martin. Frances bit her lip and found herself saying how he had let her down and that was it with men.

Jo rarely minced her words. "See it as if your fairy godmother sent him to get you through a bad time. You were in crisis; you got a mental detox and physical intimacy. He was a good friend for you to practise on. Are you going to look around for a replacement?"

Frances didn't know what to say.

Jo plunged on. "When was the last time you let go and had a fling?"

A fling? Frances was shocked. She shrugged. "I must go now, sorry."

"What do you want out of life, Frances?"

She looked blank and backed out of the door.

"You've got to want something. I think you need to look outside of yourself. Work was what you most enjoyed. Have you thought about charity work? Helping others helps yourself is something I've just discovered. Have a think and let's talk again. Give me a ring." Frances opened her flat door and fled upstairs, oblivious of Jo's cheery wave.

Frances sat in her favourite chair and put her head in her hands. Next birthday I'm going to be an old-age pensioner. A senior citizen. My body must be winding down. Soon it will be falling apart. What do I want? To be valued?

A partner? Sometimes perhaps, but every day? I've got enough money to live comfortably if I don't splash it about. I need to look forward to something in life, not spend the rest of it angry and depressed. And I don't want people feeling sorry for me. Not that anyone cares about me. Charity work? What charity? She sat and sat, full of a heavy stillness, a stasis, the aftermath of her violent feelings towards Martin. Of how pointless and meaningless their relationship had been. But then was it? He had restored some of her confidence, sort of 'awakened' her emotionally and sexually. So what was she to do now with this unused love, unemployed passion, with the hole that Martin had filled? She reached down into her bag for a tissue to mop up her tears and saw the newspaper she had bought that morning. She turned to the jobs pages.

Now that Terry had come to terms with her coming demise, she decided that she was not going to spend the last part of her life depressed. She read Nietzsche. About how slow pain forces us to descend to the ultimate depths, from which one emerges more profound, joyful, subtler, new born, and she tried to feel this in her better periods, even having moments of ecstasy, exulting because she was still here. The world around her had never seemed so beautiful. The tenderness in her friends' faces as they pushed her around Kew, Regents Park, Chelsea Physic and other gardens, filled her with joy.

All the literature about impending death, advised her to:

'Spend time with people you click with.'

'Enjoy your memories. Travel to your past and relive the best times of your life and using all your senses, remember how you felt.'

She told people: "It's not sad to die, the sad thing is not to have lived intensely, to have chickened out in life. I was intensely involved in the 'Cultural Access' charity. Building it up was the highlight of my life and I had a good marriage and have a wonderful son. And at least no one can catch cancer from me. It's all mine. Entirely mine."

The rate of her deterioration seemed to have slowed, in fact sometimes she felt quite good.

"Why not have a blog, or a twitter account, so your friends and family can get the latest from you?" Laura suggested.

"I can't be bothered with things like that. What are they anyway?"

Laura looked across at her dear friend. She was drowsy and mumbling: swollen legs propped on a pile of cushions, face turned towards the sun, which was streaming through the window. "I've not got either, or follow anyone. It's part of the oversharing era. Twitter is a micro blog, a social site that you and friends can leave comments and messages on. No longer than in one hundred and forty characters."

"I don't know how to do it." Terry looked down at her puffy hands. "I couldn't do it with these and anyway I just don't feel up to learning stuff like that."

"Why not talk to Rosie about it? I bet she tweets."

The next day Rosie set up a twitter account for her and she tweeted how she felt. She was quite overcome with the outpouring of affection from her family and friends. Later, after over one hundred and fifty others she had never met sent her tweets about the heroic way she was facing death, she started to become quite addicted.

Then came the heat wave. It was suddenly blisteringly hot. Everyone knows it should not be as hot as this, 32 degrees and not a breath of air. The forecast said there is torrential rain in the west. But it stayed there. It didn't seem fair.

People with burnt faces and more were everywhere. Laura looked at them disparagingly. "Don't they know that a tan is skin damage?" She kept in the shade of buildings when shopping and wore factor fifty, having over exposed her skin for years in Greece. Everyone seemed to be eating outside in gardens, on pavements and in parks. Suddenly Laura's tomatoes and beans were ready for picking.

One late afternoon she was at the bottom of the garden collecting salad, when the phone rang. She ran across the overlong lawn, 'not to be cut when it's too hot', Daniel had said. She picked it up, but the person had gone and looking up, she briefly saw a shadow against the thick glass of the outside door and the stained glass of the inner one.

It couldn't have been Daisy, could it? She opened the doors and ran down the path, but the street was empty...

Jo, Lynne, Laura and Beth had finished their swim. It was a beautiful day, warm with just a tiny breeze. Laura sighed, "We should be by the sea now. This great weather can't last, but we're stuck here 'til Dan takes down the exhibition."

"Mmm, the sea. Walking down a sandy beach, breathing in fresh air. How about going somewhere, Lynne? A staycation isn't so attractive when everyone's away and it's hot," said Jo.

Laura noticed a slight narrowing of her eyes and a hint of chill in her voice as Lynne replied. "Well, next door would feed the cats and Robert could pop in when he comes to see his Father. Mmm, Ok. As long as you don't insist on a marble lined hotel with hot and cold running botox in a place stuffed with people lounging on loungers, with their tiny dogs, perma tans and spray-on slag outfits? How about St David's? One of my patients was telling me about the beautiful beaches and the quaint little town."

Jo laughed. "I refuse to be offended, but this country? You can't

314

rely on the weather."

"Look Barbie-head. Europe hasn't had a great summer either. I think I just need peace to be able to think. Why don't we go for, say, five days while the weather's settled?"

Jo gave her a hug. "Sisters under the skin?" she grinned.

Who could resist Jo? She bathed people in warmth with her vivacity. With the way she fixed her eyes on you. As if no-one else mattered.

"Why not? Shall I come over this evening and we can look on the Internet for somewhere to stay?"

"Ok. I'll expect you after eight."

Lynne knew that her reaction was grumpy and ungrateful, but Jo had always made her feel an inadequate lump: anxious, narrow minded, unadventurous and afraid of losing control of her own small world. Jo's seeming so much more vivid and interesting, though chaotic. Jo shrugged off things that would have tortured or even destroyed Lynne.

The next day Jo went for a wax in preparation. It cost a fortune, but the pampering and calm atmosphere were so relaxing and Sophia, the owner, always told her that she had perfect, beautiful legs. She had cellulite, but at least if they were tanned it would not show so much.

Two days later, they took the train, away from the tangle and dirt of the city through unknown towns and little villages where unknown people were living out their lives, to Haverfordwest. Then a bus ride to St David's and their hotel.

Jo dragged her large case upstairs and started to unpack. It was so quiet. Oh good, cotton sheets. She went to the window and looked out into the street. Nothing was happening except an august afternoon. The bedside drawer had a Gideon Bible and a folded used tissue. Did someone cry themselves to sleep here? Just as lonely as she now felt? The age of invisibility. Get used to it, Jo, she thought. Lying back on the pink candlewick bedspread, she had a little weep.

Next morning after breakfast they put on their bathing costumes, beach hats and sandals. Jo was wearing a stretchy, towelling sun dress and Lynne shorts and tee as they headed for a small cove that their

315

landlady said they would have to themselves.

The endless blue of the sky and sea blurred into one another as Lynne walked along the deserted beach. The only marks on the hard golden sand were the footprints of sea birds and the only sound, their cries and the swish of the little ripples. It was almost low tide, so she scrambled over the rocky promontories between the coves, trying to be light footed, so as not to crush the mussels and winkles underfoot. Seeing an armchair shaped rock, she sat, gazing out to sea. Gulls wheeled lazily, the sea lapped gently. It was heavenly. A day to share. Why did I say that? What is this compulsion to be with a partner? Who said that human beings should always be in twos or groups? It's sad. In the States fifty per cent of adults are single. Mostly by choice. How can I possibly not be completely happy, here, now?

She walked back to Jo, lying sphinx-like on her mat and beach towel. "You're not going to burn are you?"

"I've got 30 on," she rolled over, tucking her full breasts into her untied bikini top and hooking it up.

"You're so lucky. You've got good skin. You look years younger than your age. It's my own fault, covering myself in oil and sautéing myself in my twenties," Lynne said, looking down at her own saggy, wrinkled skin. "How about a swim?"

"Later." Jo went back to her book and sunbathing.

Getting in took a few minutes, but once submerged and after a few strokes Lynne was accustomed to the temperature. Ribbons of cool and pockets of heat caressed her strong body. Her skin felt like velvet and waves of tingling energy coursed through her. She swam powerfully around a rocky outcrop into the next bay. Then floated on her back, staring up at the cloudless sky, suffused with peace and calmness.

Kicking gently, she propelled herself to the beach and lay on the warm sand, feeling like a contented basking seal. Her hair in wet rat tails, the salt drying on her skin.

A little later, she woke to feel water lapping around her feet. Sudden panic engulfed her...was she trapped? Looking around, she calmed down as she saw that she could scramble up the rocks behind and into some undergrowth. Fifteen minutes later, scratched, sweating

316

and with dirty sore feet she reached a sunken medieval lane where trees and bushes arched over, making a dense canopy with only occasional dappled light. She picked her way through the thicket of sycamore and larch, where the smaller sea holly and hawthorn struggled to see the sun. The ground underfoot was dry and stony and roots made gnarled steps as she walked up hill. Emerging from the trees, gorse buds popped and bees hummed as they pollinated the blackberries, rosebay willowherb, honeysuckle and dog roses. Though she had always dreaded doing things alone, she felt happy and could understand how solitude became addictive. I can walk at any pace, stop and start and go wherever I choose. And think. Yes, think without interruption, she said to herself.

Reaching the coast path, the sky was now grey and the sea had become an indigo blue blanket extending to the horizon, calm and unruffled by the sudden cool breeze. The little beach where Jo had lain was empty and only a few families were still in the next cove. The nippy wind and promise of rain had hastened everyone home. She looked forward to an evening of reading, relaxing and not having to cook for herself.

It was starting to rain as she reached the beginning of the shops and she saw a wild looking woman reflected back at her in their windows. Would having a partner mean that one took more care with one's appearance? Maybe...

Could I live in Brighton? Do I want the fresh air of a new life? Not really. It would just be a different setting, without my friends and London culture. If I really loved Robert would I be hesitating? What's love anyway? The sex is great, but do I want to live with him? I was expecting to be a cranky, eccentric old spinster, with a vibrator and the occasional sexual encounter. He's seventy-five. He won't be able to get it up in a few years anyway and I don't want to be looking after anyone else. Thank you very much.

After Jo had read a few more chapters, the tide was advancing so she decided to swim. She lay in the sea, trying to relax and let go of her feelings for Ethan and Ed. She breathed out and breast stroked her arms, kicked her feet, pushing her sadness out. Hoping that the

317

last vestiges of them were draining out of her and dissolving in the vast, salty sea. She was melting, reality loosening. Where were her edges? Where did she stop and the water begin? Was she seeping into the water?

Do I feel things more intensely than I used to? Or not? Do I appear ridiculous? People expect serenity of the old. That is the stereotype, the mask we are expected to put on. Did I have the perfect life with Ed? No, nothing is perfect. No one can be happy all of the time. It's the human condition. That's why we rush about disguising our emptiness, our fears. Trying not to think too deeply. But the nameless fear does not go away. There are always the frighteners in the middle of the night.

I've been surfing from one high octane moment to the next. A free spirit, only thinking of myself. My own pleasures. Am I a masochist? Why haven't I wanted to be with someone who respects and loves me, rather than one who takes me? Why do I need to bang my butt off with bastards? Hunting for the perfect shag has been my full time job. Enough is enough. I don't want to be an old crone joke. I'm a nice person underneath, with good intentions; I'm adjusting my priorities, changing direction. Doing more with my life.

I'm cold, cold. She paddled her arms, pulling herself through the clear cool water until she was lying in the tiny, warm ripples at the water's edge. No sign of Lynne. She must have swum off into the next bay. Her body was beginning to feel as if it belonged to her, so she pushed herself to her feet and waded out. Slipping on her towelling dress, she picked up her swimming bag and Lynne's things and strode off towards the next cove.

Around the corner, this beach still held a few families. Anxious parents striving to amuse their cold, fractious offspring. Shrieking gulls with their malevolent yellow eyes and cruel yellow beaks, waiting to pounce on anything edible. She deliberately took a route over the rocks; to feel her feet gripping and body tensing as it strove to balance. The sea was now grey and low cloud hid the nearby island from view.

The air smelt fresh and clean and her lungs, light and open, filled gratefully. She took a deep breath and felt like weeping in relief as the

318

band of stress, which had been tight around her chest eased.

Moving down through a family group she felt herself to be invisible.

"Jellies," said a little girl pointing to her shoes, forcing her to exist, to be part of the scene, to smile and acknowledge her observation.

There was now a large black cloud above and a few drops fell. She returned to the water's edge, where it was firmer and she could walk more quickly. Rain hissed into the bright shingle and everyone scurried for shelter.

Laura and a relaxed, tanned Jo were heading to the gym. They discussed the holiday in St David's, then Laura asked:

"What have you been up to recently, Jo? Have you been seeing someone?"

"Absolutely not. After Ethan, I haven't even been looking."

"So what then?"

Jo adopted an extravagantly neutral face and avoided eye contact with Laura. "Why should there be anything? I'm working on how to live more fully in the present while contemplating my mortality."

"Working out how to age well? You're brilliant at that already. Chronology is totally deceptive as far as you're concerned."

Laura dropped round to see how Lynne got on in St David's.

"I had an epiphany on the beach. I'm not aspiring to the sunny uplands of coupledom. Now I'm feeling healthier and happier I rather enjoy being on my own."

"You're not lonely?"

"Absolutely not. I don't do lonely. There's so much in my life and always something new to try. If I never have a lover again I wouldn't be 'bovvered.' The only down side is that couples feel sorry for you and can't see singledom as a life choice, which is why it's so convenient to have Robert. He's a partner to do things with, including sex, but I won't be looking after him when he's past it. Ken was never practical and wouldn't cook, then my Mum. I don't want to be an unpaid carer for anyone else. I mean no one gets fitter as they get older. Exhaustion, sickness and decrepitude are ahead and for Robert probably before me. It's great to be on my own. This is exactly how I want to live the rest of my life."

"You never think about your two abortions?"

"Of course not. I didn't want a baby then and I'm glad I made that decision. I'm fine with being a Pank."

"Is that an acronym?"

"Professional auntie, no kids. I've looked all this up. At least a fifth of British women are childless and the US has almost double that. I'm single and childless by choice. Don't worry!"

She marched into the kitchen and spooned some cat food into Thira and Sophie 2's dishes and returned with some tiny quiches from the oven. They refilled their glasses and wandered into the garden. It was a still warm evening and the perfume from the Madame Alfred Carriere rose climbing around the patio doors hung in the air.

"I'm learning more about myself and how to live the rest of my life, because nobody stays special when they're old, Laurs. That's what we have to learn. We have to be happy with ourselves and our lives, because no-one else is going to really care. Did I tell you I'd started going to a Buddhist meditation class?"

"Oh?"

"It's supposed to 'quell the endless chattering of the mind', and to be truthful, I do feel calmer. I don't think of Mum as much."

"Have you told Robert?"

"Yeh, last night. I think he knew what I was going to say and anyway, perhaps he wasn't sure he could live with me either. I looked into his eyes and saw a new version of myself, saw perhaps what he was seeing. I've always been independent, but I've needed someone around. I feel strong now and not scared to face even my worst fears…I think." She cleared her throat and looked away, unsure what Laura was thinking of this new Lynne.

320

Chapter 23. August. Leaving

'Begin at once to live, and count each day as a separate life.'' Seneca.
'Moral Letters to Lucilius' (4BC – 65AD)

Marie had left again and Annie and Martin were house decorating and learning to live together harmoniously in Manchester.

Helen looked around as if for the last time at her beautiful kitchen with its lime washed oak cupboards and slate tiled floor. Would the family who were renting the house treat it well? She looked out at the garden aware of each separate moment, each of her breaths. It was a sparkling clear day. She went out to say goodbye to it all. To the cottage garden planted beds, the vegetable plot, the greengage and plum trees. "I'll miss you all, and you Phillip, I miss who you once were, not what you had become. We shared all these delights." She had a little weep as she stood in the garden he would never again tend.

She had emptied the fridge and cupboards of food and given it away or eaten it. The deep freezer in the garage had been completely full. There had been dozens of containers of soft fruit they had picked more than fifteen years ago and, ugh, half a lasagne, grey with frost and age that Phillip had crammed in. The ice tray had been frozen onto its shelf. She had switched the freezer off and put it all in the bin. The good with the bad. The car was sold and the American family were moving in tomorrow. She had packed all the clothes she thought she would need and put the others into her little locked study. Turning off the heating she took a tranquillizing pill with a glass of water, then put her rucksack and bag outside and locked the door.

James was reading his 'Telegraph' at the breakfast table, munching toast and marmalade, when he saw a heading 'Silver Separation. Relate ask couples to take a marriage MOT before retiring.' He read on: 'Does the gap widen between couples the longer they live together? Concerned about the trend for divorce among older couples, Relate have launched an online relationship checker.' He usually ignored this kind of article, but then he looked up at Beth who was making pastry for a quiche for their lunch and wondered what she was thinking. Perhaps he would rather not know. He finished his cup of tea, and made an effort to be helpful by loading the breakfast things onto a tray. Having disposed of everything into the cupboard, fridge or dishwasher, he went into his office, logged on and found the Relate website.

The questions were quite pointed, such as 'Do you share interests and have fun together? Or are you drifting apart?' Hmm, no, maybe, sometimes and perhaps yes. Were the children the only territory we had in common? We've got completely different tastes in books, music and even sport. She swims and likes watching tennis. I play golf and enjoy watching that and football. She loves seeing gardens and stately homes. I'm not that interested. I could go with her though, he said to himself.

'How do you resolve arguments?' It depends on the subject. He sat and thought. Would Beth say that I bully her to get my way?

'Have you made plans together for the next stage of your life?' Well, no. We did think of a long holiday to New Zealand and Australia, but then Sybil being here put that on hold. Oh, all B's. What does that mean, it doesn't say. He sat thinking for a while. Beth's my best friend, but do I take her for granted? Talk to her enough? Or do we both live in our own worlds? Am I clinging to the picture I made long ago of her and don't look any more. Now we've all this free time together what does she want from me? I suppose I know really, to talk to her more, to do more things together and to listen when she wants to tell me something.

He heard Beth's key in the lock. She had been out to the local supermarket. Determined to waste no time, he rushed out to the hall and took her bag. "You were jolly quick. I'll come with you next time to help you carry the bags."

Beth looked suspiciously at him. "You've never done shopping."

"I can learn. Did you meet anyone you know?"

"Just Dan. He does most of theirs. I wouldn't mind if you did ours sometimes. My child's quilt was third in the summer competition and I want to get on with one for the winter event."

"Oh, jolly good! How interesting. Oh, jolly well done. Yes. You must have more time to work on it."

"Are you going to the golf club after lunch?"

"Don't think so, no. I was thinking of going to the driving range, but I'm probably too old to get any better."

Harriet and Sybil were sitting in the garden together. Harriet had made gluten and dairy free courgette cupcakes and Sybil had made the tea.

"How are you getting on here, Nana?"

"It's not like being at the Laurels. I'm a burden to your parents and it's not my home. Not my life."

"Where would you like to be then Nana?"

Sybil smiled wryly and sipped at her tea. "My darling, my life lies behind me now. Most of my friends are dead and I'm old and tired. I'm not the woman I was. I've no idea of who I am now or how to be. What use am I to anyone?"

Harriet passed the plate of cakes and, taking one, Sybil carried on. "All those hopes and dreams and ambitions I had when I was your age. I remember when Tom retired, he was so happy. The best is still to come, he said. And those years, until he was ill, were the best." Her face was briefly young and shining. "Yes, they were the best," she repeated. "Then he died and nothing could ever be the same again. Life can be cruel and now I'm a prisoner in my failing body with nothing to look forward to."

"What would you like to be doing, Nana?"

Sybil smiled. "The impossible. To have my life with Tom and all my friends back, but this time I wouldn't waste a second. I might not make different choices, but I'd appreciate every second and never complain. I suppose I'm ready to die now. My life has no point."

"We all love you. Don't say that."

"I can't stay here. I'm a burden on James and Beth. They've got their lives. I suppose they're right that I can't manage in my big house and garden any longer. I'll have to go into a home."

"Are you sure,? If you want just to have a look, I'll take you to

323

look at some. I don't start work for two weeks. If we find one you like, you'll have things to do and people to talk to. We'll all visit you and take you out. You won't be so lonely."

It was a cloudless, still morning. The leaves of the trees looked heavy and dusty, as though oppressed by their weight.

The water in the pool was still and glassy and surprisingly there were only six other swimmers. Oh joy! This was how life should always be. Lynne had come today and she and Beth and Laura drifted up and down, each with their own thoughts.

Laura was considering writing an older women's self-help resource. "So many have retirement crises and hasn't the divorce rate for the over-sixties rocketed up?" she asked her friends on their way home. "Perhaps we should start a sixty-plus women's network?"

"Perhaps you could write a little guide to life over sixty?" Beth suggested.

"What, with sections on the joys of sex with diminishing libidos?" asked Lynne. "And financial affairs and wills?"

"How about loss, aging parents, children's demands, empty nests, failing health?" said Beth.

"Coming to terms with grey hair, lined faces and stocky bodies?" Lynne pointed to herself.

"Yes, yes, mental health, invisibility, isolation and depression, I know. You've really put me off now. Far too much specialised research. I'll stick with a novel about how retired women cope. You know, I miss having young people around. All our friends are older, even if they're still working. So many have had joint or heart operations. Lots have cancer. We all seem to be frequent hospital visitors. When do I mix with younger people? Not often," said Laura.

"Why would they want to mix with us? I sometimes think we should have hazard lights and a placard 'Avoid this slow, potentially boring person with a memory like a sieve'." Lynne grinned. "Being happy in old age won't just happen, will it? We're going to have to be positive, accept all the changes and our decreasing energy."

"Thank goodness for long term companionship. There's a lot to

324

recommend it now one's looks are no longer of interest to anyone but oneself," Beth chipped in.

"Maybe, maybe," said Laura, very aware of how lucky she was and how lonely her single friends often were.

"Where's Jo, by the way?" asked Lynne.

Laura looked puzzled. "Don't know. She didn't come to the gym yesterday, she said she was busy."

"I've put my photos of St David's on a CD, but we haven't met up since we came back."

"She must be in love again."

"Found a good shag, more like."

Terry's chest had started to feel hollow and cold. She was breathless, her lungs were tight and airless and she needed an oxygen cylinder within reach. She often had visual hallucinations. Seeing people who were not there. She was taking morphine, which sometimes befuddled her and made her feel that she was floating like a hologram above her decaying body. A week ago she had known just when to see her friends. Between the morphine injection easing her pain, but before it dulled her brain. Now she had lost track of everything. Her left eye would no longer close properly and her bottom lip hung. Laura sat by the bed, holding her hand, talking gently to the propped up skeleton that was her friend. Her bones seemed to be pushing through the surface of her skin. Her hair was like wire wool. A nurse came in, lifted the sheet, swabbed her thigh and injected her poor leg, now holey and blotched with needle marks. Terry tried to pull herself higher, to keep her chest vertical. Opening one eye she mumbled to Laura, who held a glass of iced water to her mouth, with a towel under her chin. "Thanks. Looking forward to the promised coma. No more of all this." At least that's what Laura thought she said. She wondered if it was time for her to go to the hospice.

Frances had to tell someone. She knocked on the door of the downstairs flat. Jo opened it, wearing glasses and holding a sheath of papers. "Oh, hello Frances. What can I do for you? Do you want to come in?"

She looked busy. "No, no it's fine. I just wanted to tell you I've got a job! It's twelve hours a week. For a charity. The UK Benevolent Fund."

"Well done. What do you have to do?"

"It's Chief Exec. There's two other staff. They give small amounts of money to the economically disadvantaged to buy necessities. I even get a small allowance and expenses."

"Perfect. And I was going to ask you if you'd get involved with something locally. I'll tell you more when I've got it off the ground."

"Right. Let me know when you want to talk. Bye."

Frances skipped up the stairs with a lighter heart.

Laura, Beth and other volunteers had been invited to the Community Centre, to see the facility after its renovation and for their final briefing before it opened and people signed up for their classes.

Shirley, the community worker, met their small group and showed them the large hall downstairs, half of which doubled as a café for drinks and lunch. A partition could be pulled across and the tables and chairs stacked away for large classes. The equipment cupboard already held music stands and mats for yoga, pilates and exercise sessions. The rest of the ground floor had an office and unisex toilets, while upstairs there was a classroom and a brand new IT room. "Look at this," Shirley said proudly. "Fire protection, stable temperature control, electrical installations and eight work stations with PC's, a scanner and three printers."

They stared at the beautiful room. "Wow, where did the money come from for all this?"

"It's brilliant isn't it? It was all provided from Local Authority, Government, a Rotary and two Foundation Grants. We've got three years internet access paid for as well!"

"All that applying! You've been so busy!" Beth said admiringly.

"It wasn't me, there's this amazing woman, Joanne. She's like a whirlwind doing business plans, applying to trustees, government departments, community connections and getting match funding, and she's going to teach a few classes. We're so grateful to her."

326

Beth had offered to teach adult literacy and maths for the older person. "Just hope some people want to come."

Laura had agreed to teach an exercise class. "With most things free? I'm sure they will."

She rang Jo. "Why don't you come and get involved at the Community Centre? Its going to be a place to eat, drink, learn and socialize."

There was a silence. Then, "I am already."

"Oh great, what are you going to teach?"

"Language and literature classes and basic IT."

"Why didn't you come and look round today then?"

There was another pause. "I've seen it already."

Laura was puzzled. Jo was sounding very strange. Then suddenly she knew. "You're Joanne aren't you? Is it you who has been getting all the funding together?"

"Pop round for a sandwich for lunch and I'll tell you about it."

Fifteen minutes later and Jo was giving her surprising news:

"Jess is coming back with a partner and is pregnant."

"How fantastic! Why haven't you told me before? We're supposed to be close friends!"

"Well, it's made me have a think about my life. I've been far too needy and selfish with your time. Being a nearly grandmother has changed my ideas of what I want in life and who I want to be."

Laura smiled. "I loved you as you were before, despite the four inch heels and tiny skirts. Who are you going to be now?"

"Well," she said in a pompous, posh voice. "I'm bidding a fond farewell to a life depending on love and pleasures of the flesh. No more chasing raggedy bags of old nuts. It's vibrator time." She giggled. "It was actually Dan who started me thinking. Age should be celebrated, not hidden. I'm not going to be in denial any more. You won't suddenly see me in zippy-up bootees with a tartan rug over my old knees, but with the exception of hair dye, there'll be no more cosmetic enhancements. I'm going to age naturally, scrape my face into place in the mornings and glue it there with only moisturiser. I'll be an elegant, classically dressed grandmother, wearing soft knitwear, and beautifully cut trousers and jackets and putting myself about as a fundraising consultant. *And* I've got an idea to apply for funding for the centre to have 'better aging' activities. The NHS might be keen to support activities that engage older people, so they stay mentally and physically fit for longer. If we get funding to reduce costs and use volunteer staff, we can support people when their mates, partners and rellies pop off. Your exercise class, Laura, can be the core and we'll find teachers for Tai Chi, Pilates, Bridge, Singing. Use the kitchen for doing cookery classes, have lectures, quizzes, people doing scrabble and dominoes, tea dances…whatever. Exciting isn't it?"

"Of course, it's brilliant. It's how the Adult Education colleges started, only they were for the working classes to become literate, numerate and do exercise. Mind, they're stuffed full of better off pensioners nowadays… What's with this sudden social activism?"

"What have I got to be proud of? I'm a total hedonist! This is the departure lounge, Laurs. I don't want to be sorry for who I've been, when it's the end. You've always been an achiever. Not me! I've been up for every sensation and experience: on autopilot, a habit machine, scleroticised – is that a word? But have I benefited anyone else? No. I want to know who I could be and see what I can achieve before change is forced on me. You'll never believe this, I've been reading William Cowper's poetry and discovering sacred stillness and a better appreciation of daily life!"

"Wow, serious stuff! The centre isn't going to be like an old people's Home though is it?"

"You're right. It's a community centre, for old and young ones and hope they spend some time together. A forward looking move for when all their age group is popping off."

"We've had good lives, haven't we?" sighed Laura

"True. Liberated, more equal than any generation before us. Role models like Mary Quant, Germaine Greer and Vanessa Redgrave."

"Did I ever tell you that Vanessa Redgrave being a single parent was why I decided to have a baby? We were so cocky, weren't we? We thought we could have everything until we met that glass ceiling."

"Yeh, I banged my head and took the easy way out. I've envied what you've achieved. But I'm doing something worthwhile now, instead of being selfish and vain. Steve Jobs was dying when he said something like, 'death is life's change agent, clearing out the old to make way for the new?' Before it's my turn to be cleared away, I'm building on qualities of myself I've never bothered to develop. To the future!" She lifted her glass of fresh orange juice, then picked up some knitting and crouched doggedly over her needles and the pattern of a baby blanket with embroidered rabbits, her tongue out and in total concentration. "Doing this is agony, I can't listen to the radio or watch TV at the same time."

Laura grinned. "You've dropped a stitch there. Give it to me." Then to Jo's chagrin she undid six rows, before picking up the stitch. "Shall I knit a bit for you?"

Jo nodded. "Please. Just while I wash up."

The next day David and Rosie went with Terry to the Marie Curie Hospice, her oxygen cannula was no longer enough, she was semiconscious and her breathing was harsh and noisy.

Rosie rang Laura, sobbing. "Terry's in Marie Curie, she wasn't waking up. Her hands and feet were freezing and she hadn't eaten or drunk for two days. The doctor arranged for her to go."

"Rosie, you've been wonderful. You've done all you can for her, she knows that you've done your best. Does she respond if you talk to her?"

"No, No, not a flicker."

"She might be able to hear. I'll go and see her now."

Laura came home, deeply upset. "She won't last much longer. Her breathing was bubbly. It's terrible. She's too young to be dying."

"Unfortunately we all have to die some time. How about you getting a more positive frame of mind while you're healthy and alive?" Dan said wryly.

Laura stood thinking. "True. I was in a bit of a panic when I retired, because it's the last lap. I'm sort of reconciled to how it is now. It's so difficult trying not to live self-centredly and see everything from one's own perspective."

"Aren't living things programmed to be selfish? Survival and all that."

"Yes, true. Remember I told you about Daisy's third birthday party? Where all these little girls sat at the tea table and demonstrated human nature in microcosm? 'I want that. Give *Me* that. She's got more than *Me*,' they shouted and then left most of the things they demanded. It was a horrible, unforgettable experience. I think we learn to hide our selfishness when we grow up. Then it's a battle when you're old, not to let it take over again."

"You're retired and now you're not tangled up in so many others lives, it's natural to do what you've been waiting and wanting to do for so long. Enjoy writing!"

"I know I moaned about having no time when Daisy was here, but now she's not, I feel I should be adding to what's good in the world. Giving something back. All I've been doing is the governor job and two hours a week at Brookfield House."

Dan looked at her and sighed. Here we go again, he thought. "I just want you to be happier, Laura."

"Yes, sorry. I've got to keep reminding myself of how lucky I am that I met you, learn to be happy each day and stop moaning and wanting things that I can't have. Are we having that barbecue for some of our friends?"

Dan got out the teak table and chairs, unused so far this summer. They found the insect repellent candles to light later and chose their less good plates and glasses. Laura put vases of white Japanese anemones and mauve aconitum on the main and side tables, mauve and pink serviettes under the place cutlery.

The garden still looked stunning. The pots and the beds were colourful and clematis climbed everywhere. The tomatoes along the conservatory wall were healthy and bushy, orange, red, yellow and black ones, cherry, beef and normal sizes. Dan picked cucumbers and courgettes, rocket, mixed salad leaves, including nasturtiums and smiled to himself, happy with his life and the familiarity around him.

They were thirteen. "My lucky number," said Laura. "Daisy was born on Friday the thirteenth."

Annie and Martin came to stay for the weekend, Beth and James came, though they were off on holiday to Croatia the next day. (Sybil

330

had chosen a Home and, strangely, made no complaints after her first week.) Beth had heard from Helen. "She's just got to Manila in the Philippines and is volunteering to do counselling and to help people who were displaced after the floods. She had a few weeks in Australia with her aunt and cousin. She says she's happy and she's even been chatted up by quite nice men!"

Lynne brought Robert, her normal ebullience unusually restrained by the faintly amused expression on his lively, unlined face. They hadn't met before and Laura decided that he was happy in his skin and good for Lynne. Alan came, Carolyn, Alexis and Jo and a new neighbour, Huma. Frances said she was visiting her sister.

Dan was happy. He could spend the evening barbecuing and filling glasses rather than talking. Laura had been busy all day making different salads, a big bowl of summer fruit for pudding and jugs of Pimms.

She looked around at the pots of flowers, the evening primroses lit by the garden lights and at her friends, chatting as they ate and drunk and felt the glow of contentment.

As dusk fell and their bonhomie increased, they started talking about the past, an acceptable topic among consenting contemporaries. And the future? Beth was enthusing about her coming teaching. Huma had retired at fifty, but had had poor experiences of volunteer jobs. "I won't try volunteering again," she said. "After getting nil respect and thanks on three occasions, that's it for me. These organisations which ask for volunteers, forget that they may be getting not old people with no back story, but highly successful ex-managers, captains of industry, forerunners in their fields, with high powered, well organized backgrounds. All three places were chaotic and badly managed and having no control, no say to improve things, was *so* frustrating."

"Make a difference, be inspired, feel valued and supported, hey!" said Carolyn. " Yes, I tried being a volunteer reading helper, but half the time my allocated children weren't in school or had been told to do something else. Be a powerless dogsbody, more like. It was so disappointing."

Oh dear, thought Laura, I hope the community centre is more

rewarding. Beth's so looking forward to it!

The conversation had moved on to how lucky their generation had been. "We were the first young people to have pop music, drugs, the pill, feminism, to collectively challenge old prejudices," said Jo.

"And we didn't have to fight a war, we had free health care and pension schemes," Alan added. "Now how are we going to live the last part of our lives?"

"Martin Amis wants to put euthanasia booths on every street corner, for wrinklies to do the decent thing," said Lynne.

"It's true that the silver tsunami will be unsupportable. We're living too long," said Robert.

Most were less keen than they had been on long distance travel. "I've had five or six foreign holidays a year for most of my working life, but being squashed in that metal capsule for hours? The older I've got the more I just want to go to near places that I know and love," said Lynne and there were murmurs of agreement.

A popular topic was downsizing, but where? Then Alan and James who had read about the Fardknappen building in Stockholm, with single and double flats for older people, suggested it as a model for the future.

"There's a library, exercise, TV and computer rooms and each person cooks or gardens or cleans every six weeks, so it's communal living, but not too onerous."

"What if you didn't like some people, or their cooking or cleaning standards?" asked Beth.

"And is there a swimming pool, a gym and tennis court?" asked Annie.

After much discussion they decided that they should find a huge house with grounds and an indoor pool and buy it together for support and companionship.

"What happens if some of us get too weak or disabled to do our share of tasks?" Laura asked Dan when everyone had gone. He had put nine empty bottles in the recycling bin and was washing the glasses.

"Well, if you're a true friend you shouldn't mind. But it'll never come off anyway. No-one will take it upon themselves to organize it."

She was covering the leftovers with cling film and finding places in the fridge for them. "It seemed a great idea, but who wants to give up one's home?"

Chapter 24. September.

'Keep love in your heart. A life without it is like a sunless garden when the flowers are dead. The consciousness of loving and being loved brings warmth and richness to life that nothing else can bring.'
Oscar Wilde – in conversation. (1854 - 1900).

Laura and Jo were walking to the pool. "It may have been the wettest August since 1912 and dullest since God knows when, but I've had such a brilliant time watching sport and opening and closing ceremonies! Loved Cold Play last night. Did you see those disabled children carrying placards of fishes and things? They came bursting out of something and had to be helped up some steps. They were so proud and determined to do it."

Jo shook her head.

"I cried. It's been amazing, all those thousands of volunteers who have taken part and kept it secret until now. And Andy Murray won the gold, this summer. It couldn't have been better to be British."

"Weren't you saying a few months ago that it was a waste of the nine billion?" Jo looked at Laura with amusement.

"I take it all back. It's been stunning."

"I must say I've been slavering over all those hot hurdlers, sexy scullers and semi-naked bodies. What did Boris say? The beach volleyballers 'glistening like wet otters'. It's been wall to wall tight abs, Lycra butts and oily, sweaty flesh. Fab."

"Thought you were a reformed character? Apart from the fact that we couldn't get tickets for ANYTHING, unless we were prepared to pay a fortune. It's been a month or so of stunning athleticism, enthusiasm, friendliness and efficiency. I've been in awe of the athletes, the gamesmakers…all of it. We're going to watch the parade through the streets at lunch time. Do you want to come?"

But Jo was not that keen and the friend who would have been had gone to live in Manchester.

Frances had a phone call from Lydia.

"Vic is starting a job with Morgan Stanley. Can she live with you while she looks for a flat share?"

What could she say? She could not think of a reason to refuse, but having to share her flat with that self-possessed young woman? Life was going to be very different. "Yes, fine."

"How's your job going?"

Frances had been finding it very stressful checking up on the claimants' benefits and eligibility and then deciding if they were to be given grants.

"It's rather boring and tedious," she said, keeping to herself how sick she was of all the hopeless cases she was dealing with, or how she could not get used to the baffled, aggressive looks so many clients gave her, as if she was trying to cheat them. Having to explain without seeming patronising to people who spoke only a smattering of English was not her forte. "This job may be called Chief Exec, but it's too hands-on for me. I'm head cook and bottle washer!"

"Try something else. You don't *have* to do anything, you know."

"I need to do something. My neighbour downstairs has asked me to do some advice and guidance sessions at the community centre she's involved with. She says they'll send me on a course to do modules in tax credits, pensions and benefits. An NVQ course."

"NVQ? Isn't that for not very bright people?"

"Is it? Well as long as it's interesting."

Jo was proving to be an excellent fundraiser. She applied for and got community funding for a befriending project to support isolated and lonely individuals and one to build confidence, self-esteem and work ethic in young people.

She had also roped in friends to take up roles. Beth was going to teach a Wednesday afternoon quilting class in addition to return to learning on Monday and Tuesday mornings. James fat with smiles, was pleased with his role as chairman of the trustees and he and Beth seemed to be happier together than their friends had ever known them.

Laura recognised the handwriting of course. Daniel had brought in the post and put the letter on the table. "From Daisy," he said unnecessarily, sliding his arms around her and kissing her tenderly. She froze and could not respond to his embrace.

"What's the matter?" he asked. "Aren't you going to open it?"

"Open it? If I don't I can imagine that she's writing because she loves and misses me. If I do and her anger slips out and into my life again…I can't. Not now."

"A cup of tea?"

Laura felt sick with shock. "No thanks. I'll open this later."

As if in a dream she made a list of what she had to do today, then methodically worked through it, the letter lying unopened, almost burning a hole in the table.

After a shower and dinner, where they spoke about safe subjects, Laura went back into the kitchen and picked up the letter, hands shaking. She could not put it off any longer.

There was less than one side of a page.

Hi Mum,

Am living in an ashram having a totally spiritual experience. Living sustainably in a community has totally changed my life. We work the land, meditate and heal through music, breathwork and psycho-spiritual counselling. I look after the animals and work on my personal awakening, to align with higher frequencies. I have lessons with a Steiner teacher. Everyone is very friendly and we love the life here. Ruby and Lily are happy and send their love.

We're going to join another group in Chile, for a while. I'll write to you when we get settled. Don't worry, Happy Birthday for the 15th, Daisy.

Chile? She was sitting quietly crying when Daniel came to make himself some tea. "She's in a commune, she's going to CHILE!"

Nearly a year ago Dan had booked a two bedroomed cottage in Cornwall to celebrate Laura's September birthday. They wondered whom to ask instead of Daisy and the children. To their surprise Jo and Lynne jumped at a three-day break, even though they would be sharing a bedroom.

Dan and Laura had spent a night with old friends and next day, drove to the station nearest the cottage, to pick up Jo and Lynne. A narrow, deeply rutted woodland track overhung with rhododendrons and chestnut at last emerged behind a white washed cottage facing a lake, like blue glass, with two swans and nine ducks. At its side was a sandy beach, part of the coast path.

After unpacking, the three women went out for a walk along the beach and up the hill. Dan had gone off to explore further. Weaving through the trees, they reached the cliff top. Waves gently shushed onto pebbles below and the sea and sky seemed to merge on the horizon.

Lying back on the sheep-cropped grass, avoiding the poo, the warm late afternoon sun on their faces, the smell of grass and salt, the sounds of gulls and the breeze gently lifting their hair, they breathed in deeply and relaxed.

"What are you thinking, Lynne?" Laura asked.

"How much Betty loved coastal walks. But I'm getting better, I can think about her and Ken without crying now. And do you know, I might have topped myself if it weren't for you two."

Dan and Laura had brought the food for the first evening. They put coats on and ate spinach pie and mixed salad outside, next to the lake, shining with reflected cottage light. The wrinkled sea was lit with purple patches from the moon. The food and wine had never tasted so good.

The first morning was grey and cold. Their walk was to a small town of fisherman's cottages clinging to the cliff with large Victorian houses behind. The route had taken them up and down and through woods and fields where cattle were grazing. Through parkland with ancient trees, and once landscaped ornamental pleasure gardens,

337

which had belonged to the richest families. Dan pointed out bird's foot trefoil, centaury, yellow rattle and then the thrift, sea cabbage, vetch and ox eye daisies covering the cliffs. Chiffchaffs and peregrine falcons soared above

The second day Dan drove inland so they could walk part of the Saints Way. Lynne's knees had stiffened up, she groaned as they got out of the car.

"It's sitting in one position that hurts. Walking's not too bad."

Jo had gone ahead towards a fifteenth century church, built with huge twinkling blocks of coarse grained granite. Must be the alcohol that numbs her joints, how is she so unscathed by age, Lynne wondered. She massaged her knees with voltarol, and they were off, down dram ways, which had carried china clay, copper, lime and granite. "Weirs, sluice gates, launders and leats, built by powerful Victorians to provide water power for the mines," Dan read in his guidebook.

Lynne had edged closer to him. He had a soft voice and although she didn't tell them, her friends must have known that she was losing her hearing, because she found them over articulating to her and talking extra loudly.

They had a snack in a pub and drove back, the women determined to go in the sea.

Laura stripped first and putting her clothes on a rock weighted down with her walking shoes, she ran to paddle in the surf. The wind was exciting the waves; they had hardly reached the shore before another one reared up behind. She edged forward slowly, splashing her legs and arms to acclimatise them. Jo ran past and dived under an approaching wave. "Come on you two," she called, her hair sticking to her face and head, water running down her body. Lynne was walking in the wet sand, her heels sinking in and popping out with a sucking sound. She suddenly ran past Laura, by now up to the tops of her legs, and plunged into a wave, which reared over her. The drag almost stopped her getting to her feet, but then she did and she and Jo dived clean under the next wave as it broke, then turned to float, grinning at Laura, who had surfed the wave back to the shore. She waded out to them and they took the next big wave, exhilarated and exultant. The sand and sea washed pebbles giving way beneath their feet as they tried to stand in the shallows. Giggling and staggering, holding on to one another, they walked up the beach towards their clothes, wet strands of hair flying and the wind tearing into their throats as they opened their mouths to sing 'You've got a friend,'* in croaking, shrieking, rasps.

A rough rub with their towels, and clothes pulled over damp, sticky skin, Jo gazed at her companions and for a moment saw them as they had once been. Young and beautiful, anxious to achieve, to live with passion and purpose and to love and be loved. Had life been good to them? Yes, we're fit, healthy, motivated, stimulated, have friends and social lives. She thought of what Doris Lessing once said, that there was a secret that all old people shared. That your body changes, but you don't change at all. Sad, but incontrovertible.

Laura was thinking how nothing beat women's friendship. All those years of looking after Daisy and various boyfriends and being superwoman at work and home, there hadn't been enough time to spend with women friends. What a pleasure I was missing, friends are like the earth, holding our roots so we don't fall.

Lynne was feeling philosophical. Trying to live fully, purposefully has been a ceaseless task and what is at the end of our lives, anything? Nothing? What did I expect or want to find?

Glowing and happy, arms linked, they walked up to the cottage to eat scones, jam and Cornish clotted cream for tea.

The last day was warm and sunny. Dan drove Jo and Lynne to catch their train, while Laura packed up their remnants of food and their clothes and stripped the beds. The sea was smooth and blue, gently lapping on the beach. Gulls wheeled in the clear, fresh air. She was sitting, on the little terrace wall, reading, when he returned. "Not having a last swim?" he queried.

Her eyes lit up, "Thought you'd want to get off. You don't like driving in the dark."

"It's not twelve yet. Plenty of time. I might join you."

They unpacked their swimming things, put everything else in the car and changed on the beach on the car rug.

Dan swam out into deep water, the dim shapes of rocks with wafting seaweed beneath him. He lay on his back to watch cargo boats in the far distance and turned to see birds nesting in the cliffs, pale clouds above. What is it about swimming, he wondered. It's not just a physical experience; it's reflective and cognitive, spiritual almost. He glided smoothly towards the shore and lay like flotsam at the edge, the undertow sucking sand from under his body. Pushing himself backwards he went to stand, but his feet sunk deep and he staggered. And I'm only sixty-three, he thought, can't be losing my strength and mobility already? He flicked the tangle of hair out of his eyes and this time got up and out. Laura was wading towards him, her hair pulled up in a ponytail, wet tendrils escaping onto her neck. He saw that her skin was no longer young, it sagged and wrinkled in places, but she had a youthful shape and that lithe, familiar walk. She is beautiful to me, he thought. She saw him looking and smiled. They walked towards one another and he kissed her cold lips, her salty cheek. She kissed back. They hugged and she pressed her lips on his shoulder. He rubbed her back and arms until they were warm. "I love you, Laura, I want to be with you for the rest of my life. Shall we get married? Have a big party and get married?" He asked out of the blue.

Laura stiffened in shock. "Married? Me? Feminist, spinster of the parish?"

"You don't have to change your name, or call yourself 'Mrs'. It won't make any difference to our lives, just to others. To show I've committed myself to you, we're a couple. To keep all the other suitors at bay." He grinned.

She smiled back. "Mmm, queuing up aren't they."

They picked up their things and walked to the car, their arms around one another. 'The beginning is always today,'* she thought. 'The beginning is always today."

ATTRIBUTIONS

Chapter 5:
'Youth is wasted on the young,' is non attributed, though George Bernard Shaw said something similar.
Dorothy Parker 'Interior' (1893 – 1967)

Chapter 6:
Oscar Wilde 'Arguments are to be avoided...' (1854 – 1900)
Oscar Wilde (attributed) 'Anyone who lives within their means'.

Chapter 8:
Voltaire 'Illusion is the first...' (1694 – 1778) quoted by Oscar Wilde.

Chapter 11:
John Gay (1687 – 1732)

Chapter 12:
Oscar Wilde 'The Picture of Dorian Gray.'

Chapter 17:
Oscar Wilde 'A man's face is his autobiography...' 'Impressions of America.'
Oscar Wilde 'A little sincerity...' 'The Critic as Artist' Part 2, (1891)
Rudyard Kipling 'The Glory of the Garden.' (1923)
Stevie Smith 'Not Waving but Drowning' (1957)

Chapter 19:
Imtiaz Dharker, 'The Terrorist at my Table' (Bloodaxe Books, 2006)

Chapter 21:
Oscar Wilde 'Consistency....' 'The Relation of Dress to Art.' (The Pall Mall Gazette)
Oct 14 1886
'The very essence...' 'The Importance of being Earnest.'(first performance 1895)

Chapter 24:
Carole King 'You've Got a Friend' (Tapestry - 1971)
Mary Wollstonecraft – Godwin (1759 – 1798) or her daughter – Shelley (1797 – 1851) 'The beginning is always today...'